I0772353

The Sibyl of the Wind

The Sibyl of the Wind

Kristen Kandibo

ISBN-13: 979-8-9912636-0-3 (paperback)
ISBN-13: 979-8-9912636-1-0 (hardback)

Cover design by: Gretchen Cobaugh
Library of Congress Control Number: 2024916327
Printed in the United States of America

To Rhys Wilder:

my rainbow and my Star.

sibyl: a woman of the ancient world with the supposed gift of foresight; a female soothsayer or mystic

Part I
CHAPTER 1
AURA

The knock came just as the light began to creep through the window onto the hard wooden floor. This was where Aura sat. Legs crossed, eyes closed, enjoying the peace before the noise and bustle of the day. Her three children slept. Too old to wake up as early as babies do. Young enough to need the extra sleep. When the knock came she knew she would not be able to enjoy her peace again for a while. It was too early for anything but bad news.

An unfamiliar legionnaire stood outside the door to the cottage. He was dirty and disheveled and did not present his unwanted news with any bit of care or concern. "Your husband's legion has returned from the trip across the forest. He has been lost".

Lost. Not dead. Not missing. Status unknown. Either way didn't matter to them. What mattered now was *her* status. At least she had a choice in this, though no choice would be the right one.

He made the pronouncement as if he had done it so many times before that the words no longer held any meaning to him. Just produced the right sounds and syllables to get the message relayed and move on. She was just another check mark on his list, nothing more. "You have one week to make a decision for you and your children. The trials are in three weeks and the widower's ball the week prior. You will be informed beforehand of appropriate matches. You know your other option."

Death.

That was her other option. A woman cannot live on her own. Be free to cause trouble. She had kept her head down while her husband had been away. Had not been too loud or too brash. Now that he was not coming back, they had to find another to keep her in check while *she* figured out a way to keep her family safe and together. Keep her boys from being trained to be quiet and quick and sent away as scouts with the next legion at the tender ages of three and five. Keep her girl safe from being sent to an orphanage until she was old enough to participate in the trials and find her own match.

The messenger turned away without waiting for a response and Aura closed the door and walked to a chair on unsteady feet. The news had not surprised her. She had not received a post from her husband through carrier or bird in weeks. The thread that connected them through magic and matrimony had become thinner and thinner the farther away he had ventured, and she could not recall the moment that it had fully disappeared from her heart.

The guilt had been eating away at her that her husband may have passed without her even noticing, but the events of the past month had been trying and her mind had been elsewhere.

Aura's closest friend, Ophelia, had also lost her husband, and had chosen to have her life ended by the king's guard. She had been completely devoted to him and had so deeply felt the severing of their connection that she happily agreed to death in order to stop her suffering.

Was that where the guilt stemmed from? Seeing the pain that Ophelia had felt and not feeling the same? Ophelia's husband had been killed by one of the beasts of the dark woods. His body carried back and buried in the forest surrounding the village. The fate of Aura's husband was not as clear; however, the fact that he had not returned, paired with the snipping of the thread, suggested at least a death of some kind.

Aura had suffered as she watched her friend dutifully walk to the square and drink her cup of widow's tonic along with the other wives who had chosen her path. She had held the hand of Ophelia's only son, Eryx, who was sixteen and refused to let his tears be seen by anyone. Since Eryx was of the age to participate in trials he was allowed to remain in his parents' home until the time came for him to compete and find a partner. After the bodies had been buried, she could hear him taking out his sadness and anger on the furniture within their small home which stood next to Aura's own on an otherwise small isolated hill above the village. When she had visited the next morning bringing breakfast, everything was back in its proper place with only a few visible scuffs and breaks. Similar to the state of his home, Eryx only showed his grief through tiny cracks in his facade. She was curious to know if anyone had picked up on the ones that had developed in Aura following the deaths of her own parents. Would her appearance change even more now with the loss of Vitus?

Aura knew that she would not accept the same fate as Ophelia. While she had loved her son, Ophelia had expressed to Aura that she knew that he would match well and go on without her. Possibly the idea of being reunited with Felix in death was more appealing than being alone with a stranger when her son went on to create his own family.

Aura's children were much younger and still needed her. Even if they were of age and no longer dependent on her, she would still want to continue to live for herself. The past five years spent birthing and nursing her three children had mostly kept her house bound. There was still much she wanted to see and do with her life, but that would prove difficult without her husband. Though Vitus had often been away performing his various duties, the little time they did have together was often spent exploring the nearby woods, searching for waterfalls, picnicking in quiet meadows and exciting the children with stories of fairies and other magical creatures. He had promised that with his extra work they could take a trip to the coast when the weather warmed, and the boys had been fighting pirates and swimming with sea nymphs in the bath for weeks. While the loss of their father would obviously upset them, this is where they would feel it the most. In the broken promises resulting from his absence.

Aura looked up as she heard the door creak open. She hadn't moved from her place while contemplating her future. Eryx stood with a loaf of bread and a basket of fiddleheads. She still found it hard to look at him following Ophelia's death. Eryx was already taller than her, even though she was not a small woman.

Though he very much presented himself as his father's son, with his rigid posture and stern demeanor, he had Ophelia's glowing brown skin and kind eyes. Those dark eyes assessed her now as she stood frozen in place in front of him.

"I saw the man from the guard. Is everything all right?"

"Vitus is lost." She said the words quietly, as if that would lessen the blow. The two had been close and he had already lost so much.

He turned, placing the goods on the table behind him and then stood, arms rigid and head down.

"What are you going to do?" he asked, without turning around to look at her.

"Not leave you, or this realm," she responded. "Apart from that I'm not sure yet."

He faced her, concern showing through his typical stoic countenance. "You'll have to remarry. Do you think they'll have an appropriate match for you?"

They would *not* have an appropriate match for her. Aura had fibbed her way through her own trials and disguised her magic so that she could still be paired with her childhood friend whose powers, while impressive, were significantly less than her own. Luckily that was known to only Vitus, herself, and the one she should have been paired with, who had also met his end far too soon and had taken the secret to his grave.

"Albus Pennyworth supposedly won highest marks in his trial. He just lost his wife to sickness," Aura responded somewhat playfully attempting to bring some levity to the dire situation. She had never been very good at emotionally relying on others and preferred humor and sarcasm to actually dealing with feelings.

"His trial was at least seventy years ago. He won't be far behind her and you'll be right back in the same situation." Eryx replied, taking her seriously. His total lack of humor undoubtedly came from his father.

"I have a week, Eryx, and I have more pressing matters to deal with," she said, finally clearing the fog of shock from her head and moving from her place to start preparing for the day. "The children will be up soon and will need to be told."

"Told what?" Aura's sister asked as she walked down the stairs of the cottage and broke off a piece of the fresh bread with her hands. Odessa was fourteen to Aura's twenty-three. A welcome surprise after her parents thought they were done with children. Sadly, their years together as a family of four were short. Aura's father passed from an infected animal bite when Odessa was only nine, and their mother had taken the same path as Ophelia, unwilling to remarry. While she had kept a strong face for her little sister, Aura had been so internally distraught then that she hadn't noticed the absence of her courses for over a month. Odessa had come to live with them afterwards and had been a great help in raising her niece and nephews.

Eryx turned, looking at the bread in Odessa's hands and scowled. Though the two had basically grown up together, their upbringings had been very different. Eryx's father had been high up in the King's guard and was very strict with his son. The family's magic was rooted in the earth, and Eryx was taught from an early age how he would be able to use it to gain advantage in a fight. Since he was their only child, Ophelia had also shared *her* gifts with him and taught him how to grow the best plants in the garden behind their house. His full days left little time for leisure, and manners were to be demonstrated at all times.

While Aura always felt that her mother and father were strict with *her*, Odessa was the family's princess. Her parents had been older and too tired to let her do anything other than what she pleased. Aura hadn't been much better when she took over after their passing. Being either pregnant, nursing or both, and trying to raise three children very close in age to one another, Aura didn't have much energy to chase after Dessa or ensure that she was going to her lessons rather than wandering the woods.

Since they were only two years apart, Eryx and Dessa attended the same lessons and often traveled in similar circles; however, Eryx was always annoyed by Dessa's flightiness and she mercilessly teased him about being uptight and refusing to have fun. While she had mostly left him alone since his parents' passing, the animosity between them was still palpable, especially since Eryx had been spending more time at the house.

Eryx took a deep breath, retrieved a bread knife from the drawer and presented it to Odessa. She looked at his hand, ignored the gesture and then proceeded to take a large bite out of the ripped hunk.

Aura didn't have the energy to rebuke her younger sister for her boorishness. "Vitus' legion returned this morning without him. A messenger came but didn't provide any details."

Odessa's brow furrowed. "You didn't feel anything?" She shifted her eyes to Eryx then back to Aura. "They didn't carry him home?"

She busied herself by putting on a pot of water for tea. "The connection had been fading with distance. Whatever happened was too far away." Her hand shook as she lifted the lid from the canister of fragrant black tea leaves, "In regards to his body I supposed there wasn't anything to bring back."

Odessa dropped into a seat at the table and began strategizing, knowing that her elder sister would prefer that to cuddles and empty words of condolence. "What are you going to do? Not remarry. Can you go looking for him?"

"She must remarry," Eryx answered for her. "Who would care for the children? Trials are in another month. Even if they allowed us to care for them for a couple of weeks, who's to say our matches would be willing to take them in? As for a search, Vitus' legion went looking for The Witch's Kingdom. He was gone for months. If the connection has been severed what advantage does Aura have that his fellow soldiers didn't?"

"There's no one suitable that we're familiar with," Odessa replied, standing to face him. Her fair skin and sun bleached hair in direct contrast to his dark umber coloring. "They're either too old, too young or too weak. She's just supposed to marry some stranger?"

"That's usually what happens," he retorted. "She just got lucky last time."

Well that wasn't quite true but Aura wouldn't correct him.

"Do I get a say in my own future?" she asked, agitatedly, sitting down across from her sister and putting her face in her hands. "I agree with Eryx that I can't leave my children behind and go on an endless search. How did you not foresee this Dessi?"

"Maybe if she had attended her lessons," Eryx interjected under his breath.

"Everything I learned about how to develop my personal powers came from our mother," Odessa snarled back. "I wouldn't trust any of those supposed teachers with the true extent of my abilities. Maybe it was as Aura said. He was too far from our lands. We don't know about the magic that surrounds The Witch's Kingdom. I can ask the cards about the path you should take. I can also try to acquire a dreaming tonic for tonight." She got up from the table and retrieved her boots from next to the door.

"I'll join you," Eryx said sheepishly, possibly embarrassed by his earlier comment. "I have some herbs to sell. Maybe the Widow will accept a trade."

Aura stood to see them off. Odessa came to her and placed her hands on her shoulders, kissing her forehead gently. Like Eryx, her baby sister already towered over her. "We'll figure something out. You're not alone in this."

With that she turned and exited the cottage, Eryx close behind. Aura walked to the window and watched them go. Her only two allies were basically still children themselves, and she had three young ones to worry about. There was no time to grieve the loss of her husband and oldest friend. She had plans to make.

CHAPTER 2
ODESSA

Odessa thought about the look on her sister's face as she walked down the path to the Widow's house. Aura had always been the one to take control and fix problems head on. Odessa was happier to run away from them. This time would have to be different. No matter how strong she was, Aura was not going to be able to fix everything on her own this time.

Odessa had understood that she was going to have to grow up sooner rather than later, especially with her trial coming up next month. Girls of fourteen and boys of sixteen from the city and all of the surrounding villages converged on the castle grounds in order to compete against each other and find their match. A male would compete against each of the females until he was bested. Then he would be paired with the last female he had won against, ensuring that each male would have the power in the household and would be able to keep control of his wife.

Young people of both sexes trained hard in order to succeed and avoid the consequences of a total loss. If there was more than one female left at the bottom, the two would compete for the hand of the lowest male. The loser would end up in one of the kingdom's brothels.

There were also occasions when a male walked away alone. An unfortunate male who was unable to beat a single female would have to return the next year and hope for a weaker female to be part of the group. Some chose to endure the year of teasing and possible ostracism from their family and friends. Others walked away and were never seen again.

The other group of males to walk away unattached were the royals, who were typically the most powerful in the rare years they did compete. A Serenfawr heir didn't even enter the fighting grounds unless an especially talented female proved to be more powerful than all of the other male competitors of her year. Even then, she still might not be deemed strong enough to sit beside a future king if she didn't hold her own during the match. If a royal did not find a match in his sixteenth year he continued on year after year until someone appropriate was found. Female members of the royal family were passed over in the line of inheritance but males that beat them in the tournament did win themselves a life of leisure and riches.

Aura and Vitus had been lucky. Vitus had worked his way up and beaten every other female that year. Aura had been his toughest competitor but had lost to him in the end. Odessa had been five years old but had remembered the excitement of watching her first trial. While the whole competition had been a wonder, the fight between her sister and brother-in-law had been an elegant dance. They had been friends for ages and had trained together for this exact purpose.

Odessa did not have high hopes for her pairing. All of the males from her village were bland country boys with basic elemental powers. Present company included, she thought, side-eyeing Eryx who had been silent after agreeing to come along.

Maybe there would be someone exciting from another village. Someone with a different kind of power like her own. The son of the king would be competing this year. The rumors said that he was handsome and powerful and also much more personable than the king himself.

Odessa was brought out of her thoughts when she saw they were approaching the Widow's cottage. While the society did not typically allow for widows of any kind, women who had lost their husbands after the age of seventy were seen as having paid their dues and were allowed to live on their own as long as they continued to provide for themselves and their fellow villagers. A Widow was no longer seen as a threat since her beauty and vitality had faded. Their magic also supposedly withered with age;

however, their knowledge was seen as an asset to the community.

Widow Delafleur's power also was rooted in the earth. Unlike Eryx and his mother, who specialized in the growing of plants, she was versed in the collection of wild greenery and the mixing of roots, grasses and herbs to form tonics and potions. She often traded with the other earth masters for the items that she needed.

Eryx knocked three times on the small wooden door. The Widow, for all of her skills, had not been able to bear children, so she and her husband had not needed a large home. While the cottage was old and small, it was well maintained since the villagers did tend to take care of their own. They heard a muffled "come in" from inside, and Eryx opened the door and gestured for Odessa to step in first, as an annoying gesture of chivalry. She crossed her arms over her chest in refusal but then huffed and walked in knowing she would never win that particular battle.

The Widow was seated at a small wooden table covered in borage flowers. Her long white hair was braided, and she wore a long-sleeved shift dress the color of the forest at twilight.

She smiled up at them as she used her pale gnarled fingers to pick the seeds from the dried blossoms.

"How are you faring, Eryx?" she asked with sad but kind eyes. "I was so sorry to hear about your mother. She was a talented grower, though I know she passed on much of her knowledge to you."

Odessa could see Eryx shift uncomfortably, never happy to be the center of attention, even more so now that it was often due to pity. "I am glad that we had our time. The other fellows were always trying to get away from their mothers, but I always enjoyed the lessons that she had for me." He said it with a slight smile that didn't reach his eyes. "I brought you some lemon balm. We were hoping for a trade." He presented his basket and left it on the table before her, quickly changing the subject away from his loss.

"What are you in the market for?" she asked, looking back and forth suspiciously between the two teenagers.

"A dreaming tonic," Odessa replied quickly, her cheeks warming. "My sister's husband was lost on an expedition to the west. I was hoping to help lead her to an appropriate match."

"So many have been lost lately," the Widow said grievously. "Forcing young women to make such difficult choices so soon after losing their loved ones is barbaric. A child should not have to lose both mother and father within a week."

She shook her head and then moved towards a large cabinet in the back of the room. She began removing jars and lining them up on a small sideboard.

"Have a seat. I just put some water on."

Odessa and Eryx sat across from each other at the small table. The cottage was warm and welcoming. A small cauldron sat in the hearth fire. Though the Pink Moon, the first full moon of the spring, would be rising this evening, the mornings still brought a chill, and Odessa had forgotten her cloak. The kitchen took up the majority of the main living area and dried herbs hung throughout, filling the air with a pleasant aroma. A gray cat was curled in the rocker near the fire, seemingly unbothered by the unexpected company.

"How have your studies been going? You're both up for trial soon aren't you?" the Widow asked as she crushed and mixed items from the different jars. Odessa could smell ginger and rose as a slight breeze wafted the scents of the tea over to where they sat. "There hasn't been a clairvoyant competitor in quite some time. I can't remember one since your sister competed. She never seemed to embrace that side of her powers as much as you did."

Odessa agreed with the Widow's statement. The girls' parents had both been air elementals; however, Odessa and Aura had been gifted with the clairvoyant powers that seemed to rarely and randomly develop in children throughout the kingdom. Odessa loved reading the cards her mother had found for her while selling her wares in the city market. From a young age she dreamed of things that were yet to come and was always excited to share something auspicious with her parents or warn them of something that they could then prepare for. Sadly, death seemed to evade her, and she had no intuition when it came to her father's demise or apparently Vitus' disappearance.

Aura never talked about her psychic powers and preferred to embrace the powers of the wind that had been inherited by her parents and also shared with Vitus. She treated the air around her home almost like a beloved pet: using it to sweep away dust from the house, tickle the necks of her babes or warm a cup of tea with the breath from her lungs. Odessa wasn't even sure how her sister's spiritual powers truly manifested since she always changed the subject. She assumed that she could read minds and didn't want to discuss the awkward secrets that she learned. She found it curious that the Widow was even aware of Aura's more obscure powers, but it was possible that their mother had discussed them with her before her passing.

Odessa on the other hand, felt like the wind liked to spite her for favoring her powers of the mind. Her fighting skills were lacking and she could never make the air do what she wanted it to. She was hoping that the dreams and readings she did prior to the upcoming competition would give her an edge on her competitors and how to best them in other ways.

"My parents prepared me well enough," Eryx said. "At least I'm sure I won't place last."

"He's being modest," Odessa chimed in. "He's top of the class. I wouldn't be surprised if he matched with one of the top females."

"I'm sure you'll both do well. Your families raised you well and your parents placed highly in their day. I wouldn't be too concerned." She carried over two cups of tea and carefully placed them on the table.

"Black tea with ginseng and tangerine to help keep you lively. It sounds like you might have a trying day ahead."

Odessa breathed in the warming scents and then took her first sip with intention, hoping it would do as the Widow said. The tea was sweet with a hint of spice, just the way she liked it.

The Widow moved over to the window in the kitchen and closed the wooden shutters before returning to the herbs. She lowered her voice before asking, "Has your sister considered…other choices? Good husbands are difficult to find these days. Especially among widowers. Some might be intimidated by a strong willed woman like Aura. Others would not be so inclined to take on children who were not their own. Many might even be widowers of their own making."

"She will not take her own life if that's what you're implying," Odessa said angrily. "There are no other choices for a woman in her position."

"Of course not," she responded, unbothered by the outburst. "I have been providing for this village for years and have heard whispers of women who disappeared before their widow's walk or second marriage. The palace would never admit to such an embarrassment, and if the women were found I'm sure an example would have been made of them."

"But where would they go?" Eryx asked, his dark brows furrowed in confusion. "A lone woman would be noticed immediately in any of the villages within the kingdom. There is the sea to the east and the forest and the river to the west. The king's men, Vitus, my father… none of them have made it past those woods. How could someone defenseless? Someone with children?"

"No one in this kingdom is defenseless, dear boy," the Widow replied with a slight smile. "We've all heard of the Witch Queen in the west. When I was younger she and her kingdom were a rumor on the wind. In recent years it seems she has been gaining territory. The creatures of the woods and the river bow to her. The land itself no longer willingly obeys the king. Someone seeking refuge might be able to cross over without being harmed. Why do you think Talon has been sending so many men that way? He fears for his own power and the people and lands that are slowly being taken from him."

King Talon had been in power for the past nine years, ever since taking over the throne of his brother who had supposedly been killed by his own son. Talon had married his brother's wife and his only son from his first marriage was now the heir to the throne. The first family had been in power for centuries and ruled over all of the villages east of the river. They had been the ones who had held the first trials and created the rules of marriage. Prior to the establishment of the kingdom, villages had been under their own rule. While the propaganda that was circulated by kingdom officials always declared that the bringing together of the clans of olden days had strengthened the kingdom, stories were passed down quietly through generations that told otherwise: that the villages had been more connected to nature and the old gods, and the people had prospered. The psychic gifts held by Aura and Odessa had been commonplace rather than the rarity they were now.

Odessa felt a flutter within her heart at the idea of there being another path. One where she could control her own future rather than being wed to whomever the palace deemed fit. The Widow closed the top of the jar that she had filled and placed it on the table next to Odessa's empty cup.

"Cinquefoil to encourage prophetic dreaming and chamomile to bring sleep on quickly. I know you don't have much time. Whatever Aura chooses to do, I'm sure it will be right as long as she follows your guidance."

Odessa blushed as she stood and kissed the Widow's cheek. "Thank you for the tea, and the kind words."

"Oh, one more thing." She stopped before moving to open the door to let them out. With a far off look, she continued. "It was many years back, but my husband got turned around in the forest once while hunting. It was an awful blizzard, and he didn't think he would make it home. Somehow he stumbled across a small cottage situated within an old cemetery. He was desperate so he knocked at the door. There was no one there, but there was warm food on the table and a fire in the hearth. He stayed there until the storm let up. He was excited about it and tried to take me back with him in the spring once the snow had cleared. Sadly, we could never find it. I always wished that I got that chance to see it, but I did appreciate those quiet adventures we had together."

The Widow wiped gently at her eye and Odessa could only hope that she would find that same kind of love one day. "Whatever Aura chooses to do, tell her that there may be help if she looks for it."

She opened the door and patted Odessa on the shoulder as she and Eryx walked out.

As they left the small cottage and began walking down the dirt path back to the village Odessa thought about the Widow's words and how she could bring the subject up with her sister without sounding too eager.

"Stop," Eryx commanded, breaking her from her reverie. "You're not considering this. It's not worth the risk. Aura will not choose to put her children in such obvious danger."

She did indeed stop and silenced him by covering his mouth with her palm. While most others wouldn't dare commit such an act of disrespect against the village's golden boy, she had no such qualms. His brows furrowed in outrage but he didn't pull away. She looked him in the eyes and spoke calmly and quietly as if reassuring a small child. "Such things should not be discussed out in the open. I will not consider anything, nor say anything to Aura until I consult the cards and take the dreaming tonic. If the cards show me a knight in shining armor ready and willing down the road, so be it."

Eryx didn't break his malevolent stare as he pinched her bony wrist between his fingers and removed her hand from his face. He frowned at her another moment and then continued walking the path back home. Maybe it was the power continuing to grow and mature within her but she was already sure that the cards would show her what she wanted to see.

CHAPTER 3
AURA

Aura quietly prepared breakfast while she collected her thoughts. Sharing the news with the children would be worse than hearing it herself had been. Their baby girl Echo was just a year old, and though she adored her father when he was home, she was much more reliant on her mother who was her food source and constant companion throughout the day.

Callen was three, and although losing his father would be hard on him, the memories would likely fade with time. She wasn't sure if that was upsetting or a relief.

Barrett would be the most difficult. He was five years old and wise beyond his years. She was sure his powers were already starting to develop. He would tell her bits of information that he heard around the village that should not have been spoken about in a child's presence. Also, no matter how far the boys strayed from the cottage, they would always return shortly after their father's footsteps entered the house, or she mentioned something to the baby about the biscuits being done. She was surprised that he had not been the one to share the news with her about Vitus, though it seemed that the legion had only arrived back that morning while he was still asleep.

How was she going to raise her children with someone else? She had known Vitus her entire life. Their love had been rooted in mutual fondness and respect. She had felt safe sharing the full extent of her powers with him, and he had not balked or acted like she had insulted his manhood in some way. While they did not seem to have the same fervent passion as other couples, their relationship had been well suited for starting a family. She had been happy raising their children and taking care of the home while he had worked for the king's men: settling local disputes, helping villagers in trouble, and going on outings with his legion every couple of months. The home and life they had built together would be no more. Even Odessa would be leaving her to live with her husband once she was matched and married. While she would still be living at home during the courting period, which ensured the suitability of the match, by eighteen she could be anywhere. Now that Aura had time to think, she understood the pain and insecurity Ophelia had felt after the loss of her husband.

She heard the soft sound of padding feet on the wood floor and then the creak of the door.

"Mama!" Callen toddled out first and held his arms up in a request to be picked up. She scooped him up into her lap and attempted a smile.

"How is my littlest man this morning?"

He furrowed his fair brows and scanned her face. "You sad?"

While she was unsure if Barrett's chiropteran hearing had more to do with him being half air elemental or was more of a mind sharing ability, she was fairly certain that Callen's powers were psychic in nature. He was extremely adept at social cues for a three year old and also had an uncanny ability to predict what she was going to do before her mind had shared the thought with her own body.

Barrett walked out behind his brother, rubbing the sleep from his eyes. Both boys shared the same ivory skin tone which would soon be turning golden with the summer sun. While Callen's hair was the light color of straw similar to his father, Barrett's was more of a tawny blond that darkened to a light brown over the winter months like her own. They had also both inherited Vitus' deep brown eyes while hers tended to change between a light green and gold depending on the color of her garment.

"Is everything okay?" Barrett asked, likely hearing his brother's question and noticing the feelings on her face that she was unable to hide.

"No little one, it's not," she said sadly. There was no use keeping anything from him. Gossip traveled fast and he would hear it from someone else's mouth soon enough. "Your father didn't come back with his legion. He was lost somewhere in the forest and they aren't sure where."

"Is he dead? Are you going to die like Eryx's mom?" Barrett had an unsurprising interest in death as of late. While the children were not allowed to see the widow's walks, the deaths had been a highly discussed topic and he had been coming home frequently with questions after playing with his friends.

"No, I am not going to die like Ophelia," she replied, dodging his first question and cementing her own decision as she spoke it, "but that does mean that I'll have to find a new husband at the ball next month."

"But what if he comes back? Where will he live then?" he asked, choosing to deal with the logistics of everything rather than facing the more difficult thought of not seeing his father again.

"I'm not sure, sweetheart. That's something that we'll have to deal with at a later time if it happens."

"Can we go find him? So you don't have to marry someone else?"

Maybe he had been awake or had heard Odessa's suggestion subconsciously in his sleep.

"That would be very dangerous. Don't you think? Your father was big and strong. I don't think I would be able to find him on my own."

"I could find him. What if he's calling for help and I could hear him when no one else could?"

"Barrett...I don't think..." She was interrupted by the front door opening and Eryx and Odessa returning from their walk.

Barrett turned away from her and ran to the door. Callen also scooted out of her lap in order to see his aunt. Odessa scooped him up and pressed her nose to his.

"Dessi, will you come to the forest with us to find papa?" Barrett asked eagerly. "You too, Eryx?"

Eryx slammed the door quickly and then Odessa knelt down until her face was even with her nephew's.

"I will," she whispered. "We both will."

"Odessa!" Aura cried, as Eryx walked around the small home, closing the windows in order to keep their words from being overheard by anyone nearby. "This is hard enough as it is, don't tell him things that aren't true."

"I'm not," Odessa replied. "This is the right choice to make. The Widow practically confirmed it, and I know when I dream tonight it will just reinforce the decision."

"I wouldn't go that far," Eryx stated stonily from the kitchen, depositing the small packages the Widow had given them next to the stove, "and I definitely don't remember saying anything about coming with you."

"Of course you will. What are you holding on to? Going to trial and marrying some stranger you've never met? We're your family. The only family you have left."

"Dessa!" Aura scolded again, turning towards Eryx with an apologetic look. "Eryx please don't feel like you have to make any rash decisions based on our current predicament."

Eryx's face looked pained as if he knew he would be doing just that, but he turned and headed towards the door. "I told some friends that I would do some sparring with them today to get ready for trials. Don't disappear into the night without telling me. And don't have any more casual conversations with neighbors about disobeying the Crown." He gave Odessa one last warning look before walking out and closing the door behind him.

"Sit," Aura commanded her sister with a glare. She returned to the kitchen and plated a slice of freshly baked bread with butter and jam for each of the children.

"How would you boys like to have a morning picnic?" she asked, forcing a smile. She opened the door to the small cottage and carried out a blanket and the two plates. The grass was still wet from the morning dew and a layer of fog covered the valley leading down the path from the house. The sun was bright, promising a warm afternoon, but the air still carried a chill and she shivered through her light lemon colored tunic.

All of Aura's outfits were in shades of yellow and gold. As an air elemental she was expected to represent the color of the sun's light. She enjoyed choosing her outfits based on the sun's strength as it changed from day to day and season to season: pale cornsilk on the winter days when the light was barely visible through the cold and gray, joyful dandelion when spring finally arrived bringing color back to the world, honey with the sweetness of summertime, and vibrant gold when autumn came drenching the hills in beauty.

Eryx always dressed in shades of green. Aura could remember the bright green tunics that Ophelia had sewn for him in his youth. As he matured he tended to select darker, more muted tones; however, she felt he looked his best on the rare occasions that he wore something brighter that contrasted with his dark skin such as emerald or seafoam.

Those with power derived from fire and water wore warm and cool colors respectively. Aura did feel twinges of jealousy at times when she saw a fire elemental in an especially stunning crimson or a stranger from one of the ocean side towns wearing a deep cerulean. Water elementals tended to prefer to live in areas closer to running water where their power was stronger. Since the towns had become more cut off from the river to the west many had moved east to be closer to the ocean.

Members of the royal family dressed in purple, though they still typically wore some kind of stripe or symbol representing the origin of their power. The elder Widows wore darker shades, or even black, as a sign of their perpetual mourning and diminished power.

Those with abilities that were more ambiguous in origin still wore the colors of their elemental powers. Powers of the mind were rare and were better off hidden so as to not attract the attention of jealous neighbors or the Crown. Odessa had been encouraged by both Aura and her parents to keep her prophetic dreams a secret, though she couldn't seem to help showing off to her friends through use of her cards or by describing her nightly visions. Aura did not feel the need to demonstrate parlor tricks and had no problem keeping her secrets to herself. She would encourage her children to do the same.

Aura went back into the house and grabbed two more blankets. She draped one around Callen's shoulders and placed a kiss on his forehead. As she wrapped another around Barrett, she looked him in the eye and spoke quietly and seriously, "Do not speak to anyone about what your aunt and I discussed this morning." He nodded stoically, took his brother's hand, and went out.

Before resuming her conversation with Odessa, Aura went into the back bedroom and retrieved Echo who was standing up in her small wooden crib. It was typical of her to quietly look out the small window at the birds in the trees rather than immediately call out to be picked up. In general she was a quiet child, much more so than both of her brothers who had been desperate to talk before their mouths would allow them to do so. While she obviously loved the girl, Aura felt she had to work harder to gain her affections. Echo did not come with bright eyes seeking connection like Barrett or a contagious smile like Callen. She was content to be in her mother's arms while nursing but then preferred her space. Aura savored those moments between them that were becoming few and far between as Echo became less reliant on her mother's milk and happier to eat the fresh berries the boys brought home or crumbs of the sweet cornbread Aura baked since she knew it was her favorite.

"Good morning, sweet girl," Aura cooed. She groaned as she lifted the girl from her crib. If they did go along with Odessa's wild plan she would be carrying her far longer than from the bedroom to the kitchen. The other boys wouldn't be able to walk very far on their own either. If they were going to get anywhere they likely would need Eryx's assistance. The idea was ludicrous.

Though, if she chose to stay and go to the widower's ball, could she really trust someone new to care for her children? Would she be able to find someone kind enough, close enough in age who she could trust enough after meeting them on one occasion? It wasn't likely.

She walked back into the kitchen and sat down across from Odessa, opening her tunic in order to bring the child to her breast. She looked across at her sister, still a child herself, but right now the one person Aura could trust with her family's best interests at heart. She sighed and then spoke.

"Just tell me what to do."

CHAPTER 4
ODESSA

Odessa filled her sister in on everything that had transpired at the Widow's cottage, including the women who had supposedly disappeared in the past and the cabin in the woods. She had never told her directly, but Odessa had always felt strongly encouraged by her sister. Though Aura often reproached her for flaunting her gift as a seer outside of the home, behind closed doors she often asked for her little sister's thoughts on basic day to day decisions, as well as significant life choices. Aura never scoffed at even the most mundane or ridiculous of Odessa's visions. Even after her failure at not foreseeing their current predicament, Aura was still willing to trust her younger sister and her gifts, and Odessa would not let her down.

As she shuffled her cards Odessa studied her elder sister nursing her youngest child. Aura held Echo in her left arm while twisting the dark blonde braid that hung down over her right shoulder. Her worried hazel eyes shone gold against the yellow of her open tunic. Odessa couldn't imagine having three children by the age of twenty-three. While she loved her nephews and odd little niece, and did whatever Aura asked of her, she wasn't sure if she could handle losing her freedom. Not being able to wander off into the woods because someone else needed to be fed or bathed or comforted. She knew that even before having children her husband would likely require the same of her, and she was sure that she wasn't ready to do even that just yet.

Odessa finished shuffling and fanned the cards out on the table. She didn't have to tell Aura to close her eyes and focus on the questions that she wanted answered. After so many times completing this ritual her sister knew to ask simple direct questions in order to get a clearer response.

"Which path should I take?", "Where will it lead me?", "What will my future then be?" she asked, firmly and sure. She moved her hand across and tapped three cards. Odessa followed her movements and picked them up one by one leaving them face down. She scooped up the rest of the cards and placed them back in her velvet sack.

"What path should you take?" Odessa repeated as she turned over the first card. It depicted eight staffs of varying sizes that looked like they were poised to strike. A pit of fire blazed behind them, and a bright sun was coming up over the horizon. "Eight of Wands."

She tried not to look too excited as she looked up at her sister. "Well?" Aura asked impatiently.

"The general meaning is movement, especially fast movement. Travel, action…freedom."

"I suppose that doesn't leave much up to interpretation," Aura responded uneasily.

"No it does not," Odessa affirmed with a slight laugh. "Where will this path lead you?" she asked, turning over the next card. This one quickly brought down the corners of her smiling lips. It depicted a high tower on a rocky mountain surrounded by water. The Tower was cracked and leaning after being struck by a bolt of lightning coming down from the sky.

"This message is not as clear," she admitted, trying to reassure herself as much as her sister. "It could mean danger or crisis but can also mean unforeseen change or even liberation like the first. If the first card suggested that we do leave this place I don't think that this one would warn us away from doing just that. It could be suggesting that we proceed with caution on our journey but still be encouraging us to make that choice."

Aura looked unsure but gestured to Odessa to continue the reading. Odessa took a deep breath and reached for the final card. It showed a man, standing tall and dressed in armor. He held a large staff and there was a crown placed upon his head.

"The king?" Aura asked, startled.

"No," Odessa corrected. "The Emperor. He's not someone to fear, rather a symbol of good leadership. You asked what your future will be so this is suggesting that you will be in a position of power. It could even represent the head of a family."

"Which I suppose I am now," her sister said cheerlessly, gently toying with the curls on her daughter's head.

"Which you always have been, "Odessa countered firmly. "Even before now, Vitus was often away. You've managed the household, the children, me…"

"I don't think anyone has ever truly managed you," she replied, laughing.

"Well, you've tried your best at least. Others would have given up long ago. We'll quietly prepare today and go to bed early. Hopefully whatever dreams I have will further cement our decision and provide more specific guidance."

As Aura got up to get Echo ready for the day, Odessa went to put the three cards back with the others but then changed her mind and removed all the cards from the bag. She shuffled them quickly then split the deck and took the card from the top of the bottom pile. It depicted a girl of snow white hair sitting in a field of bright red flowers. The black cape around her shoulders faded into a picturesque scene below showing a calm river and a starlight road leading to a path between large mountains. Behind her head glowed a round full moon. Odessa let out a small sigh of relief and returned the card to the deck. Whenever she did an especially important reading, she liked to check in on herself. If either The Moon or The High Priestess appeared she felt that they were assuring her of her intuitive abilities. In this instance she severely hoped she was right.

CHAPTER 5
AURA

Once Aura had dressed Echo, she gave her over to Odessa so that she could think through all of the preparations that would have to be made for the journey. They would have to pack lightly with only a single change of clothes each. This time of year they would likely have luck foraging for mushrooms, berries, and other gifts from the forest. Aura was also quite skilled with a bow thanks to her relationship with the wind. She had been taught from early on not to take her powers for granted, and she treated the air around her as if it were an old friend. As a small girl she would spin in circles, releasing flower petals and seeds as gifts. She taught the children how to blow bubbles into the summer breeze and also share bits of their harvest sweets with the stronger gusts of autumn. She often pestered Odessa to do the same; however, she also understood her sister's devotion to her clairvoyant powers and the more mysterious forces that had gifted them to her, forces that Aura preferred not to acknowledge. Her elemental powers were concrete and simple. Her other powers were more difficult to understand, and they scared her in a way. She wasn't sure where they came from, how they worked, or the effect they truly had on herself and others.

As she folded and gathered and packed, Aura thought about Eryx's expression as he left the cottage. Odessa wouldn't be happy if he chose to stay. Her statement that he would come with them had been her plea even though she was sure he hadn't interpreted it that way. The animosity between them was too strong to not be hiding stronger feelings beneath, yet she knew they were both too stubborn to acknowledge anything. They might not even be aware of how they really felt about each other.

The kindest option would be to steal away into the night before Eryx decided that he was too chivalrous to allow two women to set off into the horrors of the woods on their own. If he had been any younger, things would be different. She would either have chosen to stay to keep an eye on him or talked him into coming. As it was, he was sixteen, and she knew that he would be fine on his own even if he was a bit lonely at times during his courtship. His whole life, his father had prepared him for his trial, and she knew that he would be disappointed to miss it and the chance to show off his skills. He would be matched with a top female, forget about his old neighbors, and eventually be a kind and dutiful husband and father. He would be lost wandering the woods with them without purpose. Odessa would thrive. As for herself, she would do what was necessary to provide the best chance for her children and perhaps find her missing husband while she was at it.

As she sorted through the dried fruits, nuts, and grains that remained in their basement cellar from last year's harvest, Aura felt a slight breeze tickle her neck, an uncommon occurrence in the dark, airless space. The upper door to the cellar moved lightly back and forth, as if two invisible entities were fighting with one another to keep it open. When Aura just stared rather than initiate any kind of movement, the door swung violently open and then slammed shut, startling her and finally causing her to run up the rickety wooden steps. Once she reached the main living area she noticed that the front door was slightly ajar, and she could hear voices outside, both of which she recognized.

She felt a jolt of fear go through her, but she knew she didn't have a second to spare to prepare herself for the conversation that was coming. Who knew what hints the boys had already unknowingly provided concerning their plans. She straightened her posture and headed for the door.

Callen was sitting cross legged on the ground watching a small green caterpillar weave through his fingers. She couldn't tell if he was just uninterested in the conversation going on or if he could feel some kind of ill intentions coming off the man speaking to his brother and chose not to engage.

Barrett stood tall, his hands on his slender hips, talking with the man that stood twice his size before him. His hair was a reddish brown that nicely complemented his copper tunic, and a light stubble dusted his strong chin. The fire elemental had been one of the sought after prizes of their trial year due to his good looks, a prize that she had absolutely no interest in then or now.

"Good morning, Donovan," she stated simply, trying to keep any iciness from her tone. "Boys, you forgot to bring in your dishes from this morning. Go take them in to Dessi."

Barrett opened his mouth to argue but Callen gave him a beseeching look. He appeared to understand because he bent to pick up the plates and followed his brother inside. The door quietly closed behind them.

"What do we owe the pleasure?" she asked, then winced at her choice of words. She added quickly to dispel any lewd comment, "What brings you to Goldenmount? It had to have been quite an uncomfortable journey from the city. The roads through the mountains must still be wet." Damnit she'd done it again.

The corner of his lip rose into an oily smile, but he seemed to think better of being inappropriate at such a time. Instead, he cleared his throat and said: "How could I not give my condolences to the wife of my oldest friend?"

She furrowed her brows in confusion. "Were you already in town? We only got the news this morning."

He folded his arms and looked extremely satisfied that he had gotten one up on her. "I heard last week. The palace gets birds from the legions so it can update the list of dead or missing. They're especially vigilant this time of year with the ball so close. The ball I assume you'll be attending?"

"As I said, we only heard this morning. I'm still weighing my options."

"We all know you're too full of yourself to actually take the widow's potion," he scoffed. "I'm surprised with your bond you didn't know earlier. Guess it wasn't as strong as you thought." He eyed her with a jeer as if just waiting for her to make a move that would give him an excuse to retaliate. While she already knew that she could beat him in a fight, she didn't need any scrutiny from the village or the palace and instead chose to change the subject.

"How's Flora?"

He smiled tightly at the mention of his wife. "Fine. Looking forward to seeing you when you come to the city."

Well, that was a lie. Flora hated her.

"It was her idea actually, that I come down here to retrieve you."

Aura froze. Her mouth opened, but she wasn't even sure which part of that statement to digest first or how to respond. He expected her to refuse. He knew how she felt about him. There was no way in hell she would put herself in the position to be alone with him for any amount of time, let alone more than a day's journey. As for it being Flora's idea, she had likely said something along the lines of "That bitch better not show her face here when she comes to the city" or "I bet Vitus didn't even leave her with enough coin to make the trip."

"I appreciate your kindness, but that's really not necessary." She attempted groveling and excuses rather than outright hostility. "We already set aside some money for a coach to take Odessa and Eryx for the trials. I plan to go along with them. It would be nice for the children to get away and see the city. Odessa was Barrett's age when she came up with my parents to watch…"

Aura stopped herself. She just couldn't stop putting her foot in her mouth today.

Donovan had grown up in the village alongside Aura and Vitus. As kids, the two boys had been a fearsome pair and had acted towards Aura the way boys were expected to towards females: pulling hair, pushing her in the mud when the creek flowed over and the ground became a swamp, taking unfair hits during sparring practice when the instructors weren't looking. Eventually Vitus had matured and come to his senses, realizing that a person's sex shouldn't determine how they should be treated. He also realized that Aura was stronger than both of them and winning her favor was more important than being "one of the boys." While he still refused to outright abandon his horrible friend, Vitus chose to spend more time training with Aura and no longer shadowed Donovan during his cruel pranks or laughed at his vulgar jokes.

Even after it was made clear that Vitus and Aura were romantically linked with the hope of matching at trial, Donovan still made off-color comments to her when Vitus wasn't around and even stole a kiss once when she was walking home from Vitus' house through the woods after dark. It was only weeks before her trial, and her mind had been elsewhere so she had ignored the whistling wind's warning and didn't hear him sneak up behind her. She had never told Vitus. She had been ashamed thinking it was her fault and that Vitus would be upset with her. Donovan had pulled away before she could even react, but he had whispered that he knew how to beat her when they competed and that she would be his and not Vitus'. She knew that he had selected his timing strategically in order to lower her confidence and cause her to slip up.

Unfortunately for him, and fortunately for her, she was stronger than that, and his behavior only strengthened her resolve to completely annihilate him. In a shocking twist and despite all her worrying, he ended up being the least of her problems that day. While she assumed she would have to rely on her more preternatural powers, which would have completely messed up her strategy of hiding those same powers in order to fake losing to Vitus, it turned out that Donovan was all bark and no bite. She overpowered him easily with the use of a giant windstorm that was fed on pure rage. Flora was from the city itself and had been the second most won female of the day. Following their marriage, Donovan claimed that they chose to move to the city because Goldenmount was too humdrum for him and his aspirations. Aura was certain that he was quite embarrassed about being beaten by a girl, and also suspected that Flora, whose family was somewhat influential and definitely wealthier, refused to leave Awrymor. Aura was never certain if Flora's discernable detestation for her was a result of the lascivious looks her fiance openly gave Aura whenever Flora visited during their courting period, the fact that Aura had completely destroyed Donovan at trial while he had easily bested *her*, or because in doing so it sealed her fate, causing Flora to be stuck with him for all eternity.

A look of malice flashed over Donovan's face, but it was gone just as quickly. He wouldn't want to revisit that particular day either. Instead he changed the subject back to the present day.

"Come on. Let the youngsters travel on their own. Some private time in a carriage might do them some good before they're both betrothed," he said with a repulsive grin. "I distinctly remember some moments stolen on a chilly spring evening not long before our own trials."

Aura swallowed the bile that had risen in her throat. How could a person not change from five to fifteen to twenty-five. It was unimaginable. She took a deep breath just trying to end this conversation and get him to leave.

"Odessa and Eryx are my responsibility, and I will see them to the city safely. I appreciate your concern but your assistance is not needed." Her words were firm. It was becoming harder and harder to stay respectful as he pushed more and more of her buttons.

"I'll be here for another week or so regardless. That will give you some time to come to your senses," he replied breezily. He took a step closer and let his fingers find the end of her braid. "Even if we don't make the trip together, I hope you'll stop by the townhouse. Flora always goes to visit her mother first thing in the mornings." The despicable message was loud and clear. Now that Vitus, his oldest friend, was likely dead, he had the right to her before she was married off to someone else.

He suddenly tugged the hair that he held, painfully bringing her head nearer to his own, his mouth disgustingly close to her ear. She winced but stopped herself from crying out in order not to frighten Barrett who was surely listening if not watching from some window. He whispered conspiratorially, "Don't think about disappearing. I'll drag you back by this little braid right here. I'm sure my friends in the guard would turn a blind eye if I wanted some time alone with a runaway."

He finally released her and smiled easily as he stepped backwards towards the path. He waved up towards the upstairs window of the cottage almost as another silent threat and was gone. She stood for a long moment until she could see that he was out of the woods and walking down the lower path towards the center of town. She walked back into the cottage bolting the door behind her. Odessa stood with a look of concern, the boys beside her and Echo wiggling in her arms.

"Tonight," Aura replied to all of their silent questions. "We leave tonight."

CHAPTER 6
ODESSA

Odessa awoke to cold. The open window beside her bed let in the last icy breaths of winter. The full Pink Moon illuminated her exhalations turning them into miniature lightning filled clouds. As she sat up she noticed that she wasn't alone in the dark room. A specter sat beside her silently as if it had been waiting for her to rise. It was translucent and only visible where the moonlight touched its form. While startled, Odessa was not afraid. She had been visited by this being many times before and knew it meant no harm.

The apparition stood then and turned towards the door. As it walked out into the stairwell leading to the ground floor of the cottage it faded completely to black. Odessa dressed quickly, throwing a heavy cloak over her chemise. Once downstairs, she retrieved her brown boots and hurried out the open front door.

The figure stood waiting for her, its outline now more defined in the ample moonlight. Its contours appeared to be female in nature with thin, long legs much like her own, but fuller breasts that Odessa could see whenever it turned back to check that she was following. At times she could also observe the illusion of long hair swaying from side to side.

The moonlit shadow went around the back of the house, starting down a path that Odessa had taken many times before in the light of day. It helped that she was already familiar with this particular route, but she knew that the further they walked the more foreign the path would become and therefore took note of any interesting landmarks or unique features.

As they walked, Odessa lost all concept of time. It sped up when the path became monotonous and everything looked the same, but then it slowed when there was a particular rock formation or a magnificent waterfall she was meant to take notice of. At the beginning of the journey she passed by old friends from the midnight forest walks she would take after being roused by prophetic dreams: swooping owls, masked racoons and chittering bats. The deeper they ventured into the forest the more shadowy the creatures became, the sounds they made more strange, and yet, their presence, like her guide, did not ignite any feelings of fear.

Odessa felt the cold leave her, though it was not due to exertion alone. The closed buds of early spring had bloomed and fallen as they walked, marking the passage of time. A maelstrom of petals spun around her as she walked down a rocky path, the rays of light making them look like giant snowflakes.

Finally, the being stepped out of the forest before her and lit up like a beacon, opaque and shimmering as if it had fully absorbed the light of the moon. As they stood at the banks of a river, the phantom lifted its hand and pointed southwards to what appeared to be a small island, atop of which stood a crumbling fortress. The river here was narrow, and Odessa was close enough to see another figure standing out on the parapet. Its appearance was in direct opposition to that of her guide, as it was dressed in full black robes that billowed and shifted in the midnight gusts.

Odessa removed her eyes from the figure in black and was startled by the moonlit wraith now standing directly in front of her. It took her face in its hands, the bite of cold so sharp it almost felt like she was being burned. The figure matched her in height and as it brought its forehead to her own she became blinded by the bright silver light, everything else fading from view. Before the light dimmed and Odessa was left alone in the darkness of her bedroom, she could hear the spirit whispering to her, something it had never done before. It was in a language that sounded both foreign and ancient. As her mind attempted to unscramble the meaning of the words, they faded quickly from her memory.

CHAPTER 7
ODESSA

Odessa again woke up to the cold air coming in from her window. She was sure that she had closed it before going to bed, but it was possible that the wind was in cahoots with her dreamlike visitor and had woken her so that she could put her dreams into action. She had tried to go to bed early after drinking the tea the Widow had given her with the hope that she could get confirmation of the path they were to take and get as early a start as possible. Unfortunately, her anxious energy had gotten the best of her, and she had tossed and turned for hours before finally falling asleep. If she had to guess, it was now well past midnight.

She dressed by the light of the moon, which was just as bright as it had been in her dream and then opened her door to head downstairs. The stairwell was dark, but the light of a single candle flickered off the walls of the kitchen. As she reached the bottom step she could see her sister sitting silently in a chair watching it burn.

When she reached the table, Aura looked up at her questioningly. She was fully dressed, and every hair was perfectly ensconced in her braid. The color of her face was so pale it almost matched that of the woman in her dream, though without the sparkle.

"What were you shown?"

Odessa looked down at the chair beside her but then decided that it would be better to keep her momentum going rather than get too comfortable.

"The dream told me the path to take. First through the Burnished Forest and up Steilkopf Mountain and then through the Stygian. The end of the journey was the Harridan River. There was a small rocky island there with some kind of abandoned castle." She closed her eyes trying to remember everything she had seen. "Actually, not abandoned. There was someone there."

"Someone?" Aura's dark eyebrows rose in question. "Not one of us?"

"No. I was alone apart from my guide. None of you were present. And then the figure at the end, but they were masked."

Aura dragged her hands down her face. "And we can trust this guide of yours? This place should be safe? I don't ever recall hearing or reading about an inhabited island on the river."

"Maybe that's the point," Odessa retorted. While they got along for the most part, Aura sometimes did pull the 'wiser older sister' card which didn't sit nicely with her own 'rebellious teenage younger sister' persona.

Aura considered it and then nodded. "I suppose any place would be a better option than we have right now." Odessa could see that she was thinking about Donovan. Aura hadn't shared much with her about the man. She personally had few memories of him, but she had seen the rare fear in her older sister's eyes when she had walked back into the cottage and didn't doubt that he was someone they shouldn't mess with.

"Where's Eryx?" she asked her sister suddenly, noticing that he wasn't lurking quietly in some corner. Aura had told her not to worry about calling on him before she went to sleep and that she would take care of it.

"Not coming." Aura spoke the words nonchalantly but shifted her eyes towards her as if looking for her reaction.

Odessa rolled her eyes, sure that Aura had not sufficiently used the threat of guilt in order to manipulate him into joining them. "Let me try him. We'll stop by there on our way out."

"No we won't. I didn't tell him we were leaving."

"But he's supposed to help with the children. We can't carry them all on our own." Her voice was more shrill than she liked and she wasn't keen on the fact that she sounded like a petulant teen.

"We can't ruin his life just because I don't want to remarry and we would benefit from an extra pair of hands. I'll take Barrett on my back and Echo in front. You can carry Callen. Once the sun comes up we can rest a bit and then they can walk for a while."

Odessa felt like she was sucker punched and wasn't even sure why. "We can't just leave him here. He'll think we abandoned him."

"Maybe at first, but he'll be married soon. If none of this had happened you both would have been getting ready for trial and going off who knows where during courtship. Plus you two get along like oil and water lately. The guard would find us before long just by following the sounds of your bickering." She stopped a minute and looked at her younger sister. "Unless he was part of your dream? You said none of us were there so you can't be certain whether or not he's supposed to come with us."

Should she lie? Give both her sister and Eryx an excuse for why he had to join them on their journey? They would both believe her. For all his whining about how she didn't train hard enough, he, like Aura, never doubted the messages she received. She couldn't abuse their trust like that. Even if leaving him behind was like a stab to her gut.

"No," she replied, head downcast. "He wasn't there." The excitement she had felt all day about setting off on their adventure was dulling quickly. Leaving for somewhere new, even if it was dangerous, with everyone she cared for wasn't really leaving home, but if Eryx wasn't coming, a piece would be missing. He had been a constant presence in her life for as long as she could remember and was always there when she needed him. Could she really say the same though?

With the tension between them she hadn't known how to talk to him about what had happened with his parents. Aura had done what she could for him but almost more as a mother would with food and hugs rather than as a friend, and even with her he had been unwilling to really share what he was feeling. Odessa had tried to ask him about how he was doing on one or two occasions, but he had brushed her off. She had felt it was probably just better to leave him alone.

When her own parents had died, even though Eryx had

only been eleven, somehow he had known what to do to make her feel better. He had held her hand and brought her to a meadow filled with wildflowers. She figured that he thought it would cheer her up and make her smile, but instead it had triggered a barrage of tears. At first he had looked horrified; however, when she grabbed onto him and sobbed he had let them both fall to the ground. He held her, brushing her long hair with his fingers until all her tears were spent and her body finally stopped shaking. It wasn't something either of them had brought up afterwards but that was how it always was. They would live their own lives but then if some girl was mean to her or some boy broke her heart by breaking off some silly chaste relationship, she would come to him and he would just listen.

Maybe her sister was right. He would be better off without them. Happier living the life he had always prepared for. He'd probably match with some super uptight, insanely talented female. Odessa was better off being a world away from that.

Aura had gotten up from the table and was tidying up the last vestiges of their old life. The fresh fruit and bread from the morning had been either eaten or packed and not a crumb remained. The fire had dwindled down to bright red embers. For some reason the fact that she would never again sit by this particular hearth while cuddled up with one of her nephews and a book pulled at her heartstrings. The cottage would look like they had simply gone out and not left forever for some crumbling tower. Rather than letting her mind go back to Eryx and everything else they would be leaving behind, Odessa chose to look towards the future. She donned her armor of tall brown boots that would keep her warm and cushion her feet through the long miles, and the goldenrod hooded cloak that had been her mother's.

"It's alright. I'll take Barrett," she finally said to Aura, acquiescing to her plan to leave her friend behind.

"I wasn't being kind in giving you Callen." Aura chuckled. "He's only five pounds less and has shorter legs. I likely will need you to carry my bow. And my pack."

"Alright, now it sounds like you'll be the one getting off easy. Though maybe you're just trying to make it out that way so I offer to take Echo."

"Hey, I paid my dues carrying you around for years. It's about time you made up for it." Aura smiled as she said it but then her face turned serious as she stood before her sister and held her face with one hand, tucking a stray hair behind her ear with the other. Her hands were warm and rough from all of the work she did constantly to keep everyone alive and happy.

"Thank you for coming with me," she said quietly. "I have a feeling it's something you would have done on your own one day anyway, leaving this place for somewhere better, but I'm glad that we'll be doing it together. If anything happens I just want you to know that I appreciate it."

CHAPTER 8
AURA

Aura knew it would be safe to leave in the middle of the night since no one would think them so insane as to carry three children through the woods in the dark. Even if they had thought that she might be desperate enough to do just that, no one's first thought for a route would be up Steilkopf Mountain. Before Odessa had shared the exact specifics of her dream, that had not been her first choice of a path, but if there was more of a chance for them to make it to their mystery destination by roughing it at the beginning, so be it.

They did have two things going for them already. The first was that Barrett had woken up eagerly excited to start their trek and happy to walk on his own for a while. Callen and Echo were dead weight as expected, but at least Aura had use of her arms and back and could help Odessa with more of the baggage. Without being weighed down by his siblings or bags, her eldest child moved over the rocks so swiftly they had to call him back at times so that he wouldn't lose his way.

The second was that while this path was unforgiving, with an immediate zigzagging incline followed by an uphill jaunt through a rocky streambed, at least it was one that Aura was very familiar with. In the lead up to their trials she and Vitus had visited this place once or twice a week, even more frequently that final month. They had alternated between sprinting up the mountain as fast as their legs could carry them and hauling large sand filled packs up on their backs in order to focus on strength training and stamina. They had done it over and over, and yet the path looked and felt so different with the passing of each season that it didn't get old. In the summer, the sun browned her skin and made the sweat drip off of her so much that once when she laid down in the dirt at the top of the hill she made a person-shaped stain in the dry earth. Vitus had teased her about how disgusting she was but had then done the exact same thing and made his own dirty sweat angel holding hands with hers. In the autumn, the leaves fell from the trees beautifying the path but also making the cliffs more treacherous with the threat of slipping on them. In the winter, the rocky streambed was almost impossible to conquer since each of the boulders was covered in ice making it necessary to grasp onto the trees on either side. In the spring, the trail was at its most welcoming; however, that only begged them to go harder and faster and to use all that strength that they had gained throughout the year.

Odessa would roll her eyes and feign gagging when Aura talked about "the old days" and how exhilarated and strong she felt after those hikes. Her sister's body was for gracefully strolling through flat woods like an overgrown fairy and stretching and meditating on giant rocks. Aura had accepted long ago that she would never be delicate or petite. She wouldn't be winning over her match with fluttering eyelashes or a coy smile. She would earn their respect with her drive and her willingness to take on any challenge.

Vitus' ability to keep up with her proved that he would be a good match for her. He didn't get intimidated when she made it up the mountain before he did or if her bag was a little bit heavier. Every time they made it to the top he would give her a high five or a pat on the back or a hug. Those touches that had seemed so innocent at the beginning of the training had felt more and more intimate with each climb. She knew that she was in trouble when she began to think of his bright smile and his touch as the prize for all of her hard work. He also gained plenty of points for the fact that he didn't give those big proud smiles to the other prettier, more delicate flowers who did attempt to gain his favor through looks alone. Aura couldn't say that she never felt jealous of the attention that he got back then with his wavy blond hair and muscled teenage figure. He was pleasant enough to the other girls but he always made it very clear that all of his hard work was to win her, and her alone.

As they crossed back and forth moving gradually up the mountain, Aura felt a pang of sadness wash over her for her husband as he had been then. They had continued to visit the trail during their courtship and even after they had wed, and those chaste touches had escalated quickly. The first time they had gone up after the trial, when it was settled that they belonged to each other, he had stood over her, placing his big warm hands on her wide hips. He had gazed down at her with a hungry look in his eyes, scanning her face as if taking stock of what was now his to do what he wanted with.

Those few quick moments had felt like forever. She remembered being terrified that he wouldn't like what he saw and that he was regretting the steps they had taken to ensure their match. Eventually, finally, he brought his mouth to hers, and she had forgotten everything else other than the hardness of his body and the taste of salt on his lips.

With them both still living at their parents' houses throughout their courtship, Aura again began to live for those hikes so that they could be alone and explore each other's bodies without judgment. They made sure to take precautions so that there wouldn't be any proof of their trysts in the way of children, but they didn't see any other reason to wait. The first time that he tasted her he laid her on a large flat rock, hidden by some trees, and she remembered thinking that if she tripped on a tree root and broke her neck on the way down she would have died a satisfied woman. Afterwards, he leaned her up against that same rock and gently eased inside her. Though she winced at the initial sting she kept quiet so that he could feel the same pleasure that he had given her. She bled afterwards but he didn't shy away and instead retrieved some water from the nearby stream to help her clean herself up rather than making her feel ashamed. She had felt confident that he would raise their boys to be as considerate and respectful as he was. Now, that would all fall on her.

Somehow, they had successfully completed the first part of the ascent without too much trouble. Though it was all uphill, the back and forth made it more of a gradual climb than a vertiginous one. Now they had reached the more challenging portion that required them to either hop upwards from one boulder to the next or get their feet wet in the shallow stream. Luckily it had been warm enough the past week that the ice had melted from the rocks, making their task somewhat easier. Though it wouldn't be fun scaling the enormous slabs with Callen and Echo strapped to their bodies, the fact they were still sleeping, meant that at least they wouldn't be crying or flailing about. She tried to think of Echo's small weight on her front as a simple sandbag, just one she had to make sure not to crush by falling or slamming on one of the jagged edges of rock.

Barrett had run up the mountain and now easily scaled the rocks like some kind of millipede. Aura was glad that he was acting like this was all some kind of fantastic adventure. She knew once the realization that his father would not be found in some dark cave guarded by a fearsome troll or tied to the mast of a pirate ship sailing the river he would take it hard. Maybe the change in scenery would make it more of a gradual acceptance rather than an unapologetic knife to the heart. Even if they had stayed home it might have seemed like nothing but a bad dream for a while. Vitus was often gone on the king's errands, and they were typically fine knowing that he would eventually be returning to them. Once a new man entered the picture things would have gotten ugly. She couldn't see anyone who would have stepped into that role having an easy time of it with either her or the children. They were quite the stubborn lot.

Her sister could also be included in that group, and at the moment, her pigheadedness was likely the only thing keeping her going. While Aura wasn't having the grandest of times with the burning in her thighs and the sweat dripping equally down her back and chest, Odessa sounded like she was on the point of collapse. With the steepness of the mountain and the full moon Aura could still see her clearly, even though she still had a lot of ground to cover in order to catch up. Yet another positive to this route was that if someone indeed did try to follow them there was nowhere to hide, and Aura could blow them straight off the cliff if she sensed any ill intentions. Aura would have preferred to keep her momentum going to make sure that Barrett had made it safely to the top of the incline, but she was afraid that if she didn't stop

Odessa might just give up and tumble back down the hill. She stopped and turned on the last rock she had climbed and watched her sister ascend. The closer she got, the louder her grunts and groans became, though she might have been exaggerating just a bit in order to gain her sister's sympathy.

Odessa finally reached the rock Aura stood on, and she offered her hand, making sure to plant her feet so the four of them wouldn't end up tumbling down together. Callen was snoring on his aunt's back, lulled to sleep by the sound of her exertions.

"Wishing that you listened to Eryx and were more consistent with your training?" Aura teased, not being able to help herself.

"No," Odessa answered as she took a swig of water from the canteen that she had been carrying on her hip. "If I indeed had a wish, it would be that I didn't listen to you and brought him with us so that he'd be carrying me up this hill. He probably could have had me on his back with Callen on mine without even breaking a sweat."

"He would have done exactly that. That's why I didn't tell him we were leaving."

Odessa just rolled her eyes.

"If I thought—" Aura started, but then reconsidered. "Nevermind."

"If you thought what?" Odessa asked, putting down her canteen and wiping her mouth with the back of her hand.

"If I thought maybe you were into him… In that way…"

Odessa laughed loudly, "We're not exactly well matched."

"Maybe it doesn't seem that way but he obviously cares for you. I was just saying that if I thought there was a chance that you were open to taking on that..role..with him…I would have felt more comfortable asking him to come."

Odessa looked shocked. "What, you would pawn me off on him as some kind of payment for services rendered? Carry my stuff and you can have my sister?"

"No!" Aura groaned, becoming flustered. "I'm explaining it wrong."

Odessa laughed again and patted her sister's shoulder. "I know what you're trying to say. You would feel better taking him away from his trials and future if you thought we had a connection like you and Vitus did, but we don't. Anyway, he wants a girl like you."

Aura scrunched up her face in horror.

"I didn't say he wanted you, specifically. Just someone like you. Someone like him, who would enjoy this particular form of torture," she clarified, sweeping her hand around, gesturing to the mountain around them. Aura couldn't tell if there was a hint of sadness in her tone.

"He and I are too similar," Aura argued. "Being with a girl who was just a copy of himself wouldn't be very stimulating."

"You and Vitus are like that."

"True," she responded, not really knowing what to say to that particular comment and also appreciating the fact that her sister was continuing to speak about her husband as if he were still alive and well.

They sat quietly for a moment, taking in the scenery around them. While the woods to either side of the path were dark, the moonlight unable to penetrate the heavy canopy, the trail was bathed in light, causing the rocks they had already conquered to appear a luminescent white.

"So basically you do want him for his body but only for carrying purposes." Aura stood up gingerly and held her hand out her sister.

"Ew," Odessa snorted, as she took her outstretched hand and pulled herself up. "But yes. Exactly that."

Aura thought the conversation was over as Odessa followed her up the last segment of the climb and was surprised when her sister spoke again through her pants, continuing the discussion.

"So, how *did* you know that you and Vitus were meant to be together?"

"I don't know. I guess because it was easy. He was handsome and strong and not an ass. Not too much of one anyway." She laughed. "I knew raising a family with him wouldn't be difficult."

"Does sound rather boring actually," Odessa replied.

Aura nudged her but gently so that she wouldn't fall over.

"Isn't that what love should be? Easy? Comfortable?"

"I hope not." She paused for a moment in order to push

herself up an especially large rock but this time ignored the hand Aura held out to assist her. "I want to be challenged. That's kind of why I wasn't looking forward to trials. I figured I would have gotten stuck with some brainless lout just because I don't have the best handle on the physical aspects of my power. Unless my dreams had pointed out my competition's weak ankles or poor hearing on one side I would have ended up pretty low."

"Well, here's your second chance." Aura stepped off the final rock and stood waiting for Odessa on the solid ground at the peak. They both looked down at everything they had just very painfully accomplished. The sun would be following them as they continued west and Aura could just make out the lavender haze starting to creep up the horizon.

"Either they find us and drag you back and you're a little bit stronger for climbing this mountain. Or maybe we end up somewhere you'll actually have a choice in the matter and you can find that challenge for yourself."

CHAPTER 9
AURA

Once they reached the top, they found that Barrett had spent all of his energy and was curled up on a bed of soft needles beneath a small pine that had thrived in spite of the inhospitable environment of the peak. Without the respite provided by the thick cover of trees, the icy wind bit at their quickly cooling bodies. Though Aura knew that they needed to keep moving, she took a moment to bask in the frigid air swirling around them. While the coldness of it stung, it still felt like it was welcoming her home and commending her for a job well done. Wind like this wasn't akin to a playful kitten or a comforting dog but rather a porcupine or a scorpion: wild and deadly but still respected and adored by a select few. Aura was uncertain if Odessa was also feeling the connection to their elemental master, or rather it was the closeness of the bright celestial body looming over them, but she too seemed to be silently communicating with a higher power.

They let a couple of minutes pass in silent contemplation but then Aura began to unhook Callen from her sister's back, not wanting their bodies to become so rested that they would begin to ache when they started up again. She placed her smaller son in Odessa's lap who held him close and spoke to him in soothing tones.

"How would you like to walk with me, young sir?" she asked, tickling his chin. Though still sleepy he smiled and then nodded. "The terrain should be much easier after this point," she said, turning to Aura. "Mostly flat land and a slow descent moving across the range of mountains. If you want to carry Barrett for a bit I'll take the baby."

"Just let me feed her first, or she'll be disappointed when she wakes up and notices who's carrying her," Aura replied, apologetically.

Aura removed Echo from her swaddle and moved aside her tunic, letting the wind sharply bite at her exposed breast until her daughter covered it with her mouth and began suckling. She let her body relax into the familiar feeling of the milk's let down even though nothing else at the moment felt the way that it should. She changed her and then let her drink from the other side so that she would be satisfied enough to get a couple more hours of rest, and Aura wouldn't have to worry about feeling any fullness getting in the way of the items she would be carrying.

After they had refueled with a light meal of apples, she strapped Echo to Odessa's chest and slung Barrett on her back, hoping that her already burning thighs wouldn't turn to jelly with the extra weight. As they made their gradual descent, and the sun crept higher and higher into the sky, the forest around them slowly stirred awake. It started with the birds, happily chirping as they made their way out of their nests to search for worms and grubs. Then came the squirrels and chipmunks recklessly racing in front of their path, living for the present and unaware or unbothered by the snakes and hawks looking for breakfast.

Could she be like that? Just living for today? It was somewhat freeing that there was nothing that she could plan for at the moment. No dishes to clean or laundry to hang. Rather than let her mind worry about the "what ifs", she just tried to feel the warming air on her skin, and let her eyes appreciate the random peeks of color that popped up around her. Some were familiar: the light purple of fresh lavender and the bright orange tiger lilies. Yet there were so many more she couldn't identify by name.

Since they were no longer moving uphill and Odessa had the lighter load, she now took the lead with Callen by her side. Though his legs were shorter than his brother's, he was revitalized from his nap and feeding off the excited energy that had reanimated Odessa with the coming of the dawn. As they kept pace with one another, Aura thought about how she could already see the similarities between them as second-born children. They both walked with a lightness that spoke of worrying only about themselves. Not to say that Odessa was self-centered or narcissistic, but she didn't seem to struggle with the same weight of responsibility that Aura had always felt. She could already see the same seriousness imbued in Barrett. The plight of the eldest child. The need to succeed and provide. Every daily action for some purpose.

"What do you think mother and father would have thought of this little journey of ours?" Odessa asked from up ahead.

Aura had tried not to deliberate on what her parents would think of her actions. "I don't think mother would have wanted me to make the same choice that she did," she said, pausing to take a breath, "but she also wouldn't have agreed with letting you walk away from your trials."

"If she knew about how little my fighting skills have improved since the last time she saw me, I think she definitely would have agreed."

"You're selling yourself short, Dessi."

She watched her younger sister shake her head, her white blonde braid wagging from side to side, putting an end to the conversation. Aura was too winded to argue.

Odessa hadn't talked to her after the scouts from the palace had come to watch her and her cohorts spar in order to determine their seeding. Aura had probably been more excited than she was, but she had tried to keep it to herself, knowing that it would just make her sister more likely to withhold the details. As it was, immediately afterwards, Eryx had come by to share the compliments and high ranking that the officials had bestowed upon him, modestly of course; however, Odessa was nowhere to be seen. She didn't return to the cottage until Aura had already retired to bed. She had waited up a while to see if she could ambush her in the kitchen while she made a cup of tea or by the fire where she usually studied her cards or read a novel, but Odessa had immediately gone up to her room and didn't come out. Now that she thought about it, their conversation this morning was the first time Odessa had brought it up herself, likely now comforted by the fact that her ranking no longer mattered.

If Odessa did end up competing this year, or even next year, Aura was sure that she wouldn't just end up with "some brainless lout." Psychic powers aside, while she didn't have Aura's natural proclivity to easily put on muscle, she could see that with her lean arms and long legs, that seemed to grow more day by day, Odessa could grow into quite the fighter if she only tried. Her lightness on her feet would allow her to sneak up on any opponent and once she built up her stamina and grew out of her clumsiness, she would have the speed as well. Maybe with the excess of time they would now have with one another, Aura could also help her in regards to her air control. It wasn't something that they had worked on together in ages. Aura had always had the nagging feeling that Odessa had purposefully leaned into her psychic powers just so that she wouldn't have to compete with Aura's mastery of the wind. Or listen to her advice.

As she checked in with the air now everything seemed to be as it should be.

"Do you think we'll be able to keep this up until sundown?" she asked Odessa, trying to phrase it in a way that her sister wouldn't take offense. While the wildlife on the mountain had been mostly nonexistent due to the difficult terrain and high elevation, she would rather not have to worry about being stalked by wolves or other nightly beings on the woodsier paths.

"We'll see how we feel in a couple of hours, but I think it would be in our best interest to make our way through the forest during the day, and then try to find a safe place to rest once the moon rises." She looked over her shoulder giving Aura a reassuring smile that she was holding up just fine.

"Agreed," Aura replied, finding it difficult to say much more with Barrett still dead weight on her back. After nightfall she and Odessa could take turns keeping watch and hopefully she could get a chance to take her bow out in the morning. She wasn't sure what creatures they would find in the Witch's woods but she wanted to make sure they had full bellies beforehand in case there was nothing but albino deer or three headed snakes.

Though she did have reservations about crossing over from the more familiar Burnished Forest to the darker, more mysterious Stygian Woods that were supposedly loyal to the Western Witch, she almost felt like she would be holding her breath until that change happened. Regardless of the fact that she had always been taught the contrary, she felt that once they reached that point they would be safe. That the patriarchal society that wanted her dead for no reason other than that she didn't "belong" to someone, would no longer be able to hurt her or take her children away.

CHAPTER 10
AURA

Barett slept on her back until noon and by that point her biceps, shoulders and neck felt as tight as her bow before a shot. They had a small snack, she fed the baby, and they were on their way again. Odessa offered to keep Echo and this time the boys walked together, first pretending they were outlaws on the run, which in a way they were, and then legionnaires on a conquest. Barrett would stop at times and listen to the sounds of the woods, though she knew that he was looking for any sign of his father's cries or calls for help. No matter how far they ventured from home, Aura still didn't feel anything of the marriage bond that had been such a comforting presence in her life.

Somehow they managed to keep up with the pattern of stopping to rest and switching the positions of children when they became too tired throughout the day. Finally, the light around them began to fade as the sun surpassed them on their journey west. The sharp rays that had pierced the forest canopy were now warming the people of far off lands. As the temperature dropped, Aura began to notice just how many patches of sweat darkened her tunic and how cold they felt against her skin. She tried not to think about the large tub they had at home and all of the soaps that she had left behind.

While no one would consider her a "girly girl" and she had never been one for fancy dresses or makeups or perfumes, her one guilty pleasure had been soap. She typically got them from the

Widow when they had a bit of extra money, but if Vitus was anywhere exotic and saw some new scent that she could add to her collection he would buy it for her. However tedious or exhausting her day had been, once the kids had gone to bed, she would bathe in the scents of sage and white tea, or basil and citrus or her favorite, intoxicating lilac. If Vitus was at home and still awake, he would drag his nose across her skin and try to guess what scent she had used that night. It was her favorite form of foreplay.

Now, whichever village official came to investigate their disappearance would have first dibs on her collection. She seriously hoped that if Donovan came snooping around he wouldn't pay it any attention. His nose in her soap would offend her more than if he were looking through her undergarments, which would surely be his first stop. She had saved one small bar of the white and purple spotted lilac that Barrett had picked out for her with Odessa for this year's Cold Moon celebrations. She would hold onto it and smell it when she needed a calming breath rather than use it for bathing. Right now she would settle for a nice big whiff, a change of clothes and a seat by the fire.

Aura noticed that Odessa had slowed and was scanning the woods on either side of them.

"There should be a clearing a little ways off the path here."

Aura followed her into a darker section of the woods where the pines and evergreens were spaced closer together and ferns and tall grasses tickled her above her bootline. They walked for a couple minutes more, Barrett almost swallowed up by the thick foliage as he walked between them, until Odessa stepped through two large trees and disappeared. Aura felt a shiver of fear run through her as she lost sight of her eldest child who had followed his aunt through the trees but then she pushed the branches aside and stepped through herself.

A small secluded clearing stood before her. It was large enough that the waning gibbous moon above them shone through and provided enough light that she could see the excitement in Barrett's eyes and the exhaustion and relief in Odessa's. A small circle of stones was in the center as if someone had taken shelter in this particular clearing before and had built a pit for their fire.

Odessa unwrapped Echo from her chest and sat her down on a large flat rock. After sleeping most of the day, she would be awake for a while which was fine since she was typically quiet, and one of them would have to stay awake to keep watch anyway. Her sister then stretched her long arms above her head, straightening out the cramped muscles of her back. "There's a stream a bit further down. I'll go wash and then bring back some water for cooking. Once I'm sure of the path, I can show you the way."

"You'll be alright on your own?" Aura asked hesitantly.

Odessa nodded and smiled as if too tired to get any more words out. She turned and walked out through the trees the opposite way they had come.

Aura could barely keep her eyes open as she went through the motions of getting the children down for the evening. She didn't want to drag the littlest ones down to the water in the dark so she settled for stripping them of their dirty tunics and replacing them with new ones so that they would at least be warm and dry. Maybe there would be fish and they could kill two birds with one stone and catch something for breakfast before they bathed in the morning.

When Odessa returned to the clearing safe and sound, Aura took her turn, bringing Barrett along with her. He led the way, listening for the sound of the stream though she couldn't hear it herself until they were almost upon it. They washed their arms and faces quickly with the cold fresh water and then dipped in their old clothes, watching the water turn brown with all of the dust and dirt they had accumulated throughout the day. On their way back, Barrett carried the wet bundle and Aura picked up as many logs and twigs as her aching arms could handle.

As soon as they arrived back, Aura placed the wood into the small pit and used a piece of flint she had brought to start a fire. Though no fire elemental, her manipulation of the air was typically a great help in starting and maintaining a strong blaze. Odessa boiled the pot of water that she had brought back and they flavored some porridge with a bit of honey in order to make it more palatable.

After dinner they passed around a large mug of tea to help them wind down. Aura was sure that even if she did get a few decent hours of sleep her body would still protest when it was time to go, but for now she would let herself be comforted by the warmth of the fire, the feel of the stone tea cup in her hands, and the taste of mint on her tongue. The boys, who had gotten a second wind with the novelty of a camp out, were begging for ghost stories but apparently Odessa could see that the tea was already having an effect on her oldest sister's ability to keep her eyes open.

"Why don't you sleep first? I'll stay up with them for a while and then I'll wake you when I get too tired."

Aura could only nod before she fell asleep, her head on her pack, listening to the crackle of the fire and her sister's soft, calming voice. Imagining they were all still at home, everything as it should be.

CHAPTER 11

AURA

Aura awoke to black. She felt like she had been sleeping on rocky earth, and pain radiated from her neck down her back and into her hips. She opened her eyes but all she could see was darkness. She called out first to her sister, and then to each of her children, but there was only silence. She didn't yet have the energy to pull herself up out of the fetal position her body had curled itself into, so instead she brought an arm out to feel in front of her. When she did, she touched a wall of earth that was only inches from her face, the movement causing small moist particles to land on her cheek and get stuck in her eyelashes.

Aura moved her other arm behind her and felt another wall of earth surrounding her. Panic rushed through her, providing the necessary momentum to get her stiff limbs moving. She moved up to her knees and tried crawling, but she was surrounded on all sides. As her eyes searched through the dimness in order to determine how far she would have to reach to climb up, a faint beam of moonlight began to light up the space. A figure quietly appeared above her.

With the moon behind him, she could only make out the dark shape of his outline. She called out for help, but the figure quietly retreated. A moment later, she was hit by a shovel full of earth. She tried to scream, but each time she opened her mouth she was hit by another shower of soil that caught in her throat.

Time sped up as the figure continued to shovel dirt on

top of her. As he pressed on with his wicked work, the ground that filled the hole became a never ending deluge until she was buried up to her neck. When there was nothing left but her eyes uncovered, he bent down to her level and she saw that his pale face was just a shining skull with rotting strips of flesh covered by a full head of rich dark hair. He brought one bony finger to where his lips should be in a gesture meant to silence her, and then used his skeletal hands to cover her up the rest of the way.

***

Aura sat up in the campsite gulping in the sweet air that smelled of sulfur and burnt wood. While this particular dream was nothing new, it was especially horrifying when waking up outside on a bed of actual earth without the softness of her bed or the hardness of her husband's chest to comfort her.

To her right side, the children lay bundled together, close enough to the fire to keep warm, but far enough away to avoid any falling ash or ember. She could see Echo's smaller head, covered in light brown hair sandwiched between her two fairer brothers. Her daughter had been the only one to take after her brunet grandfather in more ways than one. Aura and Odessa's father had been the strong, silent type, and the way Echo quietly studied the world around her was a painful reminder of him. She tried to avoid the images but sometimes she couldn't help thinking about how sweet it would have been to see them communicating to each other without the need for words. The baby sitting on his lap soundlessly watching the bees flit around the wildflowers or the snow fall from the sky.

Odessa, on the other hand, was completely her mother's child with her free spirit and her long hair that looked more white than blonde with the starlit sky behind her. She currently sat, eyes closed, head tilted upwards as if listening to someone providing guidance from above. When she opened her eyes to look in Aura's direction, they appeared to be without pupils for a moment, but maybe it was just the glare from the fire, or the reflection of the luminescent moon that made them look like glowing white orbs.

"It keeps showing me the same three cards."

"What are they?" Aura asked, as she undid the mess that was her hair and attempted to rebraid it. "Not that I'll be much help but maybe if you talk it out you'll figure out what they're trying to tell you."

"The High Priestess is first. That's the one that's the most obvious to me. It's usually what I see as a representation of myself."

She passed Aura the card. A hooded, dark haired woman looked out at her. She sat in between two pillars and the branches of pomegranate trees reached in from either side. A large open book sat upon her lap, though there was nothing written on the pages.

"So do you think this represents you or is it referring to some other meaning?"

"Well I thought the other two cards might provide a clue. Sometimes if I can't figure out the message of a card, the other cards that are drawn with it give some added insight into the meaning."

"Alright, what are the other two cards?"

She passed the next one over and Aura could see a man this time, decked in heavy decorative robes, carrying a staff.

"The Hierophant. He's actually considered to be the counterpart of the High Priestess. They're both teachers in a way. She encourages finding truth through intuition, while he supports gaining information through more conventional means."

"So they're opposites, yet still counterparts?" Aura questioned, somewhat slyly as she thought about their previous conversation concerning Eryx.

"Well yes because they still both encourage learning even though he suggests more conservative methods, schools, passed down traditions, etcetera and she's representative of more mysterious, divine knowledge."

"Like how you've taught yourself your own powers versus the training school for elemental powers."

"Exactly."

"So again that could represent a person or just an ideology."

"Yes. Unfortunately the third card is the same. It could go either way and doesn't really help with the other two."

The final card Odessa gave her was a man dressed similarly to the High Priestess. He wore a cloak which showed only his strong arms and the features of his face, though they were somewhat darkened and difficult to make out clearly. In front of him were a gold coin, a goblet, a staff and a sword though the objects floated rather than strictly laying on the table. A storm raged behind him and the electric energy of his movements suggested that either he was the one causing it or he was feeding somehow from its power.

"The Magician. The great manifestor. He utilizes all of the elements to turn thoughts and dreams into reality. "

"I've never heard of anyone being blessed by more than one elemental power," Aura mused.

"Me neither but who knows what powers people hide in order to keep themselves safe."

Aura nodded. The conversation was waking up her brain, now if only she could get rid of the numbness in her limbs. "What about the cloaked figure from your dream? Could they be one of the people represented?"

"Possibly. I suppose you could be the hierophant but that isn't the first card that I would associate with you. You're rigid but not definably so."

"Thanks," Aura responded dryly with a roll of her eyes.

"If we play it that way though. If the High Priestess is referring to me and the Hierophant is representative of you, then maybe the cloaked figure could be the Magician? Maybe they have some kind of mysterious unique power that caused them to hide out in the fortress?"

"Could be," Aura agreed, though not really confident with that interpretation. Sure, she had been quite the rule follower in her younger days but obviously had strayed quite far from that particular path recently. Especially since she was relying on her sister's mysterious powers to guide her on this journey. "Could you draw one more card and ask it to bring clarity to the first three?"

"I knew I liked you." Odessa laughed. "I'm not quite living up to my role as the High Priestess right now. I should be able to figure this out."

"Don't be too hard on yourself. You're functioning on no sleep and you pushed your limits today." She patted her sister on the shoulder and gave her a smile that hopefully let her see just how proud of her she really was.

Her big smile was lit up by the still blazing fire. With all her teeth showing she looked younger than her fourteen years and much younger than the serene prophetess that she had embodied a couple of minutes ago. She kept the three cards she had already pulled out, and lined them up in front of her on the well worn silk scarf they had been wrapped in. She shuffled the remainder of the deck, eyes closed, and seemed to focus on her question. She then split the deck and removed the top card from the bottom pile. Aura, who had moved closer, peeked at the card and saw another cloaked figure, this one bearded and holding a lantern.

"The Hermit," Odessa said slowly. A hint of something resembling concern flashed in her eyes but then it was gone.

"Well?" Aura asked, now getting very into the whole thing.

"Technically this could be referring to another figure. Since they didn't appear initially, maybe they could be someone who we'll be meeting further down the line. Someone who currently is in hiding or withdrawing themself from society in order to work on self-reflection."

"Again, maybe the cloaked figure from the fortress?"

"I don't think so," Odessa replied thoughtfully. "He or she seems more important. They were already present in the dream so it would make sense that they would be one of the first three cards. I see this one as connecting to the first three but maybe at a later date." She appraised Aura uneasily but then her face lightened. "Or this card could just be telling me to go to bed and reflect on everything internally. The more cards I draw the more diluted the message seems to become. I'll just let my mentor help me make sense of all this."

"And by mentor you mean your dream ghost?" Aura laughed.

"I'm sure she's more than that," Odessa responded, a bit peevishly. "Maybe one day I'll figure that out too. Sometimes my power is more trouble than it's worth."

Aura looked at the cards once more before Odessa scooped them back up. She would try to commit them to memory so if the pieces did begin to come together, she would be able to help her sister solve the riddle.

Odessa put the cards away and wrapped herself in their mother's golden cloak. Aura guided her closer and lowered her down until her sister's head rested in her lap. She lightly dug her fingers under her ash blond hair and massaged her scalp until she fell asleep. As she listened to Odessa's soft rhythmic breathing she recited the names of the cards in her mind until she could commit them to memory.

High Priestess. Hierophant. Magician. Hermit.

CHAPTER 12
AURA

Aura awoke again, this time with her back to a log and her sister's head in her lap. The fire had completely burnt out but Odessa and the children still looked to be warm and content, wrapped up in their cloaks and blankets. Directly above them the dark sky was giving way to the purples and oranges of dawn.

While she tried to enjoy the peace and quiet of the moment, the fear and anxiety began to seep back into her bones. They had now been gone a full day and it was likely that someone had noticed their absence. Eryx would know where they had gone and might try to hold off the dogs for at least a little while. With her status as a new widow, there would be people checking in on her, but she wasn't sure how many resources would be spared to hunt down a single woman and four children when it was assumed that they would be lost to the woods anyway. Unfortunately, Donovan wouldn't let it go, so they needed to get to the Stygian Woods as quickly as possible.

Fully dressed, she grabbed her bow and looked back at her sleeping sister. The clearing was well hidden. They wouldn't have found it without Odessa's mysterious helper. It would be more beneficial to them all if she let her sleep in a bit longer so that she would have the energy for the next leg of the journey. Aura would stay close and stay quiet in order to hear if anything was amiss.

She moved out through the trees and towards the small

stream that they had visited last night. Even though she didn't have Barett with her this time to lead the way, the path was clear enough in the soft light of the morning, and the forest was quieter without the voices of the frogs and owls and insects.

She would have liked to use the crystal clear water to clean her face but she didn't want to get too close and scare any animals away with her scent. Instead, she scanned the forest near the stream until she found a tree that would not be overly difficult to climb, and had a perch that would provide a good view of the large bank. The muscles that she had earned from constantly carrying her children around made it easy for her to pull herself up from branch to branch.

This part of their new life on the run was luckily not something new to her. Coming from a family of air elementals, she had grown up hunting and her father had brought money in by selling whatever extra meat their household didn't need. He had taught her the quiet and stillness required to be successful and also how to respect the air so that it would provide the additional boost to make a stronger and clearer shot. Aura had taken over the job after his passing, since Odessa had no interest and was fidgety to the point of scaring away all of the animals. As their family had grown, there was little left to sell but she usually managed to trade with Eryx and his parents, along with other close neighbors for produce and any other goods they needed.

She didn't have to wait long before her instincts were rewarded. There was the snap of a twig, and shortly after, a graceful, long legged doe strode into the clearing by the stream. If anything remained of their scent from the night before, she wasn't bothered by it. Aura kept still as she watched the deer use its tongue to lap up the gently flowing water. The stream would not only act as natural bait for her hunt, but it would also be the easiest place to process the meat so that she could wash up immediately afterwards. She waited for the doe to finish taking its final thirst-quenching mouthful and then pulled back on her string, ready to let it fly once the deer turned its head back in her direction. Before she could release her arrow, she heard the sound of rustling and the deer turned its head the other way, away from Aura in her tree. Two more deer bounded out of the woods, both smaller than the first, with their reddish brown fur covered in white spots.

Aura swore under her breath, too quiet for the deer to hear beneath the sounds of running water. She could still kill the doe but that would leave her fawns alone and defenseless in the cruel world of predators that they were still learning to navigate. She also wouldn't shoot either of the fawns. The little meat they provided wouldn't be worth the guilty feelings that would plague her for days afterwards. She couldn't do that to another mother.

Instead of waiting for another deer to walk past, she could try her hand at catching something in the stream. She was no water elemental, but the stream was shallow and it couldn't be that hard to use the net she had brought to scoop up a bass or a trout. Once the deer had moved on, she carefully made her way down the tree, moving slowly from limb to limb. Finally she jumped down to the forest floor below. As she released her arms from the last branch she felt a prick in the back of her neck. She put her hand up, thinking that it was a stray branch or angry insect but then she heard a deep voice behind her.

"It would be in your best interest to come with me."

CHAPTER 13
AURA

Aura said nothing as the stranger led her back up the path she had taken down to the stream. He kept one arm on her shoulder, leading her forward. The knife remained at the back of her neck so that she was unable to turn around and see if he was someone familiar to her, or get a hint as to what his powers might be. Until she was sure about the situation and all of the players involved, she would be the docile woman everyone expected her to be. There was still the question of whether or not the man, and any companions he might have, knew about Odessa and the children. In case he didn't, she would keep quiet until she could get out of this.

She was bothered by the fact that there had been no warning. That the whole time she had been in the tree the air had been still. Was the stranger also an air elemental therefore making it difficult for the wind to give her favor over him? Or maybe it hadn't wanted her to fall from the high branches?

As they moved farther away from the stream, she heard a whistling that grew louder and louder with each stunted step. They did unfortunately seem to be heading back towards the clearing where the others slept and she tried not to let herself imagine the worst case scenario. That any of them had been harmed or killed. When they finally reached the row of trees surrounding the glade, she could see that the leaves and branches were violently shaking as if a tornado were confined to the small space. Refusing to wait another moment, she shoved her elbow into the gut of the man behind her and lurched through the opening in the trees.

The children sat huddled together on the ground. Barrett had one arm around each of his siblings trying to keep them safe from both the high winds and any predator who would attempt to harm them. Callen was crying loudly. Echo was just watching the spinning leaves and needles as if in a trance.

Donovan had a strong freckled arm around her sister's neck. His other palm was open as if he were trying to conjure fire from it but the wind wouldn't allow it. He had likely known that if he had been the one to ambush her at the stream, she would have immediately killed him so instead he had sent his lackey to confuse her until he could get her back here.

"I told you what would happen if you tried to leave Aura," he yelled over the sound of the unrelenting wind. "You're lucky that I knew exactly which path you would take. We'll have you all back before the officials even notice you're gone."

"We're not going back Donovan," she screamed through the noise. "Let her go."

The other man had recovered from her blow but was struggling, trying to get back through the wall of trees and wind. She could see now that his tunic was navy blue in color but other than that, there was nothing about him worthy of notice. She was used to weak-minded, untalented fools following Donovan around hoping that some of his charisma would rub off on them. She knew that he only picked men who would make him look brighter, not anyone who he would have to compete with for the spotlight. Not since Vitus anyway.

Aura attempted to take a step closer but as she did so Donovan's arm tightened around her sister's throat.

"Why does it matter to you?" she questioned, unable to hold in her frustration. "Are you really putting in all this effort for a quick fuck before I'm married off? You know whoever they match me with will be stronger than you. Just like Vitus was." She didn't like talking this way in front of her children but she figured they would be too terrified to really take in anything she was saying.

A look of pure fury crossed his face but it was quickly replaced by a cruel smile that chilled her to the bone.

"Do you really think that's all I want from you? I've met a lot of influential people since I moved to the city. I'll just have to say the word and you'll be mine."

She shook her head. "You're already married, Donovan. No matter how high up the asses are that you've been kissing, they aren't going to let you have two wives."

"Flora will be dealt with," he sneered.

Though she was trying to remain calm and give him as little emotion as she could, she couldn't help the shock from showing on her face. Sure Flora wasn't her favorite person, but she didn't deserve death. She was sure he wouldn't even do it himself. He would have another one of his cretins commit the act so that it couldn't be traced back to him.

"Don't look so horrified. I know there's no love lost between you two. I will miss having you fight over me though. Maybe we could arrange something between the three of us before she's out of the picture."

The man was a complete narcissist. Anyone in his way was disposable. His brain wouldn't accept the fact that she really did hate him and was in no way playing hard to get.

Whatever feelings he thought he had towards her weren't real either. It was just the need to possess her. To have the one thing that had been denied to him. If she did marry him and give him what he wanted he would lose interest fast.

"How long do you really think you would make it out here alone? The kingdom puts these rules into place because women would never survive on their own. Vitus would be happier knowing that you had someone taking care of you."

Of course. Donovan had Odessa in a headlock because he was worried for their safety.

"If the kingdom was so concerned about our welfare they wouldn't make us take our own lives when our husbands died," she scoffed. "And Vitus more than anyone would know that I would be better off taking care of myself than married to someone like you."

She needed to think her way out of this. She was worried if she made any move against him he would snap Odessa's neck.

"If you don't give me any more trouble I'll make sure that Lucius is gentle when he has his reward. Your sister would benefit from some experience before she finds her husband anyway."

Odessa's eyes widened in pure terror but before Aura could react a vine of ivy shot out from the tree behind Donovan, wrapping around his throat. He released Odessa to pull it off, and she darted away from him and into Aura's arms.

A second later a solid dark shape jumped from the tree. It landed on Donovan's back and the two went down to the ground. The brown of his skin and the dark forest green of his tunic had perfectly camouflaged Eryx who had been hiding in the pine tree above.

The Hierophant had returned.

The man behind her, who had finally made his way into the clearing, saw that his hero was on the ground, and, as expected, disappeared back into the line of trees. Aura pulled her sobbing sister away and held her shoulders firmly.

"Take the children and hide. Don't come out until Barrett tells you it's okay."

Odessa nodded and picked up Echo and the whimpering Callen while Barrett gave her a look and a nod and then followed behind them.

She grabbed the knife that was hidden in her boot and dashed back out through the line of trees. She could see Lucius running down the path back to the stream. She increased her speed, not letting her eyes leave her prey, but also trying to avoid any stray rocks or large roots that would cause her to fall and allow him to get away. After one final curve in the trail, they reached the straightaway that led directly to the stream. She skidded to a halt, her boots kicking up dust, and watched as he continued to run, thinking that he had made it to the safety of the water. The air here was calm, the force of it still in the clearing, hopefully giving Eryx the advantage in that fight, but with the short distance and clear shot she could still reach her target.

She grabbed the handle of the knife, raised her right arm and sent it flying. She aimed for the exact point on his neck where he had held his knife to hers only minutes before. Her physical strength combined with her power to manipulate the air, propelled the blade with enough force that it made its mark within seconds, severing his spinal cord, digging itself between the vertebrae and through the muscle and tissues of his throat. He collapsed mid-run, one hand stretched out towards the awaiting water.

She quickly dislodged the blade from Lucius' still form, grabbed her bow that was lying on the ground by the tree and raced back towards the clearing. When she broke through the trees again the wind was still howling. Donovan was sitting on Eryx's chest, trying to release his arms from the vines that twisted around them. Eryx was struggling to get up. Donovan was almost ten years older, and while Eryx was well built for his age, Donovan significantly outweighed him.

Aura dropped her bow and knife. She wouldn't need them. She walked over to the men on the ground and stood over Donovan as he continued to struggle. She refused to live in fear of this man anymore. He had threatened her sister. Frightened her children. Planned to kill his wife for no other reason than she was in the way of what he wanted. If she let him walk away, he would only come back with more men and more motivation to hurt her and the ones she loved.

She stood in the eye of the storm. The wind swirling around her as she concentrated on her power. Donovan finally realized that she was there and smirked. Aura wouldn't let him speak another word against her. She watched as he inhaled and then released the air from his lungs. She held out her hand and called it to her. Every last bit of oxygen that had filled the large pink organs in his body came when she called. She saw the shift in his demeanor when his attempt to breathe in air was denied. She pulled and pulled and he grabbed his own throat against the straining vines. His skin began to turn blue, contrasting unpleasantly with his copper hair, his outside appearance finally congruent with the ugliness of his soul.

When the lack of oxygen in his blood finally shut off his brain, he slumped down upon Eryx who shuffled his way out from under him. Aura moved to turn the body over and then continued to pull from it, making sure that he was fully gone and not just unconscious. When the air flow began to slow and eventually peter out, the swirling air around her did the same. The clearing went from a screaming cyclone to a peaceful warm spring day within seconds.

"Fuck, Aura," Eryx said, staring at the lifeless body before him.

"Would you rather I left the dirty deed to you?"

"No, but just remind me never to get on your bad side."

"You saved our asses. It would take a whole lot for that to happen."

"I didn't do much," he admitted, almost embarrassed. "I just distracted him enough for you to, I'm guessing, take care of his companion in a similar fashion and then finish the job here?"

"Yes, but you spared the children the sight of it all and I really wasn't sure if I would be able to get Odessa extricated safely." She said it matter of factly and refused to imagine what would have happened if Eryx hadn't shown up at that very moment. He took a deep breath beside her as if also not letting his mind enter those dark places.

"I'm not going to say this situation could have been avoided if you brought me with you in the first place but.."

"This situation could have been avoided if we brought you in the first place? That's possible but then I wouldn't have rid the world of that man and so it was worth the scare."

She wanted to explain to him why she hadn't told him they were leaving but now wasn't the time. This mess needed to be cleaned up before anyone else caught up with them and they added another mark to the tally of crimes committed against the kingdom.

Donovan's body would need to be burnt. An elemental's body not returned to the spirit from which it came would refuse decomposition. If he was buried or thrown in the river, the process would take much longer or possibly not happen at all.

She turned towards Eryx, sweeping her eyes across his face and body to ensure he had no major injuries. She poked lightly at the top of his cheek near his eye where the dark skin looked puffy. He swatted her hand away.

"He got one good hit on me before the vines grabbed him. I'll be fine."

"After you help me get rid of the bodies you can go back to the village. See a healer or get a salve from the Widow. You can just tell everyone that you couldn't find us. Any of us," she added, looking towards Donovan's body. The fact that he was just lying there quietly as the bright sun filtered gently down through the trees was unsettling to say the least.

"You're joking right?" he asked, incredulity lacing his words. "You expect me to just go back to the village? The only reason I haven't told you off yet for leaving me behind is that I'm a little bit afraid of you right now."

"We'll talk about everything later. I just want to get all of this taken care of before some legion stumbles upon Lucius back there. It's also been a while since the wind has provided me with that much independent assistance. That kind of cyclone typically brings some serious weather in its wake." As she spoke the words, she could already feel that something was coming their way. The moisture in the air was more reminiscent of a muggy summer afternoon than a dewey spring morning. "We're going to have to find shelter. And soon."

The fire pit in the center of the clearing wasn't huge, but if they curled Donovan up, he would just about fit. Having Eryx act as her accomplice in disposing of the bodies would be another item to add to her list of things to feel guilty about, but at least he hadn't ended up having to kill anyone himself. He stayed quiet as he grabbed Donovan under his arms and began dragging him towards the pit. Aura picked him up by the boots in order to lighten the load, and they placed him on top of the ashes from the night before. She then bent down and rearranged the body until he was on his side, his knees pulled into his chest.

When she stood back up from her gruesome task she saw that Eryx looked a bit sickly, either from the shot to the face or the thought of what they had to do next. She was about to ask him to just go pull the other body into the water, but then remembered the gaping wound in the Blue's throat and decided that only one of them needed to have nightmares tonight.

"Why don't you go find Odessa and the others? If you call out to Barrett he'll find you. I'm sure Dessa's still upset and could use the reassurance that we're all okay."

He nodded once and headed out of the clearing through the trees. Aura retraced her steps back to the stream and rolled Lucius' body into the water rather than pulling it in order to avoid wetting her boots. Rather than float downstream like any other elemental would, he immediately sank to the bottom as if the cool waters were reclaiming something they had lost. Unfortunately she would have to wait to give the children their washing, though if she was right about the storm, they would be getting plenty wet anyway.

On her way back up to the clearing she grabbed any small logs or larger branches she could see along the path. When her arms were full, she returned to the fire pit and arranged them as best she could. Just like with Lucius and the stream, once the fire was lit, it would quickly feed on one of its own. She stood above the pit for a moment and let one single tear roll down her cheek. A tear for the people who might miss Donovan even with all of his faults: his mother, his wife, his friends. A tear for the society that praised violence and chauvinism over kindness. A tear for the innocence that had been taken today from her and those she loved. She lit the flame and watched the fire burn.

CHAPTER 14
AURA

By the time Aura had ensured that not one piece of evidence was left behind and had gathered all of their belongings, the gray clouds had rolled in, darkening the sky above her and bringing the return of the winds that had so abruptly disappeared.

She exited the clearing in the direction that she had so hastily sent Odessa and the children during the ordeal, and called out for them until she saw Barrett run out onto the path. She bent down and enveloped him in a hug as best she could while still carrying all of their things.

"Is he dead?" he asked, with a hard look in his eyes. "Eryx wouldn't tell me."

"He's dead," she replied reluctantly, her hands on his bony shoulders. At five he should be catching frogs and climbing trees. Not worrying about missing fathers and dead vigilantes.

"I'm glad," he said, that same hardness in his voice.

"I'm not," she spoke gently, removing a leaf from his hair. "I wouldn't have done it if I thought there was any other way. It's not a fun or easy thing to take a life."

"But he was bad. He hurt Aunt Dessa."

"Yes. That's true, and I couldn't be sure that he wouldn't hurt any of you if I let him go. But someone will miss him and there's always that small chance that people will change. He'll never get that chance."

He nodded thoughtfully and she stood and took his hand

so that they could go find the others.

He led her to an open meadow covered in purple wildflowers. Though she couldn't see anyone at first, she heard soft voices and could make out rustling among the stems that suggested the movement of a small animal.

They followed the voices to the middle of the meadow where Odessa and Eryx sat beside one another on a small log. Her legs were folded into her chest as if she were trying to protect herself from any more threats. He sat almost in a squatting position ready to hop up and take out any enemy that came their way.

Aura was curious to know how their reunion had gone; the only expression currently visible on either of their faces was one of weariness. They were quiet now but were just close enough that their arms were touching. Echo sat before them on the soft ground, shaking one of the periwinkle colored blossoms in front of her eyes. Callen ran around them in circles, the morning's horrors forgotten. As they broke through the flowers, Odessa jumped up and enveloped her sister in a hug.

"I am so sorry. I think she tried to warn me in my dreams but I couldn't wake up. I think I was just too tired and then it was too late."

"It's fine," Aura said, pulling back to look at her sister's neck to see if there were any marks on her. "I should have woken you up before I left. I was anxious about getting moving again and thought you could use the rest. We're all okay. That's all that matters."

"How much longer do we have until we get to wherever we're going?" Eryx asked, getting to his feet.

"Too much," Odessa replied, looking up towards the darkening sky. "Might as well start now."

***

Aura knew that nothing in life was ever free, but the heavy rain clouds that had been brought in by the influx of wind in the clearing were a menace. Would Donovan have done more damage to them all if he was able to conjure fire? Yes. Could she still hate this? Also yes.

The ground was so wet that her boots took on more and more mud with each step and her footprints were twice as large as when they started out. She had removed the hood from her mustard colored cloak when it became more of a nuisance than an aide. She was doing her best to shelter Echo by wrapping the sides of the cloak around her carrier; however, she was either upset by the heavy feeling or the growing wetness and was crying inconsolably. Aura's only hope was that she would cry herself into exhaustion, but she wasn't foolish enough to believe that it would happen anytime soon.

The only consolation to the whole situation was that they had gained Eryx, and in doing so, an extra pair of hands. Barrett and Callen would have been knee deep in the muck by now if they had to walk on their own, and she didn't think neither her nor Odessa would have been able to take on two at a time.

When she thought about it, the rain was also likely in their favor, since any village or city officials would have turned back rather than search for them in this. She just wasn't that important.

Odessa abruptly stopped in the path in front of her and pointed to something off to their left. Aura walked forward and tried to see through the pouring rain.

"Do you see that? It looks like a cottage."

The building was a ways off and was dark with no signs of life within. Eryx caught up with them and looked over to where Odessa had been pointing. In his haste to get to them, he had apparently forgotten to bring a cloak and the rain ran unchecked down his nose. He attempted to swipe the water from his eyes, but it was quickly replaced by more.

"You don't think anybody lives out here do you?" he shouted through the downpour. "We have to be in the Stygian by now."

Aura looked around her. She always thought that if she ever made it as far as the infamous dark woods she would be able to immediately tell. There were rumors of unusual sounds, dark shadows, and irregular creatures. Any of the king's legions who came this far out, attempting to take the land back for the kingdom or hunt out the enchantress who was supposedly responsible for its dangers, were either stopped by unexplainable occurrences; sick horses, spoiled rations, weapons that disappeared in the middle of the night; or were hunted by the mysterious beasts that ruled the land. One of those beasts had killed Eryx's father though they hadn't gotten any specific details concerning its appearance or his exact manner of death. Another reason she thought it would be better to leave Eryx behind. They didn't need him hunting down any shadow that crossed their path in case it was the one who had made him an orphan.

This forest didn't look any different to her, though she supposed with the sheets of rain falling down around her, it wouldn't be easy to tell.

"What if it's the cottage the Widow was talking about?" Odessa asked. Even through the noise, Aura could hear the excitement in her voice.

Eryx looked unsure but shrugged. He bent down to take Barrett off of his back.

"Take him and I'll check it out. If there's no one there, at least maybe we can stay until the rain lets up."

He started to walk over, but Odessa grabbed his arm.

"She said there would be a cemetery out front. I can't tell from here but that would be a good sign." She then added as an afterthought, "Be careful."

He nodded and walked off. Barrett huddled closer to her and Aura could feel him shivering through both of their cloaks. Even if the place was a dusty shack she would take it over this.

Eryx took an excruciatingly long time assessing the safety and current occupancy of the cabin while they all stood getting drenched to the bone.

"Did you get a chance to talk when he came to find you before?" Aura asked her sister, having to shout to make herself heard.

"I didn't throw you under the carriage if that's what you're asking," Odessa replied back. "I told him that we both thought it would be the best thing."

"You didn't have to do that."

"I know."

She didn't get to pry further because they saw Eryx's shape swiftly running back towards them. The look on his face was one of bafflement and wonder.

"You were right about the cemetery. There didn't seem to be anyone there but there were things about it that just seemed...off."

"Like what?" Odessa asked eagerly.

"Well, the outside of the house appeared as though it had been abandoned for years. Rotting wood on the steps, cracked windows, overgrown grass. When I looked inside, I figured there would be cobwebs and dust but it looked well taken care of. Like someone just walked away for a moment. There was even a fire lit."

"Maybe they don't keep up with the outside so that no one knows that they're there. They could be some kind of runaways as well. But that doesn't explain where they are now," Aura thought out loud. "We're days away from any other settlement, unless they got caught out hiking or hunting and haven't made it back yet."

"That wasn't all," Eyx continued, hesitantly as if he wasn't sure if they would believe him. "I thought I also saw a set of stairs leading up but from the outside it only looked like one floor. There didn't even appear to be room for any kind of attic or loft. Should we just move on? Try to find some kind of cave to sleep in for the night?"

"No!" Aura spoke at the same time as her sister. Eryx didn't even give Odessa a look as if he expected this kind of complete disregard for safety from her. At Aura, however, he raised a single black eyebrow.

"In a different situation I would have said yes, we should look elsewhere, but the fact that none of us are doing very well here and also that the Widow did mention to you a similar sounding safe house that her husband returned from with all his limbs attached makes me want to risk it."

She could tell that he still didn't like the idea, but rather than argue, he took Barrett's hand and started walking back towards the cottage.

The house was surrounded by a crumbling stone wall that went around the cemetery in front of the house and then seemed to circle around the back. At the opening stood a large circular stone arch. The perfect round shape of it made Aura feel as though it were the gateway to some other world and she felt a shiver in her bones as she walked through that didn't seem to just come from the relentless wind or the wetness of her clothing. The presence of the cemetery suggested that whoever lived in the cottage came from a family of earth elementals since they were the only ones who buried their dead. It didn't look as though any fresh graves had been dug in quite a while.

The cottage itself was made up of small white and gray stones that were missing in some parts. There were also empty areas in the tiles that made up the roof; however, as she walked closer she could see that somehow the rain still seemed to be bouncing off of those spaces rather than pouring into the cottage. Though the windows were cracked, again there were no actual gaps that would allow the rain or wind inside. Depending on the way she tilted her head she either saw emptiness within or colors and light. Anyone seeing the place from far off would assume that it was derelict and abandoned but from up close, there were things about it that made it feel like her eyes were being tricked.

As they reached the front door, Eryx looked back once to confirm that she really wanted to do this. She gave a small nod and he knocked loudly on the wooden door. When no one answered, he knocked again but still there was no movement. He looked back at her once more, looking very uncomfortable at the breach of politeness he was about to make, but then turned the knob and opened the door.

CHAPTER 15
AURA

Aura felt like she was home again.

The first thing that hit her was the smell. While she was expecting must or the scent of decay, she breathed in the warm aromas of cinnamon, cloves and oranges as if someone was heating up a pot of cider. It was something that their mother always used to do for them during the annual final Full Moon celebration; a task she personally had been too overwhelmed with attempting over the past couple of hectic years. The door opened into a small mudroom and they immediately shed their sopping cloaks and muddied boots after quickly seeing that there were no mouse droppings or splintered pieces of floor to worry about. In full view from the mudroom was a roaring fire, in front of which appeared to be a soft, white, bear skin rug and on either side long red velvet couches covered in gold pillows and white wool blankets. On either side of the hearth sat tall bookshelves with well worn volumes of all sizes and colors. She could feel her fingers already itching to grab one. The cottage was warm as if the fire had been going for quite a while and when she looked closer, there was a pot of something cooking within. She saw no signs of dripping water or unwelcome wind blowing through and disturbing the peace. Other than the fire itself there was no sign of anyone. No sound of footprints above or hushed voices.

Eryx turned towards them and put a finger to his lips. Just like he had said, there was a set of stairs off to the side of the kitchen which also had a long table lined with heavy wooden benches. As he crept silently up the stairs, which didn't even have a squeak to them, she continued to scan the room around her. Not only did the inside of the place seem cleaner than the outside would suggest, but also significantly larger.

The idea that the whole structure was somehow enchanted was a novel idea to her. Some people had elemental powers and others had more mysterious powers, but whoever had created this haven must be very powerful indeed. Either they were present and just hiding themselves and were playing with all of their minds, or else someone in that past had bespelled the whole place though how it would continue on at this level of warmth and cleanliness seemed impossible.

While she waited for Eryx, Aura contemplated removing Echo from her chest. She had finally calmed down the moment they had stepped in from the rain, but Aura figured that she would wait to unhook her until Eryx returned in case they were going to be chased back out into the rain. No use getting her dry and comfortable if she would be putting the wet clothes immediately back on. The boys were awake and alert and were examining all that the cozy home had to offer: feeling the softness of the seats and the rug, warming their hands by the fire and searching through the books for something familiar.

While Aura was still being cautious, Odessa seemed relatively sure that they were alone and would be staying the night if not longer. She had already pulled everything out of her pack in order to locate her cards. They had apparently been wrapped in multiple layers of clothing which were now scattered all over the floor. She was now rummaging through the cabinets and drawers of the kitchen. Aura heard her make an approving sound and then she began placing large ceramic mugs onto the table.

"Can you at least wait until Eryx comes back and ensures us that there's no one hiding up stairs?" Aura hissed, her eyes scanning the ceiling above. "He could be battling for his life right now with a silent assailant and you're making yourself at home."

"If there was a problem, I'm sure we would have heard something," Odessa replied, unconcernedly, without lowering her own voice. "He's probably just being neurotically cautious and looking for people hiding in impossible places like under the floorboards."

Aura looked at the wood planks beneath her feet and shuddered. "Thanks for that."

When she looked up again she was startled to see that the man in question was standing at the bottom of the steps looking between them both with wide eyes. She expected him to make some kind of dry comment in response to Aura's jab, but he either hadn't heard it or was too concerned with what he had seen upstairs. He turned his focus back to Odessa before speaking.

"Count to ten and then follow me up the stairs."

Her sister looked at him questioningly, but he just turned and went back up the way he had come. Odessa looked over at her, shrugged her shoulders and moved to the bottom of the stairs bringing her foot up to place it on the first step.

"Dessa. He said 'count to ten,'" Barrett scolded, matter of factly.

She rolled her eyes and then started counting. The boys got in line behind her and counted along. When they finally reached ten, she smiled back at her nephews and then started upwards. Aura debated remaining downstairs to keep watch in order to ensure that no one followed after them, but decided she didn't want to miss out on the excitement. Echo was still strapped to her, and she almost changed her mind when she felt the fire burning in her thighs after two days of non stop exertion but then she heard her sister's squeal.

She raced up the last remaining steps and was momentarily blinded by the bright light coming out of the room. It was as if the rain had been swept away in a matter of moments. The entire room was bathed in sunlight that streamed in from a set of glass doors that opened outwards onto a small balcony. The room was mostly empty except for a large bed. A gentle breeze blew in from the open doors rustling the light white sheets.

Eryx was standing across the room as if he had wanted to see the look on Odessa's face when she made it up the stairs. Aura hadn't seen him look so blatantly happy about something in years, and it made her sad that he either hadn't experienced that kind of joy in a while or that he felt like he had to be stoic in order to come into his role as the unaffected man. If he was still upset with them, he was letting it go, for now at least.

Aura moved further into the room in order to look outside and see if the weather had truly changed that quickly or if it was some kind of trick of the light. She walked out onto the balcony and saw that there was a set of stairs leading down into a giant garden. It was surrounded by a large wooden fence and above that a circle of pine trees blocked any view in or out. There didn't appear to be any gate leading out of the enclosure.

Within the garden she could see giant green leaves but also spots of color: red tomatoes, green zucchini, purple eggplants and yellow squashes. In the very back corner, set away a bit from the vegetation was a circular pool with steam emanating from it.

"Is it..real?" she asked Eryx, wondering if it was just some kind of illusion without any substance. He threw something at her, and she caught it easily in her right hand. It was round and soft and fuzzy. She took a breath and then brought it to her lips. The sweet and floral taste of peach flooded her mouth and juice dribbled down her chin and dripped onto Echo's shoulder.

"Can I sleep here?" Callen asked, longingly looking at the dry, clean covers.

She couldn't help but notice that Odessa's eyes held a similar yearning. She shifted her own eyes over to Eryx, who nodded as if understanding her silent question.

"There should be plenty of room for you, Barrett and Aunt Dessa but don't even think about touching those sheets before you get cleaned up."

She would go down to the garden pool first to make sure that the temperature was safe for the children before letting them wash up. She was sure that Odessa and Eryx wouldn't mind keeping an eye on them all for a couple of minutes…or an hour.

***

Aura and Echo leisurely tested out the steaming waters of the hot spring while Eryx and Odessa explored the garden and helped the boys pick out the ripest looking vegetables for dinner. The pool was the perfect temperature and Echo was fascinated by the way the water bubbled around them. Aura felt as if all of the muscles in her body were melting with the heat, and she felt all of the stresses of the last couple days evaporate along with the steam that rose in plumes above them. While the weather here seemed impossible, they still appeared to be in the same location and season, and by the time she got out, the sun had disappeared from view and the spring sky was turning to the pinks and oranges of dusk.

When she was finally able to get her legs up and moving, she took Echo back inside to start working on dinner while the rest of their party washed up and relaxed. The moment she put the curly haired baby into a set of dry clothes and set her down on one of the couches near the fire, she immediately fell asleep.

Unimaginably, the weather outside of the lower floor of the cottage was still ugly and gray but it added nicely to the comfort and coziness of the kitchen and living area. Aura filled one of the mugs that Odessa had left out on the table with the mulled cider that was indeed at a roiling boil in the pot within the hearth and got to work.

She sweated the eggplants, removed beans from their shells and cut and quartered the zucchini and summer squash before putting everything together in a large heavy pot with some tomatoes. There was some flour in one of the canisters on the counter which didn't appear to be rancid so she put together some biscuits filled with fresh rosemary, another one of her favorite scents. Then she spooned heaps of batter atop all of the vegetables, closing the lid to steam them within the stew.

When everyone was dry and in clean clothes they joined her around the table and greedily ate the dinner she had prepared. The vegetables were soft, but the zucchini still had a bit of a bite to it. The tomatoes had melted into the thick broth, and the taste of rosemary added a comforting warmth to the dish that she felt in her bones. The table was silent as everyone cleaned their bowls. The boys almost fell into them as their stomachs filled and their eyes began to close.

Aura followed Odessa and Barrett up the stairs, with Callen in tow and tucked one boy on either side of their aunt in the large bed. Night had fallen and a gentle, warm breeze flowed in through the open doors. She didn't feel that it was necessary to close them since the back was fenced in and didn't even seem to exist from the other side of the cottage. If there were any unseen enemies she was sure that the air around them was strong enough to do something as simple as shut them. The room was lit only by the same gently waning moon that had followed them since the start of their journey.

"Are you sure you don't want to stay up here with them?" Odessa asked quietly.

"No, Echo will wake up soon and want to feed since she missed dinner. Also, I feel like the atmosphere down there is more fitting to my mood."

She wasn't just making excuses. Now that her basic needs had been fulfilled and then some, the sadness and anger that she felt about her entire situation were becoming more difficult to ignore. The tiny hope that she had held onto, that she might feel something of Vitus deeper into the woods where he went missing, was proving to be nothing but wishful thinking. The fear that they could still be discovered was creeping back in, but she was trying to keep from showing it on her face so that everyone else could sleep peacefully. She hoped that Odessa's shadow woman could fight off any of the nightmares that attempted to infiltrate her dreams thanks to Donovan.

She kissed the three golden heads and then went back down stairs. As she descended, she felt the warmth leech away with every step and heard the rain pattering down against the windows. The fire continued to burn bright even though they hadn't added a single log to it. Eryx was already tucked into one of the couches flipping through a large book and holding a steaming mug. Another was placed on the coffee table between them, and she sat down across from him, careful not to disturb Echo's still sleeping form.

She picked up the mug and took a small sip and then coughed when she felt the familiar taste of liquor burn her throat.

"I found some whiskey in the cabinet. I thought you could use a splash."

"A warning would have been nice. I'm guessing you left it out of yours?" she questioned, raising an eyebrow.

He pointedly took another sip without looking at her. "It's not like I'm going to get myself into any trouble falling asleep on the couch."

Arguing further was futile, especially since she wasn't going to get up and remove the drink from his grasp. She took another sip, this time aware of the bite, and couldn't disagree that the fire of the liquor paired with the sweetness of the apple and the warmth of the spices had the same effect as the hot spring had on her body: an immediate release of tension and dissolution of all the negative thoughts that had come back into her mind.

"She lied to you," she said quietly, using the cider as a boost of courage for the conversation she didn't want to have.

"I know. She wouldn't look at me when she told me. I just wasn't sure if that meant that she was the one who wanted to leave me behind, or if it was you." He still didn't look at her as he studied the book in front of him, though he hadn't turned any of the pages.

"Neither of us *wanted* to leave you behind," she corrected. "But, I was the one who thought it would be the best thing for *you.*"

"You didn't think I was capable of making my own decisions?" he challenged, finally looking up at her.

"You're much too chivalrous for your own good. Even when it puts your own needs second," she replied, leaning forward towards him, the mug cupped in her hands. "That's why I didn't want to tell you. You've been training for trials your entire life. I couldn't take you away from that."

He sat up and turned back towards her, "You didn't want to tell me because you don't know how to ask for help."

She opened her mouth but then couldn't find a way to disagree with that statement. He gave her a few seconds for a retort and then laughed.

"You know I'm right. You and my mother were so close and she still would have to send me over to your house as a spy to see what you could use in the kitchen because you wouldn't just ask."

She gaped, dumbfounded. "I always wondered how she knew just what I needed." She smiled and then blinked the tears away that were forming in the corners of her eyes. She wished that she could go back a few months and stop all of the loss they had experienced in so short a time.

Eryx didn't say anything, and she knew he was probably thinking the same thing.

"I miss her," was all she could offer.

He nodded, and they both just sipped from their mugs as they watched the fire continue to crackle in the hearth, giving each other space to push the grief back down before continuing on with the conversation.

Finally he spoke first. "Just because I've been focused on training and wanting to be better than everyone else doesn't mean that I haven't considered that the current way of doing things isn't necessarily the right way of doing things." He tapped his long brown fingers along the sides of his mug. "Growing up, we're just meant to believe that following the rules of the kingdom is what makes us successful, but has it really worked out for any of us? Was the king's desire for more land worth my father's life? Would my mother have chosen to live if she hadn't been taught from an early age that she was something that needed to be possessed? Someone that couldn't exist on her own? Would you have been such a threat to society if you were just allowed to grieve for your husband before being forced into another relationship?"

Aura was stunned into silence for a moment. "I'm sorry. I didn't know you felt that way."

He shrugged, his dark eyes focused on the liquid that he was swirling within his mug. "You didn't ask."

They were quiet again as they eased down the remaining liquid from their cups. Even the last drop had somehow still been warm and full of flavor.

While Eryx had always been mature for his age, she hadn't realized the changes that had occurred within him over the past month, and it seemed as though the same changes had been occurring within her too. If Ophelia hadn't chosen to follow her husband into the afterlife and Aura hadn't spent the hours contemplating the unfairness of it all, would she just have taken for granted that there were only two choices available to her? Marriage or death? Would Odessa have just gone along with whatever decision she made and headed off to her own trial to start a life she didn't especially want? Had the questions she had been asking herself allowed for her to accept that there was another choice? That there might be a life outside of the kingdom's harsh rules?

Echo began to stir and before she could wake up completely and be up the rest of the night, Aura slowly laid down next to her and allowed her to find her breast under the blankets.

"What are you reading?" she asked, desperate to break the silence that still felt strained between them. After finishing his drink he had begun flipping through the pages of the tome which was immense with a faded cover that appeared to be red leather.

"It's a history book concerning the last few hundred years of the kingdom's history. I wanted to see if the island we're supposed to be heading towards was included somewhere."

"And…" she asked, impatiently. Being ensconced in the soft blankets, with Echo nuzzled up next to her in the cozy fire lit room, she knew that she wouldn't be awake much longer. Especially not with the liquor easing through her veins and turning every muscle it touched to jelly.

"There's nothing. Even before the Witch Queen made her way west there weren't many settlements this far out. The king is always declaring that he needs to "take back" the lands surrounding the river but they never really belonged to the Serenfawrs to begin with. No one really wanted to make the trek back and forth through that ridge. Thanks for that by the way," he changed his tone and glared at her through the blankets that were wrapped almost completely around her. "I had to wait for those miscreants to make it all the way up the mountain and then basically sprint after them once they made it past the peak just so they wouldn't look down and see me."

She laughed. "You should be thanking me in earnest. Odessa told me that if you had been with us, she would have made you carry both her and Callen up on your back so I'm sure you were much better off with your sprint."

"She prances about like she's some kind of tiny pixie, but she's almost as tall as I am. I remember playing chicken and giving her piggy back rides when we were younger but she's delusional if she thinks I'm going to do that now." He rolled his eyes but smiled, and she finally felt that things were right between them again.

She knew she should let it go but she had to ask. "Do you feel better or worse that it was me and not Odessa?" she asked before her eyes closed.

She didn't think he was going to answer for a moment but just before sleep overtook her she heard him sigh.

"Better."

CHAPTER 16
ODESSA

Odessa woke up in bed wedged between two smaller bodies. The light white blankets were askew and her older nephew's long skinny legs stretched over her torso. The younger one's face was only inches from her own, his small mouth open and his breath softly tickling the hair that was plastered to her face. She gently moved them away and then scooted down to the bottom of the bed in order to let them continue to sleep.

Her feet were bare as she padded across the smooth wooden planks and stood over the balcony looking down at the miraculous garden below. Based upon the amount of light already reflecting off of the bubbling pool, her guess would be that it was already mid morning. The stiffness in her back and limbs was reminiscent of lazy summer days when there was no training and there were enough hours in the day that she was allowed to sleep until her brain decided that it had been given enough rest. She was certain that it also had to do with the days carrying her entire life on her back, and the one night spent on the forest floor.

She brought her fingers up to the base of her neck where that man had almost cut off her air supply with his arm. There was a tender spot directly on her windpipe where the bones of his arm had dug into her. Luckily she had slept without any nightmares or visitors. She took that as a sign that they would be given a few days here to rest and regroup instead of immediately setting out again.

She tried to enjoy the fresh air and quiet that now surrounded her. This was what she had wanted. A new start. A different path than the one that she had been told she would have to take at fourteen years of age without any choice in the matter. She would not have to defend herself against anyone in order to show them what kind of wife she would be. Lay out her weaknesses for the world to see.

Even though her trial was no longer part of her future, she had to admit that she did feel a bit embarrassed that she hadn't listened to Eryx and trained harder physically. She had been powerless when attacked. Apart from the wind, who was likely only attempting to help her because of her sister, she had been completely helpless. Even worse than the fact that she couldn't defend herself was that she wasn't able to do anything for her niece or her nephews. It wouldn't happen again. She would give in to the air training that her sister was always trying to push on her as well as the strength and stamina exercises that Eryx constantly berated her for skipping out on. Who knew what dangers they would face when they eventually left this place and what would she do if she didn't have her sister or her friend there to protect her?

She dressed in the dandelion colored tunic that she had laid out on the balcony to dry. She wished that she had some kind of light scarf to hide the bruises developing on her neck, but they had packed light and while the cottage had provided them with a lot, that did not include any fashion accessories. She decided the best option would be leaving her untamed mane of straw colored hair down around her shoulders to at least make it so the marks were not on clear display. She adjusted the blankets around her nephews so that they wouldn't catch a chill from the breeze floating in from the window and walked quietly down the stairs.

When she reached the bottom, Aura and Eryx were already sitting at the large wooden table sipping on mugs of tea and pouring over different books that were piled in front of them. She should have known that even with the amount of energy they had both expended actually fighting off their attackers, they would still be up and functional at dawn's break.

"How did you sleep?" Aura asked, filling a mug from the still steaming kettle. She passed it over to her while keeping her eyes glued to the faded pages. The tea was strong and black with hints of jasmine, and as she sat down at the large table, she felt older somehow: like the three of them had still been children before, even though Aura was a mother herself. They had been living in their parents' houses, following the plans that had been dictated to them and now they were somewhere new, figuring things out for themselves.

"Like a rock, which is impressive considering I was sleeping between those two bed hogs." She turned towards Eryx with a smile, but it faded from her lips when she saw that he was staring at her with a look of pure violence. His dark brown eyes were focused on her collarbone, and his usually full lips were clenched together as if they were the gatekeepers of some vicious words that were desperate to be released. He got up from his seat at the table and stalked out the door without a word, slamming it behind him. Odessa winced at the sound that seemed to reverberate around the small cottage even as her heart warmed at her friend's obvious concern for her wellbeing.

"What…" Aura started, finally looking up from the tome. "Oh, Dessi," she grimaced, her eyes lowering to her neck. "I really should have drawn out that bastard's death a little more."

"It probably looks a lot uglier than it feels, especially since it's early enough in the spring that I could camouflage myself in a field of daisies," she replied reassuringly. "And from what I heard he suffered enough."

Aura winced. "Eryx told you what I did?"

"I asked." She looked down almost embarrassed. "I wanted to make sure that he wouldn't be coming back for us."

"Not in this life," Aura confirmed with a hard glint in her eye. She looked towards the door. "Why don't you go talk to him? He's probably out there beating himself up since he doesn't have anyone else alive to actually take his anger out on."

She gazed longingly at the steaming mug of tea, knowing it would be cold once she made it back to the table.

"Take it with you," Aura suggested, reading her mind even though her nose was already buried again in the book before her. Odessa wondered if that was some kind of power that mothers were given when their children were born. The ability to read minds and predict everyone's needs before they voiced them.

She picked up the mug, smiling at her sister and then walked out the front door.

***

While the weather outside was significantly more glum than what she had experienced walking out on the balcony this morning, at least the rain had stopped. She hadn't bothered to put on her boots, and she could feel the wetness of the grass on the bottom of her feet. The air still held a chill since the sun had yet to break through the clouds, and she felt goosebumps rising on her forearms that were uncovered due to the short sleeves of her tunic. She held the mug of tea closer to her body in order to stop her shivering.

Eryx was a bit away from the house looking around the small graveyard. As she walked towards him she could see that while the weeds around the bases were overgrown, the graves themselves were clean and unweathered. She walked up behind him and nudged him with her elbow.

"They all died on the same day, almost fifty years ago," he said quietly. "Maybe a father and his five daughters? It looks like the youngest was only four."

"That's horribly sad," she replied. "Maybe a sickness?"

"Even if they all caught something similar it would be unusual for them to all pass on the exact same day. I would guess something more sinister."

She didn't want to think about anyone harming a child that was between her two nephews in age. "I wonder if it's the mother who still lives here. Maybe she moved somewhere else when she remarried but still comes to visit."

"That's a lot of upkeep for a woman who would have to at least be in her eighties. A lot of power for a woman in her eighties as well."

Odessa shrugged. "A woman who lost five of her daughters and her husband on the same day would have a lot of motivation to care for those she lost, even that many years later."

Eryx nodded. They didn't speak for a moment as if giving the family a moment of silence.

"I'm sorry for walking out," he said finally. "Seeing you like that made all the feelings from yesterday come flooding back, and I didn't want to take it out on you or Aura."

"I'm sorry," she started but he turned towards her and covered her mouth with his hand, like she had done to him less than a week ago. It felt like a lifetime.

"It's fine. Aura told me that she was really the one who insisted you go off without me, and I understand her reasoning." He removed his hand from her mouth and frowned as he brushed the knuckle of one finger against the skin on her neck, making sure to avoid any of the actual bruises. "Though I'm never going to let the two of you out of my sight again."

"It sounded like Aura demonstrated to you that she can take care of herself," she spoke up, trying to ignore the goosebumps that ran down her skin, possibly not just from the cold air of the damp forest.

He looked at her in a way that made her happy she wouldn't be facing him at trials, not that she would have had the opportunity anyway. He had quite a formidable scowl.

"Yes, but it isn't just herself she's taking care of is it?"

She blushed knowing that he was right. "Teach me."

His thick dark eyebrows shot up, almost touching the coarse black hair that was shaved down close to his head.

"*Now* you want me to teach you? After years of stressing the importance of learning how to protect yourself?"

She shrugged. "Before it was about demonstrating my ability to some man." Eryx rolled his eyes, but there was also a hint of a smile on his lips. "Now it's about protecting my family."

"Some man, huh?" He scanned her face with that same quiet smile and she felt the tiniest jump in her heart. He opened his mouth slightly as if to say something more but then thought better of it and put an arm around her shoulder and started leading her back towards the house.

"No better time than the present." He looked down and shook his head as if he had just noticed her bare feet. "Let's start with your attire. You're not fighting anybody off with those squat toes of yours."

She sighed deeply wishing that she had kept her mouth shut so she could just have another cup of tea and lounge on the couch with a book for the day, but she knew there was no going back now.

CHAPTER 17
AURA

Over the next few days, they enjoyed each other's company and took advantage of every luxury the cottage had to offer. They took long soaks in the pool until their blisters had softened and the muscle aches from carrying the weight of the children finally disappeared. Aura and Eryx continued to sleep on the downstairs floor before the fire and as their bodies began to heal and their moods improved, the sky outside the cabin also steadily lightened and the days lengthened with the coming of summer.

Aura was happy to be able to spend time enjoying her children without feeling the weight of the world on her shoulders. While she felt guilty about taking things that didn't belong to her, she couldn't deny how freeing it felt to just accept the gifts that the cottage itself or whoever owned it had bestowed upon them. There was little washing to do and the house almost seemed to clean itself though it could have just been that they hadn't been there long enough for any dust to accumulate.

Everyone helped with the cooking, and it was fun having the whole family in the kitchen thinking of creative ways to put together what they had available to them, the boys included. Echo was in love with the rug in front of the fire, and though someone always kept an eye on her to make sure she didn't get too close, she spent hours running her fingers through the soft fur and watching the flames dance. At night they all sat on the couches and read from the books on the shelves. Many of the stories were folktales from far off lands that she had never even heard of. There were plenty of volumes, similar to the one Eryx had found, about the history of the land and the growth of the Serenfawr kingdom; however, there was nothing regarding the mystery island that they were setting out for or the lands across the river.

Odessa and Eryx were on much better terms now that trials weren't looming before them, and they had been doing exercises together. Eryx was a good teacher, and Aura could tell that he was starting off easy and focusing on the areas of training that catered to Odessa's strengths so that she wouldn't get frustrated.

By the fourth day, Aura began to notice that the cottage's offerings were beginning to lessen. While the plants in the garden continued to thrive, the fruits and vegetables that had been so abundant were becoming more difficult to spot within the foliage, and there were no new blossoms. Slowly but surely, the bubbling water in the pool was drying up and losing its warmth. Even the fire in the hearth which had burned steadily throughout their time there without any assistance on their part was beginning to shrink. The house was telling them it was time to move on.

Though she had known that the time would come, Aura couldn't stop the feelings of anxiety from creeping back into her psyche. Odessa had told her what they had found on the gravestones, and she had gone out herself to trim the grass around the graves and plant some flowers around the stones as an offering to the earth elementals. The idea that this man might have witnessed the deaths of his children was a dagger to her heart, and she wondered if Odessa was right in her conjectures that the mother still lived. Could she be the stranger from Odessa's dreams hiding from the king on the undocumented island?

Living without Vitus was painful but possible. Her children were the ones she would end her own life for. She couldn't help but fret about what would happen to them once they left this place. When they reached the fortress, would the stranger there be accepting of a widowed mother who wanted to keep her children? Could they trust Odessa's guide who had kept so much from them as of late? Who was the being's loyalty to anyway? Was it Odessa herself or a higher power who had some kind of stake in their future?

When Aura brought it up that night at their last meal in the house, Odessa took offense that the motivations of her shimmering visitant were being questioned.

"I've been seeing the same spirit in my dreams since I was a child. She wouldn't put us in harm's way," she argued before slurping up a long string of squash from her fork.

Aura shifted her eyes towards Eryx. The only time he typically let his stoicism slip was when he was watching her sister eat. Sure enough, his face was twisted into a look of pure horror and disgust. He bowed his head and covered his brow with his hand, likely in order to keep his own food down. It had been surprising to her that they had been getting along so well considering the fact that they were having all of their meals together.

"But she *did* put you in harm's way by telling you to leave the village and then not giving the warning that you would be attacked," he countered, his eyes still downcast, looking into the bowl in front of him.

Odessa responded while continuing to chew on her mouthful of vegetables. "Maybe when she gave us the original instructions he hadn't known he was coming after us yet, and therefore *she* didn't know," she took a pause to swallow and then continued, "or maybe she knew that even though we would be attacked we would make it out unscathed and would have one less pursuer."

Eryx lifted his head to look pointedly at her neck which was now a very unflattering combination of yellow and purple, though technically it did blend in well with all of her tunics. He used his fork to further enunciate his point. "I wouldn't necessarily call *that* 'unscathed.' I hope that once we reach the fortress she doesn't consider us being locked in some dungeon as 'unscathed' as well."

"Do you have any better suggestions?" Odessa asked, glaring at him while she plucked a cherry tomato from the serving dish of salad with her thumb and forefinger.

"There are tongs right there!"

Odessa smiled as if she had somehow won the argument through deflection and popped the tomato into her mouth. Callen reached over to take his own tomato, emboldened by the actions of his aunt, but Aura stared down her son until his small hand slowly retreated.

Aura knew that when it came down to it the decision was hers to make. "I think right now the fortress is our best option. Odessa's right. We made it this far without losing anyone. It's not safe to stay on this side of the river, even if Donovan himself is no longer a threat. We don't know who else is going to come looking for us or him. If whoever is on the island seems untrustworthy, we can cross the river fully and take our chances there."

Eryx still didn't look convinced, but he didn't argue further as if accepting the fact that it was indeed their best option. "If we go by the maps, it shouldn't take us more than a day to get to the river's edge. Will we be ready to leave early tomorrow?"

Aura scanned the faces of her loved ones as they looked to her for confirmation of their plan. She felt a pang of sadness at the fact that they would be leaving this place and experienced some kind of premonition telling her that what she had at this very moment would soon be lost to her, but rather than speak any of that she simply nodded.

"Pack your things. We leave at sunup."

CHAPTER 18
ERYX

Eryx thought that he would feel more anxious about leaving the safety of the cottage for the unknown of the dark woods and the river island but as they started out that morning he felt nothing other than a sense of peace. They were all together and back to perfect health. The forest around them was quiet and still with the first rays of sunlight softly peeking through the trees. At the moment there was nowhere else he would rather be.

The instant he had entered the empty house back in the village and realized that the Banuette sisters had left for their journey without him was probably the loneliest few seconds of his life. The loneliness had then turned to immediate panic in realizing that he had to pack up his things and start out immediately before something happened to them or they crossed into some kind of territory where he wouldn't be able to follow. It had been pure luck that he heard Donovan and his accomplice sneaking around the cottage next door as he collected his belongings and then followed them on what happened to be the right path, though the more things that happened lately, the more it seemed that it was destiny rather than luck, or maybe the scheming of some unknown power that was aiding them on their journey.

Staying in the village without them wasn't something that he had even considered. It was typical of Aura to think that while she spent every second of every day caring for everyone else, no one actually needed or cared about her. He had been a little offended that she thought he was some emotionless brute who would just cut his losses with them gone, but then realized it was more about her own insecurities than anything having to do with him.

As for Odessa, he originally thought that she had been the one to talk Aura into leaving in the middle of the night but that was definitely *his* insecurities speaking. He knew things had been tense between them lately, and Aura had been somewhat correct in assuming it had been about trials and how he was the one taking it more seriously. The truth of it was that he was scared. He was scared that they wouldn't end up together. But he was also terrified that they would.

While he knew that she believed she would do poorly, he was strongly convinced that the opposite would be true. Through her dreams she would have been provided with explicit details concerning her competitors' weaknesses and how to use them to her advantage. In his studies of past matches, he had seen many instances of intelligence and cunning winning out over bodily strength or more honed elemental powers.

Being paired with a female stranger always came with the possibility of someone being disappointed, but what if Odessa and he had matched, his oldest friend who already knew everything about him, and she was upset about being stuck with him? That would be soul crushing. Even if she *was* okay with it, the whole idea of courting was also something that he just wasn't ready for. Putting it all off for now was a huge relief, though obviously he couldn't have said any of *that* to Aura. Even though she had always felt like an older sister to him, she was Odessa's older sister first, and he couldn't expect her to hold in all of his secrets.

He watched them walking together now, twin braids hanging down their backs. Aura's was a bit darker and she walked with her shoulders up near her ears. Though she never complained about anything, and typically acted like she could take on whatever life threw at her, he saw through the facade, mostly because he acted the same way. Her posture was horrible, as if she was truly carrying the weight of the world on her shoulders and the past couple of nights, he could hear her grinding her teeth in her sleep. He was certain it was a typical thing and not just due to the added stress of the last month, though that likely hadn't helped.

Odessa, though she was probably at least two or three inches taller, walked on her toes like she weighed nothing. They had started working on agility exercises this week since he knew that with her quickness she would do well, and she had. Though he acted like her carefree attitude drove him crazy, and often it did, he typically did enjoy himself whenever he went along with one of her whims. She had been the one to push them onto this very path, and he had to admit that right now it seemed like it had been the right one to take. Hopefully that wouldn't change once they reached the mysterious fortress.

Eryx continued to observe the forest around him and thought about the conflicting accounts that he had received about this curious place. The Widow's husband had seemed to have a similar experience to their own in that he had discovered the cabin and had found refuge during a storm. The Widow herself also implied that others had traversed these woods in order to seek asylum in the queen's lands, though maybe that was wishful thinking, and they had really perished the same way his father did, attacked by one of the brutal beasts lurking in the shadows.

Eryx wasn't a fan of the idea that the forest had seen his father as someone who was a threat. If he had caught up with a group of people who had been fleeing, Eryx would have hoped that his father would have done the right thing and let them go, rather than send them back to be separated from their family members and jailed or worse. He knew that his father was loyal and proud and disobeying orders would have been difficult for him, but he was also a good person. It was likely that he was seen as a danger because of his position and uniform rather than what was in his heart.

He saw no evidence of any horrors at the moment. If anything, this area of the woods seemed more alive, almost like it was enchanted just like the cottage had been. The foliage was greener. The wildflowers were brighter and much more abundant. Though he was no mycologist, he could tell that the variety of colorful and unusual mushrooms was not typical of a normal forest. In some areas, the ground was so bright it almost looked like the drawings he had seen in books of the coral reefs in the oceans to the east.

After they had walked for a while, he began to notice the appearance of the fauna, which seemed to be accepting of the fact that they were here to do no harm. He passed by a large luna moth, resting on the bark of a tree, whose giant pale green wings and eyespots fooled his mind for a moment into thinking there was a masked woman observing them. He startled when Odessa squealed loudly and stopped short, causing him to bump into her pack, but when he peered over her shoulder he saw that it was just an enormous horned beetle casually making its way across the path in front of her feet. Echo, who was holding her hand, bent down and tried to reach out to it, but her aunt grabbed her and pulled her up into her arms before she could make contact. Echo squealed in protest but was quickly distracted by an iridescent green damselfly flying nearby. She put out her small chubby hand and the fly graced her palm for a few moments before taking flight again.

"I might have preferred the mythical rabid beasts to the overgrown insects," Odessa admitted, shuddering.

Aura looked at her pointedly. "Unless there are some kind of foot-long hornets, I'll take the bugs."

"The kids seem to be enjoying them," he noted, as he watched Callen pick up and cradle a giant caterpillar with yellow and black stripes. Barrett was chasing a beautiful blue and white spotted butterfly further up the path while Echo was squirming in her aunt's arms trying to get down in order to do her own exploring. Odessa relented, and Echo immediately began tottering after an orange and black grasshopper.

Eryx stealthily reached his arm around and tugged lightly on Odessa's braid. She screamed, pulling frantically at her long rope of hair to ensure that no one was attempting to burrow within the plaits. Aura nudged him with her shoulder but he could see that she was smiling, as she watched her three children frolic down the forest path.

The farther they walked the larger the animals became, and the more apparent it was that they seemed to be leading them towards their destination of the river. On the ground there were slow moving box turtles, poisonous looking frogs of all colors, and a stunning red sided garter snake, much to Odessa's chagrin. Above them in the tree tops were scarlet cardinals, blue jays and bright yellow goldfinches all slowly flitting from tree to tree in the same general direction.

The trail through the forest was flat and they chose to snack on the dried fruit and nuts they had taken with them rather than stop and waste time taking a larger meal. If they reached their destination before the sun went down they would have more time to assess the situation in the light of day. Eryx wasn't sure if he would prefer that the place be abandoned, so that they wouldn't have any mysterious strangers to contend with, or if the fortress was at least somewhat established and that the proprietor was as beneficent as Odessa believed they would be.

They walked until the children's legs grew tired and they were given the chance to be carried in order to take an afternoon nap. Barrett, who only ever seemed to put on weight through the inches that he continued to grow lengthwise, wasn't much to carry, and as Eryx cradled his sleeping body to his chest he thought about how glad he was that he would continue to see him and his siblings grow up. Wherever they were, he would ensure that they received the same training that he had both from his parents and his teachers in the village. Though Aura would hold the reins when it came to teaching them specifically how to work with the wind, there was still plenty of expertise that he could share. He was excited to see how each of their powers manifested.

With the children asleep, the three of them increased their pace and were mostly quiet, contemplating what the future would bring. He could tell by Aura's furrowed brow that she was still fretting about what they would find, but she had the most to lose if things went south. At this point, Odessa and he hadn't really committed any crime. While it was warned against to stay within the kingdom's invisible boundaries, it wasn't a punishable offense. If they stayed away for long enough to miss their trials, however, that would be a different story.

He could tell when they were nearing the river by the change in the sky above them. The mountains were all behind them and the sky seemed more empty and clear. The forest was beginning to open up and the trees were spaced farther apart. Above them he could see white gulls flying.

When they finally broke through the tree line, he could no longer dispute the truth of Odessa's gift. While he had never doubted her, it was different seeing it with his own eyes. Not only had she brought them to the exact spot in the bend of the river where the island was located, but her description of it matched completely with what he now saw in front of him.

The piece of land was covered in the same green trees that they had just walked through. It was as if the river had one day decided to force its way through the land, severing the small islet from the areas around it. The stone fortress took up the entire north east quarter of the island, though it also looked as though there were other outbuildings hiding within the trees further out towards the western side. He scanned the battlements looking for the person from Odessa's dream as if they would have known that they would be receiving visitors at this exact moment but there was no sign of a robed figure watching them, at least as far as he could see. If they were observing from one of the darkened windows, he wouldn't be any the wiser.

They gently woke up Echo and the boys and let them explore the waterfront while they decided on the next steps to take. He put his arms around the shoulders of his two friends and they observed what would possibly be their new home. The sun had made its way past the fortress and was starting to dip down behind the mountains on the Witch Queen's side of the river, turning the sky above to oranges, purples and pinks.

"So no matter who else we encounter in this crumbling ruin we're going to have each other's backs right?" he asked.

Aura reached across his body to grab her sister's hand. "Always."

Part II
Five Years Later
CHAPTER 19
SCORPIO

The Beggar's Tavern did not start out as the Beggar's Tavern. It was one of those establishments that at some point had been someone's seed of hope. A father and son joint venture meant to be a place of gathering for the locals and of welcoming to visitors from foreign lands passing through. A haven for those seeking a warm meal, a crackling fire and a cozy bed. However, as the years passed and the pub changed hands from one proprietor to the next, each one in turn less connected to the hands that had selected the stones for the hearth or laid the planks for the floor, the more it fell into disrepair. With the decline of the people's powers and the increase in poverty throughout the land, it was likely that the pub had not been truly owned by an individual or single family in over a century. Instead, a highly taxed mortgage was paid to the Crown month to month. Without the love or pride it had been birthed from, the Beggar's Tavern now had a name fitting of its clientele. There were those who begged for food and those who begged for shelter and those who begged for sex in the dirty and flea-infested rooms upstairs. Most importantly there were those who begged for nefarious goods, which is why the herbalist and poison monger known as Scorpio sat in a shadowed corner near the bar looking for a familiar face, or someone who could become a familiar face, if he could convince them that he had something they needed.

Scorpio was attempting to nurse the ale that he had in his cup, but the night had been a slow one and the boredom was starting to get to him. He had received one drink by providing the pub's muscle at the door with a tonic that would improve his libido and increase his stamina with the ladies at the neighboring brothel. He had been given his second when he provided the barmaid, his previous client's wife, with a concoction that she would slip into her husband's drink at last call in order to ensure that he would pass out before accomplishing his said mission. His third was given to him by the bar's proprietor in exchange for a tonic that would ensure that the wife of the doorman would not become with child when they rendezvoused after her husband was no longer conscious.

Though his local, repeat clients typically supported his drinking habit, it was the out of towners who provided him with the actual coinage he needed to continue living in comfort. Very minimal comfort but still comfort. His targets were often young stags looking for the mushrooms that he collected from the forest that made them forget their quickly approaching responsibilities as soon-to-be-married men. Sometimes there were slightly older men looking to get rid of their unpreferred pairings or cloaked females trying to do the same. Being an accessory to murder often left him with a sour taste in his mouth, but he had to survive somehow. Swordsmiths didn't feel guilt over who was killed with their blades. Why should he? At least that was what he told himself on the nights he didn't have enough ale to knock him out and the ghosts of his misdoings came to haunt him.

Scorpio hadn't always been drawn to the plants that caused more harm than good. Growing up he had been fascinated by the herbs, flowers and foods that could fix what was broken. The aloe grown in the south that could soothe and heal cuts and burns. The ginger root that would ease the pains in his stomach after too much cake. The sweet white yarrow that could bring down a fever. As he entered his teenage years he began learning about herbs that could improve one's mental or emotional state or enhance someone's natural powers.

While his father had been disappointed that he had obviously taken after his mother as an earth elemental rather than a fire master, she had been overjoyed by his love of botany and encouraged his secret treks out to the woods and the experiments that he did with the items that he found there. Her powers differed from his in that she was more interested and in tune with the culinary use of plants rather than medicinal; however, there were instances in which the two fields intersected, and they always had tidbits to share and discuss. Their hired staff limited her opportunities to play in the kitchen, but she took any chance she could to sneak to the ovens and create special treats just for the two of them. He could still remember the sweet taste of the peach cakes and lilac scones, and the feelings of love and pride they had stirred in him.

The emotional descent into darkness from losing his mother had made him turn his back on his old friends and turn instead to vegetation of ill repute: sweet looking snakeroot, striking pink oleander, and of course the infamous belladonna. These were the plants that called to him now and that always appeared whenever he needed them. He felt a companionship with them since, like himself, people avoided them until a particular dark need arose. While he still held onto the knowledge he had gained in his old life and occasionally called on those healing plants in order to cure his own ailments he often did so with reluctance. Work as a healer would be more consistent, and would come with less risk, but he could no longer see himself patting a sick child kindly on the head or providing a customer a tonic accompanied by a smile rather than a scowl. Also, desperation and the need for secrecy also made people more willing to accept his high prices. A less shady occupation would come with more competition.

The door to the pub opened and a couple walked in. The man was tall and dark-skinned and had a look on his face that would not invite small talk. The woman beside him was extremely fair and slight of build, though with her boots she almost met the man in height. Scorpio had never seen the pair before. He would have to watch them for a bit in order to determine if he would have anything of interest to them. He didn't often have couples seek him out for a joint venture.

The pair did not immediately go up to the bar; instead, they sat next to one another at a corner table looking out at the room. The man said something and the woman began scanning the floor without trying to look too obvious. When her eyes met his, Scorpio swore that they lingered a moment longer than necessary. She then lowered her head but said something under her breath to her companion who waited a beat and then also shifted his eyes in Scorpio's direction.

So either they did need something or they had come looking for him for a more troublesome reason. Either way he decided to stay put until they chose to approach him. Until he was sure of their motivation, he was safer where he was.

The door to the pub opened again, and he laid eyes upon one of his most consistent clients. Widower Dasher was approaching eighty and was a man loved by all…cats. He was a water elemental who had been a talented fisherman in his day, and he still had success making catches in the creek bed behind his house. The man seemed to have some kind of intuitive power when it came to animals which attracted them to him. That same intuitive power did not apply to humankind, since if he did he would have figured out Scorpio's game plan ages ago.

What must have been two years prior, Dasher had entered the pub looking for someone who could assist him with a neighbor's dog who was "harassing" his cats. Scorpio didn't think himself to be a complete monster and didn't go around poisoning man's most faithful companion if it wasn't necessary. He told the man that he needed some time to prepare the lethal concoction and then went to see if the dog truly was a danger by following him home.

The dog was large and gray with matted fur, but in no way appeared to be the ferocious beast that the Widower had described; however, he did growl menacingly when one of the man's cats, likely numbering close to one-hundred, got too close to his family's porch which he guarded honorably as they slept.

The next day when the old man came to collect his tonic, bringing along his freshest catch as payment, Scorpio provided him with two: one to put in the dog's water bowl and the other a bonus to help him to clear up the apparent arthritis in his hands.

Two weeks later, the man had returned with another piece of fish and a new complaint about the dog, whose fur was now radiant from the herbal that the old man had put into his water. He had forgotten the entire exchange since, rather than helping his arthritis, Scorpio had provided him with a tonic containing thornapple, which likely did help the pain in his hands but also moved along his progressing dementia. Though he did not initially create this plan with the intention of a consistent bi-weekly meal, overall it had worked in his favor and he hoped that the beast would continue to thrive for his personal benefit.

Scorpio was a bit surprised to see Dasher since he had only given him his last tonic last night and it usually took him a while longer to return to the pub seeking him out. He was also slightly alarmed by the apparent outrage on his face that replaced his usual look of general irritation. When he caught sight of Scorpio sitting in the corner he stormed over with renewed purpose and put his gnarled finger an inch from his nose.

"I bring you my best catch and you try to end my life!" he shouted in an unsteady voice, then turned towards the rest of the room. "This man tried to kill me!"

"Woah, woah, woah," Scorpio rose from his corner and put his arm around the man. "I provided you with just what you asked. Why don't you explain to me exactly what you did with the tonic."

"I went out last night just like you said. I put the poison from the red bottle into the dog's bowl, but when I got home to take the tonic that you provided, one of the kittens got in the way of my feet and the blue bottle smashed on the floor. Three of the darlings started licking it up before I could stop them and were dead by morning!" The man was clearly devastated by the loss of the felines even though the whole community would be tripled with the upcoming breeding season.

"Of course," Scorpio replied in a soft tone, trying to bring the old man's voice down to his level, "You were supposed to take the red bottle yourself and give the blue one to the dog. Unfortunately the cats' demise was a result of your own forgetfulness. I would never wish harm upon such a generous man and hopeful repeat customer such as yourself."

Take note that thornapple can be used as a pest control method for cats, he thought to himself. He could see the internal struggle going on in the old man's head as he tried to recall the initial instructions given to him and whether or not the error had been his and his alone.

"Now why don't you get yourself a drink and I'll see if I have any more of the tonics on my person to send you home with. On my bill." He steered the man towards the bar realizing if he could slip a little extra than the usual dose into his drink, he might forget all about the whole situation as long as the cats had already been burned or buried. If it worked fast enough, he could put the drink on the Widower's tab as well as his next round.

"Yes, yes that will do," the old man replied, apparently pacified. "We'll just have to get rid of that nasty hound tomorrow."

Unfortunately the last bit was said a little too forcefully and another patron from the bar turned, eyes blazing. He was tall and broad. Much bigger than either Scorpio or the Widower and likely of more sane mind and therefore not as easy to fool.

"I knew you were trying to get rid of Sir Henry!" he spat out. "All those nights sneaking around my home. I just thought if you truly had evil motives he would have been with the worms by now."

"Nonsense," the old man replied. "I'm no coward and I did try to rid the world of that beast last night, but it was my first attempt. Why don't you call on your wife and ask her who else might have been lurking around your cottage. It could have been one of many I'm sure."

Well his mind can be sharp when the situation calls for it, Scorpio thought as he slowly backed away from the two men. It was time to find a new shady institution to haunt. He snuck out the door and breathed in a sigh of crisp early spring air only to have it sharply cut off by a strong arm around his neck.

"I saw my lady pour something into the drink she served me. What was it you scrawny wretch?"

Scorpio tried to think of a solid response to get him out of his second predicament of the night but found it difficult to accomplish with no air flow to the brain. Even if the words did come to him, he would not have any way of getting them out.

While his rusty fighting skills had gotten him out of a number of better matched fights in the past, the doorman was awarded his post for a reason. He frantically looked for any other way he could free himself from the man's grasp. His eyes went above to a thick tree limb sticking out directly over the entrance to the pub. He turned his mind dark which wasn't that difficult to achieve and pictured the innards of the limb formed through years of slow and steady growth. He envisioned the small insects burrowed inside and the buds that would be opening soon with the warming of the air. Then he imagined each inner cell of the tree branch beginning to break apart until he could finally start to hear the creaking above the roar of the blood in his ears.

This is going to hurt, he thought, just as the heavy branch crashed down upon both himself and his captor and then everything went black.

CHAPTER 20
SCORPIO

Scorpio woke with a blazing headache, likely from being knocked out by the tree. It also could have been a result of too much ale if it was the next day, or not enough ale if he had been out for a while. He was in a small room with wooden floors and walls of gray stone. He was sprawled on a narrow straw cot but, apart from that, the room contained little else other than his boots, a wooden chair which held his neatly folded cloak, and a wooden side table with a glass of water which he quickly downed. He stood up gingerly and walked over to the window. He was in some kind of large castle or fortress that appeared to be surrounded by water, most likely the Harridan River. This was somewhat alarming as it meant he had been brought through the Stygian woods which he would now have to journey back through alone after figuring out how to cross the river.

As he stood pondering his bleak future, he heard a short precise knock at the door. He thought about yelling at them to go away but figured some food might ease his sour stomach. Plus, he was rather curious about his current situation.

He opened the door to find a somewhat familiar man standing there with a scowl on his face. His skin was the deep color of a freshly found truffle and his hair was even darker and curled upon his head. His eyebrows were thick above deep set eyes that, unfortunately, were focused intently on Scorpio. They stood at about the same height and for all his intimidating qualities, the stranger seemed to be not long out of his learning days. His short sleeved tunic was the color of a fresh artichoke, and the thought caused Scorpio's stomach to grumble loudly.

"The Widow wishes to meet with you," he stated without preamble. No small talk about the comfort of his bed or how he was faring after his unfortunate confrontation. The man turned and began walking down a long cold stone hallway without turning back to see if he was being followed.

"Who is this Widow and can she wait until after I've had something to eat?" Scorpio asked, trying to catch up with his long strides.

"She rules this place and questions everyone who enters these doors and you will be provided food after she deems your acceptance appropriate."

"I don't remember requesting to be accepted anywhere. Can I leave or am I being held against my will?"

"If you wish to return to your life of opulence at the 'Beggar's Tavern' please feel free. I wish you well." As they walked, Scorpio could see others milling about. In what appeared to be some kind of sitting room a thin, freckled girl with hair the color of straw sat at a small table drinking a mug of tea and looking at a deck of seer's cards. When he smiled at her, she clamped her lips together, but there was a slight twitch in the corner of her mouth, as if she were trying to hold in a laugh. Pieces of the previous night came back to him. They were the unfamiliar couple who had been sitting in the corner of the pub last night. Or was it two or even three nights before? Another faint memory of them standing over him flashed in his memory.

"This one? Really?" the man had said.

"No other," she had responded.

He had felt a tugging on the bottom of his tunic and then only darkness.

Since his companion was not much for conversation, Scorpio held his tongue and instead focused on his surroundings. His room appeared to be on the ground floor of the structure which was definitely preferable to an underground cell or something higher that would make escaping through a window more complicated if the need arose. The walls were made of gray stone and his boot steps echoed loudly on the matching floor. The hall was bright. The windows facing the outside were thin and shaded by the surrounding evergreens that appeared to keep the building from view, but the arches inside opened up to a large sunny courtyard with a single twisted tree planted in the center as if it was the heart of the whole place. While the fortress did seem to be sturdy enough and holding up against the elements, it also seemed to be growing out of the earth itself. Spring roses were wound around the pillars, and green moss crept around some of the stones. It was similar to an abandoned cottage that had been left to rot after its owners were dead and buried; however, in this case, the overgrowth seemed purposeful as if it was sheltering and providing for its occupants in some way. As an earth elemental, it tugged a bit at his heart strings.

They continued walking and then finally reached a set of stone steps that led up to a pair of wooden doors. His captor, or his rescuer, he supposed, repeated his sharp rap from before and then stepped back as the door slowly pushed out towards them. They entered what was a long semi-circular throne room. It lacked any deep velvet curtains, elaborate tapestries or chandeliers of crystal. Light came in through the same thin windows that he had seen in the rest of the fortress rather than any delicate stained glass. The place was one of function rather than fashion. There was a single, simple throne on a raised dais at which sat a small woman clothed fully in black. As they walked closer he could see that only her hands and eyes were visible. Her hands were gnarled but showed off a small citrine ring on her left ring finger. Her nose and mouth were covered but as he walked closer he could see that her eyes showed signs of cataracts and were surrounded by deep creases.

"Leave us, Eryx," she spoke, her voice gravelly but her words clear.

The young man looked uncomfortable doing so, but he turned and left through the doors, shutting them behind him.

"What do they call you?" the old woman asked curiously.

"Scorpio," he responded. "I deal in tonics, mostly of the unsavory kind if there is anything you're in need of."

"I would hope not," she responded. "We are not an unsavory establishment. I'm sure you have some more wholesome talents that would be more beneficial to us."

"None that I've explored in quite a while," he replied a bit peevishly since she had insulted his profession. "And what kind of establishment is this exactly?"

"An orphanage," she responded. "We take in those who have been outcasted by society. If you choose to stay with us, you will be fed and housed; however, we do require that you use whatever powers you have to benefit the rest of the group."

"Maybe your eyesight is no longer up to par but I'm a bit old to be considered an orphan." He tugged at the dark beard covering his chin and then gestured to the rest of his frame which, though not as broad or muscular as he would have liked, was indeed that of a grown man.

"My eyesight is just fine," she responded unphased. "And as far as I recall, one can be considered an orphan for as long as they live if they have been deprived of their parents. It is possible that I am mistaken, though that is a rare occurrence. Have we taken you away from a warm, loving cottage where your mother and father sit with a bowl of porridge eagerly awaiting your return? A mother and father who lovingly named you 'Scorpio'?"

His jaw dropped for a moment at the woman's harshness and it took him a moment to respond.

"I suppose you're correct in that I would not be missed by anyone other than my clients, though perhaps that is not something I should admit to in my current situation. Why am I truly here? Why would anyone think that a man of my appearance and occupation could bring anything of use to an orphanage?"

"Our seer dreamt of you, which means that this is where you were destined to be. Other than that, your guess is as good as mine. As I said, you can stay as long as you earn your keep. I would appreciate it if you took a break from your usual concoctions and thought about how else you could better assist us. Eryx is a Green elemental as well and specializes in the growing of vegetables, fruits and herbs. He'll help get you accustomed and can plant anything specific that you request. In the past we have gotten our healing tonics from the mainland though in time maybe you'll be able to provide some for us."

"And if I would rather not? Do any of this?" he asked, though the idea of a warm bed, a guaranteed meal, and a river between himself and anyone after him wasn't totally unwelcome.

"Better to stay put for at least a couple more weeks," she responded with a rough, dry laugh. "The river is still partially frozen. Wouldn't be a fun swim."

She picked up the cane placed next to the throne and tapped it on the floor. The doors reopened and he could see Eryx scowling as he waited in the doorway.

"We'll speak next week. I like to keep up on how all my orphans are doing."

He rolled his eyes, but he could already smell the food wafting from somewhere within and knew that he would see her again in a week's time.

CHAPTER 21
SCORPIO

Scorpio followed Eryx back down the staircase and then down a second set of stairs that were to the left of the first. These led down to another set of wooden doors behind which he could smell something that made his mouth water. He could hear voices speaking loudly and happily with one another and he supposed that implied that his fellow "orphans" had adjusted to being brought to this strange place and were not silently suffering or being tortured on a daily basis. Once the door opened, he saw that the dining room, which must have sat directly below the throne room, was still perched on some kind of cliff. It was surrounded by wide windows which gave an open view of the forested island and the river and mainland beyond.

The hall was filled with perhaps two dozen people. Some were small children and others seemed slightly younger than his own thirty years. Everyone sat at one long wooden table that stretched from right to left across the room. Bowls of food were passed from one hand to another and Scorpio couldn't stop his feet from moving to the first empty seat that he found. Eryx stuck his hand out to stop him so that he could likely begin some lengthy lecture about the rules of the table, but the girl he had recognized from the sitting room looked up and interrupted his forthcoming spiel before it could begin.

"Let him eat, Eryx. Anything you tell him before he gets food in him is going in one ear and out the other."

Eryx opened his mouth to argue but then removed his hand and gestured towards the table.

Scorpio didn't wait another second and climbed over the wooden bench without taking any notice of his breakfast companions or anything else but the different foods being passed to him. The first platter was freshly toasted bread served with a green spread smelling of garlic. The second was a bowl containing eggs scrambled with asparagus and bright green peas. Next came a bowl of meaty morel mushrooms with the simple flavors of butter and salt and, finally, stewed rhubarb with cooked oats. Once he had finished his first plateful of food, he looked up to see if there were more courses coming. Everyone else continued to eat at a much more leisurely pace while conversing with one another.

"Ham?" He asked no one in particular. "Sausage?"

"No meat," replied Eryx, wiping his mouth. "We eat what we forage or grow and we have chickens that provide us with eggs. There are people here who are sensitive to the plight of the animals in the kingdom and we respect their wishes to not cause them harm. I'm afraid you won't be getting your usual pub fare, though maybe it will do you some good."

Scorpio knew this was some dig at his lifestyle but he shrugged and reached for seconds of the delicious food that was in front of him. Truthfully, the freshness and taste had been significantly more satisfying than what he was used to; even the water was clearer and had a touch of sweetness to it. When he couldn't stomach another bite, he finally put down his fork and poured himself a cup of coffee from the carafe placed in the middle of the table. The beautifully crafted mug, the color of a robin's egg, was pleasantly warm in his hand. As he sipped the fragrant brew, which was strong and bitter with notes of vanilla and almond, he took note of those sitting nearest to him.

Directly across, sat the familiar blonde girl whose name he hadn't yet been given. Her tunic was a deep ochre, many shades darker than her pale hair which was now tied into a bun on the top of her head. She had pushed her plate to the side and had the old deck of cards that she was shuffling as she laughed and joked with the others. With a smile on her face and the morning light streaming in from the windows, she looked significantly younger than she had in the dark of the pub, maybe close to ten years his junior.

To her right sat another girl, maybe slightly older, a fire elemental judging from her dark, wine colored tunic. She was strikingly beautiful with a round face, clear olive skin and long black hair that was tied back high on her head. Even sitting, it was evident that she was significantly shorter than her friend. Her smile was warm and her eyes were a deep brown color and were focused on the person sitting directly across from her and to his left.

Shifting his eyes to not be too obvious, he could see a very white freckled arm. He moved his head to the left pretending to look around the room and saw a very pale man with hair the color of a ripe persimmon. He wore a deep rusty color which would have appeared more brown if the hints of orange weren't brought out so strongly by his short messy curls. He did not appear to take any notice of Scorpio's snooping since he was looking back at the girl across the table with an equal amount of ardor.

Finally sitting across from Eryx was another girl. Her hair was dark and cut short. Although she was seemingly tall and thin, like the blonde, her defined arms suggested some kind of strenuous work. Her tunic, which was the fair color of a tart green apple, made him think her muscles had been earned through hours digging in a garden. He did not get much time to study her since she was looking back at him with a scowl that he preferred not to engage with. She examined him right back and then turned towards Eryx.

"Eryx, are you going to introduce us to…your friend?" she asked with a raised eyebrow. Though her hair was cut shorter than any female he had met, her features were fine and her nose was pointed up at the end.

"Hardly," he stated simply in a bored tone. "Odessa and I retrieved him from the mainland the night before last. I have yet to learn his name and know little more than you about him so it would be better if he introduced himself."

So he had slept a full day, which accounted for his empty stomach and withdrawal symptoms. "You could have asked, though thus far your conversation skills have left much to be desired. I go by Scorpio and like 'my friend' Eryx here, I specialize in earth magic though typically more of the unsavory sort." He gave a wink and a smile to the short haired girl who rolled her eyes and continued to scowl. "And who might you lovely young people be?"

"I'm Odessa," the blond replied, looking up from her cards. "We met when I pulled a giant tree branch off your head, lugged your body onto a horse and then shoved it into a rowboat. The people we help tend to be conscious when we bring them here but you seem to be a special case." She acted annoyed but he could see the hint of a smile like he was a puzzle she wanted to figure out.

"This is Yakov," she continued, nodding her head towards the ginger haired man on his right. Looking straight on he could now tell that he also appeared to be fairly young, maybe even a bit more so than the others. "Yakov is our very talented smith." She took the cards that she had been shuffling and laid them across the table in front of her.

"A fire elemental. My father always wished that I'd taken after him in that regard," Scorpio said.

"My father would have preferred that I hadn't," the boy returned with a smile. Scorpio furrowed his brows in question, but Yakov didn't elaborate and instead reached out to select one of the cards. He turned it over and handed it back to Odessa. It depicted a long broken branch or stick being held by a spectral floating hand. She scanned the card and then smiled.

"Ace of Wands. Inspiration, inner vision, exploration. Do you have some new projects you're starting today?"

"Always," Yakov replied. He then looked over at the girl sitting next to Odessa. "This lovely lady is Lavender, also a fire elemental in her own way." He grinned at her playfully and then continued. "She's my apprentice of sorts and we've recently started working with glass and ceramic creating some pieces for the meal hall. We already have a full armory that we, thankfully, haven't had much use for. We definitely do more eating than fighting."

Lavender nodded at Scorpio with a small smile and then reached for her own card.

"The Lovers," Odessa read, then wiggled her eyebrows at Lavender teasingly. She paused as if to think for a moment and then continued. "Attraction, harmony, partnership."

Scorpio could see a blush spreading on the girl's cheeks and spoke up to divert attention from her. "I've never seen a smithy's workshop and the blade that I had on my person was mysteriously missing when I woke up here so I could use something to hold on to."

Eryx of course entered himself into the conversation. "As Yakov mentioned, we haven't had any use for weapons being here and you likely won't either. Until a threat arises, and until we know we can trust you, which I have my doubts about, to be honest, you will remain unarmed. I'll be showing you the garden after breakfast but you're welcome to visit with Yakov and Lavender later on."

Scorpio rolled his eyes with a sigh. He didn't appreciate being babysat by an overgrown teen but also didn't want to step on toes if it meant free food and a place to sleep. Odessa turned to her other side and slapped the back of the cantankerous girl seated to her left.

"This diamond in the rough here is Heren. He's an earth as well."

Heren stared at him with a look of defiance, likely to see his reaction and whether or not he would comment on Odessa's choice of pronoun. He tried his best to look unphased and asked instead "Does that mean I'll have someone else to spend my time with other than Eryx here?"

"Sorry to disappoint you but I don't go near the garden. I specialize in stones," he replied, lowering his gaze to pick at some dirt under his fingernails. Now that Scorpio was no longer a threat, he was apparently no longer interesting.

"A healer then?" he asked, trying to hide his excitement. There were many types of healers. Some healers used plants to create tonics. Others used crystals to heal through the flow of energy. When he was younger he had read about the benefits of combining different healing techniques in order to have greater results; however, he hadn't had any luck sensing energy within the few crystals that he had found on his excursions into the woods. The final type of healers were those with psychic powers who could use their mind to heal an injury by reconfiguring the cells and tissues within but those were extremely rare.

"No," Heren almost looked sad before plastering back on his look of uncaring boredom. "I come from a long line of finders.

We sell what I find in order to buy what we can't get ourselves here." He closed his eyes and put his hand out to grab a card from the spread.

So his air of haughtiness likely came from a privileged background. Finders were rare and were often wealthy due to the expensive stones that called to them from the earth and quarries.

"Four of cups," Odessa said, her features morphing into a frown. She looked up at Heren as if asking if he wanted her to continue.

"Out with it," he returned. "We don't have all day."

"Four of cups, jealousy, resentment, a need for grounding."

"Then a grounding I will go." He picked up his dishes and got up to leave. "See you for dinner." He left the table without a second look.

Odessa watched him go and then turned to Eryx with a teasing smile on her face. "Well, is today the day you let me read for you? Give us privy to all of your secrets?"

"Maybe tomorrow," Eryx replied in a manner that made it clear that she would receive the same answer tomorrow and every day forward. He then started to get up from the table himself. "Come on Scorpio, there's lots of weeding for you to do."

Scorpio started to stand but was stopped by Odessa grabbing his wrist. There was something familiar about her he couldn't quite put his finger on. He was sure they had never met before, and she would have been too young for him to come across her in his previous life. "Let him pick a card. Give us some of *his* secrets at least."

Eryx nodded and Scorpio moved his hand back and forth across the cards. He stopped when he felt a slight tingle in his fingers and tapped the card below. Odessa slid the card out and turned it toward him. Her hand shook as she placed it in his hand and looked at him with a face of horror.

The card depicted a skeletal figure in a suit of armor. He sat upon a white horse and rode over a body lying in the dirt. The words on the bottom of the card read Death.

CHAPTER 22
SCORPIO

Scorpio tore his eyes back up from the card to look for Odessa's explanation. Her face was still a mask of horror but Lavender had her head down and was slightly more flushed than before as if she were trying to hold in a laugh. Eryx's expression remained blank, though he wasn't sure if the boy had more than one facial expression. When his gaze returned to Odessa, her lips were clamped shut but twisted as if she were trying to regain control over them.

"Put the man out of his misery so we can move on with our day," Eryx said finally, rolling his eyes.

Lavender and Odessa finally bent over the table in synchronous giggles.

"Well, you're officially a member of the club," Odessa spoke, wiping the tears from her eyes. "Your expression might have been my favorite one yet."

"You mean you chose that card on purpose? How did you even know which one I was going to pick?" Scorpio responded incredulously. The old woman had said something about a seer. It made sense that Odessa had been the one she was talking about. She *had* pointed him out in the pub. Even so, predicting which card he would choose seemed quite the trick.

"I didn't," she responded, finally calming down and becoming more serious. "You chose the card, not me. It's just that everyone who makes it here tends to be going through a transformation. That's what the card means. Not literal death. It's the death of a prior self or an old life. It's not actually a bad thing."

In his mind, Scorpio had already been on life number two so he was now apparently on number three, moving through them like a cat. Hopefully this one would be an improvement over the last.

"No better time to start living than the present," Eryx said as he pulled on the back of his tunic. He stood up reluctantly and nodded to the others before moving towards the door.

"Hey Scorpio," Odessa called back to him. "This is a good place for second chances. Make the most of it." He nodded again and thought about how exactly to do just that.

***

Eryx led the way back up the set of stairs to the ground floor corridor. There they went out through an archway across the way from the courtyard. A set of steps covered by trees led down perhaps fifty feet until they reached a clearing and the front of a large glass building that appeared to be falling apart.

Eryx walked to the door and turned to look at Scorpio with the smallest hint of a smile. He was surprised that the man was even capable of joy; however, once he stepped through the doors he felt an even larger smile spreading across his own face.

The interior of the greenhouse was enormous and every inch of it was covered in green. A large metal staircase to nowhere was placed in the very middle. Fruiting vines wound their way to the top, with snow peas, pole beans and cucumbers growing abundantly. Along the sides, as far as the eye could see, were pots of all sizes containing eggplants, tomatoes, peppers and summer squashes.

"How is this all even possible?" Scorpio asked, stunned as he walked the aisles of greens and reds, purples and yellows. "Even being indoors the glass doesn't provide much warmth. It's barely spring. How is everything so advanced this early in the season?"

"Yakov alluded to it before, but Lavender's powers are extremely unique and have been valuable assets to both him and I. She is a fire elemental but rather than creating it, she has the ability to transfer it from one place, object or person to another. When you go see the forge, you can find out more about how they have been working together there. She's been able to absorb solar energy and transfer it to the plants. I've been able to grow the food we need much more quickly and also have success with some plants that otherwise wouldn't grow well in this season or location. She hasn't been with us long, only since fall, but she was eager to help us while gaining control of her power. Before she arrived, our meals were not as colorful."

"Potatoes and mushrooms?" Scorpio conjectured.

"Potatoes and mushrooms," he affirmed.

"So your meals weren't so far off from my pub fare until recently then. Except still lacking the meat." He bent over to examine an aloe plant. "So you do have some species here that could be used for something other than ingestion."

"I've done some research into healing, yes." Eryx was looking at him searchingly. "Just the planting and maintenance of this place takes up most of my time but I'm able to do something for the small bumps and scrapes that tend to occur, especially amongst the children. Is that an area you would be able to provide some assistance with?"

"I wasn't always the bad guy," Scorpio acknowledged. "I don't think anyone starts out that way." He smelled something on the spring breeze coming in from an open window and walked further down the path leading towards the back of the greenhouse. "Some plants heal and some plants harm and some do both. I've studied them all."

As he walked, the scent intensified, though he couldn't identify it. It seemed like a conglomeration of many things. Sweetness and earthiness and spice. Finally, in the back right corner, he found a giant raised garden bed in the shape of a spiral. Each segment contained a different herb: sage, onion grass, thyme and cilantro all in their own box but part of the greater whole. As he moved his fingers across each herb they called out to him and pulsed with their particular energy. Rosemary; nostalgia, sage; clarity, lavender; peace.

While an individual of any background could collect herbs and use them for their intended purpose, he and others like him could sense a plant's true purpose and use it accordingly. Mastery included learning how to combine species in order to get the maximum results. This is what he had studied as a boy and what had helped him to create a lucrative business over the past few years.

While Eryx was also an earth elemental, Scorpio expected his gifts were more based upon caring for the plants themselves. Being in tune with the plant, like a mother and her baby. His type could feel what a plant needed in order to thrive: how much sunlight and water, the optimal temperature, the appropriate soil.

"Do you prepare the food as well?" Scorpio asked him.

"It's typically a joint effort. Luckily for us, about two years ago now we picked up an older woman, Matilda. Too young to be an acceptable Widow, a huge threat to the establishment, clearly," he said, rolling his eyes. Scorpio was again surprised the Eryx was now making jokes but maybe it was due to the fact that he was in his natural environment.

"Too young to be a Widow but not too old to be an orphan," Scorpio returned, attempting to hold onto the levity of the moment.

"Exactly. Anyway, she spends a great deal of her time with the children but then plans out and directs the others in making the meals. She tells me what she needs, and I plant it. She's a valuable asset."

"It seems like you have a lot of those," Scorpio said, thinking out loud. Growing up he had spent most of his time alone, which was partly due to his own reclusive nature as a child, but also because he was encouraged to work on learning and developing his power independently. It was to be used to one's own advantage, not shared. The mentality here seemed to be one of cooperation and from what he could tell during his short stay, it was benefiting everyone. Maybe he could do some experimentation here himself. Though Heren hadn't been especially welcoming, a joining of knowledge between the two of them would likely have very beneficial results for both parties as well as the rest of the people living in the orphanage. Orphanage? He refused to refer to it as that. Compound? Fortress?

"Let me show you the rest," Eryx said, interrupting his thought process.

"There's more?"

"I told you there would be weeds. They know they're not welcome here." He walked towards the middle of the greenhouse and stopped at a pair of glass french doors at the very back. The look on his face was one of apprehension and guilt.

"As I mentioned, the herbs and vegetables in the greenhouse take up most of my time along with some of my other responsibilities. I'm afraid the outdoor gardens have been neglected to say the least."

If the greenhouse was a beloved cat who was fed fresh milk and tuna from a silver bowl, then the outdoor garden was a stray dog who was occasionally thrown scraps when someone was in an especially generous mood.

Four large square plots surrounded a dry central fountain. Overgrown forsythia grew along the back edge and thorny rose bushes along the sides. There were tulips and snowdrops and daffodils but there was also goosegrass, bull thistle and spurge. Scorpio walked closer to the fountain and observed the statue within. Two females and two males stood, backs facing. Each faced a particular square of the garden. The first female had long hair that cascaded down her back. Her face was sweet and smiling. She wore a crown of flowers and very little else, but plants growing up from her feet providing her with some coverage. She held hands with the male to her right. Scales carved down his arms and he was attempting to pour water from a large pot into the fountain below; however, there was no water to be poured.

A short haired female came next. She had harsher features than the other woman and was covered by a short tunic. A small flame was present in her left hand. Her right was joined with the final figure who was a bearded male. His lips were rounded and he was blowing onto his upturned palm. He wore an airy toga draped around his body.

"We figured the fortress must have been hidden for quite a while for this to still be here," Eryx stated, gesturing to the figures. "The palace would have destroyed them ages ago like all the others."

"Who are they?" Scorpio asked, continuing to study the various details. He could see a small circle on the wrist of each of the first two figures above their conjoined hands.

Eryx looked at him like he had three heads. "The first four."

Scorpio looked back at him like he had four heads. "If all the other statues like this were destroyed how would I have seen them before?" He examined the figures on the other side and noticed that they each had a small pair of parallel lines on one shoulder.

"Fair enough." Eryx conceded. "We just heard about them in stories growing up. I assumed it was common knowledge in Fysia." He turned towards Scorpio, brow furrowed. "Where did you say you were from again?"

"I didn't." Scorpio replied matter of factly. "Where did you say *you* were from?"

"So, the statues," Eryx avoided the question like Scorpio assumed he would, and turned back to the figures. "They come from the creation myth explaining the turn of the seasons as well as the origin of elemental power."

"Go on," Scorpio encouraged him, gesturing with his hands.

"You've really never heard this?"

"Maybe I just love the pleasant cheery tone of your voice."

Eryx rolled his eyes but continued. "The story starts with the sun being alone in the universe. He decided to create the earth but didn't want to have one entity there to rival his power so instead he divided the power between four demi-gods."

He stood by the first female decked in flowers. "There was Prim, goddess of the flora." He moved to the next male figure holding her hand. "Quiro, god of the rain and rivers."

Scorpio followed him around to the other side of the statue and Eryx gestured to the final two: "Next was Ignitia, goddess of flame and heat, and finally Frigus, god of air and cold."

He completed his circle around the statues and continued. "The sun was happy with what he had created until he noticed that the demi-gods had become attached to one another. Prim and Quiro had shared their powers and he had helped her to create plant life all over the surface of the planet. While he was a god of frost, Frigus had stoked Ignitia's fires with his air and helped her to spread warmth, and support life on the planet. The sun felt threatened and therefore he separated the lovers. They were sentenced to chase each other through each year for eternity never to be reunited."

"The seasons," Scorpio postulated. "Spring and fall. Winter and summer. But why would the kingdom care about an old story? Or these?" he asked, gesturing to the statues.

"Many reasons," Eryx answered. He opened his mouth and then closed it again as if debating whether or not to continue. Scorpio gestured at him to keep going and Eryx sighed but then relented.

"The females and males were equals. Frigus and Quiro didn't have greater power in order to control their mates. Worship of the demi-gods predates the myth itself. Where I'm from, the people still leave small offerings to the gods they received power from and find ways to celebrate the turning of each season. The myth is basically a slight to the first family and the decline of love in the kingdom due to the required power differentials."

"How do you know I'm not some loyalist to the kingdom who will report your traitorous ideas?"

Eryx scanned his features, his mouth upturning with a hint of disgust at his long stringy dark hair that had gone quite a while without a wash. "Excuse me if I'm a bit harsh, but you don't strike me as someone with any loyalties at the moment."

"Harsh indeed but I suppose it's true. Your secrets are safe. You said this fortress must have been here for quite a while but how long have you been here exactly?" Scorpio asked, attempting to sneak in a question while Eryx was off his guard.

"A while," he responded, not budging. "Anyway, it's yours. Grow whatever you'd like here as long as it's to our benefit rather than our demise. If there is something that requires a more specific type of climate let me know, and I can try to get some planted in the greenhouse. Once you acquaint yourself with Lavender, I'm sure she'll be willing to help as well. She's the most eager to make friends. I'll collect you for lunch." He turned and went back into the greenhouse to start his work for the day.

Scorpio looked at his new gift. The garden had the potential to be something incredible, but potential only got you so far. It would take work and he was ready for it. He placed his knees in the dirt and began.

CHAPTER 23
SCORPIO

It didn't take long for Scorpio to get lost in his task. While he was used to foraging for the wild mushrooms, herbs and flowers that he needed, it had been a while since he had owned a sizable piece of land and done any planting of his own. He didn't have the same skill set as Eryx, but he wasn't too bad with a rake and a trowel. The work provided the same quiet focus that he felt while hunting for chanterelles or experimenting with a new concoction.

As he pulled each weed up by its roots he thought about all of the information that he had been provided with about his new temporary home. It would be temporary since he knew something like this couldn't possibly last. All of the people he had met so far were living outside of the societal rules dictated by the kingdom. As far as it being an orphanage, the Widow being in charge of a home for children seemed legitimate enough. It was all of the others that worried him. None appeared to be married and all likely were running away from something. So was he, but he knew it was better to keep to the shadows than attract attention by conglomerating in one place.

The place itself was a mystery. He wasn't sure exactly how far they must have traveled to get him. The pub was on the outskirts of the forest but he had no idea if they had traveled north or south to reach the river. The forest itself was something most people found impossible to navigate. It was rumored that the Witch Queen of the west had enchanted it, making it impossible for the king's armies to cross it and invade her territory. If her magic had allowed them to reach the river and find safe haven here, maybe it was because she wanted them to. That thought wasn't exactly comforting either.

There was also the question of why the seer, who must be Odessa, had seen him. Scorpio hadn't met many people with psychic powers, though he supposed it was possible he had and just hadn't known. He wasn't exactly sure how the powers worked. Did they lead them to him simply because he had a power that they could make use of? A job they needed to fill? Or was it something else? Something to do with a bigger picture?

By the time Eryx came to retrieve him for lunch, he needed a break from his own mind that kept going around in circles. The dining area was quiet since they had worked into the early afternoon. He followed Eryx through a door to the side of the room that led down a small stairway into the kitchen. A woman perhaps twice his thirty years sat working at a large counter top accompanied by Heren and two young boys. She wore a tunic of light orange that matched nicely with the dark red hair that was wound into a tight bun on the top of her head. She was tall and slight but her strong arms suggested that she had no problems with kneading a dough or lifting up large sacks of flour. When the boys saw Eryx approach, they quickly stood up from their stools and began taking off the aprons they wore on top of their yellow tunics.

"Sit down please and finish your tasks first," the woman scolded. She pointed to two plates that were sitting on the countertop off to the side. "We fixed you boys some sandwiches since you missed lunch. Heren told me that there was another mouth to feed. I'm Matilda."

Heren looked up from the asparagus he was snapping the ends off of and Scorpio gave him an appreciative nod.

Eryx grabbed the plates and motioned for Scorpio to sit on the bench at the work table. The plate contained a sandwich made of thick crusty bread, a white spread speckled with green herbs and what looked like cucumber, tomatoes and peppers.

"Do you have cows here as well?" Scorpio asked after taking a bite of the sandwich, which again, was much more satisfying than he would have thought. The spread was creamy and tangy and also held a bit of a pleasant smokiness to it.

"It's eggplant," Matilda replied smiling. "We have traded for dairy at some of the smaller markets but it doesn't stay fresh for long and isn't usually worth the journey."

Scorpio nodded but didn't reply in order to continue eating. The two boys sat in front of a large pile of potatoes. The first, who was taller and thinner, peeled each spud and then handed it to the other boy who was a bit shorter and broader. Neither one appeared to have yet reached their teen years. The taller boy looked at Scorpio with a frown on his lips and suspicion in his eyes, but the younger boy gave him an open smile that he couldn't help but return.

"So tell us about yourself," Matilda prompted as she flitted around the kitchen collecting ingredients. In front of them on the workspace were glistening red apples, bright golden pears, two enormous heads of crisp green lettuce and six eggs that were precariously perched near to the edge of the table. Scorpio opened his mouth in warning when one nearly became a cracked and splattered mess on the floor but just before it leaped off the precipice, the older boy flicked a finger and he felt a soft breath of air as the egg rolled back to join its companions. He brought his hands together in a silent clap of appreciation for the catch but the boy just scowled back.

"Not much to tell," he began. Truthfully, there weren't many things about his current life worth discussing. "Eryx and Odessa rescued me from some peril that I got myself into."

"A tree branch fell on him," Eryx cut in as he ate his sandwich slowly and in an annoyingly polite manner. Scorpio could detect the slightest hint of a laughing smile as he chewed with his mouth closed.

"A tree branch did not fall on me," he corrected. "It was not a passive action committed by the tree. I used my power to sever the branch because.."

"Because…." Eryx prompted, eyebrows raised. Heren had stopped his snapping and was curiously watching their exchange.

"It's not important," he finished, realizing Eryx was actually trying to stop him from sullying his own reputation. It had been a long time since anyone had looked out for him. It wasn't something that he was used to.

"I'm sure it was for some nefarious reason," the surly boy said, eyes narrowed.

"Barrett," Matilda warned as she began chopping the lettuce and putting it into a large bowl. "If it was destined that Scorpio join us, then we're going to treat him with kindness and respect. Everyone deserves a second chance. Just because you may have heard something that wasn't meant for your ears, doesn't mean you should make judgments based upon it."

"What kind of name is that anyway?" he responded, obviously not paying any attention to what was said. "Can we go now?" he asked petulantly, turning to Eryx. " The potatoes are finished."

"We can. I hope your arms aren't too tired from all that peeling," Eryx responded with a wink.

"Just adding to these muscles" the younger boy broke in, putting down his knife and flexing his arms playfully.

"I'll be working with the boys this afternoon but Yakov will be expecting you," Eryx said to Scorpio, as he got up from his stool and headed back up the stairs with the two boys in tow. "There's a path right out the kitchen door that will lead you down to the forge. It's a large outdoor stone structure. You can't miss it."

"Thanks," he replied, meaning it. "For everything."

Eryx only nodded back with a slight smile. "See you at dinner."

CHAPTER 24
SCORPIO

Scorpio didn't immediately move to get up from the table. He was exhausted from spending so much time working out in the sun. Over the past couple of years he had usually slept afternoons away after making deals late into the night. Foraged the forest floor in the early hours of the morning when the sun was still making its slow journey up and around the mountain ridge. Matilda's food had filled his belly and the warmth of the people around him had given him cozy feelings that made him want to curl up in front of a fire and sleep for days.

"Would you like some coffee before you head out again?" Matilda asked, as if she had seen the exhaustion on his face. The apples and pears had been cut up and added to the bowl of lettuce, and she was now roasting a pan of pecans over the fire. The toasty scent added to the feelings of coziness brewing inside of him.

"Yes, please. Or else I might fall asleep right here."

Matilda took the nuts off of the stove and left them to cool. She grabbed a ceramic jar from the back of the kitchen and then reached inside a cupboard to retrieve a large, heavy, mortar and pestle. It was big enough to flex the muscles in her lean biceps. She filled the bowl with dark fragrant coffee beans from the jar and then pushed it across the table to Scorpio.

"From what I've heard, you should be well versed in the art of grinding. The aroma will be a good pick-me-up on its own."

She said it without any hint of malice, but he still flinched internally, aware that she had probably not chosen to take such a nefarious path in order to survive. He picked up the pestle and began using it to crack open the beans, releasing their smoky and nutty scent.

"I guess word travels fast around here." His eyes flicked over to Heren.

"Do I look like the gossiping kind?" he asked, not even looking up from his new task which was cracking and peeling the eggs that had apparently been boiled at some point before he had arrived in the kitchen.

"I don't usually judge books by their covers," Scorpio responded, now grinding the coffee beans into smaller and smaller pieces.

"Do you *read* books?" Heren replied, now looking at him pointedly, eyebrows raised.

"Are you two sure you aren't somehow related because you sound like my children, bickering with one another." Matilda walked back over and plucked the mortar of crushed coffee beans from between his hands.

Scorpio could see echoes of his own teenage self in Heren's aloofness and superior attitude, but he wouldn't admit that. He also wondered about these children that Matilda had, who were likely grown, and if she missed them, but didn't want to pry. Instead he just said petulantly, "I do read books, I just didn't manage to take any with me."

"Very well," Heren responded, rolling his eyes. "And some words of advice: If you don't want your history being known here, don't talk about it. Barrett is the king of gossip. He hears everything. Literally."

Scorpio's interest was piqued. "How? He's an air elemental so does it somehow carry the sound to him?"

"No one knows for sure, he's not exactly mister chatty when it comes to his own business. Odessa is his aunt so it's likely there's some kind of mind power there as well."

"I thought you weren't the gossiping kind, Heren," Matilda cut in teasingly, placing a mug of coffee on the workspace. Scorpio cupped his hands around it and fought the urge to sigh in pleasure at the warmth and the scent.

"The man deserves a warning at least." He had peeled all of the eggs and now cut them into neat slivers.

"What happened to his parents?" Scorpio asked, lowering his voice as if that would help. Hopefully the boy would be too busy with Eryx to be listening in on this particular conversation.

"Apparently the father disappeared and then the mother also when she went off looking for him," Matilda provided. "Sad story. Callen's two years younger and they have a little sister as well."

"Callen was the more cheerful looking fellow?"

"Yep. If Callen likes you, no one can really argue about your place here. He definitely takes after his aunt. Very intuitive about people. Knows what you're going to say or do before you're even aware."

Scorpio pocketed that bit of information. The boy had smiled at him openly so maybe he truly wasn't a threat to these people and his days of grim deeds were over. The thought was a relief, and his future suddenly seemed a bit brighter.

"That must be a lot for a girl so young to have three young kids to watch over," he postulated, sipping on the hot, bitter beverage.

"Eryx is a big help and the rest of us all play our part as well. I'm sure you'll have plenty to teach them once you get settled." She removed her apron and hung it on the back of a chair. "I'm going to head out for more water for those potatoes. It was nice talking with you. Enjoy your time with Yakov, he's a darling."

She was out the door before he could thank her for lunch or ask if she wanted any help with the water, but she looked like the type that would refuse help anyway. He was left alone with Heren who was putting together the remaining parts of the salad.

"Did you find anything exciting today?" Scorpio asked, as he savored his last sips of coffee.

Heren looked up seemingly surprised at his interest.

"Just some moonstone." he responded, reaching into his pocket and tossing something over. Scorpio caught it and examined the small, rough edged holographic stone. "It's meant to invoke feelings of calm during times of change."

"I thought you weren't a healer."

"I'm not," Heren replied snidely, "but in order to sell them you have to be able to talk them up."

"Do you think you could teach me?"

"Why?" he questioned, eyes narrowed in suspicion.

"While it might shock you, I actually do know a lot about the healing properties of plants. Maybe we could work together to learn the same about crystals. Isn't that what people do here? Collaborate? Combine forces? Teamwork?"

He could tell Heren was trying to stifle a smile. "You're very annoying but I'm also getting bored searching the same places over and over again on this island. Maybe if we go together they'll let us search the river banks on the mainland."

"You trust me that much already?" he asked, arching an eyebrow.

Heren's pale cheeks reddened as if he realized he was being a bit naive. "I suppose it's like Matilda said. If Odessa decided you should be here and Callen doesn't see you as a threat, then maybe I should give you the benefit of the doubt. I'm sure I could kick your ass anyway if the need arose," he ended, smiling.

Scorpio let out a loud guffaw. "I highly doubt that but go ahead and think it if it makes you feel better." He was definitely looking at a version of his younger self. He finally got up from his seat and attempted to hand Heren back the small shimmering stone.

The teen pushed his hand away. "Keep it, hopefully we'll find way more once we get off the island."

Scorpio clapped him on the back and left the kitchen for the next adventure of the day feeling much more nourished, both physically and emotionally, than when he had arrived.

CHAPTER 25
SCORPIO

The smithy was a small circular stone structure with a large smoking chimney in the direct center. There were two doorless entryways that allowed some air circulation throughout the building. An oversized, ancient looking anvil sat in the direct center, and Scorpio assumed that it had been there as long as those statues in the garden. Long before any of the current inhabitants of the island were born. A roaring fire blazed in the forge, and he stayed silent in the doorway as he watched the pair inside work on their current project.

Both Yakov and Lavender wore thick black aprons to protect their clothing and glasses upon their faces to avoid flying debris. Neither wore gloves, though since they were both fire elementals it wasn't necessary. Lavender's silky black hair was wound tightly into a bun atop her head. Though she was covered up by the apron he could get a fuller picture of her than when she had been sitting at the table. She was considerably shorter than both Odessa and Heren, maybe only an inch or two over five feet. What she lacked in height, she made up for in curves. The middle string of the apron was tied tightly around her thick waist and the bottom was pulled taut over her generous hips.

Yakov stood at the anvil, hammering at a large piece of steel. The biceps in his pale, freckled arms were twice the thickness of Scorpio's own, and he wielded his tool easily. Lavender's blushes at the table were understandable if she watched him use them like this on a daily basis.

At the moment, she did not seem to be distracted at all by her partner's physique and was instead concentrating fully on the blade that was being shaped. Once Yakov had taken a couple of hits, he handed the blade to Lavender. Scorpio watched in amazement as she absorbed the heat from the flames and funneled it evenly into the blade, turning its color to a blazing red, so that Yakov could continue to smooth out and shape it. Anytime the flame lost its strength, Yakov fed it with his own power, refilling the small space with glowing orange light.

Scorpio quietly observed their intricate dance until Yakov handed the blade to Lavender and nodded. She heated the blade one last time and then slowly seemed to absorb the excess heat back into her own body. Her cheeks flushed, and a small bead of sweat ran from between her thick, dark brown brows and down her nose. When she was satisfied, she handed the blade back to Yakov and cooled herself off by funneling the heat back into the forge's flames.

Scorpio clapped and they both turned, obviously surprised that they had been observed.

"Well done. You two do make quite the team."

Lavender blushed again. Funneling heat energy didn't cause her much stress, but apparently compliments or any acknowledgement of her forging partner affected her greatly.

Yakov smiled. "We can't take full responsibility for it. The Widow is exceptionally good at figuring out people's strengths. She encourages us to work together in order to maximize the benefits to the whole group. I shudder when I think that Lavender here could be wasting her gifts in the kitchen."

"It seems like Matilda has that covered," Scorpio replied with a grin.

"So you've met our resident mother then. She'll be even more efficient at feeding us all with this." He ran his finger down the blade which Scorpio now realized had the shape of a butcher knife. "We'll still have to make the handle but that's easy enough. Would you like to see it?"

"Eryx won't have your head for giving me a weapon?" he asked, somewhat jokingly.

"He's all bark, no bite," Yakov laughed, but then seemed to rethink his response. "Actually, I'm sure he would have plenty of bite if truly provoked, but thankfully it's been peaceful here since I arrived."

Yakov kept his head down and studied the blade as he began walking towards him. Though it hadn't been evident as they'd worked, the Red walked with an extremely irregular gait that seemed more inherent than caused by a specific injury.

When Scorpio tore his eyes away he saw that Lavender was watching him carefully with the tiniest hint of a threat in her gaze. Though the room had been sweltering a moment ago, he felt an icy chill go down the back of his neck and goosebumps pop up along his forearms.

He nodded at her and tried to school his features back into nonchalance before Yakov noticed his surprise. "How long have you been here exactly? If you don't mind my asking, that is."

Yakov held the smooth unfinished knife out to him, and he took it cautiously. The blade felt strong and sharp, and it only made him want to get his hands on one of the actual weapons, though this could definitely do some damage against the toughest of butternut squashes.

"I'm one of the few here who doesn't mind answering that question," he laughed as he made his way over to a stool in the corner and took a large sip of water from a mug. While the skin of fire elementals didn't burn, they needed a much higher intake of water to stave off dehydration, especially after using their power. "Odessa and Eryx came to retrieve me from the city almost two years ago, right after I failed my trial. It was a good thing too since I didn't have anywhere else to go."

"The king didn't offer you a place at the palace?" Scorpio asked, unable to hold in his surprise.

Yakov looked at him like he was mad but then relaxed his features into a more considerate expression, "What would they want with me?"

If he was going to be around people again, people who wanted to get to know him rather than just ask him what flavors paired best with arsenic, he needed to figure out how to keep some things to himself. He tried to back pedal a bit. "It's just when I was younger I heard rumors that the king helped those boys who didn't match at their trials. Gave them small positions until they were able to compete the next year."

Yakov looked at him curiously and then opened his mouth but then closed it again as if he thought better of what he was going to say. "I've never heard of anything like that. Talon isn't exactly known for his generosity." His eyes darkened for a moment before clearing again. "Though I suppose the pair of them were pretty much waiting for me as I left the arena. He wouldn't have had the opportunity."

Scorpio turned the blade over and over in his hands, "I must say I'm surprised that you placed last. You seem to have quite a handle on your power and I wouldn't want to be up against you in a fight either."

Yakov smiled. "The man you see now is very different from the boy I was then." The smile stayed but no longer reached his eyes. "My parents had a very difficult time accepting me as I was."

Scorpio remembered now the comment he had made about his father. "They were concerned about your ability to handle your power because of your physical differences?"

Yakov nodded. "My father was. He assumed the weakness in my legs automatically meant that my mind and level of control would be weak as well. He didn't let me train because he was concerned that if my power grew I would do damage to him or the house. My mother just coddled me. I didn't walk until I was ten. She did love me but I think they were both counting down the days until I wasn't their problem anymore."

"I'm sorry," Scorpio said, honestly. His relationship with his own father had been difficult but not as tragic as what he had just been told.

Yakov shrugged. "Everything happens for a reason. If I had done any better I would have paired with a female and might be married and miserable. As it is I have my own forge, with a wonderful partner," he winked at Lavender who was sweeping the floor of debris "and friends who accept me for who I am. I'm much happier with the makeshift family I've made here than the one that was stuck with me."

Scorpio attempted to cough out the lump that was forming in his throat, and Yakov went over to get him his own mug of water. Once he was sure he wouldn't burst into tears on the man's behalf he finally replied, "Everyone here has been overly kind, even to someone who might not deserve it."

Yakov patted him on the shoulder, "Don't be too hard on yourself, this kingdom isn't an easy place to live if you're on the outside."

Scorpio needed a change of subject. No one, especially Yakov, needed to see him in a fetal position on the floor. "Lavender, Eryx told me that you help him out in the greenhouse when you aren't needed here."

"She's always needed here," Yakov grinned at her again. These two needed to get a room if they didn't have one already.

She rolled her eyes while giggling. He was pretty sure he hadn't heard her speak yet. When she did her voice was quiet but also deep. She must have been the top prize at her trial, if she attended it. Her voice had a bit of an accent to it which he associated with the southernmost lands of the kingdom.

"It's been a little more complicated to be honest. In the beginning when I started working in the forge, if I transferred a little too much heat to a blade, Yakov just let it cool off a bit before attempting to work with it again. I was able to figure out the right amount to add and to take away fairly quickly. Plants are so much more sensitive. Many sadly lost their lives and shriveled up in front of me before I figured out how to minimize my output. It's not easy holding back." She smiled, self-deprecatingly.

"Plantricide. A very serious offense." Scorpio nodded but then put a finger to his chin. "Could be helpful with taking out large amounts of weeds though."

"Actually, that would be a much easier task than trying to bring things to life. If I helped you, could I make some requests for the space?" she asked hopefully. "I would love to be able to get my hands on some body oils or perfumes." She fluttered her eyelashes at him, and he knew that her elemental powers weren't the only ones she possessed.

"Sounds like a fair trade," Scorpio responded, holding out his hand to shake her much smaller one. "Is lavender on the top of your list? Is that your given name or did you choose it yourself when you came here?"

She took his hand with a much stronger grip that he would have thought she was capable of. "I would tell you but then I'd have to kill you." While she smiled at him, the chill in the air returned and the hard glint in her dark eyes told him that she wasn't kidding.

CHAPTER 26
SCORPIO

Scorpio had watched Yakov and Lavender for a while longer before Eryx retrieved him in order to show off the areas on the island designated for bathing. Once he had washed off the last few days of filth, and tied his now clean hair into a bun at the base of his neck, he was ready to go back to his cot and sleep for days.

At dinner, he sat in the same seat he had taken in the morning and was welcomed by Yakov clapping him on the back and a hint of a smile and eyebrow lift from Heren. He somehow managed to keep his eyes open throughout the meal while shoveling in as much food as possible. Though he didn't have enough energy left to participate in conversation, he didn't mind observing the dynamics of the others who he had become more acquainted with throughout the day, attempting to figure out the connections between them all.

Odessa was the only one at the table he hadn't spent much time with. For a seer, a power which in the past he had associated with the quiet, mysterious types, she was an open book. Her smiles were easy, and she seemed to be equally comfortable with everyone around her. She was unphased by Heren's haughty eyerolls or Eryx's general air of disinterest, though Scorpio was beginning to think that was just a facade for someone who actually cared very much about everything and everyone.

He made it back to his room before the spring sun had made its way past the western horizon. While his body ached the next morning from his work in the garden, he felt refreshed and motivated to continue clearing up the misplaced stonework and trimming the overgrown hedges while planning out in his mind what he was going to do with the land once it was all cleared out and ready for planting.

His first week passed generally in the same way. After seven days of moving stone around, pulling up especially thick weeds whose roots were untouched by Lavender's lethal abilities, and even chopping lettuce with Matilda's new knife, the aches and pains in his arms were beginning to result in fresh muscle, though it would be a while before he reached Yakov's proportions if that was even possible. Eryx had shut down Heren's idea of looking for crystals on the eastern banks and he didn't want to make trouble; however, he thought if he causally brought it up with the Widow during their talk today, there wouldn't be anything Eryx could do since she was the only one who seemed to outrank him.

She was seated in the same place with the sunlight streaming in through the small narrow windows around her. He hadn't seen her anywhere else on the grounds. For all he knew, she had her meals brought to her and slept in the chair. It seemed like a sad existence to him but with all of the young people coming in and out, she probably had many more visitors than any of the other Widows or Widowers around the kingdom.

"Ah, Scorpio," she croaked, and he could tell she was already mocking him. "Eryx tells me you've adjusted well so far? Have yet to take your chances with the river?"

She had already brought it up, might as well make his plea. "About that actually, Heren asked me if I would go with him to check out the eastern banks for crystals since he's exhausted his searches here. I've been focused on clearing out the garden, but I'm sure Matilda would appreciate it if we found some wild mushrooms for her to use in the kitchen as well."

"I'm guessing Eryx doesn't trust you enough yet to let you go? Thinks you'll leave and take Heren with you for some kind of ransom?" He could hear the hint of amusement in her tremulous voice.

"I'm sure he has his reasons but, I promise to return Heren safely and soundly. To be honest, if he doesn't get off this island for a bit I'm afraid he might leave of his own accord." It wasn't a lie. Wherever Heren had escaped from, he wasn't exactly happy here, and maybe if they were away from Barrett's hypersensitive hearing, he'd be willing to talk it out.

"That's very perceptive for someone who's only been here for a week." She sighed. "I take pride in the fact that most of my people have found their place here and have opened up, but Heren is still very reserved."

Better to keep going while he was ahead. "We talked about collaborating on improving our healing abilities. Before..." he stopped himself. "When I was younger, I did some experimenting with the healing properties of herbs. While Heren isn't naturally attuned to using crystals to heal he is familiar with all of the names and qualities and knows which ones to look for. Maybe a big project like this could make him more willing to stay. Make him feel like he was important to the community." He was wringing his hands and rambling like a school child desiring approval.

She nodded slowly. "And do you feel important to the community yet? Important enough to stay?"

"Yes, surprisingly." It was the truth, though before she had asked he mostly knew he was going to stay because *he* felt better, not because he was actually helping anyone else.

It almost looked like she had been holding in a breath that she released when he answered though that didn't seem right. She couldn't be *that* invested in him already. Maybe she just didn't like being wrong.

"I will tell Eryx that you and Heren may go explore the bank. Just don't go too deep into the woods. If he can't see you from the parapet, where I'm sure he'll be watching, he'll go out after you. He's a bit protective, that one."

"You could have fooled me." He shook his head then turned, thinking he had been dismissed.

"Before you go," she called out, stopping him. "Have you ever done any research into healing psychically?"

He turned around confused. "No. I don't have any powers of the mind."

"Something Eryx and Odessa mentioned suggested otherwise."

Now he was completely baffled. "What exactly did they mention?" he asked, slightly peeved that they had been discussing him behind his back.

"The tree that fell on you. How did you do it?" she questioned. "I'm guessing it wasn't just divine intervention or extremely good timing."

"I just…" He stopped to actually think about what he had done. "I imagined the parts of the tree breaking apart and then they did. Is that strange? It's well known that Green elementals can control the movements of plants when they need aid."

"Yes," she countered, excitement in her tone, and he could tell that this was what she lived for. Debating and figuring out the complex puzzles behind "her orphans'" powers. "But what you did goes against the plant's desire to self-preserve. The plant didn't choose to break itself for you. You broke it."

"What does that have to do with psychic healing?" he questioned, seriously curious now to where she was going with this.

"If you used your mind to change the inner composition of the tree so that it broke, maybe you could also do the opposite. Fix a tree. I'm sure you've studied the anatomy of plants and therefore picturing the innards of the tree was easy for you. If you familiarize yourself with human anatomy, maybe you could not only cause harm to a human in the same way, but also heal them." She had been gesturing with her arms in an excitable manner and he was surprised that she hadn't gotten up from her seat though maybe she was unable to do so.

"There are a lot of "what ifs" there," he had to state, though he couldn't lie, the idea did excite him.

"You've got plenty of time on your hands. Start small. Next time you're in the garden, nick the stem of a daisy and then see if you can piece it back together. Practice that for a while and do some research as to how the human body works. Have you been to the library?"

Of course there was a library. "No, but I'm sure someone can show me."

"Alright then. Good luck. I expect an update next week."

That was a dismissal. The woman wanted him to regenerate human flesh like it was no big deal. He shook his head as he passed through the large wooden doors, unable to ignore the flare of excitement in his heart. He was being encouraged to go to the library and read books on end and then do plant experiments. His younger self wouldn't have questioned this was where he was meant to be.

CHAPTER 27
SCORPIO

Scorpio awkwardly opened his mouth for the seventh time in a row as he tried to think of a way to start a conversation with Heren that wouldn't be too intrusive. His companion wore a short sleeved, teal tunic, that brought out the flecks of lapis in his blue-green eyes. With the clear water around them, he would have been truly striking if not for the ill-disposed look that barely ever left his face.

Scorpio was rowing them from the small inlet of the island to the eastern banks, which should have been a very quick trip but with the awkward silence between them felt never-ending. Every time he thought of something to say and then decided against it, Heren rolled his eyes and went back to picking the dirt from under his nails. It had been so long since he'd actually had to make small talk. His time at the fortress so far had either been speaking with people in a group, or talking while working, which was much easier for him to manage. Maybe something general would be acceptable.

"So, tell me about yourself," he finally choked out.

"Ten minutes of gaping like a fish and that's all you could come up with?"

"It's not like you've come up with anything better."

"That's because I don't really see the need for pleasantries. It's not like this is some kind of courtship outing where we have to get to know each other. Unless that was your intention?" he added, batting his eyelashes.

"Sorry, smartass teenagers aren't really my type."

Heren's face fell.

"I'm sorry. I didn't think you were serious. I'm just a little old for you and…"

The downcast look was immediately replaced by a smirk, "Maybe this will be fun after all. Don't worry, grungy old men aren't my type either."

Scorpio splashed him lightly with the edge of the oar. "So what is your type?" he asked, ignoring the jibe and zeroing in on the possible topic of conversation.

"None of your business," Heren replied, frowning and crossing his arm over his chest.

It was his turn to roll his eyes. He couldn't contain the sigh that poured out of him. *Was I this insufferable as a teenager? Probably.*

By the time they arrived on land he almost kissed the sand beneath his feet but didn't want to invite more scorn. The beach lining the river was narrow and transitioned quickly to the grass of the forest. He took one last look at the island and noticed a small form watching them from the upper wall of the fortress. He gave Eryx a wave and a thumbs up before following Heren through the thick wall of pine trees.

"So how does it work with you and the crystals?"

Heren side eyed him but then answered without any hint of contempt or teasing in his voice. "It's hard to explain to someone who doesn't experience it. Kind of like a humming, but it's more of something I can feel than something I can hear," he paused to think for a moment. "Like if there was a very loud sound so far away that it didn't reach your ears but you could still feel the reverberations. Like the way my grandfather used to still complain when my brothers were yelling and beating on each other even though he was deaf." He smiled a moment as if remembering his past life but then returned to scowling much to Scorpio's dismay.

"Some plants call to me the same way. Not all of them because I would go mad, but either the ones I'm specifically looking for or sometimes the ones that I think want to be found. The way I think of it is that they sing and call to each other, but humans don't have sensitive enough ears to hear them. I wish that we did."

"I like that," Heren nodded, the smile was back though more subdued. "Whose voice do you want to follow first?"

Scorpio closed his eyes and listened. A sound like the tiniest baby bee buzzed in his left ear. "I've got something unless you want to go first?"

Heren shook his head. "Lead the way."

***

The spring day was perfect for traipsing through the forest and Scorpio hadn't realized how much he had missed being on the hunt like this. The rewards that came with cultivating his own space would be great when the time came, but answering the call of the wildflowers and mushrooms held much more excitement for him, especially when he didn't know who it was that he was going to find.

The silence between them felt more comfortable now after what they had shared so he was surprised when Heren spoke up.

"How's it going with Lavender? I heard she's been helping you out in the gardens." The question was innocent enough but Heren asked it in such a way that it seemed like there was more than just simple curiosity behind it.

"Fine. I'm only slightly terrified that she'll either boil me from the inside out or suck all the warmth from my bones, but I surprisingly haven't managed to piss her off yet so all's good."

"So she told you?" Heren asked with a shocked expression on his face.

"Told me what?" he asked, slightly concerned. "I was joking. Kind of. She hasn't actually spoken to me much. I usually just ramble on about types of vegetation while she works."

"That's not surprising," Heren bit his lip as if deciding how much to share. "I guess I should warn you. For your own sake, in case you say something idiotic which is fairly likely."

"Thanks for the vote of confidence," he replied grinning. He had a feeling that in his previous life Heren had spent his time surrounded by court ladies who constantly talked about people behind their backs while claiming to be "not one to gossip".

"She obviously doesn't like to talk about it, but that's why she's here. Her marriage wasn't going well. They were having difficulty conceiving. Her husband said some very offensive things about her appearance and her abilities as a woman." He shook his head in disgust.

"She found him in bed with someone she thought was her friend and sucked almost all of the heat from their bodies. She stopped herself before killing them. According to her she didn't mean to hurt them, but her husband had refused to let her further develop her abilities once they started courting. He wanted to make sure he held all the power in the relationship. She lost control." He shrugged but then added with a touch of malice, "I hope all his toes fell off. As well as other things."

Scorpio shuddered and instinctively cupped himself over his tunic. "Her and Yakov seem to be close." He chose his words carefully in case Heren's interest in the beautiful fire elemental was something more than friendly.

"Yakov's a flirt, and Lavender feeds off of it after being constantly insulted for years. She told me she isn't ready to jump into anything serious with anyone else quite yet."

"And are you…" he stopped, trying to decide whether he should push while Heren was in a chatty mood or hold back so he didn't shut down again.

He sighed dejectedly, "I'm just a little tired of being the fifth wheel."

"Fifth? Odessa and Eryx are a thing?" That was surprising.

"They're the complete opposite of Yakov and Lavender who are all for show but don't actually have feelings involved. Not yet, anyway." Heren looked like he wouldn't be happy at all when that did happen. "If you weren't paying attention, you would think they were just friends, but they get visibly jealous if anyone else tries anything. Odessa is welcoming and easy going with everyone, but when Lavender got here, and the Widow suggested that she work with Eryx in the greenhouse, she would make me go down there to pick up vegetables for dinner or get herbs for her special teas basically every day to make sure that nothing unsavory was going on."

"And that wasn't typical?"

Heren laughed. "No. Unless it's her day for kitchen duty, she just reads in the library or walks around the island getting 'inspiration'."

"Inspiration for what?"

"Who knows," he rolled his eyes but smiled as he thought of his friend. "She even went to sparring practice which she hardly ever does and watched them with a deranged, panicked smile on her face. It was pretty hilarious actually. Once we all became friends and Lavender told us she wasn't looking for a relationship she backed off."

Okay, this trip was actually turning out to be very informative. It seemed like it would be worthwhile in regards to their original purpose as well. The consistent splashes of color that caught his eye every few seconds were infinitely more numerous than what he was used to in the woods that made up his old home. There were sweet purple violets, brash black-eyed Susans and charming blue bachelor buttons. When he spotted a bleeding tooth mushroom, he almost squealed like an eight year old girl being gifted a pony and carefully snatched it up, depositing it safely into his satchel.

When he saw the way Heren was staring at him as if he was deeply concerned, he thought that maybe he had indeed squealed out loud. He quickly attempted to return to the conversation at hand. "So what about Eryx? I supposed there aren't that many males here for him to worry about."

"As I said, Yakov is a huge flirt and so is Odessa. I wasn't here when he first arrived, but before Lavender came, whenever the three of them were in the same room, Eryx would just sit there and sulk."

"More so than he does now?"

He smiled. "You haven't seen anything yet. I'm pretty sure he played into the whole thing with Lavender just to get back at Dessa. There was way more touching and adjusting positions during that one sparring practice that Odessa actually showed up to than in any of the ones in which she did not."

Scorpio couldn't help but laugh. "I wouldn't paint him as the passive aggressive type."

"The whole thing is extremely passive aggressive. Next time they go out to collect someone, just watch him at dinner when she talks about all of the 'handsome men' who talked to her on the road. You'll be able to hear his teeth grinding." He bent down suddenly and picked up a small dirty stone. He removed a sea green cloth from the pocket of his tunic and began clearing the grime off of its surface.

"Why don't they just admit to it? Seems like it would be so much simpler," Scorpio questioned, still focusing on the elusive plant that seemed to want so desperately to be found.

"I don't know, I guess they've been friends since they were kids. Don't want to complicate things."

He shook his head sadly. "What a waste."

Heren raised an eyebrow. "What, are you pining after some lost love?"

"Maybe." He kept his gaze looking forward, the buzzing was so present now it was almost as if a giant hummingbird was beating its wings within his chest cavity. It was competing with the topic at hand that still managed to get his blood pumping all these years later.

"It didn't work out?" Heren asked gently. He posed the question so softly that he almost didn't hear it over the call of what he now was sure was a flower.

"Saying that would imply that there was an 'it'. There wasn't. It was a ghost of a wish before my life went to shit."

He knelt at the base of a large oak tree and there it was, mocking him, as if conjured by the memories that were being dredged up. A single lady's slipper orchid sat nestled between the gnarled roots. Its pink and white striped purse reminiscent of a true lady's anatomy, not that he would know from experience.

Heren crouched down beside him but the beauty of the irregular flower didn't distract him, unfortunately, from the topic at hand. "Do you still think about her?"

"Every day."

***

Scorpio almost left the orchid behind but Heren protested, complaining that they had come all that way for it, and there had to be some reason that it had called out to him so strongly from that distance. He was fairly certain that he knew the reason; it was his traitorous heart wanting him to feel something again, but he relented and packed it up carefully in a large clump of soil so that

153

it would survive the journey back. On the return trip, they picked up a wide variety of mushrooms, for both culinary and medicinal purposes, as well as a large batch of stones that Heren seemed satisfied with, although as they were now, they all just looked like large brown lumps to him. Once they were cleaned off, Heren would share what he knew and they would try to tap into their energy somehow.

They arrived back at the boat as the sun was making its way over the peak of the western mountains. They would make it back just in time for dinner so that he could stare at all his companions and think about the plethora of informational tidbits his new friend had shared with him. It seemed now that was what they were. Friends. At the thought he stopped on the sandy beach and bent down on one knee. Heren had been placing their things into the boat but when he turned back to look at him, his face had a look of first confusion and then absolute horror.

"What are you doing?" he asked cautiously.

"Heren. Will you relinquish your position as the fifth wheel in order to join forces with me in making up two halves of the horse's ass?"

He looked like he was going to actually cry for a moment before collapsing into a fit of laughter that Scorpio quickly joined in on. When he could finally catch his breath again Heren nodded. "I think that is probably the best description anyone could ever possibly come up with for the pair of us."

The smile remained on Heren's face for the remainder of the journey, and the brilliant sunset was no match for its beauty.

CHAPTER 28
SCORPIO

A few days later, Scorpio knelt in the garden sorting through the seeds Eryx and Odessa had brought back with them from their latest outing. They had kept some of the stones that Heren had found on the mainland for healing research, but Eryx had sold the extras in exchange for coin which he then spent on some of the seeds Scorpio had requested. He was already planning on collecting seeds from the wild flowers in the woods over the summer and fall so that he could dry them for next spring. He always preferred to harvest his own seeds so that he could be sure of the age, quality and specific variety, but for now, purchased seeds would have to do. It scared him a bit that he was thinking so far ahead. He never stayed in one place for very long, but the idea of not being here with people who had accepted him so readily into their lives was depressing. He wanted to enjoy things as they were for now and not worry about what the future might bring.

Eryx had been fairly chatty when he had returned from the two day trip. He surprisingly seemed to be opening up to him. Maybe it was because he was also a Green elemental and they had a wide variety of safe topics they could talk about. Many of the other lost souls they had brought here were considerably younger, and the only other male close to his age was Yakov. While the cheery smith seemed to have no problem with Eryx, *he* was definitely more closed off in his presence, which Scorpio could now attribute to his feelings for Odessa and the pair's past flirtation.

When Scorpio had attempted to stray from the subject of germination and instead segue into the topic of how he and the seer had enjoyed their time together on the journey, Eryx had immediately "remembered" that he had forgotten to tend to a strawberry plant that had been ravaged by a stealthy rodent. He would need to approach it more gently next time. Or get him drunk. The thought of a glass of ale had him salivating and in the next moment made him queasy. He hadn't had a drink since he'd arrived, which was over two weeks ago. It was probably best if he kept his momentum and stayed sober, especially since he hadn't felt the need to drown his sorrows in alcohol with everything else going on. Plus, he wasn't even sure where he could get a drink even if he did want one. It definitely helped that he wasn't regularly frequenting pubs and was in bed most nights before the moon had fully risen in the sky. Maybe getting Eryx high on hallucinogenic fungi would be more feasible.

He laughed to himself at the thought but then startled when he turned and noticed a humongous creature only a stone's throw away from him. Its small beady eyes were assessing him as if deciding how easily killable he would be and if the effort would be worth the meal. Its black wings were big enough to wrap him up like a swaddled babe. It had a large growth on its head and below that a razor sharp beak, which it likely intended to use to dig into his flesh. A ring of white feathers that looked more like sheep's wool wrapped around its neck.

In Scorpio's current position, on his knees in the soil, the avian monster had about a foot on him. He stood up to at least level the playing field in what would likely be a fight to the death. It cocked its hideous wrinkled head at him as if daring him to make the first move.

He jumped a foot in the air when a hand clamped down on his shoulder.

"Relax, it's just Hopscotch. Echo's Condor companion."

"I'm sorry," Scorpio replied, trying to quell the nervous shivers that his body apparently thought would confuse or threaten the formidable fowl. "I must have misheard you because none of those words seemed to make sense with any of the others, starting with the word 'relax'."

"He won't hurt you," Eryx laughed. "They're scavengers."

"You can't know that," he replied. "It's basically a bear with wings." The behemoth was watching their exchange moving its head back and forth between them as if deciding who looked like the tastier morsel.

"Just be happy that we haven't had any bears make it over to the island yet or I'm sure they'd follow Echo around as well."

"And Echo would be? Some seven foot strong man who likes to wrestle with beasts?"

Eryx scanned the space around them and then looked pointedly towards the back of the garden. Scorpio turned and saw a tiny young girl with curly dark brown hair that fell messily around her shoulders. She sat on the crumbling stone wall in front of some overgrown hedges that he hadn't gotten around to trimming yet. Her knees were pulled into her chest and she just sat curiously watching them and the massive bird who Eryx seemed to think was her pet.

"So let me get this straight. You watch me like a hawk, no pun intended, when I take Heren across the river. While I haven't yet had the opportunity to see him in action, his attitude alone has done some serious damage to my person." Eryx smiled knowingly. "And yet, you let this giant mythical creature keep company with that wee little thing." He raised both eyebrows questioningly.

"We tried to separate them. It didn't go well." He grimaced, apparently remembering, while rubbing a small scar on his arm that looked suspiciously like a beak mark.

"Did her parents leave her in its mother's nest?" he whispered, not wanting to upset the girl, but honestly assuming that was the most likely explanation.

"No. They only discovered each other last year. She's an air elemental with some powers of the mind that apparently allow her to communicate in some way with animals. She's had interactions with others but maybe because of the combination, she and Hopscotch seem to have the greatest connection."

"Hopscotch" was slowly stepping closer to them and moving to the side as if trying to get to the bags behind Scorpio's knees. He attempted to shoo it away with his hands but the creature was unphased and he jumped back as one of its wings brushed his pant leg. Suddenly its head turned around as if someone had called to it, though the girl hadn't moved or opened her mouth. It began slowly making its way over to her, dejectedly looking over its shoulder as if disappointed that Scorpio hadn't wanted to be friends.

"Does she speak?" Scorpio whispered again. "To people?"

"Yes," Eryx replied, though the way he said it made it seem as though it wasn't the most outlandish question to ask. "It takes a while though. For her to get comfortable with someone. And it has to be on her terms. Nothing personal. Mostly facts about animals. Her favorites are the unusual ones. The ones that are more difficult to love."

"So no puppies or kitties then."

He shook his head and watched with a bit of sadness in his gaze as the pair left through an open space in the hedges.

Scorpio had been planning on visiting the library anyway. He would have to do it soon before his list of books got any longer.

CHAPTER 29
SCORPIO

While the library was part of the main fortress, in order to access it one had to go down a set of stairs into the cellar. They were similar to the stairs leading down to the mess hall on the other side, but since that side of the fortress hung over the water, it was not below ground. When Scorpio reached the bottom of the stone steps there was one door to the right of him and another to his left. The door to the right was fully open and as soon as he walked past it to look inside, he was certain this was the room he was looking for. Another set of stairs led upwards and within each step was a small shelf packed with books of all shapes and sizes.

He bent down and smiled as he recognized some familiar tales from his childhood. It made sense that the lowest and most accessible shelves would be for the youngest readers. He was about to continue up the stairs when he remembered the other door within the small hallway. He looked back and saw that it was slightly ajar. Eryx hadn't warned him against going inside, or even mentioned it at all when he told him where to find the library. He supposed that meant it wasn't very important and probably wouldn't be the hiding place of his beheaded wives; however, if there was something seedy going on, or a hidden damsel in distress, his snooping might be very important indeed.

He made sure no one was coming down either flight of stairs and then slowly crept back down the hallway. He had almost reached it and was about to peek through the small crack when it abruptly and loudly slammed in his face. He jumped back in surprise and was about to grab the handle to see if it had been locked as well but then shook his head. Obviously, whoever was in the room wanted to be left alone, and he wouldn't disturb them. What would he say anyway? *I was just snooping around and wanted to make sure everyone in there still had their head?* It hadn't taken long for the stories he had been reminded of to ignite his overactive imagination.

He went back to the stairwell and any thoughts of the secret room faded away quickly when he saw what opened up before him. The library reminded him of the rest of the fortress, in that it was part stone and wood but also part living thing. The floor was the same limestone that made up most of the building and the walls were almost completely made of wooden bookshelves. The stairs leading up to higher levels had railings wrapped in wooden vines. The wood in the bookshelves was not sanded and overly shaped but instead was curved and full of imperfections as if someone had just cut out pieces of a tree in order to make room for the books.

While the ceiling was covered with wooden beams, the wall facing the outside was open. Though he had concerns about the elements coming in and destroying the precious paper, a heavy canopy of trees seemed to protect what was inside. He could see the place getting quite drafty in the winter months; however, there was a small stone fireplace set into the bookshelves and a number of armchairs surrounding it which would make for a cozy spot to indulge in a novel. The fire was lit so he assumed someone must be browsing nearby.

It was currently late afternoon and he could see that as the sun went down he would have more difficulty reaching the books on the higher floors, so that was where he decided to start. He would have to come earlier in the day or else bring some kind of torch with him, though with his luck he would probably trip and the whole thing would go up in flames.

As he climbed the steps he felt almost overwhelmed at the amount of books and knew that his nights were about to get much longer. There would be no more falling asleep early after a day of hard work and waking up refreshed. He could see himself passing out on the floor of his room over a compendium of botanical or anatomical research. He might even sit by the fire and hide a romance novel between the pages of something large and scholarly so no one would know how truly pathetic he really was.

When he reached the top of the stairs, he was pleased to see that the first aisle he looked down appeared to have to do with zoology. When he thought about it, it made sense that the upper floors might have more of the complex subjects he was looking for.

He found a book on exotic birds and another on nocturnal creatures, which seemed like something Echo would be interested in. He tucked the latter under his arm and began skimming through the former in order to see if there was a chapter on scavengers while he turned into the next aisle. When he looked up from the page in order to see what types of books were contained within the next set of shelves, he was startled to see that he wasn't alone. A woman stood at the end of the darkening aisle. Her face was in shadow, her braided hair looked golden as it reflected the light of the small candle placed at her feet, and she wore a tunic the color of yellow honeysuckle. He stood stock-still for a moment, his brain attempting to understand what he was seeing, but then she turned towards him, finally also noticing that she wasn't alone.

She jumped in surprise but then her look turned to one of concern as she saw the expression on his face.

"Are you alright?" Odessa asked him, her voice morphing her back into the seer he was familiar with. Her hair had seemed darker in the light and he had filled in the face with the one that he had wanted to see.

It took him a moment to find his own voice. "I just," he let out the breath that he hadn't realized he had been holding. "I thought you were someone else."

"Who?" she asked uneasily. She tried to appear simply curious but her eyes held a shred of panic within their fair blue depths.

"No one," he forced a smile trying to calm her discomfort. "The darkness up here was just playing tricks on me. What are you reading?"

She visibly relaxed at the change of subject. "I had a dream last night about a child in Andros. The dreams typically give me a good understanding of where we're headed, but it's always helpful to see what else I can find about routes, possible dangers along the way, safe stopping points, you get the general idea."

He nodded, thoughtfully. "So that's how you found me? The dream just showed you who I was and where to go?" He then added a little more hesitantly, "Do you know why?"

She shrugged. "I don't, but I've always obeyed the messages, and they always seem to have a positive outcome." She pointed to the book he was carrying. "I see that you're studying up on vultures as opposed to how to poison us all in one bout."

"My brain is already pretty dense when it comes to that kind of knowledge," he admitted sheepishly, swiping a hand through his long dark hair. "On the other end of the spectrum though, the Widow wanted me to look into healing, so I was searching for information on botany as well as human anatomy and possibly even psychic abilities. Would you know where I could find any of those kinds of books?"

She grinned. "You found the right guide. I've read every book in this library that mentions powers of the mind." She backed out of the row of shelves and pointed to a small table with two wooden chairs. "Why don't you put those down there to free up your arms and we can get started."

***

By the time they returned to the table, after she had shown him where to find everything he was looking for, there was barely enough space left to work. She plopped down into one of the chairs with a geography book she had retrieved for herself and gestured to the one across.

"It's fine, I can bring these back to my room. I don't want to disturb you anymore than I have," he protested.

"It will take you at least five trips to bring them all back and forth. It's no problem at all."

He wasn't used to working in such close proximity to someone else but as he began going through the books and jotting down information that seemed pertinent, everything else around him began fading away. Whenever he came back to himself and looked across the table, he couldn't help studying Odessa's face while she wasn't looking. His eyes traced over her features and took stock of all of the ways that she definitely did *not* resemble the other woman he had thought she was in the dark stacks. But also all the ways that she did.

CHAPTER 30
SCORPIO

The moon quickly moved through its phases. The Strawberry Moon became the Buck Moon and the air on the island became thick and oppressive. Scorpio spent his days sweating while he toiled in the garden, perspiring in the kitchen when it was his turn to help with meal preparation, and soaking through his clothes as he and Heren ventured around the island as well as the eastern bank. On one excursion on the northernmost part of the island, they happened upon Eryx leading a training session with some of the children and teens in a large open field. As he and Heren looked on, Scorpio could tell how much Eryx enjoyed this particular role that he had taken on. He stood with his arms crossed, focusing on the two students sparring before him, who Scorpio recognized from his first day in the kitchen. While he didn't see any of the children very often, other than during mealtimes and occasionally in the greenhouse while Eryx trained an apprentice, these two had stuck out to him due to what he had learned about the nature of their powers.

The older boy seemed to be struggling against his smaller, yet more solid, younger brother. If Scorpio remembered correctly, the younger boy was some kind of intuitive who could predict an opponent's movements. The older boy looked extremely frustrated as every time he threw a punch, the younger boy blocked it and then found some other location to tap him with a light hit or kick.

"This is pointless," he whined. "How am I supposed to beat him?"

"The purpose of this isn't to 'beat' him, Barrett," Eryx replied, calmly. "Callen is a great opponent to spar against because you have to think of a creative way to get ahead of him. You can't rely strictly on the air since it won't take sides in your case. He can sense your movements before they happen so he knows where to block and strike. What other ways could you get to him? This is how people get ahead in their trials, by being creative."

"You didn't even go to trial," Barrett argued. "We probably won't have to either so I don't see the point of this."

Scorpio grimaced, but Eryx didn't seem offended in the least. "We don't know what the future will bring. Your ability to protect yourself could be even more important due to the path we've all chosen." The amount of patience the man had was impressive, though it wasn't surprising from what Scorpio already knew of his character. "And yes, I never did get to have my chance at trials, but that doesn't mean I wasn't prepared. In fact..." He looked back at Scorpio and Heren who though he hadn't acknowledged, he had apparently clocked as being there, "I haven't had much sparring practice myself lately with an opponent my size. Would either of you be willing to join us?"

Scorpio opened his mouth to try and come up with an excuse, but Heren quickly stepped behind him and shoved him forward. "It's been a while since I've sparred with anyone. I don't know if it will be very exciting to watch," he warned.

"You're also a Green so that will level the playing field and since we've never fought." Eryx paused, turning back to his small audience. "It will be more difficult for me to predict his movements. Though I don't have Callen's impressive abilities," the young blonde haired boy smiled broadly, "if you pay attention, there are tells about what someone's next move will be: the look in their eyes, the tensing of a limb. If you're fast enough, and learn to hide your own tells, you can get the upper hand."

Scorpio took a breath. It *had* been a while since he'd sparred. Half a lifetime ago to be exact. He'd had his fair share of fights since then but the thing about sparring was that you wanted it to last. To prolong the fight as long as possible to hone your skills and show off what you knew to your trainers and peers. To get as many hits in as you could without actually hurting your opponent too badly, which was basically the point of the trials as well. With an actual fight, you just wanted to do the damage and for it to be over as quickly as possible.

They walked towards the center of the field, away from the rest of the group. Eryx had his lips clenched together but it didn't hide the grin that shone through his dark eyes, probably at the thought of showing off. He wasn't taking his own advice. He was overconfident, and Scorpio would use that to his advantage.

They shook hands in the middle of the field, Scorpio keeping his expression blank while Eryx lifted his eyebrows asking him the silent question of if he was ready to get his ass kicked. He nodded slightly and angled his body strategically away from his opponent. They circled each other for a moment. Eryx looked at his shoulder as if he were going to strike him there but then sent a kick to his upper thigh instead. Scorpio stumbled a step but then returned to his original defensive position. They continued circling. Eryx looked down as if he was going to kick him again but then went for a punch to his kidneys.

Scorpio continued to let himself get bruised as he took in Eryx's patterns. There was a quick second each time before he attempted to trick him with his gaze that his eyes would catch on the area he was really going to target. Then he would look somewhere else and then strike the original spot. Scorpio let him get in a few more hits and then began blocking every one that was sent his way. After he was comfortable, he began getting his own hits in every time Eryx moved against him, leaving areas of himself exposed. Eryx's look of determination never left his face but Scorpio could tell that when it came to getting in hits while simultaneously defending himself, he was rusty. His moves got sloppier and he could no longer keep up with hiding where he was going to strike.

Scorpio took a step forward ready to go in for the kill. With Eryx losing steam, he began a volley of attacks using his hands, elbows and feet. It was like the two of them were confined within a small three foot bubble and every time Eryx took a step back, he pushed ahead, forcing the close contact. Finally, he threw one last punch, then crouched and swept his leg under Eryx's knees, knocking his young challenger to the ground.

Eryx lay on the flattened grass panting, his tunic soaked; however, the smile on his face was bigger than Scorpio had ever seen it. If he knew beating the shit out of him was the easiest way to bring him some joy, he would have done it ages ago. He bent down and offered his hand. Eryx took it, slowly pulling himself up. They walked over to where Heren stood near a large flat rock, his arms crossed against his chest. Eryx stripped, pulling the dark tunic, which now appeared black since it was fully drenched in sweat, over his head. Heren didn't bother to hide the appreciative look he gave his glistening, muscled chest. Scorpio thought about removing his own tunic, which was uncomfortably sticky, but didn't really want to be compared to that ridiculous work of art.

"Can I trust you two idiots to keep your hands off of each other while I go get some of the crystals and healing concoctions we've been working on?" Heren asked, shaking himself out of his impressed stupor.

"For now," Eryx replied, still smiling, "but I can't say we won't be doing that again very soon."

Masochist. "Speak for yourself, I think it's going to be awhile before I can move my arms again."

Heren stalked away, apparently satisfied that at least one of them was unwilling to go for round two.

"How did you learn to fight like that?" Eryx asked, eyes bright as he offered him his canteen of water.

"Same way everyone does." While he had to admit he did enjoy pushing his body like that again, especially since the fight had ended with him the victor, the subject matter still wasn't something he wanted to discuss.

"So you did go to trial then? Did you match with someone?"

Scorpio shrugged, looking out at the line of kids who were now pairing up and playfully sparring against one another. "Does it matter?"

Eryx knew he had crossed a line with his last question, though Scorpio wouldn't hold it against him. The younger man looked at him sideways as if deciding what to say next. "Maybe you could come out here some afternoons. I know you're already busy but it seems like the garden is pretty well set, other than the upkeep of the weeds which Lavender and I could help you out with. Barrett wouldn't be able to use his argument of 'You never even went to trials' with you."

He wanted to say no. He had grown comfortable with the pattern of his days currently; however, there was also something inside telling him that a day might come when these kids would have to fight. Even with all of his training as a child, when the time came he hadn't been able to protect himself. Maybe if he helped them, showed them a specific move or counter, it would make all the difference.

CHAPTER 31
SCORPIO

Scorpio sat in one of the armchairs in front of a roaring fire in the library. An afternoon storm raged outside, and every couple of minutes the bang of thunder shook the shelves. Even though the lightning was obscured by the trees that kept the rain from pouring into the room through the large open window, he couldn't help but fear that one unlucky strike would hit one of said trees and the whole place would go up in flames.

He had come down to the library alone, after seeing the dark clouds heading in and not wanting to make the trek back from the garden in the downpour. He had picked up a steamier version of the familiar fairytale of the longhaired girl locked up in a castle that he had been waiting for the perfect opportunity to dive into. Luckily he had the foresight to tuck it into a large text on crystallography before being joined by Odessa and Echo who sat together in one of the loveseats opposite. Though not a sound came from between the younger girl's lips, she appeared very focused as Odessa attempted to teach her some of the more complicated words from the book on nocturnal animals that he had already read through in its entirety. As they sat there, enjoying the warmth and the soothing sounds of the crackling fire and falling rain, Echo occasionally looked up and gave him a shy smile. He was glad that she wasn't put off by his appearance, which likely wasn't the most comforting sight to a child. He figured that the few men this particular child was familiar with had nothing but kindness in their hearts, and therefore, had likely paved the way for him.

The next time he turned to look out at the rain, he saw the giant condor stalking back and forth just outside the structure beneath the trees. The scene was extremely macabre and he was glad that he had chosen something light rather than one of the darker fairy tales his uncle had tried to scare him with as a child. At least the bird knew that he wasn't welcome inside. He couldn't imagine the size of the excrement piles that it would surely leave behind. As if the beast had heard his thoughts, it turned its hideous head to look at him. Scorpio turned back and stuffed his nose into the book.

The rogue had just made his second trek up to visit the princess who had been locked in the tower, not by a witch, but by the king's rival who was planning on making her his bride.

"As he reached the top of the window and leapt off of the sill and into the room the handsome thief saw that the princess was wearing nothing other than her long golden tresses which covered her voluminous breasts but parted in the middle to reveal-"

Suddenly the image that Scorpio had in his head was abruptly swept away by another. He was at the entrance to the throne room and the Widow sat speaking to one of the teenage boys. Jonal, if he remembered correctly. Through the thin windows behind her, Scorpio could see the darkened sky and the wall of rain that made occasional splatters on the deep sills. The wind howled loudly as it attempted to make its way through the narrow slots.

Jonal had his hands behind his back and though the Widow couldn't perceive it from her position, Scorpio could see that he held a small blade without a handle. Maybe one he had stolen from the forge before it had been completed? The Widow's head leaned upon her fist on the chair as if she didn't even have enough energy to sit up, much less see what the boy was doing. Scorpio wanted to shout but he wasn't even sure if this was real. He didn't seem to be in his body within the room and instead was like some kind of spirit viewing the scene. Suddenly, Jonal lunged, depositing his blade in the Widow's side. He couldn't be sure how deep it went, the boy seemed eager to just get the deed done and over with quickly rather than assuring serious damage. As the Widow cried out and slouched over, Jonal grabbed her hand as if to remove the ring from her gnarled finger. He stood quickly and ran out, quietly closing the door behind him.

The vision faded and Scorpio stood up, both of the books dropping to the floor. Odessa was also standing up across from him, though Echo's face only held a look of concern.

"What was that?" he asked, confident that it wasn't some dream that he had due to the alarm written on the seer's face.

"She sent it to you as well?" she asked, confusion joining the terror in her gaze.

"She sent it?" he replied, unable to keep the shock from entering his voice, that a woman that old had enough power to send that kind of vision to multiple people.

"I can't explain right now," Odessa replied, turning as if to run from the room. "Stay with Echo, I have to go to her."

He grabbed her arm roughly, "What are you going to do for her? Let me go, if anyone can help her it's me. She did send me the vision as well."

"I'm coming with you then," she replied stubbornly, ice in her sharp blue eyes. "This is my fault. I should have seen it," and then quietly almost to herself, "Why do I never see these things when it actually matters?"

"It's not safe. For you or her if that boy is still running around looking for somewhere to hide." He gestured towards Echo. "You need to protect her. I'm sure he could help you," he added, nodding his head at the bird who already looked more alert.

Odessa still looked hesitant and opened her mouth to say something else but then closed it as if accepting the fact that he was right, "Please hurry and let us know once she's alright."

Scorpio wasn't quite confident enough in his abilities to know that she would be "alright". Her heart might not survive this kind of excitement, especially when combined with the loss of blood from the wound. Rather than say any of that he just nodded, giving Odessa a pat on the shoulder before racing down the library stairs.

CHAPTER 32
SCORPIO

When Scorpio opened the door to the throne room, Eryx was already there. He carried the cloaked woman and was making his way towards him.

"Why are you moving her? Let me try and heal her here."

Eryx shook his head pushing past him. "I'm bringing her to her chambers. It's safer."

"Safer than what? She's already been stabbed!" he argued. "Let me take her and you can go and find Heren so we can try to help her together."

Eryx shook his head again as he climbed the stairs down to the main part of the fortress and then began jogging quickly through the long hallway, the Widow's body limp in his arms. "We're not bringing Heren into this. We need to keep it contained. Did she send you the vision or did someone else tell you what happened?"

"I saw it with my own eyes. Odessa was there with me and saw it as well. We were in the library." The rain continued to pour down and it was the only sound other than their footsteps echoing on the cold stone floor. He hoped that everyone else was safely hidden away and that the Widow was the boy's only victim.

"Are you going out after him?" Scorpio asked, when Eryx didn't reply.

"I don't have a choice. I don't know what we're going to do once I find him but he knows too much. I'm guessing he took the ring for money."

Scorpio was loosely acquainted with Jonal from sparring practice. He had been at the fortress for a couple of months. Out on the field he had been asking Scorpio a lot of questions lately about trials and hadn't seemed satisfied with the idea of being left out. Maybe he had taken the ring when he saw his opportunity so that could go back to the mainland and try his luck there until he was eligible to compete in the spring. Scorpio didn't know his backstory but he did know that Jonal would have had a much easier time had he stayed through the winter.

They reached the end of the hallway and Scorpio found himself in the place he had originally come from. They went down the set of stone steps and instead of turning to the right to re-enter the library, they turned left towards the mysterious room at the end of the hall. Though he was sure it had been closed when he had run up the stairs minutes before, it now stood wide open and he followed Eryx as he turned to avoid hitting the Widow's head on the stone wall.

There were no windows and the room was lit only by a few candles that were placed sporadically around it. While it was in the cellar of the fortress, and therefore made completely of stone, there was a warmth to its appearance that came from the decorative rugs, tapestries and blankets resting on a few chaises and armchairs. There was an enormous four-poster bed towards the back in the center, and to the right a large wooden table which still curiously held three mugs atop it. Scorpio ran ahead and pushed the mugs to the side so that Eryx could place her body upon it.

He took a step away and looked between Scorpio and the door as if unsure of his decision to leave him. "Is there anything you need before I go?"

Scorpio shook his head, "Go after the boy before anyone else gets hurt. I'll get what I need to make a poultice once she's stable. If you do see Heren along the way, though," he added pleadingly, terrified that the woman's life was his responsibility alone. "I understand why you don't want to worry anyone but another set of hands would truly be helpful."

"No," Eryx said, eyes downcast as if he wasn't really happy with it either, "Before she passed out, she told me you. Only you." He looked at the woman's body once more, lying silently on the table, and then ran out the door, closing it loudly behind him as if he couldn't stand the sight.

Scorpio took a deep breath and readied himself for his task. He and Heren had been successful using crystals in combination with herbs in order to soothe burns, heal cuts, and minimize bruising; however, he had been too nervous to attempt to use his mind to correct anything on any of his companions. He was still concerned with the mechanics of it and didn't want anyone to end up with an excess of skin or an unsightly bump because he didn't know what he was doing. In this situation, closing of the wound was more important than anything else, and while he didn't want to be a defeatist, the Widow was probably the best person to experiment on. Her body was hidden the majority of the time and if she didn't make it, she had lived quite a long life already.

The knife was still in the wound. Scorpio exhaled, glad that Eryx had known better than to remove it. Before he pulled it out he wanted to get a clear idea of the size of the blade as well as how deeply it had been inserted.

He parted the large billows of heavy black fabric and found the end of the knife which was indeed square and unfinished. He could only hope that since the boy hadn't had a firm thick handle to grab, the knife might not have gone that deep. He sighed in relief when he got through to the woman's skin and saw that there was a good inch or two sticking out between where the knife was inserted and where the hilt should have been. Rather than removing the garment, he further ripped the gown apart in order to get a better view of the wound and a clearer picture of which areas of the Widow's body might have been damaged by the attack.

As he pulled the fabric away, he was pleased to see that the injury was in the fatty dip between her waist and her hip and that the blade itself was stopped by the bones of the pelvis. There was a water jug next to the bed so he grabbed it and tore another piece of fabric from the gown in order to gently clean the area. Only then did he notice something strange. The woman's skin was smooth, unlike the deep wrinkles that he had seen so many times on her hands and around her deep set eyes. His brow furrowed and he searched for the arm that was concealed within her long sleeve. Sure enough, though it was evident that this was the same woman from the vision, since her ring finger was bloodied from the boy forcefully removing her ring, her fingers themselves were long, thin, and young in appearance. He shook his head, now thoroughly confused, but still understanding that whoever it was under the robes still needed saving.

He tore a bit more of the fabric to continue cleaning the wound and saw the corner of some kind of mark lower down on her hip. He pushed the fabric aside and felt his stomach drop to the floor. A pink mark appeared burned into the woman's skin. Three wavy lines were contained within the top half of a circle. Going through the middle of the circle was a vertical line and from it were two smaller lines pointing up which formed a "v". A single horizontal line went across the bottom quarter of the circle, bisecting the initial vertical line and another curved above it forming a half circle. While he knew he didn't have a second to lose and he needed to focus on the wound, that was still bleeding inches away, his eye kept returning to the mark, following the pattern, desperately trying to find a way that it differed from the mark on his own body that had been burned into him so long ago.

176

Part III
Fourteen Years Earlier
CHAPTER 33
STEFAN

Stefan walked barefoot through the forest behind the castle. He was searching for *Chorioactis Geaster*, the elusive golden twilight mushroom. The mushroom was a dark brown pointed sphere that opened up into a bright orange star the color of apricots. Its culinary and medicinal properties had yet to be determined but Stefan was confident that if he could get his hands on the mushroom, it would speak to him as all plants did. Some had even postulated that the mushroom could magnify elemental powers, especially those of the earthen variety. Something that he could definitely benefit from as he prepared for his upcoming trials.

Though sunlight had been streaming through the trees when Stefan had begun his search, darkness chased him as he followed the call of the mushroom through the woods. It was not something he could hear, even though this mushroom in particular supposedly made a hissing sound upon opening, rather it was something that he could sense. Sometimes when he was searching for a particular plant he could also follow their scent which seemed to be magnified for him alone. This particular mushroom smelled of soil with hints of cinnamon and smoke. But the closer he seemed to get, the more the smell transformed into something rotten and old. He couldn't tell if it was even the mushroom that was flooding his senses or something else. He had never gotten this close before and did not want to lose the scent, so he continued on despite his difficulty to see the path through the darkening forest floor.

Suddenly the canopy opened up and the full moon shone down in the middle of a clearing, highlighting the object of his search. To his surprise, it was not just one mushroom but at least a dozen arranged in a perfect circle. As he laid eyes upon them, they began to open, producing a loud collective hiss and releasing their spores into the stream of moonlight. Even after all of the mushrooms completed their awakening, the hissing continued. Stefan turned slowly. Behind him was a creature with the head and torso of a man and the lower body of a snake. His face was cloaked in shadow but his eyes glowed red and large antlers sat atop his head. The snake's scales glowed the color of fire in the moonlight and they rippled as the creature whipped its tail back and forth preparing to strike.

Stefan ran, trampling the beautiful array of stars that had opened up on the forest floor. He could hear the creature swiftly slithering and hissing at his back. He turned around to see how far it trailed behind him and lost his footing; however, rather than falling to the forest floor and being at the mercy of the beast he continued to fall and fall, the light around him becoming darker and darker until there was nothing but black.

***

Stefan woke up in bed gasping for air. He swiped the long sweaty strands of black hair out of his face and breathed deeply. As he went to reach for the glass of water he had left by his bed, he startled at the sight of his father sitting on the chaise in the corner of his room. He couldn't remember the last time his father had been in his room, if ever. He wore a lavender colored shirt beneath a leather vest. His mahogany cloak was carefully draped over the seat next to him as if he had been sitting there a while. He was looking out the window, likely at the training field below, and had not so much as stirred when Stefan had violently woken up from his dark dream.

"I won't insult my intelligence by asking if you're ready for today. I'm sure that you aren't," he started without so much as turning his head. His light brown hair was cut to his shoulders, a golden crown sat upon his head.

"Then why are you here?" Stefan asked uneasily. He sat up fully and got out from under the blankets, shivering when his feet touched the cold floor.

"Your trainers have done the best they could. I have done the best that I could. Yet you would rather be off tinkering with your plants and tonics than prepare to lead this kingdom. Tell me, in your nightmare, were you bravely fighting a foe or looking for some exotic species?" He now looked at his son with a raised brow.

Stefan had been preparing to defend himself but closed his mouth when he realized that even in his dream, he had immediately run from the beast rather than attempt to challenge it.

"That's what I thought."

"I may not even have to fight today," he argued, attempting to placate his father. "If there is no top seeded female I can have another year to prepare. I'll try harder. Be more focused."

"And if there is one? It's imperative that you find your destined match."

"I'm a Serenfawr and I've been training since I was a child. Shouldn't that be enough?" He got up and reached for the purple tunic hanging over his chair. Two forest green lines circled the opening of each sleeve. The seamstress had sewn it with the hope that he would fill it in as he grew. He had yet to live up to her expectations and the excess of fabric billowed around him like a gown.

"You don't think they train elsewhere? The girls especially hone their skills tirelessly to get the best match. This year, you are the prize they are all fighting for. You need to start acting like it." He looked at Stefan, swimming in his tunic, and shook his head. Stefan turned his head away when he felt tears form in the corners of his eyes. He was used to his father's scoffs about him not being a fire elemental and the constant pressure he put on him to train, but the clear disappointment in his gaze was hard to take.

"It's not only that," his father continued, rubbing his hands over his face. "A seer has warned me just this morning that

I am not long for this world. If you find a match in this year's trials, I can be assured that the kingdom will be passed to you."

Stefan's jaw dropped, multiple feelings and ideas coming at him all at once. He was shocked that the king would even want him to inherit the throne, especially now that he had proved to be such a failure. He was amazed that his father seemed so resigned. He was terrified that he would actually have to leave the comforts of the woods and his greenhouse and interact with people.

"If the seer saw what was going to happen, is there any way to stop it?" he asked, trying to keep the desperation out of his voice.

"She did not see the manner of my death. Only that I was dead and that the petals of the pink magnolia swirled around in the breeze as my body burned. It is not something that can be stopped, only a warning so I can take the necessary steps to ensure that you are next in line to rule."

The magnolia trees around the castle had already been in bloom for a week or two so unless the seer had seen a vision from another spring in the future, his father truly did not have much time left. As a fire elemental, his body would be given to the flames. Stefan's own personal future would be a deep, dark earthen grave.

The king pushed himself up from the chaise and rearranged his cloak around his shoulders. He came to stand before Stefan who, though half his father's size in build, had just this year matched him in height. "We have not always seen eye to eye, but I do try to do right by my people. While you have your quirks, you are intelligent and," he paused, his eyes softening a fraction, "I can see that you have your mother's heart. Try your hardest today. Whether or not a match is made, I will do my best afterwards to share with you our family's secrets and what your duties will be as king."

He grabbed his son's shoulder lightly, the first affectionate touch Stefan could remember since the trials had loomed so heavily upon them both. "I will have more than I thought to attend to today but I will make sure to watch your fight."

Stefan nodded but could not decide on the next right words to say. His father dropped his hand and went to leave but then stopped and turned. "If anything happens to me… there is a room on the uppermost floor of the library. It will show itself to you once I'm gone. All the answers you need will be there." He turned again and closed the door behind him.

Stefan continued to dress and ready himself for the most important day of his life thus far. He would fight his hardest and show his father that he was indeed worthy of his legacy.

CHAPTER 34
STEFAN

Stefan attempted to exit his room as quietly as possible. He had donned a hooded green cloak in order to observe the earlier matches and gauge the competitors. There was no point in any last minute sparring with his father's guard. He was not going to get any bigger or stronger in the remaining few hours and he would rather conserve his energy for his turn on the field.

As Stefan walked past the large dining hall he ducked his head to avoid being seen or stopped by anyone inside. Unfortunately, there was no avoiding his mother who called out to him from her seat at the table.

"If you're trying to be discreet, don't wear a cloak that I sewed for you myself," she teased without looking up from the pamphlet in front of her. She sat at one head of the table and he took a seat catty corner to her on the right side. She was dressed in a green velvet gown with a purple cloak arranged behind her. Her black hair was braided intricately and tied into a knot at the back of her head beneath her silver crown. She pushed a plate over to him which held a long, yellow, bar-shaped tart that smelled of lemon and lavender.

"To calm your nerves. I snuck into the kitchen early this morning before anyone could scold me for it." She smiled at him with a mischievous look in her eyes and then patted his hand.

The tart was the perfect balance of sour and sweet with hints of florals and he did immediately begin to feel some of his anxiety ease. "Is that the list of trial entrants?"

"It is. Would you like a look?" she replied, continuing to scan the list. "Might give you a bit of an upperhand."

He thought about it but decided the list of names and figures would only bring his anxiety back and likely wouldn't do much to help him once the trial began. Too many what ifs that he would get hung up on.

"I'll pass. I'm going to go down and watch the earlier matches. See if I can pick up any new techniques." He finished his tart and fidgeted with a stray thread coming from the embroidery on his tunic sleeve.

His mother cupped his face and brought his gaze up to hers. "The trial is important. I won't say it's not, but don't feel like you have to be something you're not just to impress your father." She opened her mouth to continue and then paused as if trying to decide how to best phrase what she was going to say next. "If there is a possible match for you, don't feel like you have to utterly dominate her. There are some tough females out there, present company included."

"So you don't believe in me either. You think I could lose."

"No," she replied laughing. "I just don't want you to feel like you need to put some poor girl six feet under ground. Literally. During the match."

"That's not a bad idea," Stefan pondered. "Would get things over with quickly."

"It would be a horrible idea. Definitely not a good start to a partnership. Plus, it's doubtful the top seeded female that you would be facing would allow it."

He wondered then if she knew about his father's admission and thought it was highly unlikely. While the king hadn't seemed outwardly distraught about his predicted demise, Stefan knew that his mother would be doing everything in her power to stop it, even if she knew the seer's predictions were typically infallible. He definitely did not feel like it was his place to tell her. He wouldn't want to see her cry and also didn't want to upset any of his father's plans. His mother might even attempt to put an end to the day's events which would not be helpful in the long run.

Stefan's father had been more than twice his mother's age when they were matched. Claude had almost reached his thirtieth birthday before he had found a female that was worthy of the place at his side. Stefania had been quite the formidable fighter and some around the kingdom had joked that he would have lost the fight if he hadn't had the extra decade and a half to hone his skills. While it was expected for couples to wait to consummate their marriage until the female reached her eighteenth year, Stefan was born shortly after and was named after his mother as a thanks to her for providing an heir. For whatever reason, no other babies came after. Though Stefan figured it must have been awkward at first, with his mother being so young, his parents did grow to have a loving relationship.

He would never admit it to anyone, but Stefan was almost more concerned about the aftermath of the trial than the actual fight. Of course he was nervous about letting down his father, embarrassing his family's legacy, and looking like a complete and utter fool if he actually lost to a girl. Even more worrisome though was the idea of winning, and then having to actually court and marry someone he had never met. He had no experience with girls, or even other boys his age. He couldn't see himself not liking *her*, whoever she might be, but he found it very unlikely that she would have any interest in *him*. Other than his name and title of course.

The sound of running footsteps interrupted Stefan from his wool-gathering. His cousin Oliver burst into the room and dramatically bent over his knees panting.

"I thought I'd missed you. Father said I could go with you to watch the earlier matches."

Stefan groaned inwardly. Oliver and his father, Talon, had been the reason for his hooded appearance more than his mother.

Stefan's father had a younger brother who was born as a surprise "blessing" when Claude was already in his second decade. Apparently, he was like a second father to Talon, whose true father was white of hair and too close to the grave to put in much effort to the raising of his second child. Talon was eleven when Stefan was born and he didn't take well to the decreased attention given to him by Claude who was also distracted by his new duties as king following their father's passing. This was all told to him by his mother after Stefan complained to her numerous times about Talon's teasing and the tricks that he played on him including beating and battering him during sparring matches.

Stefania was obviously upset by her son's harsh treatment; however, he could tell that she also didn't hold Talon completely accountable for his actions, and pitied him for his sad upbringing. His uncle also tended to be on his best behavior in his sister in law's presence. While Stefan had a short reprieve from Talon's torment in the years leading up to the elder's trials and subsequent marriage, his wife died in childbirth and Talon again blamed Stefan for events that he had nothing to do with.

While he would have liked to return the favor and take his aggression out on Oliver, Stefan liked to think of himself as a better person than that, and also figured that his cousin would have it rough enough with Talon as a father and no mother of his own to protect him. That being said, the seven year old water elemental took a lot out of him, and he often found himself getting drenched one way or another.

Stefania smiled and raised an eyebrow at him waiting for his response.

"Alright, get your cloak. We don't want to bring attention to ourselves."

Oliver nodded happily and ran out back to his room.

"I know he gets on your nerves sometimes, but he's a good boy and he looks up to you. You know what it's like to grow up without peers and under all that scrutiny."

"Yes mother," he responded begrudgingly. Before getting up to leave, he scanned the queen's face. Her eyes were bright and her cheeks full, though there were the lightest of laugh lines around her mouth. He was afraid that if what his father said was true, some of that brightness would dim before he next saw her.

"What is it?" she asked, brows furrowing in concern.

"Nothing." he replied, bending to kiss her cheek before setting off. "Nothing at all."

CHAPTER 35
STEFAN

The city of Awrymor was situated on the eastern coast of the kingdom. A small peninsula jutted out of the mainland containing a crescent shaped bay. Over the past few weeks, the harbor had been packed with visiting ships. Some were from the royal fleet carrying the teenage competitors from seaside towns who paid the coin to have their first taste of freedom on the giant vessels. Others were privately owned schooners transporting the wealthier young widows and widowers who had come to attend last week's ball with the hope of finding a new match. Many of this latter category had stayed on in order to be wed in a short ceremony, register with the necessary offices and then become acquainted with their new partner while exploring the city. The largest number of ships were the merchants intent on selling their wares at the biggest market of the year.

The peninsula was connected to the mainland by a very thin strip of land that was gated and heavily guarded in order to ensure that traders carried the obligatory paperwork and that other visitors entering the city were identified and had no ill intent. From there, travelers had to make the trek through the city proper to where the castle itself was located. Awrymor was often referred to as the City of Air and Sea due to its coastal location and its high elevation. Serenfawr castle was built on the top of a mountain which required visitors to either climb numerous flights of stone stairs or pay to ride the lift which consisted of a number of small cars that were moved up and down the steep incline using a combination of an advanced pulley system and concentrated air magic.

The castle itself was massive. While during the rest of the year vendors sold their goods within the lower city, from the first full moon of spring, referred to as the Pink Moon due to the blooming of the delicate moss phlox, to the Full Flower Moon, the peak of the season, the gates of the stronghold were open to all. The crowds today were the largest they had been since the gates had been open, and Stefan found himself constantly bumping into people as he attempted to move through the market which took place in the immense courtyard encircling the main structure. He could feel Oliver's light tug on his cloak as they navigated their way through the crowd.

Stefan had known better than to save his shopping for when the attendance for the festival was at its highest. He had inconspicuously browsed the booths three days earlier when the majority of vendors had already set out their wares, but most of the competitors were still due to arrive by ship, horse or carriage. He conversed with the traders about where they had traveled from and the origins of their goods. His purchases included dried herbs and spices from the warmer southern climates, specimens of exotic mushrooms still attached to rotting logs, and potted plants that were hardy enough to survive their long journeys over land and sea.

His most thrilling find had been a potted lady-slipper orchid. This subgenre differed from the typical orchid because it contained a set of fused petals which together formed a slipper shaped pocket. The purpose of the pocket was to trap insects and encourage the process of pollination. This particular orchid had delicate white petals with a purse of speckled fuschia. While there were a number of curative uses for the plant, he was thinking that he could give it to his betrothed. If she did end up being an earth elemental like himself, maybe it would help them to bond over their common interests. If her powers differed than his, it would be a way for him to teach her about the things he loved. The name of the flower reminded him of the old fairy tale of the servant girl who had disguised herself as a princess and attended a ball where she danced with the prince and then left behind her glass slipper.

Hopefully in his story, the princess wouldn't have any reason to run away.

As he got closer to the amphitheater, Stefan tried to pick out who he thought might be the top female seed. He should have looked at his mother's brochure after all. It might have given him an idea about what color tunic to look for or whether the girl would have the pale skin of the northern towns or the darker coloring of the sun bathed regions. A slender girl wearing the deep red of chili peppers spoke with a brawny one with a tunic of light glacial blue. Another was dressed in bright clover, had tight black curls and nearly matched him in height. The sea of colors began to make his eyes swim and his stomach churn. He turned abruptly in order to find a place to sit and collided with someone wearing a vivid marigold yellow.

The brightness of the tunic did nothing for his unsteadiness so he brought his eyes up to the wearer's face. He opened his mouth to apologize for his clumsiness, but his words caught in his throat as his heart leapt in his chest. The girl was no more than half a foot shorter than him and was athletic in build. Her honey colored hair was braided over her left shoulder and was nearly identical in hue to her shining gold eyes that were focused on him with a look of concern. Thick dark brows contrasted with light brown freckles that acted as a bridge from one sunburnt cheek to the other. Her features were strong and he could tell that she wasn't the kind of damsel who needed saving. When his brain finally realized that he had stopped breathing, he filled his lungs deeply, and in doing so, took in the light scent of lilacs.

"Are you alright?" she asked, as she attempted to see his face, which was partially masked by his hood.

"I'm sorry," he managed to squeak out. "Was just a bit overwhelmed by the crowds. That's all." He realized then that he had steadied himself using her lean upper arms and immediately removed his hands but only after noticing how warm and smooth her skin felt under his calloused fingers.

"I can sympathize," she responded, widening her mouth into a smile that he was infinitely happy to have caused. "Our village is probably the size of the courtyard and all of the people could squeeze into that fountain with room to spare."

She gestured to the space next to her and he noticed that she was accompanied by a much younger girl with hair many shades lighter that hung in a messy array around her, almost reaching her waist. Her blue eyes crinkled at the corners as she smiled openly, displaying teeth that did not quite fit her small mouth.

Oliver had come around to Stefan's side to see why they had stopped moving through the crowds and latched on to the last bit of conversation.

"Oh he's not from a small village, he just doesn't leave…"

"My room!" Stefan interrupted him, pulling his cousin to his side and pinching his arm in silent warning. For some reason he didn't want this girl to know his true identity. Not yet anyway. "I'm a bit of an agoraphobic." Now instead she would think he was some kind of weird hermit which actually wasn't all that far from the truth.

She narrowed her eyes and looked up at him as if she didn't quite believe the story but then shrugged and pointed to his hood. "Explains the getup."

"Yes, you know the whole 'I can't see them, they can't see me' kind of thing."

She looked up at him again questioningly, and her eyes scanned his face as it was something worth studying. He racked his mind for something, anything that he could ask to keep her here, but then something caught her attention behind him and she took a step back. She waved in acknowledgement to someone over his shoulder and then turned her eyes back to him. Even in those few seconds he felt a coldness in the loss of her gaze.

"Well good luck today if you're competing. There are some beautiful trails behind the amphitheater if you need to catch your breath."

She had visited his woods. Walked on the paths that he took every day, and she thought they were beautiful. She looked up and smiled at him once more, reaching out to squeeze his upper arm as if trying to provide him some comfort in the melee. Then she was gone without even telling him her name.

CHAPTER 36
STEFAN

The first trials of the day typically didn't bring in too many crowds. Many of the visitors were sleeping in after long journeys or still making their way up to the castle from their lodgings in the lower city. Unless the king's scouts had been totally off in their predictions, the competitors who were scheduled earliest in the day didn't bring much to the table in regards to the mastery of their powers or their hand-to-hand combat skills. Stefan was happy to sit and watch since the more inexperienced participants he witnessed, the better he started feeling about his own abilities. He was sure his self doubt would return as the more skilled contenders took the field.

The amphitheater had been built into a natural dip in the mountain. Audience members sat on large steps that were made of earth and soft grass. Each step was separated from the next by a wall made of large blocks of limestone. Towering trees surrounded the outside and were also interspersed throughout, providing some shade. Merchants sold food and drink in order to fill both the bellies of the crowds and the pockets of their jackets. Stefan usually loved to sample the foods that were not typically part of the usual castle fare: roasted nuts smelling of cinnamon, cones of spun maple sugar, corn patties stuffed with cheese, and sweet bubbly cider. After the events of this morning, he could barely stomach the smell of some of his favorites. Oliver had no such qualms and had made him buy something from every vendor that walked past touting their wares before the tournament had even begun.

Stefan scanned the playing field that he would be standing on far too soon for his liking. It was like its own strange little ecosystem. A variety of different types of trees were spaced in strategic places that would not deduct too much from the audience's view. The ground was mostly earth, but there was also a small pond surrounded by fine golden sand. One side of the playing field was a steep outcropping of rock that led further up the mountain. Fires blazed in stone pits in equidistant stops around the perimeter. Each opponent would be given an equal opportunity to draw power from the elements.

The weather couldn't be more perfect. This early in the morning there was still a chill in the air, and he was glad that he had the warm wool cloak covering him as he sat next to Oliver on the cold stone. The sky was slightly overcast; however, streams of sunlight were beginning to poke their way through the clouds as if the sun was also antsy to bear witness to the day's events.

Stefan looked back up the hill to the top of the amphitheater to see if there was any action coming from the large stone outbuilding which acted as the preparation area for the competitors. The small building was separated into two main areas that were conjoined by a small hallway which led out so that each pair could walk out side by side down the main path of the theater. While the competition obviously pitted players against one another, it also could result in the start of a partnership and whether or not each pair ended up matched in the end, it was a way for them to get a first look and feeling from one another. It also engaged the audience by helping them to make wagers about what the outcome of the match would be, and whether or not the pair would be walking down another aisle in the near future.

Finally the crowd began to hush as there was movement above. While the pair that made their way down the aisle must have been the appropriate age, they barely looked like they had reached double digits. The girl had dark black hair that was separated into two childish pigtails and had an extremely pale countenance that contrasted unattractively with her tunic of dark maroon. Her almost skeletal frame suggested that she hailed from one of the northern regions and had suffered during the long winter months.

The boy had slightly more meat on his bones. Height wise, his head came up no higher than the girl's nose. He was dressed in a midnight blue tunic and displayed a confident smile as he walked down the path to the arena, unlike the girl who wore a face of grim determination. Even considering the slight advantage the boy had due to the power of water over fire, Stefan put his money on her. If he were in the boy's position he would not be wearing such an easy smile. But perhaps he had some kind of unique power or special mentoring that would give him the upper hand.

Once they reached the center of the playing field, the competitors stood across from one another and listened to the referee explain the rules. The man wore a well-pressed, dark green tunic, emblazoned with the Serenfawr crest.

"No weapons on your persons?" he asked, doing a quick scan himself. While many used weapons during training to hone their skills, they were left off the field in order to guarantee that no one would be mortally wounded or severely maimed.

"Your goal is to get your opponent past the line on their side of the field."

A touch of worry flashed across the face of the Blue. It wasn't a small distance. The size of the arena was to ensure that the contest was not over too early, and to make certain that each player would have time to fully demonstrate their skills.

"The competition is over when I declare it," he continued, his voice deep and serious. "No more hits after the whistle blows."

Once it was determined by the referee that one party was significantly more powerful than the other, even if they had not necessarily achieved their goal of moving them past the line in the earth or sand, the match was ended and their fates were decided.

There had been instances where serious injuries did occur, either in the earlier matches where competitors did not have enough control over their power, or in the later matches where they were highly skilled but let their emotions or egos get the best of them. In most cases, the referee ended the matches before things got too ugly and so that the competitors left with minimal scrapes and bruises.

Stefan could feel Oliver almost vibrating in anticipation next to him. He elbowed him softly.

"If you're going to be my second in command one day, you need to learn to project cool indifference. Do you ever see my father wiggling in his seat?" His voice was serious but he also said it with a smile Oliver couldn't see.

Oliver stopped shaking his leg and attempted to school his features into something more serious. He looked eerily like his father for a moment but then snorted.

"I would very much like to see your father wiggle. Maybe we could put a garden snake in his trousers."

"Watch yourself. That could be considered high treason threatening the king like that."

Oliver looked so aghast that Stefan quickly added, "Maybe we could just get him to drink lots of ale before his next audience with the people and then bribe hundreds to come spouting long drawn out grievances so he has to wait to relieve himself."

"That seems even more cruel," Oliver laughed. "Does the king even drink ale?"

"That is a good question." Stefan replied honestly. He couldn't remember many times in which he had seen his father relaxed and enjoying himself. He wasn't the type to whittle the nights away drinking or holding boisterous parties other than the mandatory festivals that centered around the trials. While he had gotten a reprieve from thinking about his father's earlier words in the excitement of the day, he felt it cutting into him again, realizing that he might never have a night spent with his father drinking together in toast of a battle won or a milestone achieved.

Stefan's thoughts were interrupted by the sound of the whistle. The referee stepped away and the players began circling each other in the middle of the field. The boy was still smiling yet it didn't reach his eyes as he observed the tiny hell cat in front of him. While he appeared to be waiting for something to happen and figuring how to best deflect it, the look of resoluteness on her face suggested that she was plotting her path to victory and deciding how best to begin.

The girl stopped circling, though she did not stop the movement of her feet. She bounced lightly from foot to foot and then suddenly the boy jumped as a leaf caught fire near the toe of his boot. He laughed in nervous surprise and backed up a step. Another tiny fire caught near his other boot, again causing him to take a further step back.

Stefan was intrigued at the girl's strategy. She likely knew that in a physical fight she would not have the upper hand; however, she was immediately taking control of the situation by making the boy follow her lead. The boy seemed to have realized this at the same time Stefan did. He took a step forward in order to regain some control but was thwarted by a long line of flame that spontaneously appeared in front of him. The boy jumped back again and this time the girl moved forward quickly, walked through the flames, and planted a side kick in the middle of his chest. He grunted in pain and stumbled back in surprise, the look on his face now one of sheer panic.

Suddenly, the grass on either side of the boy began to blaze, forcing him to back away along a single narrow path. The girl's elemental powers were not as minimal as Stefan would have assumed, her being the lowest seed. It was likely that her tiny frame had convinced a lazy scout that she wasn't a threat. There was even the possibility that if she indeed clenched this match she would also be the victor in her subsequent matches, throwing off the whole day's schedule.

The boy would not have it easy. Being beaten by the lowest ranking female meant that he would be mocked to no end, though if the girl was truly misranked he might still have an opportunity to fight again and be matched with someone else. Stefan could remember one of his earliest memories of trials when he was no older than four or five years old. His father had disguised himself, just as Stefan did now, and had brought him to the earliest match of the morning. That match had played out in a very similar fashion with the unskilled female still managing to best her poor male challenger. As the two left the arena the boy had been booed off the field as the female waited for her next match. He had held his head high, knowing that any sign of emotion would be viewed as a further weakness and result in additional derision. As the boy walked past the place where they sat inconspicuously in their cloaks, Stefan could see the unshed tears that he was trying so hard to keep from streaming down his dirtied cheeks.

When he had asked his father about the boy's fate he had told him that in the past, the boys would be sent back to their villages and would often be quietly, or publicly, disposed of by fathers or brothers who felt that their family had been shamed or by their peers who now knew where to find an easy target. Once Claude took the throne, he had quietly decreed that any male that placed last in the tournament would be given to the kingdom. Some mothers had cried and some fathers had raged but many were relieved to not have the daily reminder of the shame of the loss or wonder if their child would make it through the year to have another try at the next year's tournament. While the jobs they were given at the palace were not glamorous, and for some the humiliation still resulted in them taking their own lives, many throughout the years had been successful growing their power and had found a match if they did feel confident enough to compete again the next year.

Stefan had searched for that boy. In the stables, in the kitchens, in the garrison. His devastated yet determined face had permanently imprinted itself on his brain, and he knew that if had seen the boy at any age, he would have recognized him immediately. In the ten years since, he never did. Though he preferred to spend his time in the woods or in his makeshift laboratory every time he trained, he did so with that boy's face in his mind, determined that he would never be the one to fail and deal with that degree of humiliation. While Stefan knew that, with his lineage, he would never have to fight the lowest seed female and be in the same position as those haunted boys, if he did not do his best against the highest, the embarrassment would likely be just as great.

Stefan's attention was brought back to the current match by the jeers coming from the small but growing audience.

"Put out the flames, boy! Then you can snap her like a twig!"

"Just hit the bitch!"

He saw a small flicker of pain on the girl's face and Stefan flinched. If he hadn't wanted to remain incognito, he might have used his name and title to quiet the crowd. They would have done what he requested, and then probably laughed behind his back about his own "twiggy" appearance. The nasty comments were something about the trials that he absolutely loathed. If it hadn't already been beaten into them from childhood that females were lesser beings and that boys lacking physical strength were contemptible, the taunts and sneers competitors were subjected to during the trials would quickly indoctrinate them to those ideas. Though his ancestors were the ones to develop this system, those views were not something he personally put credence in. His mother was strong and capable and did not need to be put in her place by his father. When he did wed, Stefan didn't plan on attempting to control his wife or beating her into submission.

The encouragement from the crowd propelled the boy forward. He ran at the girl with a swing that connected loudly and painfully with her nose. She fell backward and was obscured by the wall of flames.

With his opponent down, the boy finally appeared to notice his elemental advantage. He closed his eyes and made a motion with his hands as if beckoning the ground-water below. The fires began to steam and lessen but did not go out completely. He then slowly and menacingly closed the gap between himself and the waif. The crowd had roared in approval at the turn of events. Now they quieted, waiting to see how the boy would further assert his dominance.

Stefan felt his stomach drop as the boy moved closer and closer to his prey until he was almost directly on top of her. While she had the look of a fighter, the girl was still a child who couldn't weigh more than 80 pounds. There was really only one true advantage she had over her competitor.

"Kick him where it hurts!" Stefan shouted, rising from his seat.

The boy stupidly looked towards the crowd rather than protecting his prized jewels and the girl took the hint and brought her foot up sharply. The boy squealed and grabbed himself in a way that would have been more helpful if he had done it ten seconds prior. Forgetting her likely broken nose, the girl shot up, jumping over her opponent, who was now down on one knee, using his shoulder as leverage.

After taking a moment to recover, the boy jumped to his feet and turned to chase the girl the way she had gone. The crowd was roaring now, some taunting, others trying to direct him through the maze of trees. The girl used her slightness to effortlessly weave through the playing field. As she ran she lit small fires, slowing her pursuer's progress. The boy was sweating and panting now as the sun had gained strength and was filtering through the trees. The crowd was in an uproar now, demanding more violence rather than the game of cat and mouse.

Suddenly, the girl tripped over a root and went sprawling. She regained her footing quickly, but the boy had taken those few seconds to decrease the amount of space between them. Though the girl was acting the part of the terrified prey, something in her expression suggested that she was still the one in control of the situation. As the boy gained on her, she turned towards the small beach in the far right corner of the arena and began trudging through the shallow water. She climbed onto a giant rock that protruded from the center of the small, man-made pond, trying to regain her advantage in the Blue's domain.

Stefan, as someone who had sat in this same place year after year and was intimately familiar with the playing field, had figured out her strategy; however, either the boy's lack of preparation or his blind rage was leading him directly into her trap. Some of the members of the crowd may have picked up on it, but it was difficult to hear those warnings among those who continued to egg him on and the others who hurled insults at the girl as she sat soaking wet and shivering atop the rock. While Stefan was sure that at least some of it was an act, the goosebumps and tinge of blue developing on her lips suggested she wouldn't last much longer.

The boy's smile was genuine now as he took advantage of being in his element and began swirling the waters around the rock, having them splash up at the little wet rat who had moved farther into the center. Suddenly, a large wave crashed against it, soaking her further, and causing her to scuttle to the edge like a frightened crab. The boy smiled wickedly as he stalked towards the boulder and then sent another wave crashing over, carrying the girl with it.

The boy stood a moment waiting for her to resurface around the other side but the pool remained still. His smile faltered and the members of the referee's team poised for action. The Green quietly held his hand up in a "wait" gesture and had more of a curious look upon his face rather than one of concern. The boy slowly moved his way around the back of the rock and as he did, the girl silently shot up from the water like an attacking water snake and shoved him from behind with all of her strength. He splashed into the water as the referee blew the whistle signaling that he had crossed the invisible line that had been drawn below the surface.

The boy stood up coughing and sputtering in surprise as the girl started making her way back to the beach. She walked confidently, soaking and shivering with her broken, bloody nose held high. The boy would not attempt to retaliate after the blowing of the whistle as rule breakers were not tolerated by the officials or the crowds. She would hopefully be given some time to rest before having to face her next opponent. While she appeared to be physically drained, her cunning and fire power might still allow for another win. If the boy knew what was good for him, he would attempt to keep his cool and observe the next couple of matches. It was possible that he would be given another chance in the arena and he would be more likely to succeed with some hours of recovery spent actually studying the layout and looking for weaknesses he could exploit in the other competitors.

Stefan looked over at Oliver who was on his feet clapping and cheering, fully amused by the whole show. For someone who had another nine years until trial, the whole thing probably seemed like a fun adventure that he would eventually get to partake in. Stefan just hoped that he would not be as easily fooled by a tiny wolf in sheep's clothing or what more often tripped up male competitors: a pretty face.

CHAPTER 37
STEFAN

Stefan sat with Oliver until the sun reached its zenith in the sky. The air had warmed and would continue to do so. The pixie-like girl from the first match had out-smarted two more competitors. She had finally been bested by the fourth, who must have been watching her previous matches and was not fooled by her wiles. Stefan was pleased to see that the air elemental, who was more than double her height, seemed smitten by her cunning, and even though he successfully overpowered her, he didn't use unnecessary force. She appeared so thoroughly exhausted by that point that Stefan thought she seemed happy to throw in the towel, but he commended her for getting that far.

Unfortunately, the boy had not had the same success. He lost his second match to a dark haired earth elemental who used the water he brought to feed her vines, which in turn, pulled him past the barrier, cementing his fate as an unmatched male. He walked out to jeers so filthy that Stefan had to cover Oliver's ears with his hands.

Though he continuously scanned the people moving in and out of the amphitheater, he saw no sign of the Gold whose face refused to leave his brain. His mind would find some distraction in the matches but then a flash of dandelion, or sunflower or canary yellow would catch his eye and he would turn only to see someone who was not her. His neck was beginning to hurt from violently turning his head back and forth throughout the morning. Each time the doors opened for the next set of competitors to walk down the aisle he held his breath, fearing that she would be one of them and that she would end up paired with the male walking next to her. He couldn't deny the fact that he was relieved when she still hadn't made an appearance by the early afternoon. It was possible that she wasn't even here to fight. She could be too young. Or too old. The person waving to her from behind him could have been her fiancé or husband, though he thought he would have noticed if she wore a ring. He would have liked to sit and continue watching the matches, but he was starting to sweat in his cloak and he needed to return Oliver to the palace so that he could ready himself for his own potential fight.

In order to avoid the crowds, which by this point were twice the size as they had been this morning, Stefan led Oliver back through the wooded trails behind the amphitheater which led to the castle gardens. He crossed his fingers beneath his cloak and held his breath at each turn in the path hoping that the honey haired girl and her young companion would still be back here exploring. Sadly, the only other people they ran into were other Greens exploring the Serenfawr lands, and newly matched older couples who were still getting to know each other following the ball.

Stefan had always pondered the reasoning behind "courtship". Younger couples were given a few years to become comfortable with one another, while widows and widowers were given no more than a couple of weeks. It would make more sense if the pairs who couldn't find any common ground during that time were given the chance to rematch with someone else, but he supposed that would make things even more complicated for the kingdom.

His father often complained about how much money was spent on trials. The treasury paid the salaries of the referees, the scouts who were sent out to the villages, and the record keepers who kept track of all the matches and pairs. Wagons and ships were sent out throughout the land ensuring that the less fortunate could make it to Awrymor. The palace also hosted some of the wealthiest and most prestigious families within the grounds. All of that in addition to footing the bill for the entire festival.

Now that he was going to be experiencing the whole thing firsthand, he wasn't sure if the concept of courtship made things better or worse. If he was to wed his match immediately following the tournament, they would be going in blind. There would be the hope that whoever she was, would grow to love him throughout their years of marriage, even if she was unimpressed with him at the start. With courtship factored in, she would have months and months to discover that while she would end up a princess, she was also going to be tied for life to an awkward, bookish, gangly prince. Either way, there was no turning back, so he supposed it didn't really matter in the long run if his fiancé wore a hopeful smile or a resigned grimace as she walked down the aisle.

As they broke through the forest and found the opening in the hedges leading into the gardens, he saw the head gardener speaking with the small water elemental from the first fight. His boots were singed, his tunic was ripped and dirtied and all the confidence Stefan had seen in his face at the start of his first fight was gone. If it had been the year before, Stefan would have concealed his face within his cloak and took the long way around so that he couldn't be beckoned by Gregory; however, if he was to start taking on more responsibility, he might as well begin with the simple things, like forming connections to his subjects.

"That was a tough first match you were given," he opened with, removing his hood and nodding in greeting to the ancient gardener.

"Good afternoon, Your Highness," Gregory greeted him, bowing slightly. If Oliver and the boy hadn't been present, he would have done without the title and gesture. Stefan had followed him around endlessly as a child and the man had been nothing but patient with him. Even these days when he preferred to be in the woods or the greenhouse, he always found at least one question to ask the old Widower as he passed through.

The boy's eyes opened wide in surprise and then he bent deeply at the waist. Stefan was afraid he was going to kiss his boots, so he put his arm on his shoulders in order to encourage him to stand.

"I'm sorry if my performance didn't live up to your expectations, Your Majesty," he expressed, his eyes downcast in embarrassment.

Oliver opened his mouth, likely to correct his use of the title but Stefan cut him off. "Stefan is fine for now, I'm not king yet. "

The boy looked unsure as he raised his eyes to him but then nodded. A look of excitement returned to his face temporarily, but then the grief returned. "Do you think you'll match with your queen today? I was hoping to watch you compete, but it looks like I'll be here instead." He gestured to the gardens around him and raised one eyebrow towards Gregory who stayed quiet, a small smile on his withered lips.

"I'm not sure," Stefan replied honestly. "We'll have to see how the day goes. It might be after nightfall, if at all." He knew the boy was hoping that he would tell him that he could come watch, but it would be much safer for him here, away from any bullies who would recognize him as this year's runt of the litter. "I know this probably isn't the way you wanted the day to turn out, but if you ask me, you got the best deal out of everyone."

The young Blue elemental screwed up his face to argue but then must have remembered who he was speaking to and changed his look to one of polite incredulity. "How so, your…Sir Stefan?"

"Well to start, you get to stay here at the palace and rather than being stuck in the kitchen or the horse stalls, you get to be here in the garden. While you might not be in the right frame of mind at the moment to really enjoy the place, it will grow on you quickly."

Stefan gestured around, hoping that the boy would take in the bursting coral colored peonies, the bright yellow daffodils and the purple tulips spread throughout. His face brightened a bit as if he was indeed noticing his surroundings for the first time but then he frowned again.

"Even if I do find that I like it here, I still brought shame to my family." Stefan tried not to let the anger show on his face. That the boy's family hadn't prepared him better. That his own family had started this ridiculous tradition in the first place.

"They'll get over it. Who knows? By next year you could be twice your size. While he's still as strong as an ox, I'm sure Gregory will need your help lugging around stones and soil. Though he's a Green like me, I bet he'll be able to teach you some tricks for expanding on your own powers that you could use next year." When the boy still didn't look convinced, he added, "Did you really want to marry that girl?"

The boy looked panicked for a moment as he tried to decide how best to answer the question, "I would have gladly performed my expected duty for the kingdom."

Stefan waved his hand around dismissively, and then brought his head closer to the boy's ear. Gregory turned his back as if he were distracted suddenly by an overgrown branch of a rosebush. Oliver didn't get the hint and bent in to listen.

"Honestly, if you had bested her, would you have been happy walking out of that amphitheater prepared to court that feisty Red?"

The boy blushed hard enough that his face would have matched the color of his tiny opponent's tunic. "Possibly not."

"That's what I thought," Stefan replied, smiling at him conspiratorially. "Stay here, work on growing your powers and I'm sure by next year you'll be much higher on the scout's lists. My father even allows the unmarried boys and men some time during the week with my trainers."

With that final comment, the boy finally looked as if he might actually be excited about his unexpected situation. "I was really only trained by my father and older brothers who were fire elementals and not much help. My mother was a Blue but she passed when I was born." Stefan's heart clenched but the boy continued on as if it was just a fact of life. "I'm sure if I have some time with your trainers I'll do much better. Though I could never dream of matching your skills." Stefan held in the self-deprecating laugh that comment deserved.

"Yes, well, speaking of my own skills, I should start getting ready in case I do need to compete. I'm sure I'll see you around here. I'm still not done with learning all that I can from Gregory myself." The old man clapped silently behind the boy and Stefan felt his own cheeks turn red at the praise the man was giving him for stepping out of his own comfort zone. He clapped the boy once more on the shoulder, and he had to admit that he did appear to be in much higher spirits then he had before his intervention. Maybe he would be able to handle his new position after all.

CHAPTER 38
STEFAN

Stefan dropped Oliver off with his tutor and then went back to his room to change into something less sweaty. He selected a dark forest tunic with some purple designs stitched into the collar and sleeves that highlighted the green of his eyes. It was one of his favorites and though it was a bit short and old, it flattered him better than the oversized things that the seamstress had been sewing for him lately. He looked into the tall mirror beside his dresser and examined his long skinny arms, and his much too pale face, and his dark hair that he should have gotten cut since it was a bit too long in the front, and the back, and around his ears. He was very obviously his mother's son and while he did love her greatly, he didn't think that his appearance was likely to inspire any feelings of lust or fear in any of the other competitors.

"Hoping that you really aren't as scrawny as you look?"

Stefan startled at the sound of his uncle's voice in the doorway. He thought that he had closed it behind him, but his thoughts were so scattered at the moment that he could have left it open or just not heard it creak as Talon let himself in. His room had seen more visitors today than it had in years.

He didn't let himself get upset by the comment and instead tried to smooth out some of the wrinkles from his tunic. "I watched a lot of matches this morning. The winner wasn't always bigger or stronger. Also even though I don't have the same build as you or father, I have height and quickness. I'll win." He said it with a confidence that he definitely didn't feel, and he was sure that Talon could see right through him.

"Don't try to convince me," the older man said with an easy smile. "If you lose, that's money in my pocket."

Stefan turned around, shocked, even though he shouldn't have been.

"You literally bet against me."

"It's a sure thing for me," he laughed. "No one else in the kingdom would commit such an act of treason of betting against the crown prince. Also, few people ever even see your face. They probably think you're some kind of reclusive genius. I'm the only one who knows it's not as glamorous as all of that. You're just," he stopped to look him up and down, "pathetic."

Stefan took a deep breath and turned away. There was no point in engaging. The only reason Talon was here was to trip him up. He would have done so even if he hadn't betted against him. Stefan would have preferred that he not even care enough to show up. This was his way of telling him that he would be there cheering on whoever his opponent would be. It wouldn't have bothered him half as much if Oliver wouldn't be sitting there next to him. While he looked up to his older cousin now, it was only a matter of time before he started picking up on his father's hostility towards him and imitating him in order to gain Talon's affections that were at this point non-existent.

Now that Stefan was out of the way, Talon had taken his place at the mirror and was admiring his own reflection. While he shared strong features with his older brother, Claude was more than twenty years his senior, and Talon lacked the creases across his brow and around his eyes that Stefan's father had showed more and more of as of late. Though the king kept his fair hair long, and his beard full, most likely because he was too busy to deal with the constant upkeep, Talon's sandy brown hair was always trimmed neatly and fashionably, and he never showed the slightest hint of stubble. His wife had died seven years prior at Oliver's birth, and since then he hadn't found any females worthy of him either at trials or any of the widow's balls. Stefan assumed that since he already had his heir, he wasn't interested in settling down again and preferred having his freedom to dance and flirt with any woman he desired.

Stefan couldn't help the anger that had ignited with his uncle's comments, and it only grew as he watched him forget that he was even present in his own bedroom. He also felt a bit braver after his interaction with the boy in the garden. "Are you still going to treat me this way when I'm king? My father might be too busy to notice, and my mother might turn a blind eye, but once I can do something about it there will be consequences."

"You? King? My brother isn't so foolish that he would bequeath an entire kingdom to a boy who isn't even brave enough to visit a brothel," he responded, rolling his eyes while still keeping them focused on his own reflection.

That was true, but he didn't see how one thing had to do with the other. Talon had tricked him into going down to the city for his sixteenth birthday but told him that they were going to a new apothecary. Again he should have known better, but as soon as he realized what was really occurring within the walls of the upscale looking abode, he immediately turned around and strode out. The girl who had let them in looked like she couldn't have been many months into her teenage years. It was despicable and he was in no rush to become more experienced in that matter. He would find his match and his queen, and they would go through that journey together.

"My father said-"

"My father said," Talon imitated, raising his voice an octave. "Your father said what?" he asked, finally turning towards him and grabbing Stefan's tunic, pulling him closer until their faces were only inches apart. There was the usual mocking tone to his voice, but his eyes also held a hint of uncertainty. Stefan had let Talon's words affect him, but he realized quickly that if his father had warned him about what was going to happen, it was possible that he had not shared the vision of his death with his younger brother and that there was likely a reason for that.

"My father said I should ready myself and get back down to the amphitheater in case the matches go quicker than usual," he responded, looking away rather than attempting to challenge him. He would prefer to start the tournament with full strength rather than covered in bruises.

Talon held onto him another moment and Stefan brought his eyes back up to see that his uncle was looking for something in his expression. He attempted to make himself appear timid and afraid which, truthfully, wasn't that difficult to do. Talon eventually let go, shoving him once before stalking towards the door.

"Pathetic," he repeated once more, shaking his head and spitting once on the floor before finally leaving.

Stefan took a deep breath. He would fight someone today, not only to prove to everyone in his family that he was capable of beating the strongest female, but also to ensure that he would find his queen, and sit on that throne. Once that happened he would banish Talon to the farthest corners of the kingdom so that he could never threaten or beat on him again. He would fight someone, and he wouldn't wait a moment longer to do so.

CHAPTER 39
STEFAN

Stefan stopped for no one as he went back down the stairs of the servant's quarters, through the garden and into the woods. He was no longer hiding behind his cloak and as he stalked back down to the amphitheater, he kept his spine straight and his nose in the air like the haughty prince they were all expecting. He didn't hide in the woods or within the walls of the castle because he didn't know how to talk to people or make friends. He did so because everyone was below him and he had better things to do. If he acted unsure or understanding, there was no way the officials would let him compete before the expected time. He had to be pompous and rigid and unforgiving so that they would obey his commands.

It was likely his father and mother wouldn't even be present yet, which he was sure the officials would be especially nervous about, but that would also make it that much easier for him to do what he needed to without being questioned. His mother would be disappointed, but his father needed the time to get his affairs in order anyway. If Talon didn't make it down in time, that would be all the better, though he would probably be furious that he hadn't had time to make all of his wagers.

Stefan broke through the forest and as he did so, he scanned the audience which had grown significantly larger since he'd left. The sun had started to make its descent but it was now the hottest time of the day. There had been years past when trials took place in raging thunderstorms as well as the much rarer spring snow squalls. He was lucky that the weather was calm and clear and the light breeze felt good on the back of his neck as it gently fluttered the hair over his ears. Once the fighting started, he knew that sweat would be dripping, soaking his tunic. His best chance for a competitor would be with a water elemental who might cool him off and who he could use to feed his power rather than a Red who would only make things worse.

The people who had gathered on the steps were chatting and laughing with one another. There were no shouts or jeers to be heard. He likely didn't have much time before the next match started, so he picked up his pace while still trying to appear arrogant and in control. He made it to the back of the outbuilding and knocked loudly and firmly on the backdoor where the male competitors were expected to enter. He only had to wait a moment before a male wearing a dark red tunic pushed the door open a crack. While palace officials obviously were still expected to wear the color of their elemental power, they were all typically a dark tone, with the Serenfawr symbol stitched on the front pocket in white or gold. The symbol consisted of a letter S that had the illusion of a snake's head at the top and a pointed tail at the bottom. A sword cut through, the hilt above, which made it closely resemble the symbol of infinity. Though they were employed by the Crown, the color purple was still only worn by those with royal blood.

"There is already a competitor on the premises," the man started, obviously not noticing the dark purple stitching around the edges of Stefan's own tunic.

Yesterday, he would have said something. He would have apologized for coming at the wrong time or attempted to explain himself. But today he said nothing and instead crossed his arms over his chest and tried to make his face look like the one that his uncle had made when he had called him "pathetic".

He waited a beat while the man looked at him with confusion. The Red's eyes drifted down to the violet trim on his collar and then back up to his unruly dark hair, finally landing on his narrowed green eyes. His face immediately changed from annoyance to deference and he bowed low and quick.

"I apologize, Your Highness," he groveled. "We weren't expecting you so early. There are still a number of matches and competitors to get through before we can be sure that you'll have a worthwhile female to compete against."

The official was bent over within the doorframe so Stefan reached around him in order to push the door open fully and squeeze his way inside before the man could shut him out again. "I'd rather not wait."

The space was small yet comfortable. A spot for challengers to have a quiet moment before facing their destiny. Stefan heard the door slam and saw that the official had not come in after him, likely searching for reinforcements. The only person within was a boy in a bright red tunic who, though he was shorter than Stefan by a number of inches, probably doubled his weight. The boy looked immensely confused and since there were no other officials present at the moment, Stefan chose to abandon his princely persona for a moment and put him at ease.

"I'm sorry to interrupt what I already know is a stressful day for us all, but I'm afraid that your match is just going to be pushed back a bit."

The boy's face reddened for a moment and he opened his mouth as if to argue but then he took notice of Stefan's regalia. He bowed quickly and then attempted to exit the room the way Stefan had come in but was stopped by three officials who were entering, the first of which pushed him back into the room.

"Horace, your match will be starting shortly. We'll keep things moving quickly so that the prince won't have to wait much longer for his own match to start."

This official was significantly older than the first and wore a deep mustard color that made his wrinkled tan skin appear even darker. His eyebrows resembled tussock caterpillars and Stefan found it hard not to laugh at the image of them crawling around his face. The man smiled at him with an expression that he assumed was meant to be placating and reassuring but instead just looked condescending. Stefan noticed that his posture had slipped so he straightened his spine and stuck out his less than impressive chest.

"I will not wait a moment longer. We pay you and the scouts generously in order to ensure that the order of competitors is correct. I see no reason that I should have to wait. You will locate the highest ranked female and bring her down here immediately."

"Your Highness," the older man started again in the same tone as if he were talking to a child. "It is tradition that members of the royal family compete last in order to ensure that the most powerful female is found if there even is one who isn't matched by the end of the day. We also wouldn't want to deprive the crowd of their grand finale," he said with a wink.

"So that's what this is about?" Stefan replied, raising his own eyebrows which sadly were much less impressive. "You're concerned that the vendors won't have as many audience members to sell nuts and pies to?" The man's face fell. "That's all this is to you? Entertainment and not the respected and time-honored legacy of the Serenfawr family?"

"Your Highness–" the man started but Stefan continued on his tirade.

"Maybe I should tell my father that the officials and scouts really shouldn't be given so much coin if they can't even figure out who the most powerful trial-aged female is. Maybe your salaries should go to the peanut sellers since their sales are apparently why we're all here."

The man had his mouth open but apparently couldn't think of another argument and the two officials behind him were grimacing at the situation and the suggestion that their salaries would be reduced. Horace had stepped as far back into the wall as he could; however, his eyes had been bouncing back and forth with the exchange.

"It's highly unusual," the third official, dressed in navy blue, cut in, "but I don't really see a problem as long as the king has been informed of the change. Whoever the girl is, she can fight again after the match against the prince to ensure that she wouldn't be better suited for a lower seeded male. If any other females come out on top afterwards, he can have two matches. If that agrees with you, Your Highness."

"That will do fine," Stefan replied, shortly, not yet giving in to the urge to release the breath that he had been holding. He added quickly, "My father is extremely busy but he has given his blessing for the change in schedule. He requested that he not be disturbed at this time." He stared unblinkingly into the eyes of the graying, caterpillar browed man, waiting for a challenge but the man sighed and nodded.

"This may take a while, Your Highness, but we will move quickly."

The man turned and left, the look of resignation still on his face, with the other two following in line behind him. Stefan was left to fret about the consequences of his actions and how little time he had now before he would have to show everyone what he was made of.

CHAPTER 40
STEFAN

Stefan paced back and forth within the windowless space. A thin layer of sweat already clung to his tunic. He had lost count of the minutes since he had been waiting, but it had been more than a few. When the walls began to close in on him and the thoughts within his head began to swell, he decided it would be better if he waited outside. The building he was in was connected to the one directly next door by a combined wooden roof and the afternoon shadows allowed him to observe the crowd outside without being seen.

He took in the soft afternoon light breaking in through the trees, the deep green of the grass in contrast with the bright white of the limestone. The sea of colors being worn by the people who were eagerly waiting for him to make his way down the aisle. He could tell that someone had informed them of the change. Rather than seeing any angry or annoyed faces, which he would assume would be the case if they didn't understand the reason for the delay, everyone seemed excited as if they were about to see something monumental. He supposed it was a rare occurrence that anyone got to see a match between a future king and his possible consort. He hoped that they weren't disappointed.

He startled when one of the doors behind him slammed open but when he turned, he saw that it was only the third official who had sided with him in moving up the fight. The Blue sighed in relief when he saw him standing there.

"The girl has been located, Your Highness. We've given her a few moments to prepare."

Stefan waved him off with a gesture of nonchalance, but the confirmation that he would be meeting the woman he might eventually wed, shot a jolt of panic through his heart. He could feel the need to bounce on his feet; however, he took a breath instead, wanting to cling onto the appearance of control that was starting to become easier the longer he held onto it. As more time passed, he closed his eyes, breathing in and out, in and out, and focused on nothing but that, until finally he heard the soft creak of a door behind him. He didn't turn but instead kept his face forward looking out into the audience and the playing field beyond. The door closed and then there was only silence and he thought maybe whoever it was had gone back inside. Then he heard the sound of a throat clearing.

"Excuse me, Your Highness, I'm afraid there's been a mistake."

A gentle breeze danced around him carrying the scent of lilacs with it and that, combined with the deep gentle sound of her voice, confirmed who it was that was standing behind him. A stubborn lump formed in his throat and he remained silent. She must have assumed he either hadn't heard her or hadn't found her comment worth acknowledging so she continued.

"The officials instructed me to come down here, but I haven't even faced any of the other competitors yet. I'm not sure that I'm quite worthy of this match."

He would be strong and firm. That would be the kind of man that she would want rather than the awkward, stuttering male from this morning who she probably didn't even remember.

"Are you suggesting that my officials don't know how to do their jobs? That my scouts haven't been assessing and judging your skills since the day you were born?"

"No, Your Highness," she replied, her voice raising an octave, "I just know that historically, the top female would have had to defeat any other high performing males before given the opportunity to face a Serenfawr on the field. I wouldn't want you to waste your efforts on someone unworthy."

"Thank you for the history lesson concerning my own family's legacy." He kept his tone sharp in order to keep his voice from wavering. He took a silent deep breath and finally turned towards her. She was looking down at her boots and he could tell that she was not embarrassed or scared but rather already exasperated with him and trying to hold in her anger. He couldn't help the corner of his mouth from inching up but then pressed his lips firmly together. She looked towards his feet and then slowly moved her gaze up his body until her eyes met his.

He was struck again by the color of them. When he looked into his own eyes in the mirror, he would see the moss on the stones and the rolling hills of green that stretched out across the Serenfawr lands. In her eyes, he could see the sun coming up over the ocean or the gold in the castle treasury.

For a second, he felt like maybe she had gotten lost in his eyes the same way he had fallen into hers, but then a look of surprise and confusion took over.

"It's you," she stated in disbelief. She narrowed those enchanting eyes and continued more harshly. "Was this morning's chance meeting just some kind of ruse so that you could assess the competition?"

Did she want to hear that no, he had been legitimately overwhelmed and she had been the beacon he'd found in the raging waters of the crowd? That wasn't very kingly behavior.

"Watch your tone," he said instead. "I can't exactly just wander the grounds unaccompanied with a crown on my head, now can I?"

"I just thought," she started, then shook her head and swallowed. "Instead of seeking me out in the crowd you could have just as easily let me try my luck against the other competitors and observed my skills that way. You can still do that," she added almost urgently.

Was she so concerned about facing him? She didn't seem like the kind of girl who would show fear in the face of a non-lethal competition. Especially considering the fact that she was the top seed. *He* likely had more to worry about. There must be another reason.

"What's done is done," he said instead. "If you're so sure that this will be a waste of my time, stop wasting more of it."

CHAPTER 41
STEFAN

As soon as they stepped outside the sheltered corridor, the trumpeters started up the kingdom's anthem. The girl walked on his right side, and though he wanted to turn back and see whether any figures were presently in his family's box, he kept his head facing forward, his arms at his sides and his back straight. While the excessive amount of people hadn't seemed quite so intimidating as he had looked down from the top of the hill, their smiles and cheers began to overwhelm him again as he passed through the crowd, and he was thankful for the small boundary created by the officials on either side.

The girl took a step closer to him as they continued to move down the hill as if she had somehow sensed his discomfort. It was small enough that anyone watching wouldn't even have noticed the movement, but he was hyper-aware of the amount of space between them even with the distraction of the raucous crowd.

"Are you alright?" she asked under her breath, her head bowed, only loud enough for him to hear.

"Fine," he replied, smiling and waving to a small curly haired child that stood between two officials. "I thought we already discussed that my apparent panic this morning was just a ploy."

She nodded and didn't say anything more. He was much too aware of the proximity of her hand and how easy it would be to grab a hold of it. Unless this day did end in their betrothal, he likely wouldn't be getting any more comforting touches from her: at this rate, even if it did.

The aisle led them down to a small break in the stone wall that enclosed the playing field. They walked towards the central point where the official in charge was waiting for them. This particular one wore the typical uniform but was much taller and broader than any of the others had been. There was always the possibility that things could get out of hand, so it was helpful to have a moderator that could break up the fight using physical force if necessary. This referee in particular, who wore a pleasing cobalt blue color, was likely chosen because he carried neither the power of the earth nor the air and therefore wouldn't be an interference when it came to the elements involved.

Rather than listen to him explain the rules, which he knew by heart, he watched the girl, whose name he should have asked when they'd been alone. She stood tall and was trying her hardest to pay rapt attention to the official with a look of interest, but she kept flicking her eyes to the side to look at him. He supposed he couldn't blame her since he was just openly staring at her standing across from him without any regard or respect for the Blue who was speaking to his left.

His initial impression of strength remained. Her face was round and didn't suggest delicacy in any way but certain features did give a hint of softness. Her eyes for one, but her lips as well which looked plump and supple even as she sent a scowl and a questioning side eye in his direction. He would have liked to see them curve into a smile again, but wasn't quite sure how he could make that happen. Focusing on her lips was probably the worst idea at the moment because he would start wondering about how they would feel, or even taste, so instead he looked down at the rest of her. For strategic purposes of course.

Her legs beneath her dark leggings appeared to be strong, so she would be fast. He had already felt the muscles in her arms but as he looked down to examine her hands, he saw that she was moving her fingers almost unconsciously. The first thing that came to his earth-centered mind was that it was like she was playing with invisible dirt or sand, but then, as he felt the slightest of breezes, he realized that maybe she was just feeling the air, either as a calming mechanism or in preparation for the fight ahead. Abruptly, she stopped.

When he looked up, he saw that she was full-on glowering at him again as the official rattled on obliviously. With the change in facial expression, her lips only became more pouty and full and he couldn't help his gaze from straying back to them. He swallowed hard and then closed his eyes for a moment to regain his composure. When he opened them, he saw that her expression had changed to one he couldn't quite place, and it looked like she was staring at his throat. Their eyes found each other again and for a moment, all of the hostility seemed to dissipate, replaced by something else. Curiosity? Wanting? He would have been happy if that moment had lasted forever but then…

"Your Highness," the official whispered to him. "I asked if you were ready to begin."

"Of course," he replied, a bit shakier than he would have liked. He could see the hint of a smile form on her lips but it was gone quickly as if she remembered where they were. He stuck out his hand for her to shake. Her hand wasn't much smaller than his own and he could feel similar calluses and wondered what had created them. In closer proximity, he could smell her intoxicating flowery scent and he didn't let go when she tried to pull her hand from his grasp. She looked at him questioningly and when he felt her tug again, he released his grip.

The official made his exit and she backed up from him as well. He could see her scanning the arena, likely deciding upon her strategy. Though it was expected for him to be the winner, well expected by everyone other than Talon apparently, and maybe himself, she would still have to put in effort to be considered a possible match for him. If he bested her without much effort, it was likely they wouldn't be paired even if she did win against all of the other males. Good stock and all of that.

They stood five feet apart from one another. The whistle blew and he gestured to her, trying to gain back his air of unbothered arrogance. "Ladies first."

He could feel the air picking up around them as if it were excited to be put to use. He tapped into the elements around him. The soil, the vines and the roots of the trees. Possibly even the rocks if he needed that kind of brute force. They were on a fairly equal playing field. He would have had the advantage over water, but the disadvantage over fire. Air and earth didn't cancel each other out in any way so it would depend on their physical abilities as well as the skill in which they manipulated the elements to their benefit.

When he looked up at her again she looked hesitant, as if she weren't sure what to do. Maybe it would have been a better fight if she had gotten the opportunity to fight some of the other males. There wasn't any turning back now though. He didn't want to harm her without knowing that she could indeed defend herself, but he also knew that he couldn't just stand here if she wasn't going to make a move. He would try to go easy on her until she found her confidence.

He took a step forward and, rather than retreating, she held up her arms as if ready to fend him off. He started off with a slow punch and she easily deflected it. He went again with the other hand and she did the same. He continued with hit after hit slowly increasing his pace. As he did so, he noticed that she was moving backwards with each hit, even though he wasn't aggressively pushing her that way. She had to know that her boundary line was in that direction and therefore she was doing herself a disfavor.

"You can hit me back you know," he teased, more confident now that he wasn't doing too poorly. "Though I wasn't exactly listening, I'm sure the official must have mentioned that any damage done to me during the fight won't be seen as an act against the Crown. You won't be spending the night in the dungeons."

"Yes, I was actually trying to be polite to the man, even though I'm sure that I'm as familiar with the rules as you are." Though she was moving quickly in order to parry each of his attacks, she didn't seem the least bit breathless.

"Well then? I watched a number of fights this morning. Even the lowest seeded competitors put in more of an aggressive attempt. You were doing more damage to me with those nasty looks than you are now." He threw in a kick to attempt to throw her off but she deflected it effortlessly with a flick of her forearm.

The wind was picking up around them as if discouraged by the fact that she wasn't allowing it to assist her.

"Are you saying I injured your heart? It was starting to seem like you didn't have one." He was happy to see that she smiled with that comment and he felt himself do the same.

"Maybe if you show a little effort here you'll find out." He meant to encourage more levity but with that her face fell as if she had recalled what this was all leading to. The realization hit him quickly, and he stopped with his attacks.

"You're not fighting on purpose." His own smile slid from his face. "You aren't scared, you just don't want to prove that you're an appropriate match for me." The crowd was cheering loudly around them competing with the roaring of the wind and they were so far apart with the landscape surrounding them that he was sure no one else could hear their words.

For a moment it had felt like the earth had fallen out from beneath his feet. Had he made such a negative impression in such a short amount of time or... He remembered her face as she had waved to the person in the crowd behind him. A light in her eyes. "There's someone else."

She looked stunned that he had figured it out so easily and opened her mouth but apparently couldn't figure out what to say. Confessing that she was planning on hiding her power and attempting to fool the officials would most definitely land her in a cell, especially if she admitted it to the crown prince himself. Yesterday, he would have done his best to act understanding and put on a show to help her lose while making himself look like the impressive victor. Accepted the fact that she didn't want him even if it had killed him inside. But again, it was today. His father was going to die, and he couldn't run a kingdom alone. If she hated him for it, so be it.

He took a step closer to her, but this time she did not move back, likely understanding that the softer their words, the better. With such little distance between them, she had to angle her head up to look at him and he was emboldened by the few inches that he had over her. "There are things at play here that are significantly more important than some juvenile attachment," he expressed, through gritted teeth.

"Of course you would say that," she responded fiercely with a harsh laugh. "I've known you for less than a day, and I can already tell that you're far too egotistical to know what it even means to care for another person. You sent those officials on a wild goose chase to find me for no other reason than your own impatience and sense of self-importance."

If he'd initially wanted to placate her and attempt to get her on his side by explaining the direness of the situation, that desire was gone now. He lowered his voice to a growl in order to let her know that he meant business. "You *will* fight me, and you will perform to the best of your abilities so that our pairing can be properly assessed."

"That's what I've been doing all along, *Your Highness.*" She said it in a mocking tone rather than one of reverence or respect. "Your strength and skill are just too much. I'm simply overmatched." She shrugged but there was a challenging glint in her eye as she took a step away from him.

He was no fool. She was top seed and her lean muscled body supported that fact, as did the wind, which continued to whine as if it were a dog who was left behind on a walk. If she didn't want to fight back, he would make it so she'd have no other choice if she wanted to make it through alive.

He tried not to make it too obvious as he shifted his eyes behind her and found a spot about fifty feet back from where they stood. It was a place of barren earth with two large trees on either side. The line that she desperately wanted to get behind in order to end the competition was still another twenty feet farther off from that. The crowd had quieted, and many were straining their ears or necks in order to hear and see what was going on between them in order to understand why he had halted his barrage of hits. If it was any other set of competitors he was sure they would be shouting insults, but it was too dangerous with him down on the playing field and not worth the risk. He felt a sudden thrill at the plan he had in mind. They had wanted a show and he would give it to them. He let a small menacing smile appear on his lips and then he bowed slightly and positioned his hands to restart his offensive.

Though she again refused to strike out at him, all of the demureness and hesitancy was now gone from her expression and he knew that if besting him had been part of her agenda, he would have been in trouble. It was like he was baiting a lion, especially with the golden hues of her eyes and hair, some of which was coming loose from her tight braid.

Though it was difficult to push her back with hit after hit while also keeping his focus on the area behind her, he felt an exhilaration in putting everything that he had learned to use. He wished that his family *was* sitting in the royal box so that they could see that he knew how to use what he had at his disposal. His long skinny limbs and his Green powers, which had always been such a disappointment, were going to help him to win his match and make it a good show at that.

Though the particles of soil wished to come directly to him, he redirected them to either side of what was now a shallow pit. The roots of the trees had moved out of the space which had caused the earth to fall slightly, moving into the small caverns that were left behind. Now above the soil, they worked like tentacles, flinging dirt out of the space and helping to quickly widen and deepen the hole. The crowd was roaring again, and it was difficult to tell if they were reacting purely to the fight, or to the pit that was partially hidden by the large trees above.

Though he had often had difficulty when paired with other males in training due to his limited strength, against the girl he felt confident and quick. As they danced backwards towards the hole, he felt like maybe he could do this. He was showing his father's people that he was smart and strong and capable and he could take over the role of king when the time came.

If anyone had been trying to warn her, they were drowned out by the chorus of the crowd, and he had kept the attacks so constant, that while she hadn't allowed him to make contact with any of the parts of her body, she also hadn't been able to spare a glance behind her despite him trying his hardest not to make it obvious what he was doing. Fifty feet had become forty and then thirty and then fifteen He urged the tree roots to move more quickly as they got closer and closer. Finally they were only steps away, and he felt a quick twinge of guilt about what was about to happen, remembering his mother's words. If this was to become a partnership, it had already started off on the wrong foot and couldn't get much worse so he might as well get it over with. The girl must have seen something in his gaze because she attempted to turn around and look behind her. With her attention diverted he sent a kick straight to her abdomen and she fell backwards into the hole with a look of pure horror and surprise on her face.

The trees had been the most hard working of servants, but their job was not yet done. Either the girl would use her power in some magnificent way to get herself out of the situation, or she would suffocate. Stefan approached the edge of the ditch and stood with his arms crossed as she lay at the bottom looking up at him with a look of hatred, not far from the one Talon had given him earlier. He noticed one of the officials starting to approach from the corner of the playing field, but he held up a firm hand to keep him from coming any closer.

He crouched down so that he could speak to her without anyone else hearing. "Your beau isn't going to have much use for you six feet under ground. How are you going to get yourself out of there?"

Rather than answering, she aimed an offensive gesture at him so he just shrugged and replied, unphased: "Suit yourself."

He stepped back and gave another silent command to the trees, who went back to work, this time refilling the hole they had created. He stood and waited. The wind whipped around him as if furious with him for what he had done, but unsure of how to help her without her specific command. There were many ways she could get herself out, or at least use the wind to blow the dirt back out of the hole as it piled atop her. He understood that she didn't want to demonstrate any elaborate uses of power; it would make any later matches in which she wanted to purposefully lose ring false.

The crowd was whooping and cheering now, pleased that their prince was winning the match. He waved and smiled but didn't look too closely in case her parents, or small companion, or lover he supposed, were looking on with worry and concern. This probably wouldn't be the best first impression for his future-in-laws; however, he hoped that they would get along well enough once they started reaping the benefits of becoming part of the royal family.

He had stepped far enough away that he couldn't see exactly how covered she was, and didn't really want to get any closer to see more of those hostile looks. The trees had been working for a while so he knew that she would have to make a move soon before her mouth and nose became covered up. He was distracted for a moment by a flash of steel as Talon and Oliver made their way into the royal box surrounded by the king's guard. Though they were too far away to see, and Talon probably was all smiles for the crowd, he was likely furious at the change of schedule. He saw Oliver wave down at him, and he waved back with a smile.

After he brought his hand down, he suddenly realized that the wind that had been circulating around him had abruptly stopped. A sliver of dread worked its way up his spine. The official had not come any closer following his halting gesture but he too seemed to have felt the shift and started jogging over to the center of the field. Stefan looked back towards the hole, where the trees had stopped their work, now that it was filled to the brim. His stomach dropped the moment he realized that she had either refused or had been unable to get herself out. He ran the last few steps to the edge of what had become her grave but was stopped short by an explosion of soil and air that sent him flying. He both heard and felt the back of his head hit the ground. Then there was only black.

CHAPTER 42
STEFAN

Stefan was awakened by the sun streaming into his eyes through the trees above. His head ached, but when he moved his hand to feel where his skull had collided with the ground, it didn't come back with any blood upon it. He also felt a strange burning at the bottom of his torso, below and to the left of his belly button. Had she stabbed him while he was passed out or was it just a piece of sharp rock that had become deadly shrapnel in the explosion?

He sat up on his elbows and looked towards the hole. Apparently he hadn't been out for very long because she was still making her way out of what was now an enormous crater, as if something immense had fallen from the sky. She must have pulled all of the air around her into the soil and then pushed it outwards taking everything with it. He was saddened to see that the two trees had been uprooted and were now tilted on their sides, exposing all of the gnarled roots below.

The girl herself looked like a creature rising from the depths of the underworld. The serpent from his dream paled in comparison. She was absolutely filthy and it was difficult to tell where her clothing ended and the skin of her arms and neck began. Her jaw was clenched and he could almost see steam pouring from her nostrils. The worst part was her eyes. Gone were the golden orbs he had become so fond of over the past day. All that remained were two empty sclera whose focus was on him and him alone.

He sat up much too fast and backed away from her until his back hit the face of a large rock, similar to a crab retreating from a hungry seabird. He let out a string of expletives, not princely at all in nature.

"What are you?" he asked, wincing at the sound of his voice, which had somehow returned to prepubescent octaves. He was suddenly very aware that they weren't alone and that Talon was likely doubling over in laughter at the sight of him. When he moved his gaze to scan the crowd, he saw that everyone appeared to be almost in a trance, including the guards, officials, and surprisingly, the attending members of his family.

He was sure that she attempted to roll her eyes but since her pupils were currently nowhere to be seen, it did not have the desired effect. Instead it just made her look more like a predator as she tilted her head. She moved closer, until she was standing directly above him and he felt even more threatened by her, as he was still on the ground with the large rock blocking his retreat.

"Isn't this what you wanted?" she asked, mockingly. "For me to use my powers?"

"What did you do to them?" he asked, his eyes returning to the audience members who stayed mostly silent but would smile or laugh in glee at random moments.

"There was a sudden influx of butterflies. It must have been due to the disturbance when you so generously released me from that hole," she said with a knowing smile on her lips. If she had smiled at him like that earlier, it would have made his heart flutter. Now, with the emptiness of her eyes and the nonsense she was spewing, it was just terrifying.

"What butterflies?" he asked, looking around and not seeing a single insect to speak of. "I didn't even get a chance to help you before you blew yourself out."

"They didn't quite see it that way," she stopped for a moment as if deciding how much she really needed to share with him, likely in order to get her desired result. "My power allows me to project images upon the minds of others. The closer it is to reality, the easier it is."

"But you aren't actually using it on me right now?" Her explaining it to him didn't make it any less horrifying. The idea that people like this could be walking around, changing the entire fabric of reality, was something that he had never considered and would never want to think about again.

She shook her head. "The projection I've sent to everyone in attendance puts you in a very favorable light. The young prince, asserting his dominance without actually letting his female competitor be harmed. I can ensure that they won't see either of the more damaging truths. Number one, that you were actually going to let me suffocate,"

"I…" he started but she ignored him.

"And two, that you're now cowering on the ground like a frightened rabbit."

He let out a breath of resignation. "So what must I do then? Allow you to lose without putting up a fight so that you can cheat? Pretend that you aren't supposed to be my match."

She laughed and it was a cruel sound. "Do you really still believe that? That I'm supposed to be matched with you? If they all knew the extent of my power," she gestures towards the officials and the crowds, "they would never let us wed."

He knew that it was true. Of course he would be the first Serenfawr to actually be outmatched by a female. She'd probably be forced into an arrangement with his uncle, though he wasn't even sure if *he* would be able to compete with a power of this magnitude. Though she had made a fool of him, he still wouldn't want that for her, to be stuck with his father's prick of a brother. It also wouldn't help his own position if Talon was engaged to someone with this type of magnificent skill while he was the brunt of everyone's jokes and forced to wait another year or more to find an appropriate match. He didn't want to think of the damage that Talon would do with someone with this kind of ability at his disposal.

"Fine," was all he could respond with, brushing the hair back from his face and forcing himself to stand, even though everything hurt. There didn't appear to be anything he could say that would change her mind. If she had been any other female she would have used her power to gain her place at his side but whatever future this particular girl had imagined for herself did not include him. The image of his own future that he had unwisely begun to dream of burst abruptly in his mind.

"Do we have to actually finish the fight or can you just…" he gestured to her eyes and the crowd around them. "I'd rather not."

She nodded and walked around him, giving him a wide berth until she stood with the demarcation line directly behind her boots. Her eyes were downcast as he turned and approached her. They stood in silence for a moment and when she looked up again her eyes were normal. So normal that for a moment he thought that maybe he could have imagined the whole thing. The crowd suddenly roared to life as their vision cleared, their prince about to claim victory. Her eyes held a look of gratitude mixed with a hint of sadness as she stood before him. He took a single step, placed his hand on her sternum and pushed her over the line.

CHAPTER 43
STEFAN

Typically, the match that occurred between the most powerful pair of competitors was the last of the day, so it was immediately followed by the city-wide party where all of the youths could finally relax and enjoy themselves before the terror of their now decided futures set in. If the day had gone differently: if he had not moved up their match, if she had not been so set on pairing with whatever brawny village boy had stolen her heart, if she was not some immensely powerful, stubborn, beautiful goddess, if none of those things had been true, their match would have ended with pomp and circumstance and celebration. As it was, there were still a number of trials that needed to be completed, and he and the girl, and possibly the country bumpkin of her dreams, were the only ones who knew that she was going to "lose" her final match and would not be the next Serenfawr queen. He was sure the people would be as disappointed as he was. Even though she had fought with minimal effort, he had enjoyed himself for the first half of their match and felt like anyone who had not heard their heated words would have thought that they would make a handsome pair.

Oh. Well.

Luckily, since the audience would be forced to hold onto their hats for a while, he was able to escape from the playing field rather quickly and easily. Though it was severely frowned upon, he grabbed a dark cloak that was lined in vermillion from the inside of the dressing area, left behind by a competitor or official, so that he wouldn't be stopped by anyone on his way back to the palace. He wanted to avoid Talon and Oliver who would interrogate him as to why he had fought out of turn. He didn't want to set eyes on his father or mother who would commend him on a job well done but also cause an immediate embarrassing flood of tears. He should probably see a healer for the bump on his head and sting below his belly button but it was nothing he couldn't fix on his own using specimens from his own garden. That was also the place he would be able to find something to lighten his spirits or knock him out thoroughly enough that he could forget the whole ordeal. Valerian root? A little bit of henbane? A lot of henbane?

When he was younger, Stefan had preferred exploring the forest and studying whatever called to him, but over the past couple of years he had also started cultivating his own plants to create different healing tonics. His greenhouse wasn't large. His father agreed to have it built in the back corner of the palace garden with some gentle coaxing from his mother. He would have preferred that Stefan spend his hours training or making friends and connections with some of the other aristocratic youths who came to visit for weeks at a time.

Stefan much preferred the company of the quiet plants and happily buzzing insects to the pompous, spoiled children, though he was sure that he wouldn't have put on such a believable act today if he hadn't had those models.

He made it to the small, glass structure without being seen. Even so, he didn't want to linger for long. The gardens had thankfully been empty as he'd walked through and he would rather not see any lovers perusing the roses when he left to go self-medicate in his lonely bedroom.

He snipped some flowers and leaves of delicate white yarrow to help with the burning on his lower abdomen and then went to the back where he had set up his makeshift laboratory. He already had some valerian root that he had dried over the winter. It would be the safest choice to deal with his headache and help him sleep through the raucous festivities he wanted absolutely no part of. His father would not be happy with him if he accidently took himself out of the line of inheritance with something stronger. The line between medicine and poison was thin and one that could easily be overstepped.

He was about to walk out with his clippings when he was stopped by the aconite plant next to the door. He had actually been successful for once in engaging his father in conversation about how the deep indigo colored petals could be used to make a poison to spread on arrows when hunting wolves or other predatory beasts. Even Talon, who had been eating with them at the table, had looked impressed.

Anyone passing by wouldn't have noticed the missing branch; however, being someone who was long limbed and clumsy, he paid very close attention to all of the more poisonous plants in order to ensure that he wouldn't be scratched or poked by one. A single branch had been neatly cut. There were no shears lying nearby, and it hadn't simply fallen off since there were no petals or stems lying on the ground.

It was unsettling and he would ask Gregory the next time he saw him if he had seen anyone poking about. At the moment he wasn't ready for any of the polite questions the man would ask him concerning the day's events and would rather deal with the problem tomorrow.

The palace was eerily quiet. Considering the weather was perfect, everyone was either watching the matches at the amphitheater or exploring the festival out on the grounds. He was almost stopped by a guard at the back entrance due to the red lined cloak he had covering his face but was quickly recognized once he removed the hood.

Being in the greenhouse had calmed him as it usually did, and thinking about the missing Wolfsbane had gotten his mind off of his fight for a few moments; however, the frustration came roaring back the moment he opened his room and saw the orchid he had purchased sitting mockingly on the sill of his window. The golden afternoon sun lit up the petals making it impossible to ignore. Ironically, his own princess had indeed run from him without even telling him her name just like in the familiar story. Sadly, this maiden hadn't left behind any glass slipper of her own and, unlike the princess in that story, she most definitely wouldn't want him to search the kingdom to find her again.

He picked up the delicate flower, imagining how her face might have lit up upon seeing it. Maybe it would be worth it just to give it to her as an apology for practically burying her alive. An excuse to be in her presence for another moment before she was gone forever. Maybe if he turned on the charm, he could still get her to change her mind. Did he even have any charm to turn on? The thought entered his mind of her giving him a pitying look as some dimwitted yet handsome brute put his arm around her, leading her away from him before tossing the plant over his shoulder, the pot breaking into a thousand pieces, just like Stefan's heart.

He stalked over to the sill and pushed the taunting blossom over the edge, letting it drop to the empty courtyard below with a clang before he could do something he would truly regret. He felt immediately contrite and stuck his head out of the window to see it sadly lying on the ground, some thirty feet below surrounded by dark soil and shards of terracotta, its strong roots now unburied leaving it vulnerable. As vulnerable as he would have been if he had carried it all the way from the castle for her like a lovelorn sop.

Turning away from the depressing sight, he returned his focus to what needed to be done. He would have to go down to the kitchen or ring for a servant if he wanted some hot water to mix with the valerian root but wasn't quite ready for the human interaction that it would require. Instead, he started working on the yarrow paste. If there was thanks to be paid for the lean muscle in his arms that had allowed him to refrain from making a total fool out of himself today, it was due to his trusty mortar and pestle that he now used to grind the leaves of the plant into a paste. Once it was satisfactory, he pulled up his tunic to look at the wound. Rather than a scratch or irritation from some kind of rock that had hit him in the explosion of dirt, he instead saw an ugly, red burn.

At first when he looked at it from above, it just appeared to be a red circle with raised scratches. When he walked over to the mirror to get a closer look, there appeared to be a method to the madness. In it, he saw a bare tree coming up from the earth. Lines representing the wind and a sunset, or sunrise he supposed, over the horizon. He had never seen anything like it before.

The first time he had noticed it had been the moment she had exploded out of the hole. Did it have something to do with her magic? If anything, he would have associated a burn with a fire elemental, and it was obvious that she was strictly a Gold even though she did have the highly unusual power to project into other people's mind on top of that.

Stefan knew very little about those elusive powers that didn't seem to generate from any of the elements. He had been surprised this morning when his father had admitted to speaking with a prophetess since he didn't even know that they had one in their employ. The only place he had ever come across people with psychic types of powers had been in stories and fairytales.

The girl had been wise enough to know that her power was not one she should share with others, and it seemed that she had only shown him because she had needed to demonstrate it in order to convince him that she was more powerful than him. Though she did seem to have remarkable control of the wind, he thought that his Green abilities today had been rather impressive. Based on elemental powers alone, he could have had her beat if given enough time. He would have kept fighting for her if her dead white eyes had not been a factor. He could only imagine how she could have used her mind tricks to humiliate him if he had pressed further.

He ran his fingers over the ridges of the mark. Would she know what this was? He had spent more time reading up on past trials than actually sparring in preparation for them. Nothing like this had come up in any of the pages. As his skin was exposed to the air, and his tunic was no longer rubbing on the raised skin, the burning feeling faded and the irritated raised lines began to smooth out. As it did so, the color of the mark intensified and became darker. Would it eventually heal or would it be some kind of tattooed reminder of the day? Something that he would have to look at and be reminded of her face fifty years from now? The thought wasn't a pleasant one.

Something inside of him told him that asking a family member or trial official wouldn't be the best idea. They would ask questions that might lead to what really had occurred during the match. With that option unavailable to him, he had only one other choice. If she wanted him to keep her secrets, she would have to share some of her own, namely what this mark was and why she had inflicted it on someone she wanted nothing to do with. He pulled his tunic back down and covered it with his own dark green cloak, shut up the small voice inside of him that said he was only looking for an excuse to see her again, and strode back out of the room.

CHAPTER 44
STEFAN

Since it was still only early spring, the days did not yet extend late into the evenings and the afternoon sun was already making its retreat across the castle and into the mountains of the west. The trail through the forest was even darker than the gardens and paths immediately around the castle, and had largely emptied out. The same could not be said of the amphitheater which was now filled to capacity. Typically, by this time the people were at their most drunk, most excited and surprisingly most kind. Unlike the earlier matches, the competitors at the end of the day were much more skilled and therefore put on a better show. Also, in many cases the audience had already seen the teens fight and be crowned the victors against other less talented youths and were more invested in their matching.

Each row of large, grass-covered steps was filled not only with friends and family members but also those who had already fought and matched and who now sat in their newly formed pairs. He could see shy, awkward smiles and hear polite small talk and the sharing of personal tidbits. It seemed so strange to him that pairings forged from years of training in violence and trickery could so quickly and easily become sweet, young love. He wondered if there were some resentments already festering beneath the surface. He observed a tall, gawky, red headed boy wearing teal, attempting to flirt with his match, a curly haired Green with warm tawny skin. Would she mix up the salt and the sugar when he was taking his morning coffee five years from now since he had knocked out one of her teeth? Was he still thinking about another girl who had beat him in the competition that he would have preferred as a match?

Stefan knew with complete certainty that if *his* girl, he didn't know her name so that was the only way he could refer to her, changed her mind and won her final match of the day, he would accept her as his future queen with open arms, even with her terrifying power and unchecked arrogance. He would bring her flowers, and jewelry, and cakes every morning and would never look at another woman again. This feeling was only amplified when he saw her emerge from the building at the top of the hill. Fire elementals had lit lanterns in the trees within the amphitheater as well as in the playing field itself, and she was lit up not only by the softly glowing light and the receding sun, but also the gentle, sweet smile on her face. The smile that was directed at the boy next to her.

He was around his own height and nowhere near as brutish as Stefan originally assumed. His tan skin glowed and his dark blonde hair was neatly cut short unlike Stefan's own unruly, overgrown mess. They were a little too perfect together in his opinion, especially with their matching yellow toned tunics. He smiled down at her as if neither one was concerned about the outcome of the fight. Stefan pulled his cloak further over his head and stepped back in order to hide beneath the shadows of the trees. He should just leave now and spare himself the sight of them, but he couldn't get his feet to move.

None of the tension or hesitancy that she had been exuding during *their* fight was visible now as she stood in the grassy, open field, surrounded by the lantern lit trees and the fireflies that had awoken just in time to witness the final match. As they shook hands, he leaned in to whisper something in her ear and she laughed as she playfully pushed him away.

As she stepped back and waited for the fight to officially begin, her eyes casually grazed the crowd and stopped when they reached him, as if even with the falling darkness and the distance between them and his hiding place within the trees, Stefan had called out to her somehow. He didn't uncover his hood or raise a hand but instead just held her gaze, sure somehow that she knew he was looking back at her. She stayed that way until her attention was stolen by either the referee, who was the same one who had presided over their match, or her annoyingly handsome friend. She nodded as if expressing that she was ready to begin but the easy smile she had displayed previously had dimmed as if Stefan's reappearance had disturbed her. *Good.* He preferred that to a complete lack of feeling.

The wind was present; however, it would be a neutral party in this fight. It gently rustled the leaves of the trees as if wanting to observe the match but not overly concerned with the outcome. The scents of fried cakes and roasted meats floated closer to Stefan, making the knots in his stomach tighten. Maybe he would feel the desire to eat once the final fight had ended and he was completely and devastatingly sure of his lonely future.

Down on the playing field the boy gestured to the girl, encouraging her to make the first hit, and this time rather than refusing, she immediately ran towards him, starting off with a high kick. They moved with each other as if this was a dance they had perfectly choreographed and practiced many times over. The wind slowly picked up blowing leaves and flower petals around them as if it wanted to participate by creating the perfect atmosphere for the performance. Though the girl was holding her own, she was also demonstrating the same almost undetectable move that she had done earlier, in that she was moving slowly backwards, as though being pushed in that direction. Stefan was positive that if it had suited her particular agenda, she could have easily pushed back or even made her opponent see flames or horrific creatures in order to force him in the right direction. Stefan knew for a fact she wouldn't be taking that route to victory. Her wish was to be a village housewife so that was what she would be. He could tell that whatever she dreamed of in life would happen for her. Not because of luck but because of sheer will and determination.

Stefan was mesmerized by the fight. The boy faded away quickly to nothing but arms and legs as he didn't let his vision stray from the girl's face. She appeared to be very focused but was having fun at the same time, and he would catch a satisfied smile grace her lips whenever she connected with a part of the boy's body that he had left unprotected. Stefan felt the urge to leap over the stone steps, push his fairer rival aside and move with her like that. He felt like she had done him a disservice by holding back during their match. It was probably the first time in his entire life that he had felt such a strong urge to fight, like his body would do anything if it meant doing it with her. Touching her, even if it was nothing but those short lived hits and blocks.

As they moved farther and farther back into the playing field, he felt his anxiety rise. Anytime the boy took a single step backwards he thought that maybe, just maybe, she had changed her mind and would continue to push ahead. Or that the referee would see something that would suggest that she was too strong for him and therefore he wouldn't be an appropriate husband and guardian for her. He took a step out of the woods thinking that maybe she would see him and rethink her decision. Remember the fact that she could be royalty, but she was too focused on the task, or else it was now too dark outside of the field to notice him and she didn't look his way again. They were ten feet from the demarcation line and Stefan was holding his breath waiting for something to happen, anything that would stop the inevitability of her crossing that line.

While the air on the playing field remained calm, the wind in the trees he was standing between began to whistle and whine, lifting the pine needles that danced around his feet. He found it strange, but didn't see it as the warning it was since the air had never shown favor for him before. He didn't notice the king's guard stealthily closing in on him from either direction as his eyes watched the girl take her final step over the line, ensuring that she would be left alone and safe, even though none of the three youths involved could truly understand the importance of her choice in that moment.

As the crowd roared around him and the wind's ominous call remained ignored, Stefan felt someone grab his arms forcefully and tie his hands uncomfortably together behind his back.

"I'd rather not harm you, Your Highness," a gruff voice spoke. "But we prefer that you'd not make a scene."

His heart was officially broken. His father was likely dead and he had been too distracted to understand the true significance of a missing branch of Wolfsbane. Why fight when he felt like he had nothing to fight for.

CHAPTER 45
STEFAN

"Stefan Cladius Serenfawr. You have been tried and found guilty of the following crimes against the kingdom: treason, patricide, regicide, growing and administration of a deadly poison as well as improper display of colors in an attempt to mislead."

Stefan thought that last one was a little excessive but the guardsman who had seen him enter the castle wearing the red cloak had been brought up to testify that he had been engaging in "suspicious behavior" close to the time of the king's death and that he had also been coming from the direction of the greenhouse.

Stefan had not needed much time to figure out who would have been able to direct everyone specifically to his greenhouse where the missing branch had been fairly obvious when pointed out, and who stood the most to benefit from his father's death and his imprisonment. That particular person had somehow ensured that *he* was still in the royal box watching the matches while Stefan had stealthily made his way back to the castle shortly before the king's body had been found; a thinly sliced wound across the back of his neck filled with the deadly poison as if someone close to him had casually walked behind him and gently eased the knife across.

Stefan could see that man now, standing with the crown upon his head. A somber expression graced his face, except Stefan could see the amusement and glee in his eyes whenever they met his own. Stefan himself stood before an open grave, not unlike the one he had pushed the girl into a week prior. He now understood that things had happened the way they were supposed to. If she had been paired with him, Talon might have waited to commit his unfathomable act and the girl might have been standing beside him now or may have already been thrown from the cliff at his back. The thought made him shudder and he could see his uncle turn his lip up the slightest bit at the sight.

Stefan had always known that he would return to the earth upon his death as a Green, but traitors to the kingdom were returned to their elements while still alive. Golds were thrown from the cliffs, death only coming when they hit the rocky ledges below. Though Reds couldn't burn until death came for them, they still had lungs that could fill with smoke until their bodies shut down, eventually giving them to the flames that waited. Blues were typically excellent swimmers, and adored by the waters which liked to keep them afloat. They still drowned when held under by heavy stones and chains.

He supposed he deserved his death after almost afflicting the same torture on the girl, whose memory had kept him warm in the loneliest, most secluded cell of the dungeons below the castle. He wondered if she had heard news of his imprisonment, trial, and forthcoming execution and whether she was bothered by it or felt he was guilty and was getting his just desserts. He hoped that she had seen something in him that would make her question the verdict at least, though he hadn't shown her much of the good in him during their brief exchanges.

He had tried not to fantasize too much about her somehow fooling the guards into releasing him but his mind preferred imagining those scenarios to focusing on his impending death. Anytime he had heard the opening of a cell or footsteps on the hard stone floor, he would feel the faintest glimmer of hope in his chest but then when no familiar face appeared, he would feel even worse than he had the minute before.

Throughout that whole impossibly long week, he had not received one visitor. He understood that Oliver would not have been allowed anywhere near him and was likely being fed information from his father about how evil of a person he was, undoing all of the kindness Stefan had shown his younger cousin. He had been slightly surprised that Talon himself hadn't shown up to taunt him. He likely knew it would be smarter in the long run to keep his mouth shut.

The only one who had surprised him in her absence was his mother. That had hurt the most. Though he knew how much she had loved his father, he was still surprised that she had accepted his guilt so easily and immediately disinherited him without a second thought, truly leaving him with no one.

He looked down into the hole below and could feel the agitation of the soil within. Its attachment to him and desire to keep his heart beating paired with the hunger for his body's return.

The crowd of onlookers was sparse. He imagined that Talon had crowned himself while the city had still been full of life so that he could be the center of the celebrations, but had waited to announce Stefan's execution until after everyone had left in their boats and carriages in order to avoid an angry mob. Stefan had felt the excitement of the crowds during his match and though he hadn't ended up being paired, he still had found favor with the people. He didn't believe that they would be happy with Talon's decision, but Stefan knew that keeping him around would be a danger to his uncle. This way the only threat would be Oliver when he came of age. His mother was not a Serenfawr by blood and even if she had been, a woman would not be allowed to rule in her own right.

Apparently she still would not be showing her face, even as her only son was interred in the lonely open field where naked patches of dirt were the only hint that the bodies of traitors laid beneath. His only mourner appeared to be the wind, which had not stopped howling since the moment he had been removed from the dungeon to make the trek up to the highest point of the mountain.

"Do you wish to make any final statements before your body is returned to the earth?" the executioner asked.

Stefan shook his head once. He wouldn't give Talon the satisfaction of seeing him grovel or cry. Instead he looked directly at the so-called king and spat on the ground, like his uncle had done when he had called him "pathetic". He hoped that the message was loud and clear.

The executioner stepped up to assist him into the hole, but Stefan looked at him with the most princely scowl he could muster before turning around and hopping in himself. He stood with his arms crossed, staring at the wall of dirt before him, and tried to keep himself calm as the guards began shoveling mountains of soil upon him. He took in deep breaths of air while he still could. The wind continued to scream at the observers above but, in the small space, it was quiet and gentle and ruffled his hair as if it were trying to comfort him. He closed his eyes and tried to relive the hope he'd had for his future the week before. When he'd first laid eyes upon the girl who'd been a beacon of light and had somehow wormed her way into his heart in such a short amount of time.

Now that his uncle could no longer see his face, as he wouldn't dirty his boots by coming any closer to the bare earth, Stefan let out some of the tears he had been holding in. Tears for his father who he wished he could have gotten the chance to really know. Tears for his mother who had lost everything in so short a time. Tears for himself and the future that he had been deprived of due to someone else's greed. He cried and pictured a set of golden eyes and a soft smile as the hole filled. He took deep breaths of the gentle air that continued to dance lightly around his ears until his mouth and nose were covered. He started to cough, his lungs trying to rid themselves of the dirt that was starting to settle within them. He had kept his hands loose in order to cover his upper orifices. They helped very little as more soil filled the air in clouds of dust.

Even though he had tried to keep calm, he couldn't help the rising panic as every breath became labored and his eyes watered in order to combat the intrusive particles. Finally with two more shovels, his head became fully immersed in the element that had previously been such a welcome companion, and he saw and felt nothing more.

CHAPTER 46
STEFAN

Bugs. There were bugs crawling in his hair but he couldn't reach up to remove them. He could barely shiver in terror as he felt the spiders and worms and beetles crawling through his thick dark tresses which they probably thought was nothing more than richer soil.

He opened his mouth to scream but only sucked in more dirt. He thought about how the girl had used the burst of air to release herself but knew that even though the wind had seemed to warm towards him, he didn't know how to control it. He wouldn't be able to do anything against the earth that wanted to feed off of his muscle and skin and bone.

He felt something else skim the top of his ear. Though the insects couldn't possibly hurt him more than the dirt that was slowly suffocating him, their presence felt like an additional horror that would truly drive him mad before death came for him. Would the fact that he was a Green mean that it would take an excessive amount of time for him to drown beneath the ground? Would his heart beat until his body slowly disintegrated?

He felt a tickle on his other ear and then something moved inside it. His stomach lurched but he tried his very hardest to keep the contents inside rather than release them into the soil around him. Luckily, the food given to him over the past week had been just enough to keep him conscious. Nothing more than that.

He thought he could hear a muffled sound, like someone speaking to him underwater, but maybe it was just in his head. Then the bugs were in his eyelashes clearing the soil from his eyes. He suddenly found that his hands were free and he used them instinctively to rub the dirt from them. He then realized that the insects had been helping free him and the top of his head was no longer covered.

"Stefan," they called to him. "Hurry."

Everything below his neck remained paralyzed due to the pounds of soil surrounding him. Then he found he could move his fingers and then his hands and then his arms. He began pushing away as much dirt as he could. Though his eyes still stung and he could only see blurry shapes as he attempted to blink out the particles, he could see that it had not been the work of courteous insects that had freed him but rather a pair of pale white hands. They worked in tandem with his own and soon enough he was able to kick his feet enough to loosen the soil around him. He grabbed onto the hands who were attached to a darkly clothed body and together, they successfully extricated him from the pit of death.

He bent over his knees, continuing to wipe the dirt from his eyes and then coughed out the dust that remained in his lungs. He didn't think that he had been below ground for very long. He figured that the onlookers must have left so he was startled when his vision finally cleared and he saw that he was still surrounded by the small crowd. They looked unsurprised that he was now standing before them and didn't move to return him to his grave. Rather, they remained strangely quiet, similar to how the audience had reacted during his trial as if they were observing something that he was unable to see with his own eyes.

He turned around quickly, expecting to see depthless eyes of white and a honeyed braid. The eyes were present, though hidden within a dark scarlet cloak which was now marred by patches of wet earth and grass. The braid hanging down, however, was the darkest of browns, identical in color to the wall of soil that had so recently been his only sight. He almost didn't recognize the woman in the Red's cloak and the tightfitting trousers until she took a step closer and placed her hands on his face.

"I don't have time to explain any of this and I know I might appear strange but it's just how I access this aspect of my power. It's still me."

Without her perfectly curled hair or her voluminous dresses or the crown atop her head, his mother looked shockingly young and unfamiliar to him. Like this person was someone who had been hiding within her all along.

"You're projecting into their minds," he said. He was still feeling a bit dazed and finding it easier to state facts rather than figure out which question he wanted to ask her first.

"How did you know?" Her brows furrowed in confusion but she quickly shook the expression from her face. "Forget it, neither of us have time for questions."

"I thought you hated me. I didn't do it. I didn't kill father," he asserted, shocked that his eyes had the capability already to form tears as they made clear paths down his dirtied cheeks.

"I know, love," she responded, as tears fell from her empty eyes and down her own round cheeks. "I never thought you did. I only stayed away so that he would think that I believed it. So that I could be here when you needed me the most."

"Where are we going to go?" he asked, happy that she did seem to have a plan. Then, her face fell again and he knew.

"I need to stay. It's the only way he won't know you aren't buried down there and won't come looking. You're going to go as far from here as you can. You know how to take care of yourself in the forest. Hide out for a while until you can better disguise yourself, then head west."

"But what about you?" he countered. "How do you know that he won't see you as a threat as well? That he won't remarry and find a new queen to take over your title?"

"My title and position will be preserved," she responded, and he could tell somehow that she was no longer looking at him.

He stared at her in horror and then looked over at his uncle who wore a bored expression as if he was wasting his time here now that Stefan was no longer in his way. Around his ring finger was a gold band that he hadn't noticed before.

She nodded. "It was the only way I could keep us both safe. I'll know if he hears anything about you still being alive. I'll be alright."

"This isn't right," was all he could say. "I can't leave you."

"You have to and you have to now," her tone was urgent and harsh like the one she used when he had stolen a sweet or ran off to the woods when he was supposed to be with his tutors. "I haven't used my power in quite awhile. It does tire me out and we still need to make this believable before you go."

He nodded and together they refilled the hole until it was impossible to tell whether or not a body lay beneath. She picked up a dark green cloak from the ground. It was thick and heavy and while it wasn't made of any plush material that would draw attention to it, it was well crafted.

"I was very productive in my grief," she smiled and he was happy to see that she still had her spirit even with all of the upheaval in their lives. "This will keep you warm in the forest during cold nights. I've filled the pockets with your favorite sweets as well as some more nutritious fare. You don't have enough meat on those bones as it is."

He tried to smile back but he was just struck again by how much he was losing and how he wouldn't get to really know the woman who he had always assumed would be there.

"I'll come back for you," she opened her mouth to argue but he shook his head. "When I'm older and stronger, I will come back."

She nodded and brought his face to hers, kissing his dirtied forehead. He put his arms around her, taking in one last time the smell of lemon, burnt sugar and vanilla. He then forced himself to walk away without looking back towards the small group who thought they had seen the last of him. He would come back one day, not only to rescue the one person in the world who was committing herself to a life of misery for his safety, but also to return the favor to those who had ruined his life.

Part IV
Fourteen Years Later
CHAPTER 47
STEFAN

This couldn't be happening. She had been here the whole time, hiding behind her cloak and probably laughing at him. And now she was going to die and he would never be able to yell at her for any of it unless he got his shit together and healed her.

He had felt unsure of himself when he thought he was trying to heal an ancient Widow. Now instead it was someone whose face he had seen above every yellow-colored tunic and beneath every golden braid for the entire second half of his life. He suddenly felt light headed and sat down hard in one of the soft plush chairs within the dimly lit room.

He could do this. Odessa had looked surprised, like she hadn't seen this coming, but maybe *she* had known somehow that this would happen. She obviously had access to one psychic power, why not more? He had unknowingly been preparing for this moment for months given her encouragement. Maybe that meant that she had also seen his impending success in regards to healing her wound.

He took a deep breath and stood. She was no one. It was just a faceless body with an injury that needed healing. He could deal with all of his feelings after the job was taken care of.

He walked over and covered up the small patch of marked skin so that he wouldn't be further distracted. The wound had bubbled up again around the embedded blade while he had been having his crisis and he wiped the area clean once more. He filled his lungs, focused his mind, and then slowly pulled the blade out. Her body shifted slightly, but she didn't rise or give any other sign that she had regained consciousness.

Blood immediately began pouring from the wound, so he pressed down firmly with a piece of the ripped fabric. He closed his eyes and tried to picture what the wound looked like from the inside based upon the diagrams he had seen in the books. Dark red muscle, thick yellow fat and pink layers of skin. He imagined first the clotting of the blood and the forming of the tough outer scab. Even if he got that far, it would ensure that she wouldn't bleed out, but he wanted to do his best so he visualized the multiplying of the tissues repopulating the space until the walls of the wound threaded themselves back together.

He held his breath. Sent a prayer up to any god that was listening and then slowly peeled back the bloodied cloth. The wound looked red and angry but it *was* closed and the bleeding had stopped. He only hoped that the cut had truly healed within, like he had imagined, and the cavity wasn't still filling with blood. He would also have to monitor her in order to ensure that there was no infection.

He had actually done it. He had manipulated a human body using his mind. What other powers did he have hiding beneath the surface? Had he inherited the ability from his mother somehow?

Thinking about his mother brought his mind back to his patient. He again gently cleaned the area and pushed back the fabric, uncovering the small circular mark. He had always imagined that she had been the one to mark him, but instead was it something that had somehow magically happened to both of them spontaneously and simultaneously?

His heart stilled for a moment. Maybe it wasn't even her. Just because the symbol matched his, didn't mean that the person who lay on the table was who he wished it to be. It would make sense that it truly was her and she had been using her power on him, on everyone, since they'd arrived. Every other time he had been in the old woman's presence, she had looked small and ancient. He had noticed the white in her eyes beneath the veil but he had assumed it to be cataracts, rather than a side effect of her power. He hadn't imagined the wrinkles on her hands or the gravel in her voice, but the soft, smooth, pale skin before him now looked like it belonged to someone else entirely. Was her body unable to hold onto the illusion because she was unconscious? There was only one way to find out.

He recovered the wound as he was sure someone else would come back and check on them. He truly wasn't sure at this point if she had been hiding her identity from everyone, or if there were a select few in her inner circle who were aware of the facade. The empty mugs on her table did suggest the latter and he had a pretty clear idea of who they might belong to.

He looked around the room quickly and listened for any sounds coming from the stone hallway outside. When he didn't hear anything, he moved over to the top of the table where her head lay. The heavy, voluminous hood of the cloak and the gauze within made it difficult to peer inside, especially with the darkness of the room. He took a moment to steady himself and weigh the options. Did he really want to do this? Would it be better if he waited until she woke up so that she could come clean to him herself? Or would it be better if she didn't know that he had realized her trickery, giving him the upper hand for once? Even if he looked, she wouldn't necessarily know about it. It might be better for him to see her now, while she was still unconscious, so she wouldn't be able to see his face when he saw her for the first time. He knew his reaction would be awkward to say the least. What if she woke up right when he was lifting the veil off of her face or even worse, lovingly staring at her sleeping form?

"What are you doing?"

He felt like he jumped a foot in the air, though it might have only been an inch. His heart was pounding so heavy in his chest he was sure it would wake the girl, or woman now he supposed, from her slumber.

Odessa stood with her arms crossed over her chest. Though she looked like she was trying to act calm and collected, her eyes were wide and unblinking, willing him to step away from the table. He breathed in and tried to make his voice sound as calm as she was attempting to look.

"I was successfully able to close the cut but wanted to check her pulse to see how her heart was faring."

"Oh," she responded, obviously relieved but still nervous. "I'm sure that she's fine if you took care of the wound. I can take over from here."

"She is rather old," he replied, baiting her. "With that kind of stress along with the fact that she's still unconscious," he shook his head, "I would feel much better knowing that her blood is flowing the way that it should be."

Even in the darkness of the room, he could see that she was debating what to do. "What if you just listened to her chest through the cloak?" she finally asked, hopefully.

He shrugged as if considering. There was no way now that he was going to remove the veil anyway with the seer in the room. He would never be able to hide his reaction from her, and he was now very certain that she knew the truth about who lay enrobed in the heavy cloak. With the amount of attachment she seemed to have for the woman, he was sure that she would have been willing to do anything to ensure her survival, unless, it seemed, it compromised her secrets.

"I suppose that would work, but if I can't get a good listen I'll need to find a pulse point."

She nodded eagerly and he moved back over to the side of the table. He swallowed hard as he brought his head down and was immediately hit with the scent of jasmine which he hadn't picked up on earlier. He sighed in relief as he heard a strong steady beat as well as the calming sound of her lungs inflating and deflating.

He nodded at the seer who also seemed to relax a bit. He shook his head in astonishment that he hadn't figured it out earlier. He had noticed a slight resemblance but had written it off since he had looked for her features in every woman he'd met. He should have paid more attention this time.

"What is it?' she asked. He realized he must have been staring.

"Just make sure that she rubs it with lemon juice or lavender oil to help with the scarring. I can acquire some aloe for her as well."

Odessa opened her mouth and screwed up her face as if she were going to ask him something else but then appeared to think better of it.

"Thank you," she said instead, and it sounded like she truly meant it.

He nodded, and forced himself to move towards the heavy door, though his feet felt like they were walking through mud. He wanted to sit by her side and attend to her every need. Even better just move her to the bed and hold her to him until she felt safe and secure enough to wake up.

He would go along with the ruse for now and wait to get the answers he so desperately needed. He *would* confront her tomorrow.

CHAPTER 48
STEFAN

A week. Seven full days. More hours and minutes than he could count.

Every second had been spent with her as the focus. Sometimes it was flashes of that first day together. Moments that had kept him warm and made him feel less alone during that first year after he ran away. That time when he had been too scared to venture out of the forest and hadn't seen another face unless they sported a beak or a furry muzzle.

At other times he thought about the more recent past. Analyzed every conversation that he'd ever had with "the Widow". He hadn't had many interactions with those older women who were given the freedom that the younger ones were never allowed. He knew that supposedly, once a woman reached a certain age, their power diminished. He thought it was just the power that they typically had over men, which faded with the addition of wrinkles and liver spots, rather than their elemental powers. It didn't really make sense to him that a relationship between a human and the elemental spirit they were attached to would fade after so many years spent together in symbiotic harmony. He hadn't been all that suspicious when a door had creaked open on its own or when the wind had gently flowed in through the narrow windows and danced around her flowing robes. Maybe he should have been.

He wished that he could recall all of the discussions that they'd had but without knowing it was her, Stefan hadn't felt the need to replay them over and over in his mind. He did know that she had been teasing him from the start about his name, his trade, everything, and if he hadn't thought that she was old and haggard, he might have had the notion that she was flirting with him. Had she been? Was she even aware of who she had brought into her fortress? It was possible that she hadn't even recognized him as being the same boy she had fought with on that day. A boy who was supposed to be dead. Though her face had never faded from his memory, to her, he had just been someone who had almost gotten in the way of her plans. Someone who had supposedly been executed not long after. Why would she remember his face?

The other question that weighed on his mind was why was she doing all this? It obviously couldn't just be because she was worried about being a single female since there were plenty of young men and women on the island, including himself, who were living outside of the kingdom's rules. What had happened to the golden boy who she had been so excited to marry? Had he died or was he still alive but just hadn't ended up being the perfect match that she had expected? Had he turned out to be one of the loathsome men who had come looking for him for a way to get out of their marriage? Not that he had been any better in supplying them with what they needed for their dirty jobs. He was sincerely glad for the end of that particular chapter of his life, but it would still be a long while before he could forgive himself and somehow make it up to the world for all of the pain he had caused with his poisons.

Though his first thought had gone to her being the victim, he supposed it was also possible that she had committed some atrocious crime and was now hiding from the punishment that awaited her. He knew from first-hand experience that she was very capable of taking care of herself and could certainly cause some serious damage to anyone who threatened her. There was only one way to find out the answers to all of his questions. He just hadn't yet been given any opportunity to ask them.

He had lurked around the library waiting to see if her door would open. It had not. Odessa and Eryx had shared with everyone what had happened. They hadn't explicitly provided all the details of what "Scorpio" had done for her, but instead expressed that she was healing slowly and wasn't yet well enough to walk or sit in the grand hall. Her weekly meetings had been postponed indefinitely.

He had studied Odessa's face from her usual seat during mealtimes when she wasn't looking, but hadn't had the courage to actually ask her about what she knew. He was very certain now that she had been the small fair-haired girl who had also been standing in the crowd that day, which no longer felt so long ago. If she had been there, she might have seen their fight and been able to put the pieces together. Fourteen years later, he was still terrified of anyone finding out who he really was, resulting in him being dragged back to those dungeons, sentenced to death for the second time.

Eryx had definitely been avoiding him. He was still present at mealtimes and training sessions but Stefan had seen him very rarely in the greenhouse and if he did, he always had one of his apprentices or Lavender with him acting as some kind of buffer. At those times Stefan politely managed to ask how the Widow was faring, and Eryx would say she was doing well but wouldn't meet his eyes, filling him with trepidation. Either Eryx was afraid of what he had uncovered and didn't want to address it, or she was not doing well. He hoped that if he had made a hideous mistake in her healing, they would come to him and allow him to fix it. If it was so horrible that they could no longer trust him, maybe that was the reason she hadn't come out of her room. There was also the possibility that she had left the island in the dead of night to find a real healer or…no he wouldn't think of more dreadful possibilities than that.

Suddenly something small and hard hit him in the back of the head removing him from his never ending parade of thoughts. He turned and saw Heren staring at him, arms crossed with a look of exasperation on his face.

"Was that you or another one of those Mydas flies?" One of the giant insects had found his beard to be an appealing place to make its home the last time they had gone out to the woods. Rather than help him remove the creature, Heren had excused himself, laughing so hard he almost soiled his pants. Stefan shuddered at the thought. He had found it hard to be in the presence of insects after being in such close quarters with them on the worst day of his life.

The corner of Heren's mouth quirked up and then he bent down to pick up a small brown and honey colored stone from the ground next to his feet, "It was just a rogue piece of Tiger's eye, no need to shave off all of that hideous hair covering your face."

"It would take a lot more than another one of those giant, disgusting beady-eyed bastards for me to do that," he replied, though he had considered it for a second when he'd had to pluck the insect out himself. The feel of its large writhing body between his fingers had almost made him throw up.

"And why is that?" Heren asked, slyly. Though he would shut down anytime Stefan even attempted to ask him a question about his *own* life, Heren was constantly prodding him about his secrets. Even though they still barely knew anything about each other's pasts, over the last few months they had learned quite a lot about each other's quirks and habits. Though he would never actually admit it, Heren was probably the closest friend Stefan had ever had. It almost hurt *not* to be able to tell him about his past, especially now that everything was coming full circle, but the idea that Heren would let something slip to Matilda or Lavender made Stefan sick to his stomach. He didn't want to end up resenting someone he thought of as a friend just because it was in Heren's basic nature to connect with other people through sharing confidential tidbits.

"Because I'm sure I look even more *hideous* without it."

Heren shrugged. "I guess I can't argue with that, it's definitely possible." He looked Stefan up and down and then laughed. "I don't spend so much time around you because of your looks."

"Why *have* I been awarded that particular honor?" he asked, as the two of them began walking again through the forest. It was coming up on the Harvest Moon and the humid heat that had been so constant the past couple of weeks was finally easing up. The wildflowers that were now blooming along the forest floor, as well as in the occasional random meadow they passed, were those that would complement the colored leaves that would soon be gracing the trees: black eyed Susans, fiery marigolds and bright, happy sunflowers. Though surely there were others his eyes hadn't picked up on, he couldn't help but notice the abundance of yellow that seemed to be following him wherever he went.

Heren quieted for a moment, likely thinking for just the right snarky comment. He also seemed to be taking in the floral bounty whose colors were further emboldened by the patches of afternoon sun.

"I suppose you do have quite a bit of knowledge in that oversized head of yours," Heren finally replied with a teasing look in his bright eyes that were almost turquoise in the late summer sunlight, "though you have been a bit quiet lately."

"I've had a lot on my mind," was the only excuse he could think to give.

Heren scoffed, "Like what? The only excitement that's happened here in ages was the attack on the Widow and that was days ago, unless…" Stefan turned his head towards his friend and saw a barely contained grin on his face. Heren faced forwards but his eyes were shifted to the left, assessing him curiously, "Is this about Odessa?"

Shit. "No, it's not about Odessa. She's basically a child." Technically his father had been around his age when he had matched with his mother who had been significantly younger than Odessa was now, but he didn't really like thinking about that.

"Okay, she and I are the same age so please tell me how you really feel."

"I think we've already discussed that I'm not romantically interested in you, sorry Ren."

Heren feigned gagging, "Alright but you have been staring at her. I'm not the only one who's noticed either. Eryx has definitely been bent out of shape about it."

Double shit. "Did he say something?"

"No, but he's been all quiet and brooding. You've been in your own head too much to notice but mealtimes have been extremely awkward."

Stefan ran a hand through his hair, "Could you say something to him maybe? That you heard from someone else that I thought Odessa had teeth like a horse?"

"That's a bit rough," Heren replied, shaking his head at him, "but maybe I could help with the situation if you tell me why you've been so blatantly obsessed with her as of late."

He sighed deeply and turned away to start back up the path so that Heren couldn't see the lie on his face, "She just reminds me of someone."

"The one that got away?"

He shrugged noncommittally and kept making his way down the path but stopped when he noticed that Heren was no longer beside him. When he turned, he saw that he had stopped walking and was looking at him strangely.

"You didn't know Aura did you?"

"Aura?" he repeated, with what he hoped was an unaffected question but the name had caught in his throat. For all he knew, Aura could be Odessa's childhood pet goat. Somehow he knew that wasn't the case.

"Odessa's older sister," Heren clarified, his eyes focused on his face as if looking for the answers written there.

"Older sister," he repeated, unsure if it was a statement or a question. It shouldn't have been a shock but somehow it still was. He saw a large rock to his left and sat down hard, suddenly feeling like the wind had been knocked out of him. After fourteen years he could finally put a name to the face. He knew he was making a scene but couldn't help it as he placed his head in his hand trying to catch his breath. When he opened his eyes and raised his head, he saw that Heren was kneeling in the dirt in front of him, his eyes as big as saucers. His mouth was open as if all of the questions in his head were competing to be asked first but a clear winner had yet to be declared.

"When? Was it before she left here or after? Does Odessa know? Did you know that…" The words flowed so quickly from his mouth that it was difficult to determine where one question ended and the next began.

Stefan stopped him with a finger to his lips. The idea that someone might be listening caused an immediate flurry of panic. None of Heren's questions were ones he could provide the answers to either because he didn't have them or it was too dangerous.

He stared into Heren's eyes as if trying to express the direness of the situation. "It was a long time ago. That's all I can say about it."

The look on Heren's face immediately went from one of shock and excitement at the promise of a secret to a chilly one of defensiveness. He stood up and crossed his arms. "You don't trust me."

Though it wasn't easy, Stefan managed to stand up from the rock, "I trust you more than anyone else here. Than anyone else in the world other than my own mother." *With his life perhaps, definitely not his secrets.* He could see Heren's face soften a bit. "Part of the problem is that the secret isn't fully mine to share and if someone else overheard, I couldn't be sure that the information wouldn't put anyone in danger."

Heren looked unconvinced but when he spoke, his tone wasn't harsh, "You're telling me that you explaining your unrequited romantic feelings for a woman could result in someone being injured or worse?"

"Yes, I'm sure it seems a bit dramatic when you put it that way but it's true." He knew if he told him outright not to tell anyone else, he would get annoyed again so he added, "There's no one else in the kingdom who knows of my feelings for her so it's imperative that we keep this to ourselves. Our secret?" He raised his eyebrows pleadingly and extended a hand for Heren to shake.

Heren looked at it for a moment before extending his own, "I suppose".

Stefan still wasn't convinced that Heren would be able to keep it to himself so he added sheepishly, "Thank you. For telling me her name, I never knew it."

"Pining after a girl whose name you didn't even know? Even I'm not that pathetic," Heren scoffed, shaking his head, but his tone was teasing rather than cruel.

"You're friends with me so you aren't that far off."

Heren smiled, "Maybe it will be more fun holding this over you than actually telling anyone else about it."

Stefan sighed, "Something to look forward to." Though he said it sarcastically, there was truth to it. Even while Heren didn't know the whole story, there was something freeing about having shared at least some of his deepest secrets with someone who cared enough to make fun of him.

CHAPTER 49
STEFAN

After another night of tossing and turning, Stefan sat up in bed just as the sun was beginning to peak over the eastern mountains, turning the waters of the river orange and gold. He had shed most of his clothing throughout the night as he'd moved from his back to his chest and then to his side and worked up a sweat doing nothing other than trying to get comfortable. Now, however, the damp sheets combined with the cool morning air gently flowing in through the window were making his skin break out in goosebumps. He thought, not for the first time, how much nicer it would be to wake up with someone beside him, sharing body heat and groggy kisses. Recalling and analyzing dreams while tucked under a warm flannel blanket. Staring into bright hazel eyes while playing with golden strands of hair splayed across the white pillows

These were exactly the kinds of thoughts that had kept him awake all night and unless he did something soon, they would continue to do so. He dressed quickly while thoughts of what else might happen beneath the sheets in quiet early mornings made it a bit difficult to pull on his pants. He put on his nicest juniper colored tunic that Eryx had picked up for him after selling some of the tonics he'd made at the market, and smoothed down his hair the best he could. He combed his beard using a rosemary and cedarwood oil that he'd been working on for the past couple of weeks. He had been happy with the final product and thought it was nicely befitting of a Green. Masculine and earthy. He was already thinking of more combinations that he could put together that would appeal to the different elementals. Something smoky and spicy for the Reds. Salty and sweet for the Blues. And for the Golds? He knew exactly who to ask. Even in the small number of times he'd been close enough to get a whiff of her, he knew that she had a penchant for florals. Maybe he could open with that.

He gently creaked open the wooden door to his room and peeked out. The stone hall was empty and all of the other doors remained closed. Everyone else was enjoying the first crisp breaths of autumn while curled up in their blankets. He wondered if everyone here was as lonely as he was or if there were some couples within the walls of the fortress who made secret morning treks from their lover's room back to their own. The thought put a smile on his face.

He turned to the right and headed towards the stone stairway that led to the bottommost floor. He had given her a full week to recover and he was tired of being a coward, running away from things rather than taking action. He would knock on her door and if she wasn't there or refused to answer, he would just spend his morning in the library nursing his wounds with one of his favorite romantic fairy tales. He had another vision of him curled up with one of those books in front of the library fire. Red and orange leaves dancing in front of the open window and Aura's feet in his lap as she read her own book. Did she enjoy romance as well or would she laugh at him?

He was surprised to hear muffled voices as he slowly crept down the stairs and was even more shocked when rather than coming from the library, they seemed to be emanating from down the hall where the wooden door to Aura's bedroom stood open. There was both a male and female voice. His stomach dropped for a moment as his brain automatically went to the most unsavory idea: that Aura had her own lover who was just exiting her room after a morning of quiet canoodling. As he moved closer he quickly identified the male voice as Eryx's. But it definitely sounded more worried than sexually satiated.

"Why would she have taken her? Do you think it's some kind of ransom situation?" Her voice was deeper than when he had last spoken to her as a teenager and he could also recognize some of the Widow's inflection in it, though it was smoother than the crackling rasp he had been hearing the past couple of months.

"Both boats were gone. I'm assuming that Cassandra went off in the night to try and meet up with Jonal and that Echo followed." Though he was stating basic facts, there was a twinge of guilt in his voice as if Eryx felt personally responsible.

If Aura was emotionally affected at all by the information, she didn't sound it. "Have you seen the bird?"

"No, he wouldn't let her go off on her own."

"I wouldn't think I'd ever say it but that's comforting. If there's a chance of finding her, it's with him."

Stefan was about to back away and wait until Eryx asked for help so that they wouldn't know he was eavesdropping but then remembered that he was supposed to be taking initiative rather than running away. He didn't give himself any time to think about the fact that this was the first time he would be addressing her again after learning her true identity. He took three large determined steps down the hall and rapped on the large wooden door before letting his head peer around the other side.

Sadly she had apparently had the time to cover herself in her robes; however, any hint of the old woman had disappeared. She was taller, and the gold of her eyes shone through the gauzy veil rather than the Widow's cloudy white orbs. He wasn't sure if that meant that she had chosen not to use her powers on him, that she hadn't been able to do so since he had surprised her, or that since he knew the truth his brain couldn't unsee that it was her hiding beneath the heavy layers of fabric. It was the first time he had seen those eyes in over a decade and for a moment he couldn't think of a single word to say. If she thought that maybe he hadn't realized her true identity, he was surely letting her know now that he had. Apparently the fact that he had let himself into her chamber left her speechless as well, and they both stood staring for a moment before Eryx cleared his throat. When Stefan finally shifted his gaze, he was looking between them with a puzzled frown on his face.

"I was going down to the library when I heard voices." His own voice was hoarse and it didn't help that he hadn't had his morning coffee. "Can I help?"

Eryx looked as if he was going to say no but then Aura spoke, though she directed her comment at Eryx rather than directly answering him, "It would be better to have two of you in case Echo lost Cassandra's trail and they went in two different directions."

"Odessa could–" Eryx started but she cut him off.

"Odessa will tell me once she wakes whether or not she dreamt of this. I will not wake her now and interrupt any dreams that may come to her. She is fully capable of going out on her own." She reluctantly turned her gaze back to him, though he noticed her eyes were lowered as if she couldn't handle more eye contact at the moment and he was almost thankful for it. "Scorpio has spent enough time on the mainland banks to know if anything looks out of place and therefore which direction they may have gone in."

Eryx looked as if he wanted to argue but closed his mouth and nodded as if she was his general and he was nothing but an obedient sentry. Her no-nonsense demeanor wasn't a surprise to Stefan and yet, he still found himself extremely aroused by it. He turned away before she could see the heat rising in his cheeks.

Eryx was already turning into the stairwell as he went back through the open door. As Stefan turned to close it behind him, he stole one more glance into the room and saw her wringing her hands and watching him.

"We'll speak once they're found." It was spoken quietly as if conceding to him.

He couldn't tell if he was excited or terrified.

CHAPTER 50
STEFAN

"We couldn't have asked one of the water elementals to swim across first and fetch one of the boats?" Stefan asked, unable to keep the tremors from his voice as he slowly walked out of the river onto the mainland. His feet sunk into the soft loam, and he carried his clothing and boots in a sack above his head though he was sure that there would at least be some damp spots even if they weren't completely soaked.

"Cassandra and Jonal were both Blues. That's how he got away so quickly. Cassandra took a boat but I'm sure it was just because she didn't want to get her clothes wet and catch a chill in the middle of the night. The only other water elementals on the island are young ones."

Eryx dumped his own sack on the sandy shore and began pulling out his clothes. The whole time they were in the water, Eryx had swam with his biceps tensed and arms fully extended above his head. Sure enough, his dark green tunic was pristinely dry. When he finally made it to a large rock on the shore where he could catch his breath, Stefan pulled out the juniper tunic he had chosen so carefully and found that it was soaked and wrinkled.

Though he was hating Eryx a bit at the moment for his impressive physicality and swimming abilities, Stefan was glad that the younger man was speaking to him again. He could still tell that there was something simmering under the surface by the fact that he refused to look him in the eye. Even though his relationship with Eryx wasn't as easy and carefree as the one that he had with Heren, it was still something that had become important to him. Heren had become like a younger sibling, their relationship reminiscent of the one he might have had with Oliver if given the chance. Even though Eryx was not much older than Heren, his maturity made Stefan see him more as an equal. He had been a much harder egg to crack but they had made definite progress since that first spring morning. Even though he obviously couldn't bring up Odessa or Aura at the current moment for a multitude of reasons, he hoped that once he did talk things through with the older sister, he would be able to explain himself to his friend. For now he would just keep the conversation going on neutral ground.

"Did you pick up on an attachment between the two before any of this happened?"

Eryx shrugged his glistening muscled shoulders before pulling his tunic over his head. "The only times I saw them together was during training and I was more focused on their fighting technique rather than any eyes they might have been making at each other."

"Fair enough," was all Stefan could think of to say. No wonder Eryx was having such a difficult time making his move on the seer. He didn't seem to have a romantic bone in his body. Though Stefan had only recently started helping Eryx out with the training of the younger ones and was still learning the names of many of them, the fact that Cassandra was a Blue did help him picture her in his mind. He had seen both her and the boy during kitchen duty. She was freckled with light brown skin and dark curly hair; sweet and pleasant, though often quiet and lost in a daydream. He could certainly see her as being the type to get carried away by romantic promises.

Jonal, if he had the right boy in mind, had been constantly complaining about whatever task Matilda assigned to him and often attempted to sweet talk anyone impressionable enough into taking over his duties. He could see Cassandra believing that his niceties towards her were amorous rather than self-serving. He hoped desperately that both her and Echo would be brought back safely. And that Jonal would get what he deserved. The fact that the boy had unabashedly attacked the woman who helped save him from whatever pit he'd grown up in told Stefan that there was no goodness left in him. If Jonal had been any more practiced with a blade, any future Stefan might have with Aura would have been robbed from him; he feared for what he might do if he ever saw the boy again.

The two boats were side by side and it was lucky that the girls had been discovered missing so early since the small crafts were perilously close to the lapping waters. They each took one by the rope tied to the front and pulled them up into the woods where they were hidden by the overgrowth. Though it was highly unlikely that anyone would actually come out of the forest or be sailing down the river, the possibility was still there.

Stefan studied the pairs of footprints that were clearly outlined in the sand. There was one larger pair and then a second one to the left which was accompanied by prints that could only belong to Hopscotch: three times the size of a chicken's with deadly points where the large black nails would be. He took a few steps into the woods and as he did he felt the familiar pull of something calling to him. For a moment he thought to just ignore it, but then the realization came to him and he followed the hum for a few steps. Sure enough, the call seemed to be coming from the same direction that the footprints were headed as if something knew his reason for entering the forest and wanted to provide assistance.

"They headed in this direction. We'll stay together unless there's reason to believe that they split up?"

Eryx nodded and Stefan felt pride and a sense of belonging that he didn't question him, falling into step behind him as he listened to the call of his mysterious helper.

***

Something about the familiar woods felt different as he followed the pull and noticed the small signs that the girls had left behind. The footprints were not as clear as they had been on the sandy beach, but beside them he noticed what looked like the purposeful dropping of bright red winterberries. At first he assumed that it had been Echo who had left them; it was also possible that it was the bird's doing.

Though his body warmed up a bit as they moved through the forest trails, the strands of his long hair refused to dry, chilling the back of his neck and scalp. He stopped for a moment to tie them into a messy knot. This day was not going at all the way he had hoped, but he was pleased that his beard still felt soft and the scent of the oils mixed nicely with the natural aromas of the forest surrounding them. If he could prepare enough oils over the next couple of weeks, hopefully Eryx and Odessa could sell them and get him a knit hat and some thicker outerwear for the colder months that would arrive much too quickly.

While he loved the beauty of the fall and the quiet cozy season leading up to the Cold Moon, he could do without the dark and dead months that followed. Those had always been the most difficult for him in the years he'd been on his own. Even though people were at their poorest, the food from the fall harvests dwindling, the tensions between them meant that he still had plenty of business. The pubs were still full, depressed men spending coin they didn't have to get away from their wives and children and starting fights as a form of entertainment. If he could have afforded to just spend those months hidden away in a cave like a bear he would have; however, he needed the income to spend money on bland pub food since he was no hunter and the forageable plants at that time were minimal to say the least.

Though the gray skies would be ever present through the Wolf, Snow and Worm Moons, he could see that time being tolerable this year as long as he was with his friends. The hours wouldn't pass so slowly if they were spent reading in the library with Odessa or playing cards with Heren. His bones wouldn't feel as cold if he were sharing a cup of coffee and preparing a hearty soup with Matilda or watching Lavender and Yakov do their magic in the forge. Maybe his nights wouldn't be as lonely either if he could stay focused on what he was supposed to be doing and find the girls.

"Hold up," Eryx said from behind him, bringing him back to the present moment. He turned and saw the younger man looking at him from a few paces back. "Are you sure they went that way?" He was down on his haunches studying the path before him. "It looks like there's a split in the trail and I do see a partial print. Looks like one of Cassandra's."

Stefan closed his eyes to see if he had strayed off course after getting lost in his thoughts. Whatever was calling was definitely coming from the opposite direction of the trail where

Eryx stood. As if to reassure him he saw another winterberry a few yards away in the direction that he was headed. "Maybe Echo and the bird missed the turn that Cassandra took?"

"It's possible," Eryx replied, getting up from his crouch. "Echo's no huntress and Hopscotch is a scavenger so it isn't like he has any exceptional tracking talents himself. Especially if he was staying with Echo down on the ground rather than flying. Truthfully I'm surprised they got this far."

"We'll split up then?"

Eryx looked unsure as if he still didn't trust him to not run away, "I'm not going to find one of the girls and take them away with me somewhere," he promised, rolling his eyes.

Eryx sighed, "I know that. I'm not worried because I don't trust you, I'm worried *for* you."

Stefan knew that was only partially true because Eryx *didn't* trust him when it came to Odessa, but apparently he did when it came to anyone else. He was a bit surprised that Eryx would even voice a concern for his welfare and didn't know how to respond at first.

When he took too long to answer Eryx continued, his head bowed, "I have a hard time letting my friends go off on their own. In the past it hasn't ended well."

Stefan was definitely interested in *that* story but knew it wasn't the time or place and didn't look like something that Eryx wanted to elaborate on. He smiled at Eryx in what he hoped was a reassuring gesture. "I'm fairly certain I can take care of myself. I have a new sparring partner who has kicked my butt into shape these last few weeks. We'll save time in finding the girls this way, which is more important. They can't be much farther off."

Eryx nodded, "Just promise either way we'll both be back to the fortress by nightfall. If we haven't found them, we can consult with Odessa and see if she received any messages about their whereabouts."

Stefan clapped him on the shoulder before turning to go down his own path, "I'll see you at home."

CHAPTER 51
STEFAN

Though it was still early morning and the sky had been bright when they had landed on the shores of the mainland, the forest grew darker the farther he walked. He had heard rumors concerning the Stygian and the dangerous creatures that lurked within but in his experience thus far, there had been nothing deadly or frightening about it. In addition, Heren and he typically foraged in those parts closest to the river which would assumedly be the scariest parts. As he now ventured closer to the base of the mountains and his old home, he noticed a definite drop in temperature and felt like he was being watched from every direction.

The pull was getting stronger and was close to the feeling that he usually got when he was almost upon the plant that desired to be found. With it was a growing trepidation warning him to be on guard. He slowed his pace a bit and tried to control his breathing. Darkness flashed to the left of him, but by the time he turned his head, whatever was there had gone. The sounds that he was typically used to hearing: the frogs, bees, and birds had disappeared as if they were also hiding from whatever was lurking nearby.

If it wasn't for the silence of the woods around him, he might not have heard the whispered voices of men coming from up ahead. He immediately wanted to turn back but was afraid that Echo was in trouble and retrieving her once she was taken would be a much more complicated task. Rather than continue to follow the clearer path, he moved deeper to where the pines and firs would provide some coverage and headed in the direction of the soft voices.

It didn't take him long before he reached the clearing where six men sat around a small fire roasting some kind of meat. They wore the royal insignia on the shoulders of their tunics and even though they looked haggard, exhausted, and bloody, Stefan couldn't feel anything but deep, overpowering fear at seeing them. The sight of the six ordinary men before him was more terrifying than any beast or ghastly spirit these woods could conjure. He closed his eyes for a moment and took deep breaths, not letting the air from his lips make an audible sound. He pushed back visions of the men finding him and dragging him back to his uncle who would ensure that his death this time was permanent.

"Are you going to just stand there, prince, or make yourself useful?"

Stefan knew he must have jumped about a foot in the air but was glad that he hadn't cried out. He snapped his head around for a moment to see who had addressed him but there was no one there. Somehow, the voice had seemed to come from inside his own head. He quickly turned back to the circle of men, but if they had noticed him, they didn't show it.

What *he* noticed, however, was a small pair of eyes peering out from a thorny raspberry bush. They were not the glowing or haunting eyes of a mythical woodland predator but rather those of a scared little girl who was trying to stay hidden while likely torn and bleeding from the thorny branches. He moved his gaze upwards as the flapping of a wing caught his eye. Hopscotch was in the tree directly above her; the enormous bird's beady gaze was directed right at him.

"'Just stand there' it is."

The voice came again and he tried to turn his head around much more discreetly but still saw no one. He looked back up into the tree and saw the bird shaking its head. He wasn't sure how the men below hadn't seen it yet, but he supposed they would have to crane their necks and look directly up into the sun.

Wait. It wasn't actually the bird talking to him, was it? How was he supposed to talk back to it?

"Hello?" he whispered, as quietly as possible.

"It won't help any of us if they hear you whispering to yourself, you twat. Just direct your thoughts towards me."

He narrowed his eyes and looked up towards the bird. *"How did you go directly from 'prince' to 'twat'. I don't talk to animals, how am I supposed to know how to do this?"*

"I needed to get your attention and I was sure calling you prince would do just that. Calling you twat was just the honest truth."

Stefan couldn't blame the bird for feeling how he did. He *had* scorned him at their first meeting. *"We can work on repairing the hurt between us at a later time. How can I help?"*

"I can scare off the men if you can extricate Echo from the bush. If something happened to me, I wasn't sure that she would be able to get out on her own."

"That should be easy enough. Are you sure they'll be scared and not charmed by your handsome visage?"

"Birds talk, prince. I've kept your secrets to myself but it would be very easy to let something slip."

"Understood," Stefan replied. Though it would be helpful in this one particular situation, he would have preferred being ignorant of the bird's intelligence and psychic abilities. Now he would likely be brushing his feathers and bringing home dead animal carcasses to win his favor. He sighed loudly and Hopscotch gave him a warning look before bounding out of the tree and into the circle of men. If given the chance, they would happily carry Stefan's head back on a pike as a trophy for Talon, and yet he still felt sorry for them as they screamed in terror at the deadly taloned beast coming after them with his giant wings and sharply pointed beak. Even the sound it made was closer to a lion's roar rather than the sweet song of a bluebird or the sharp caw of a crow.

None of the men tried to use their powers in any way. It might have been the surprise of it all or the exhaustion that had so clearly been written on their faces. He was certain that Hopscotch was not the first beast that had crossed their path. It did worry him that they had even made it this far towards the river and their home. As they scattered in various directions, Hopscotch flew up into the sky in order to make sure that they didn't return.

Stefan waited only a minute before quietly creeping into the center of the clearing. The men had left behind a number of personal items including some weapons. Stefan slipped a pair of small daggers into his boots and went over to the raspberry bush that Echo must have jumped into after hearing the sound of deep voices. He crouched down next to her and tried to speak in soothing tones so as not to frighten the girl further.

"Echo," he began, looking into her terrified eyes, "I'm going to get you out. We have to do it quickly in case the men come back. I think it will be easier if I have the bush move on its own so just don't be afraid if you feel something moving. It isn't snakes or anything else like that, just the branches."

He would cut the bush if necessary but would prefer not to; he might accidently cut Echo in the process or the bush could react negatively and grasp onto her more tightly. He wondered then if the raspberry bush had been the one that had been calling to him the entire time, or if it had been a conjoined effort between all of the plants who had observed Echo on her journey. Even though he had lived with his Green magic his entire life, there were still so many aspects of it that remained a mystery to him.

He spoke to the bush now, and it gently and carefully rearranged its limbs until he was able to reach in and pluck Echo out of the center. Once she was safely tucked into his arms, the bush curled back into itself and he sent it a silent thank you.

He bent down to place Echo back on the ground, but she tightened her grip around his neck and hid her face in his chest. Her dark brown curls smelled of the sweet fruit; he would make sure to pick some for her before the season came to a close. He could see the multitude of bloody scrapes on her arms but nothing looked too deep and it would take too much time to heal each and every one now.

"I can carry you for a while. It would be safer if we got moving. I know your wounds might sting. If you can wait, I have plenty of ointments I can put on them when we get back to the fortress that will make them feel much better."

She nodded and held on tighter. He was glad that his beard smelled fresh and woodsy since her face was buried in it. He was surprised by the fact that she was so willing to be held by him and his heart warmed at the fact that she saw him as someone she could trust.

"If you do get uncomfortable or want to walk on your own you can just give me a pinch, alright?" he asked, making sure that she could express her boundaries without having to verbalize.

She nodded and he started back towards home as quickly and stealthily as he could.

CHAPTER 52
STEFAN

When they arrived back at the rowboats, they were not only greeted by a pacing Hopscotch but also a relieved Eryx and a sheepish looking Cassandra.

Stefan finally crouched down to place Echo on the soft sand, and she immediately went over to her furry friend to check in. His back and neck felt stiff and he was sure his arms would need a full day to recover before he did any serious gardening. Even so, he immediately felt the absence of Echo's small warm body, especially with the chill coming off of the river as the late afternoon sun moved away from them towards the Witch's kingdom.

He hadn't even realized how long it had been since he'd been in such close proximity to another human being. He wondered if it had been a while for Echo as well since she seemed to spend so much time on her own. Maybe she would be more willing to open up to him after today. She had remained silent on their journey back but once he had been sure that they weren't being followed, he had softly recited some of the facts that he'd learned from the books about animals in the library and then some stories he had loved from his own childhood that he'd long ago committed to memory. After so much time spent alone, he found silence to be difficult for him, and he hoped that his whispered words had been a comfort to the girl.

Echo did seem to be in good spirits despite her injuries. She had moved away from the bird and Cassandra was crouched on the ground before her, apologizing profusely for leaving, and praising her for her bravery. He could understand why Echo might have felt strongly enough about the older girl to follow her. Though a bit misguided in this case, she did seem like someone sweet and gentle enough for Echo to feel comfortable with.

"You didn't heal her."

He immediately turned towards Eryx and opened his mouth to explain when he realized it had been the bird who had spoken. Rather than explain his choices twice, he spoke up so that both could hear.

"When I found her, Echo was stuck in a pricker bush surrounded by the king's men. Hopscotch distracted them while I got her out." Eryx raised one dark eyebrow at that admission but he continued. "There were no life threatening injuries and I wanted to make sure we got back before dark. I'll examine her when we get back to the island and I have the supplies I need."

Hopscotch didn't look satisfied, though Stefan wouldn't even know what that would look like on his ghastly face. The bird didn't push the point and didn't attempt to speak to him again so maybe Echo's unworried countenance had put him at ease. Maybe he would be lucky and the bird would ignore him now that the situation was no longer life or death.

"I didn't think I would live to see the day that you two would willingly work together on something. How were you able to coordinate your efforts?" Eryx asked with a smile.

"It's a long story," he replied, not wanting to admit that he was able to communicate with the bird through thoughts alone and that the bird knew enough to ruin him. "Let's go home."

***

Once everyone had safely made it back to the island, Eryx escorted the girls to their rooms. Stefan ran down to the makeshift laboratory he and Heren had been working on in order to grab the tonic that he thought would disinfect Echo's wounds with the least amount of sting.

When he made his way back up to the main fortress, he found her in her room sitting on the edge of her bed with Odessa assessing the scratches.

"She'll need a bath to ensure that the wounds get cleaned, and that there aren't any thorns left behind," he said from the doorway, not wanting to crowd the tiny space.

Odessa looked up and smiled, "It's nice after a day like today when I *do* get those reminders that my power is good for something. Thank you for finding her and bringing her back to us."

He smiled sheepishly, "Just doing my part like everyone else." He took the small glass jar he had brought up and placed it on the table next to the door. "Once she's cleaned up just rub this on the scratches. It's a mixture of honey, chamomile and thyme."

"Might taste good in a tea as well," Odessa replied, thoughtfully, as she gently moved her fingers over Echo's small legs. They were scratched up though slightly less so than her arms due to the leggings and boots she had worn. She turned to look up at him. "You're not going to heal her yourself?"

He sighed, "I'm still not totally confident in my psychic healing abilities and I wouldn't want to experiment on Echo, especially since her injuries aren't life threatening. I haven't yet been assured that the job I did on the Widow was to her satisfaction." He raised an eyebrow, as if waiting for Odessa's confirmation of just that.

Odessa lowered her eyes back to Echo, her cheeks pinkening beneath her light freckles. "I'm certain she'll tell you that she was more than satisfied the next time you see her, but if you're not comfortable helping Echo in that way I'm sure this will do just fine." She reached for the tonic, screwed off the top of the small jar and brought it to her nose. She inhaled deeply and then made a satisfactory noise, likely as a way to move on from the topic.

He contemplated telling the seer that visiting the Widow was next on his list just to see her reaction but was interrupted by someone pushing him into the room.

Odessa moved her chair back from the bed and the two young air elements knelt before Echo in the space she had vacated.

"That was very naughty, Echo," the younger boy, Callen, scolded, bopping her gently on the nose.

The older one, Barrett, if he remembered correctly, was following in Odessa's footsteps gently moving his eyes and fingers over the scratches.

"It was very brave, but also foolish," he added. "Next time come get one of us and we'll help."

Echo nodded and Stefan was surprised that she seemed so comfortable with the older boys.

"Are you going to help her?" Barrett asked, turning towards him. "Isn't that what you're good for?" It was said with the same loathing tone the boy usually directed at him, but there was also a hint of worry behind it.

"Scorpio has done enough," Odessa said, getting up from the chair, and shooing them out the door. "Your sister needs a bath and a rest. You can come see her in the morning."

Well that was new information, and unexpected at that. The two brothers were blond haired and tanned from the summer sun, and Echo had dark curls and much fairer skin. He should have put two and two together based on the fact that they were all air elements with some hint of other abilities. Another memory came back to him suddenly. One that hadn't seemed that important all those months ago but was now glaringly obvious.

Odessa is his aunt…

"I need to go," he told Odessa suddenly, feeling a bit sick and needing to get some of his questions answered before he discovered that there were even more to ask. He turned around to go but then stepped back into the room and bent down until he was at Echo's level.

"Feel better. If the tonic doesn't do the trick, I'll make you whatever you need." He moved his head until he could whisper into her ear. "Just tell Hopscotch and he'll relay the message." She raised her eyes to finally meet his own, and he was hit with the golden honey color of them that put any doubts he might still have to rest.

CHAPTER 53
AURA

Aura paced back and forth in her grand suit in the lowest level of the fortress. She had specifically chosen this room because it had no windows or chimneys that would allow her true voice to escape the four walls. It was always dark and always damp and always cold but the rugs and furniture she had brought down from other parts of the fortress had helped to warm up the space. It was also larger than any of the upstairs rooms, so she had plenty of room to pace. She still wore her robes, not only as a buffer from the cold but as a precaution in case "Scorpio" still planned on coming to speak with her.

She scolded herself yet again for even saying those words to him. She could have just let him go off with Eryx and continued pretending that they were nothing more than strangers to each other. She knew that he didn't need any kind of motivation to do his best to find Echo. She had pleasantly discovered through their one-on-one conversations, as well as what the others had said about him, that he did indeed have the heart she was so sure was missing all those years ago. She could have, should have, wished him good luck on the search and then continued avoiding him for as long as possible.

It was the look he had given her upon entering the room. The same one that he had given her at least twice the day they met. The one that contrasted so severely with his general attitude towards her. The look that said he saw her and that she was something worth looking at.

She couldn't remember the last time anyone looked at her like that. Maybe the boys when they were babies; when she was still the focus of their universe. Maybe Vitus, before life became too busy and their only stolen moments together were in the darkness after everyone else went to sleep.

It had been years, and this morning the fallen prince had stared at her like that again when she was covered from head to toe in black, possibly with crows feet around her eyes if the glamor was still working. She had an inkling that that ship had sailed and that there would be no more hiding from him now that he had figured out the truth.

The only positive thing about the situation was that she wasn't waiting for him to give her the confirmation that Echo was safe. She was sure that even under her robes, she wouldn't have been able to hide the relief. Eryx had stopped in a couple of minutes ago to debrief her on the situation. She hated the fact that she couldn't just go out herself to locate her daughter. She was sure the wind would have led her right to her, and maybe Echo wouldn't have had to suffer through the entire ordeal. She shuddered to think of what would have happened had those men seen her.

A sudden wave of exhaustion hit her after a day spent as coiled as one of Echo's tiny curls. If she hadn't thought that he was coming, she would have passed out in her bed the moment Eryx let himself out. As it was, she would be too jittery to sleep even if he never ended up showing his bewhiskered face.

What was the point of this anyway? She didn't owe him any kind of explanation. She didn't owe him anything at all. He was thriving here because of *her*. She had been the one to convince the other two that bringing him here was a good idea. Both Odessa and Eryx initially had their reservations, even though her sister typically followed her visions without question. It would have made things much easier if she had explained his true identity and their past but it wasn't something she wanted to get into. Nor did she feel that it was her place.

When he'd first arrived, he'd looked pale and unkempt and soft, likely from all of that greasy brown pub food. Now he looked…good. Too good, if she was being honest. She could feel herself becoming overly warm beneath her hood and went to the back of the room to calm herself down and ease her breathing. She opened one of the drawers next to her bed and ran her fingers over the different options. Autumn was rapidly approaching and, though it wasn't normally her first choice, she could go with the cinnamon apple that Odessa had brought back for her last week. She shook her head. She needed something stronger. She found a small circular bar with deep violet petals embedded within it and brought it up to her nose.

She inhaled deeply, breathing in the light calming scent of peonies. She imagined herself walking in a garden of large, bright, round blossoms on a warm summer day. Pinks and purples and…

Two quiet knocks on the door and the soap flew from her hands. She crouched to the ground and retrieved it from the place it had fallen next to the bed, frowning at the small bits of dust now marring the surface. She tsked at her own skittishness and put the small white circle back before straightening her robes. She walked to the door, unlocked it and then backed up as many steps as she could in the time it took him to open the door.

***

"They're yours."

The words had flown out as if he had been unable to hold them within the confines of his mouth a second longer. Aura slammed the door behind him and then propelled a dagger that had been lying on the large wooden table towards his throat, the point softly embedded in the dark hair of his beard. They both fell silent for a moment as she stood with her hand in the air, all of the anxiety that had been present a moment ago evaporated with his statement. While she tried to hold onto her usual air of calm authority, she could feel her whole body trembling in either rage or fear, she couldn't tell which.

His eyes widened and he slowly raised his hands in a gesture of surrender. "I'm sorry. The realization just came to me and I'm not always the most tactful." Had he thought she was going to give him some sort of prize or pat on the back for figuring it out?

"I have not put up with this charade for the past five years just for you to open your mouth and ruin everything," she growled. "Why is it that every time you show your face, my best laid plans go up in smoke?"

"So you do know me then." He spoke quietly, his dark brows raised above eyes that were the color of dark moss in the candlelit room. He seemed more startled by this bit of information than the dagger that still hovered before him. "Do the others know?"

"Of course that's what you're most concerned about. Your own hide." She dropped her hand and the dagger dropped to the stone floor with a loud clatter. He startled at the sound but then bent down to retrieve it from its place on the floor. "Yes, and no, no one else knows. I know how to keep the secrets of others to myself. Unlike some people." She looked at him pointedly, crossing her arms over her chest.

He paused for a moment and she could tell he was trying to weigh what to ask next. "How?"

Aura turned and sat, suddenly devoid of energy after the flash of anger and panic she had felt at his realization. "You know by now how we find our people. Odessa sees them in her nightly visions and then goes out to seek them using whatever clues she's been given. She told me that morning what she had seen. A man passed out beneath a tree limb outside of a pub. We were both a little taken aback to say the least. Her visions typically show people who are put in harm's way due to no fault of their own. We don't have many drunkards or poisoners in our midst."

She was glad to see that he now at least had enough decency to look ashamed. When he first arrived he probably would have given one of his annoyingly charming one sided smiles.

He studied her for a moment and then crossed his arms over his own chest, "That still doesn't explain how you recognized a man you hadn't seen since you were a teenager through a vision that wasn't yours."

She could lie and tell him that she hadn't recognized him until he had arrived at the fortress, but she had never been very good at lying. He would hear it in her voice, even if he didn't have a clear view of her shifting eyes or her flushed cheeks.

It was a topic that she didn't want to bring up, yet there wasn't any other way around it.

"She told me about the mark on your lower abdomen. You were wearing green and around the right age. I knew it had to be you." She kept the words flowing so that he wouldn't get stuck on the one she wanted to move past.

"You knew," he corrected her, "because the mark matched your own." He was gradually making his way closer to her, fidgeting with the blade in his hands.

Odessa had been only five years old when Aura first laid eyes upon the infamous prince and therefore, hadn't been the confidant that she was to Aura now. There were many rumors surrounding his powers and overall temperament. Many said he was dark and moody and kept to himself. Others said he was a spoiled mama's boy who chose not to bother with anyone of lower status. Aura's first impression, well actually her second impression she supposed, was that he was indeed an overgrown petulant child needing to be put in his place, which she had done with some pride. Her *first* impression, when they had met outside on the castle grounds, had been that he seemed a bit awkward but also handsome in a quiet, bookish kind of way. She had been disappointed to find out that the boy she had met first hadn't really existed.

It seemed that the years he spent fending for himself had altered his highfalutin persona. She had been surprised by his transformation, even thinking at his first meeting with "the Widow" that she had been wrong about his true identity. Though he obviously had much less wealth and status than he did as the heir to the kingdom, he was more comfortable in his own skin and came across as confident and easy going. She supposed that once he'd lost everything, there was nothing left to lose.

By the time Odessa was old enough to prepare for her own trials, the secret that Aura had kept for so long felt like a scab that had been covered over with too many layers. She had not even shared the true details of the fight with Vitus. He knew that she had concealed her true powers during *their* match but assumed that the prince had easily overpowered her.

The mark was another reason she kept what had gone on between the two of them to herself. Once her and Vitus wed, she had hidden it for as long as possible and then attributed it to being an unusual birthmark. He had a strange fascination with it as if he didn't quite believe her story, but luckily didn't connect it to an event that to him seemed of little matter or consequence. Concealing the mark from Odessa had been much easier since she had little reason to disrobe in front of her younger sister. When Odessa had seen the mark on the man in her vision, she hadn't realized the true importance of it.

"Yes. I figured you must have seen it when you healed me," she responded, slightly unnerved by his growing proximity.

"So it worked then? I did indeed heal you? It would have been nice to get an affirmation that you were alright. Maybe even a thank you. Instead you left me to nearly go out of my mind for a whole week's time. Finding out that you were not some elderly Widow and that you were the girl who…" he paused there as if struggling with something and then more quietly, "and then that I may have lost you again." He walked until he was nearly standing in front of her but then turned and began pacing back and forth.

Aura was confused by his words and thought she must have misheard but was also agitated that he was suggesting that she was somehow in the wrong. "For a first try, your healing abilities left little to be desired but I'm sure either Odessa or Eryx told you that I was fine. To be honest, I was also avoiding this very conversation."

"You? Avoid something? What a thought," he scoffed.

"What is that supposed to mean?" she asked, rising to her feet in order to gain some leverage in their duel of words.

"You could have been a princess!" he fumed, stopping his pacing to stand nose to nose with her, though with their difference in height it was initially nose to chest until she raised her gaze to meet his. "Possibly a queen! If we had been matched all of this could have been avoided. Years of misery, for the both of us. Maybe my father could have made me king before his death. Who knows what could have been different."

He ran his hands through his hair and then turned away from her and began pacing again.

"And what if nothing changed? What if your father was killed and we were both held responsible? I am putting quite a lot of faith in the fact that you're innocent of that particular deed, by the way."

He stopped his pacing but faced away from her. "I did not kill my father," he growled, a threat. "And I'm sure we would have been fine. If my mother was able to get me out of that particular predicament on her own, I'm sure that with the two of you working together it would have taken very little effort. You could have had a mother-daughter tea party on the lawn while everyone was frozen in place."

Aura opened her mouth ready for another volley but found herself speechless. He had shared that his mother likely had some psychic powers that he had obviously inherited through his ability to heal human flesh, but it took her a moment to recover before she choked out. "The queen can project as well? Did anyone else know?"

"No," he responded, turning towards her again, some of the fight having left him. "I didn't until that moment. I don't think anyone was even aware that she had any powers of the mind, unless maybe my father. I'm guessing she kept hers hidden for the same reasons that you did yours."

"So your grandparents must have…" she started, thinking out loud, but stopped herself.

"My grandparents must have what?" he asked, stepping closer again. She was sure that his new found confidence also had something to do with his much improved appearance. At their first meeting he was awkward and long limbed, but he'd grown into his body nicely. He was still on the leaner side rather than beefy; however, he had put on some muscle since he started his training with the others. The lower half of his face was still covered in a heavy black beard, which oddly was a nice juxtaposition with his delicate nose, prominent cupid bow lips and long dark eyelashes. His hair was a bit too long for her taste but she imagined it would be soft if she ran it through her fingers.

"Nothing," she responded, attempting to look away but finding it difficult.

Though she was still masked, he found her chin and held it in place.

"What?" he asked through clenched teeth. "Whether or not we intended to be such intimate allies, it seems that we are the only ones we have to share all of our secrets with."

She took a deep breath at the word "intimate" but held his gaze through her gauzy veil. Though he drove her completely mad, she was also strongly aware of the warmth of his hand still on her chin and the intensity of his eyes that flickered with gold in the candlelight as if in reflection of her own. Her cheeks already felt flushed and she knew that the next secret she was going to reveal would only make them worse.

"True mates," she responded, noticing how his eyes furrowed in confusion at the term.

"I don't understand. What would my mother's power have to do with her parent's marriage?"

She held his gaze and continued. "There is nothing written, but stories have been passed down throughout the villages. It happens rarely nowadays but certain unions in which both parties have equal power tend to result in children with stronger powers, in many cases powers of the mind, even if neither the male nor female had them to begin with."

"And this is how your powers were passed down to you? Your parents were true mates?" She could see the wheels turning in his head. "But your husband," he dropped her chin at this, seemingly remembering that at some point she had belonged to someone else. "Your power must have been stronger than his. How did your children inherit psychic powers as well?"

"We believe that once the powers are acquired, they can be passed down through non-equal unions, lessened by half, just like any trait a parent might pass on to their offspring. All three of my children have their unique psychic powers. They'll likely dwindle with each passing generation. You seem to have inherited some of your mother's power; it just took a while for you to develop it."

"Thanks to you." He again met her eyes and then turned pensive again. "But there is no way to know if the partners are true equals until children are born and their powers develop."

This was the part she was dreading. "Not quite," she said hesitantly, taking a step back. "There is something that occurs when two equally matched partners put each other at risk, a warning of sorts."

He took a step forward to match her own and again spoke through gritted teeth. "And what would that be?"

"I think you know," was all she could think of to say.

"Say it," he replied, further encroaching on her space.

"A lover's mark."

CHAPTER 54
STEFAN

Stefan had never been so angry with someone in his entire life. Not his father nor his uncle nor any of the hooligans who had broken his nose over the years. This woman had first rejected him almost fifteen years ago. She had then knowingly lied to his face over and over again while being fully aware that they had some predestined soul mate connection that she had just casually told him about and only because he had asked her directly to her face.

And yet, despite how immensely infuriating she was and how badly he wanted to storm out the door and share all of her secrets, all he could think about was how he still hadn't seen her face.

"So you knew then. All those years ago. That you weren't more powerful than me but that we were equals." He almost found it hard to believe, even now. That there was something inside of him that put him at her level. It angered him that he had just accepted the fact that he was weaker, likely because he had been hearing it his entire life. If someone had suggested to him that he was strong or helped him hone his Green magic into a more effective weapon, maybe he would have tried harder to win.

She was wringing her hands as if she was a bit ashamed for her bravado that day and possibly her decisions afterwards. "I didn't know until after the match ended and I saw the mark for myself. I thought maybe you had realized it as well when I saw you lurking in the trees behind the amphitheater but then you disappeared. I didn't realize until much later why that was."

A hint of sadness had entered her voice and he wondered then if she had mourned for him.

"You still lost that second match." He didn't say it accusingly. He also didn't form it into a question because he wasn't sure he wanted the answer.

She sighed deeply and perched on the arm of one of the soft chairs.

"I like to be in control of my own destiny. I had a plan. I imagined my future a certain way. It included being matched with someone I cared about. Someone I could trust. Someone who lived in my village who wouldn't make me leave my parents or my sister. Someone who wouldn't hurt me or try to manipulate me when they found out what I could do."

"I wouldn't," he started to protest.

She held up a hand, "I think I know that now, but I didn't then. You also didn't give me reassurance with your," she paused to think of the appropriate word, "behavior that day."

He wanted to explain all of the reasons for that "behavior". It hurt to consider the fact that she might have chosen a different path if he had treated her differently. The whole conversation was pointless because there was no changing the past. When he didn't respond she continued, her voice more gentle than before.

"It did weigh on me. You probably think I was too full of myself to care." She laughed a bit in spite of herself, and he had to turn away so that she wouldn't see how the light pleasant sound affected him. She swallowed before continuing. "It was something that I had to live with. The fact that I had walked away from you and then you…"

He needed to move the conversation away from this. Away from them. It probably wasn't going to be the most positive direction to go in but he needed to know.

"What happened to him? Your husband?"

"I still don't know for certain," she responded quietly. "He disappeared while out on an expedition west. That was when we left Goldenmount. To search for him and to avoid the other options. Eryx and Odessa have kept their eyes and ears out for any sign of him to no avail. Odessa hasn't dreamt of him either."

"And this?" he asked, gesturing towards the long robes and the veil that still covered her face.

She was quiet for a moment, apparently deciding how much she wanted to divulge.

"There was someone who followed us. When we left the village. It didn't end well."

Alright so maybe she was hiding something physical that she was ashamed of. He felt his blood begin to boil at the thought.

As if she could sense his growing anger she quickly clarified, "I took care of it. Of him. But the anxiety never went away. The idea that someone who knew him would hear that I was still alive. That I would be questioned about what happened and then my children would be taken away. No one would give a second thought to an ancient Widow caring for three orphans. An unwed woman raising her three children alone? Especially a woman who might have information about the disappearance of another woman's husband? Much more likely to invite trouble. It killed me to have to abandon the children in the same way as Vitus did. They were too young to let in on the secret. But I knew it would be the safest thing for all of us. Especially once Odessa started getting her visions suggesting that we take others in."

"You didn't abandon them," he replied, his anger continuing to grow with the fact that this was what she'd been forced to resort to. Living separately from her children because of the ideas and actions of men like him. Because of his wretched family.

"They don't know otherwise," she replied, head down, and even though he couldn't see her face, he could feel the pain and despair radiating from her. It made him want to pick her up and cradle her. Have someone take care of her for once even though he knew it wasn't him she needed or wanted. It never had been.

"I think I need to go." He turned away from her before he did something they would both regret.

"Stefan, wait." He stood shell shocked for a moment, hearing his given name for the first time in more than a decade.

He felt the warmth of her hand on his arm and turned back around to face her.

"I'm sorry that things didn't go the way you wanted back then and that I haven't been honest with you since you arrived. I understand that this has been a lot to digest, but I would appreciate your discretion in regards to my identity, especially concerning my children. Everything I have ever done has been to keep them safe. You can be angry with me. Just please don't put them at risk."

The look she gave him was so pleading that he knew she still couldn't trust him. He looked down at his feet, trying to keep the disappointment out of his voice. "I know you don't think very highly of me but I'm no monster. Your secret is safe with me just as you have kept mine to yourself."

He looked up again and held out a hand needing at least to touch her if she wasn't going to let him see her face tonight. She put her hand in his and, rather than shaking it, he brought it to his lips. While he tried to keep his face as stoic as possible, something jumped in his heart at the feel of her smooth skin. He gently let her go and passed her dagger back to her.

He walked backwards towards the door, wanting to keep her in view until the last possible minute. "Sleep well," he said gruffly before finally turning towards the door that she had reopened for him. He knew that he would do no such thing.

CHAPTER 55
AURA

Aura felt like she had just finally nodded off when she heard a light tapping on the door and the sound of a key turning in the lock. Down in the cellar room she was never able to tell when it was dark or light. Only her daily breakfast meetings with Odessa and Eryx kept her internal clock on track. She had been especially off since the incident last week due to the fact that she'd taken a break from her weekly consultations with all of the fortress' inhabitants. She was hoping to finally get above ground today and see the sky through the small windows of the throne room. Now that she and Stefan had talked things through, there was no need to continue hiding. At least she could go back to hiding in plain sight.

Avoiding Stefan wasn't the only reason that she had kept to herself the past week. Though physically there was no sign of the trauma she had endured, she couldn't say the same about her emotional state. She had heard plenty of complaints about Jonal's work ethic, but she never expected him to become violent. She would never blame Odessa. And yet, she found it worrisome that her trusted shadow woman encouraged her sister to bring him into their home without warning them of his intentions. There currently weren't any other individuals who she was particularly afraid of; however, who knew if behind their smiles they were also hiding contempt for her or any members of her family.

She heard the door creak open and threw her blankets over her head.

"Rise and shine, Goldenrod. We already told everyone at breakfast that you'd be seeing some of them today. Wouldn't want to disappoint."

Odessa's voice was light and almost musical as she walked over and sat on the corner of Aura's bed. Eryx hadn't said a word but she knew that he was there as well, likely placing the tray on the table which would contain her breakfast as well as a pot of tea and three mugs. Though she loved Dessa dearly, and wouldn't have survived all of this without her, she was envious of how perfect the situation had turned out for her younger sister. Odessa got to live out her dreams of visiting every corner of the kingdom and then coming back to a home full of people who loved and adored her. She pulled cards freely and used her power in a way that benefitted all.

Aura's life wasn't all bad. She had always preferred the quiet and had difficulty making friends. She liked pouring over the books in the library and studying different powers in order to help the others expand their abilities and learn how to use them in conjunction with others to get the best return. She liked being the puppeteer behind the scenes and in truth, she felt more comfortable interacting with so many people behind her robes where she could pretend to be a wizened old woman rather than just…herself. It did get lonely though. She missed her husband. She missed her children. She missed the air and the sunshine. At least a couple of those things she would be able to get a glimpse of today.

"Tell me what you brought with you and maybe that will entice me." She slowly slid the covers down only as far as her nose and breathed in deeply. She smelled warm fall spices mixed with some kind of herbs.

She heard a metal lid being removed and placed on the wooden table and the smell intensified.

"To start, we have a ginger apple scone with cinnamon butter, accompanied by a mushroom, shallot and goat cheese frittata, both of which Odessa ate with her hands." Eryx said it as if he were just stating the facts but she could hear the tiny hint of disgust which made her smile. She wondered if he was comfortable enough with the others to tease her sister in front of them or if he saved it for when it was just the three of them.

"Goat cheese?" she asked, finally swinging her legs out of the bed. "That's quite a rare delicacy."

"We've actually been doing quite well at the market lately," Eryx explained as he sat down and began sipping his tea. "Yakov and Lavender have been working on pottery and glassware and weapons and Heren and Scorpio have provided us with plenty of crystals and herbal concoctions. Apparently they're working on a whole line of elemental specific oils. We should have plenty of money for some treats as well as warm clothing for whoever needs it."

She had noticed that Stefan smelled especially woodsy and delicious when he was in her room last night. Delicious like a slice of Matilda's warm rosemary bread. Not delicious as in she wanted to run her tongue down his neck, though it had looked very smooth and appealing beside his dark beard. She grabbed one of the wool blankets from the bottom of her bed and wrapped it around herself not only to shield herself from the cold but also to hide her slight blush.

She got to work quickly on the frittata which tasted earthy and fresh with a bit of tang. When she had taken a couple of bites, Odessa pushed over her cup of tea and watched her with an excited look of anticipation.

"What? Did you poison it?"

Odessa rolled her eyes. "No, I'm just curious to see what you think."

"Is it a new blend?" In the winter time when the days got too cold and everyone was at their wits end from boredom, Odessa often got experimental with whatever dried herbs Matilda had on hand and tried concocting different teas to see if any were more effective in helping her sleep or encouraging prophetic dreaming. In the summer, she was usually too busy making flower crowns or fairy houses to spend much time in the kitchen.

Odessa just shook her head, her eyes wide and her lips grinning in anticipation. Aura hesitantly brought the cup to her lips and took a small sip. She narrowed her eyes in thought. The tea had the familiar base of chamomile with a touch of sweetness but then also something a bit like mint but more savory. It nicely complimented the taste of the herby frittata.

"Thyme?"

Odessa nodded excitedly. "Scorpio gave me a honey based tonic for Echo's wounds, but I thought it would taste good as well. Maybe we could get him to make a line of infused honey that could be medicinal as well as flavorful."

She felt herself warming again just at the mention of his name, which was ridiculous, but at least she would be able to attribute it to the warm beverage in her hands.

"Don't you think the man has enough on his plate?" Eryx chimed in, sounding a bit agitated. "Tending to the gardens, searching through the woods for mushrooms as well as small children, helping me in the sparring ring. I don't think we need to add another item to his list."

"He's already spending time in the laboratory with all of those herbs around him. I'm sure it wouldn't require much time. I could help."

"I'm sure he'd love that," he said quietly under his breath. Too quietly for Odessa to hear. *What was that about?*

He turned towards her then, possibly attempting to change the subject. "Last week, you said that you had woken up when he was healing you and were able to keep the glamor but yesterday morning he looked at you strangely. Differently. Are you sure you were awake the whole time? That he didn't see something he wasn't supposed to?"

Halfway through his sentence, she stuffed the scone into her mouth and chewed slowly while looking down into her steaming cup of tea. She took a long swig and then swallowed before answering.

"Very sure," she nodded her head for emphasis. "I remember waking up when he removed the blade and only relaxing again once everything was all covered up." All lies. Her head had been pounding that day even before she was stabbed. She had been thankful to pass out and not deal with any of it after swooning from the thought of the blade entering her body, not even the blood loss itself.

"He did attempt to remove your hood when I was walking in, but I stopped him. He said he just wanted to check for a pulse," Odessa added.

Sneaky bastard.

"Next time I meet with him I'll be extra observant about how he behaves but I'm sure there's nothing to worry about."

Eryx looked unconvinced but didn't press further. As she sipped her tea she wondered if there was anything she *could* tell them about the situation, but it seemed much easier just to leave things as they were. It wasn't like anything more was going to come of what had happened between her and Stefan. The past was the past. She would continue to play her part as the Widow and he would keep himself busy with the various roles he had taken on. She would give him pointers if anything came up in her research in regards to his power and that would be it.

She continued to nibble on the scone which was light and spicy with a touch of maple sweetness, reminding her of fall days when she would whip the autumn leaves in circles around the children, making even Echo giggle with glee. She let herself get lost in the moment until she looked up and saw Odessa shuffling her cards.

"Put those away," she said, swatting at Odessa with her hand. "You know Eryx isn't going to let you pick for him and I've gotten the same card every day since we walked into this place."

She had found it eye opening at first. The magician card had helped her figure out how she could spend time with her children one-on-one while also assisting all of the other people that Odessa brought to the fortress. While initially they had been confused about how one person could manipulate all four of the elements, it began to make sense as she took on her role of conductor, directing the others and helping them combine their powers in ways that would benefit the whole community.

The card had been a comfort for a while, encouraging her and validating that she was doing the right thing. Eventually it got to a point where it just felt stagnant. Like everything else in her life.

"You don't have to look, but what if something *does* change and you don't get the message," Odessa replied, obviously ignoring her.

"Why is it that you can force me into it but you don't give him the same treatment?" she asked, nodding her head at Eryx.

They both looked a bit flustered at that as if neither one wanted Eryx's thoughts and feelings out on the table. She basked in the attention being off her for a moment but then the awkwardness became too much. "Oh fine, let me pick one."

Odessa smiled and fanned the cards out in front of her and she touched one randomly without much thought. It didn't matter how much or little focus she put into it or if there was any particular question in her mind. The hooded man always found her.

Odessa slid the card over and wiggled her eyebrows at Aura before turning it over without letting either of the other two see it. As she brought her eyes to it, her smile froze and her head turned a bit in shock and puzzlement.

"Hm."

"Cut the act," Aura said, finishing the last swig of tea. "I know it's him."

"It's not," Odessa said, challengingly. She lowered the card back to the table and passed it to Eryx without turning it over. He looked at it, raised one eyebrow and then put it back down as well.

"She's right. It's not."

Something fluttered in her chest. She had been so tired of the same thing happening day after day after day, but the thought of something changing was also terrifying, especially if it was for the worse.

"Is it bad?" she asked, not yet wanting to turn the card over.

"No," Odessa said, reaching over and grabbing the last bite of her scone while she was distracted. Eryx shook his head at her in disappointment.

Aura pulled the card over and turned it over slowly. Two figures stood each holding a cup, their free hands intertwined between them. It didn't help the fluttering feeling in her chest.

"So you're going to procure some wine or mead on your next outing and bring it back for us to share?" she asked hopefully, though she couldn't keep the slight nervous squeak from her voice.

"That doesn't sound like a horrible idea," Odessa replied thoughtfully, "but there's more of a symbolic meaning behind it. The cups are a metaphor for a bond or connection. It could be a reconciliation or a new mutual attraction. Maybe," she seemed to think for a moment but then shook her head. "I don't want to make any suppositions but just take this as a sign of hope. You've been feeling stuck, this might mean that something positive is coming your way."

For her, gaining things typically only meant there were more things to lose. She and Stefan did have their reconciliation yesterday. Maybe that was what the card had been referring to and that was the end of it.

She got up from the table and turned away from them in order to start preparing herself for the day, "I'd rather just take the wine."

CHAPTER 56
AURA

Aura closed her bedroom door behind her and listened for anyone potentially in the library or coming down the stone staircase. She liked to retain the air of mystery and often kept herself hidden from anyone walking in the hallways so that no one knew where she spent her time outside of the throne room. It was easy enough to blend into the stone background if she only passed one or two people who were set on getting where they needed to be. She didn't often venture outside since there were too many variables to consider. Too many places someone could be hiding or watching from afar who she wouldn't be able to manipulate as easily.

She silently walked down the long hall, her black robes gently rustling against the limestone. She stopped and looked into the small courtyard and saw that the leaves of the tree in the center were beginning to turn yellow. Another year would be coming to a close before she knew it. She reached the end of the hallway where it split into the two staircases and could hear the soft voices of late risers still finishing their morning meal. She wondered if Echo was in there, if she was healing well, and if the tonic Stefan had made was easing her pain. She hoped that the boys would keep an eye on her today rather than leaving the full responsibility to the giant condor.

She turned to go up the staircase leading to the large room where she would spend her day. She had asked Eryx to bring

Cassandra up first so she could get a feel as to whether or not the girl would try to flee again. He assured her that she had been apologetic and contrite; however, she wanted to speak with her directly and motivate her to stay with them. She was thinking of possible tasks the girl might be interested in as she walked up the final stone steps but was surprised by a chair placed next to the door with a body sitting in it.

Stefan had a book open in his lap and a mug of coffee in his hands. His hair was tied back and his beard was neatly trimmed. He wore a clean, basil colored tunic and the scent she had smelled on him yesterday was stronger as if he had just applied it.

He looked up as she approached, fixing his green eyes directly on hers and her mind immediately went to the card she had drawn this morning.

"Good morning," was all he said before taking a sip of his coffee and returning to the large book in his lap which had watercolor sketches of flowers and herbs alongside large paragraphs of text.

"Can I help you?" she asked, wondering if Eryx had mixed up the schedule. She had definitely not put him on it for today. She had needed some time to recuperate after last night, though she supposed she could introduce Odessa's idea about the honey if there had indeed been a mix-up.

"Nope," was all he said, smiling into his cup.

"Did Eryx tell you to come up here?" He hadn't mentioned anything when she'd seen him less than an hour ago.

"No, I was actually going to bring it up to him though, see if he wanted to take turns. I tried to grab him after breakfast but he said he had somewhere to be." He shrugged but there was a knowing glint in his eye.

"Take turns with what?" she asked, thoroughly confused.

"Guard duty," he replied, gesturing vaguely to himself and his seat.

"I don't need a bodyguard," she scoffed.

"Apparently you do."

"Don't you have more important things to do?" she asked, not liking the idea of his time being wasted here, on her, while he could be doing something more important.

"I always spend some time during the week researching and brainstorming. I'm sure I can work out a schedule with the rest of your…" he stopped to think for a moment, "inner circle?"

"This really is unnecessary," she argued, but then heard someone else's steps coming hesitantly up the stairs behind her. She huffed and turned to him once before Cassandra reached the top of the landing.

"We will talk about this later," she whispered, angrily.

"Perfect," he responded happily, "I'll come to you."

"Wait no, that's not–"

"Good morning, Cassandra," he interrupted, turning his gaze to the stairwell. "Just give the Widow a moment and she'll be right with you."

She slid into the open door and stomped all the way down to her large chair attempting to get herself focused for a day of interacting with others. She didn't realize until she sat down that she no longer felt anxious about being harmed again, now that she knew someone was just a quick shout away. Maybe that was why Stefan was out there rather than actually being afraid for her safety: moral support. She tried to ignore the tiny flame of warmth blossoming in her chest as Cassandra let herself in and she got to work.

***

When she made it through the morning and her stomach started to grumble in anticipation of a late lunch, she sat for a couple of minutes trying to figure how to tell Stefan that she appreciated his help today but that he really didn't need to continue watching over her. She was sure that the incident with Jonal had been a rare mishap and that it wouldn't happen again. Also, whatever talk they were going to have was not happening and he should just get on with his day. She took a deep breath, peeked her head out the door and was disappointed to see that rather than Stefan, she saw Heren now sitting in the chair polishing a dirty stone.

Usually after her meetings she just waited until her last "orphan" went on their way and silently returned to her room. She couldn't just walk past Heren because then he would sit here all afternoon, but if she let him see her she would be forced to make small talk. Her decision was made for her when something made Heren turn in his seat and he saw the small crack in the door. He darted up and pulled the door open, almost setting Aura off balance.

"Let me get that for you," he said, smiling and holding the door open wide. "We're all glad to see you up and about again. Eryx and Odessa told everyone you were healing well but I think we were still all a bit worried when you didn't resurface."

Aura felt a small knot of guilt in her stomach. She hadn't realized that anyone would be concerned for her though Stefan had also seemed agitated by the fact that she hadn't come out of her room. Rather than provide excuses, she replied, "I hope you haven't been here long."

"I brought Scorpio lunch and told him I could take over for a bit while he helped Eryx with the kids and their training." He bent down to retrieve a small bag from beneath his seat. "We've been spending so many hours out in the forest that I haven't had much time to actually take stock of what we've collected and get them ready for sale or use. It was nice to have some quiet time by myself."

He stood up again and held out his arm for Aura to take.

"Please don't feel like you have to stay with me. I'm fine on my own."

"Nope," Heren said, shaking his head. "Scorpio gave me strict orders to take you down to the library. That's a long trip for a woman of your age, especially one who's still healing."

Alright, maybe they would be having that talk just so she could smack him.

Aura reluctantly took Heren's arm. She had to admit that she had been rather pleased with the change in Heren's attitude the past couple of months. When he first arrived, he was untrusting and hostile. Once he realized that the people here weren't going to harm or judge him, that they weren't responsible for what happened to him in his past life, he had turned into himself, doing as little as possible to earn his keep but not truly being part of the community. Something about Stefan's arrival had changed that. Maybe it was because he had been an outsider as well and someone Heren could claim for himself as a friend. The two of them formed a bridge together into the rest of the group and Aura was glad for it.

Aura didn't like to think about the other people like Heren who didn't fit into the kingdom's strict social rules. He had never explicitly described what happened to him, but he was not in good physical shape when Eryx and Odessa retrieved him. His hair was cut crudely as though someone had just cut it straight across without care. Odessa helped him style it in a more pleasing way shortly after his arrival which is what likely made him warm to her slightly, even if he refused to let any of them in more than that. Though his features were strongly feminine in nature, he expressed that he did not want to be thought of in that way. They quickly spread the word to the rest of the inhabitants who had no problem addressing him in the way that he requested.

Whether it was his new found confidence or sense of belonging, Heren now stood straighter with male swagger. As they walked arm in arm, Aura could also scent something earthy and sweet on him.

"Eryx told me that Scorpio was working on creating some oils. Have you been helping with that as well?"

"I have," Heren replied. "The one I'm wearing now is vanilla and oak. Eryx has been growing some vanilla orchids in the greenhouse which has been useful for us as well as Matilda. I think when we start selling them we're going to pair them with a stone that could also benefit the specific type of elemental: lapis for water, red jasper for fire, you get the idea. Make them a bit more visually appealing and help us jack up the price a bit."

"Sounds wonderful. It's nice to see everyone working together in so many ways. You and Scorpio especially seem to do well bouncing ideas back and forth off of each other."

"Oh, speaking of," he said, trying to be nonchalant but not quite succeeding, "have you heard any news of Odessa's sister?"

Aura tripped over a loose stone through her robes and Heren tightened his grip to catch her before she tumbled.

She assured herself that the glamor was still in place before replying "No, why dear? Have you?"

"No," Heren replied, and he almost sounded disappointed. "I guess the whole incident with Echo made me think about her." It wasn't lost on Aura that they had been talking about "Scorpio" and not Odessa *or* Echo when Heren's mind had strayed to the topic. Another thing to question him about later.

"I didn't realize that Odessa talked about her much. It seems like it's a bit of a sore subject," Aura replied.

"She doesn't. She just mentioned her once or twice when she first introduced me to her niece and nephews. Just recently…" he seemed to be thinking through what to say and Aura could feel her nerves building. "You know what, nevermind, it's not important." She wasn't sure if she was frustrated or relieved that Heren had brought the subject to a close. They reached the stone stairwell going into the cellar, and he stepped in front of her like a gentleman to make sure that she wouldn't trip and fall down the stairs.

When they finally hit the bottom, he reached into his pocket and pulled out a bright orange stone that had swirls of white forming small circles around the diameter. "Before I forget, I wanted to give you this. Carnelian. It should help with healing, especially for the hip area and can be used for protection."

She took the stone, rubbing the smooth surface between her fingers. "How do I use it?"

"You can rub it like you're doing now, or if your injury still hurts you can rub it on that area. If you have pockets on that side you can keep it there so it's in close proximity throughout the day."

"Thank you, for the stone and the company," she said and meant it.

"Thank *you*," Heren replied, smiling. "Stay well." He turned and headed back up the stairs two at a time. Aura waited until he reached the top and then headed down the hallway towards her chambers. Though the day hadn't gone the way she planned, she had to admit she was feeling a bit lighter at the fact that she was appreciated and had been missed.

CHAPTER 57
STEFAN

Stefan had dinner with his usual group of companions, but his nerves made it difficult to focus on the conversation. As he finished his meal, he observed Eryx take a small covered plate from Matilda and walk out with Odessa beside him. He took a piece of buttery lavender shortbread with him as he discreetly followed them to the cellar. Stefan stayed in the staircase as the two knocked and entered Aura's room, and then he quietly crept down the remaining stairs and into the library.

He lurked by the library steps for quite a while, examining the children's books as he waited for the pair to leave. He stayed busy searching for some fictional tales that he thought would entertain Echo. She seemed to enjoy the stories he told her on their trek back to the beach, though he knew that she preferred learning about the kingdom's more curious nocturnal creatures. As a compromise, he looked for tales of dragons and gargoyles, banshees and ghosts, thinking that maybe she would let him read them to her as the nights became longer and the autumn winds blew eerily outside the large window; Hopscotch guarding them from any creatures lurking outside the walls of the fortress.

He hadn't set eyes on the bird today, likely because Echo had been instructed to stay in bed so her scratches and scrapes could heal. At breakfast, he had enlisted Barrett and Callen to help Odessa watch over their sister. While their aunt was capable of consistently applying the tonic, they were to entertain her with card games and puppets and ensure that she was comfortable and well fed. Surprisingly, Barrett had accepted his duty without a single retort. He even looked proud when Stefan checked in on them after lunch and saw that Echo looked rested and content, her redness fading and no signs of infection.

Though Echo seemed to be enjoying the extra attention from her brothers, who were usually too busy to provide her with much, he knew that her mother was likely having more difficulty being fussed over. She said that she didn't need anyone watching over her, but he knew that she must have felt some apprehension about returning to her duties since she kept to her rooms for over a week, despite claiming to be fully healed. He couldn't blame her; he had hidden himself in the woods for over a year after his ordeal. If he'd had someone there watching his back, maybe the transition back into the real world wouldn't have been so difficult. He didn't mind providing that for someone else, especially since it also made him feel better, knowing that she was safe.

He startled when he heard the quiet creak of the door opening down the hallway and quickly scurried up the steps so that the pair wouldn't see him as they went on their way. Once he could no longer hear the sounds of footsteps or quiet whispers outside, he grabbed the books that he found and made his way down the hallway.

He knocked softly and the door immediately pushed out towards him as if she had been expecting him at precisely that moment. When he slid his way in, he was surprised to see that she was actually halfway across the room, adjusting the hood atop her head, which must have been off considering she had just eaten.

"Can you just take that thing off?" he asked, depositing the pile of books he had brought with him on a small side table. "It makes me dizzy."

"It makes you dizzy?" she repeated, incredulously.

"Yes. I don't know, when I looked at you before, you were stooped and haggard and looked like an old woman. Now you're wearing the same thing, but you're taller and you sound different and my eyes can't keep up with what my brain knows." It was true. He felt a bit queasy when they had talked last night. This morning he struggled while looking up at her and kept his eyes down towards his coffee or the book in his lap. The flickering candles in the dimly lit room weren't helping either. He wasn't just saying it so that he could see her face even though he wanted to, badly.

He moved farther into the room and sat down on one of the soft armchairs in order to try and make the room stop spinning.

"Interesting. I suppose that makes sense. You're the only person who has crossed over in a sense from not knowing to knowing. Close your eyes."

His head was already between his knees but he did as he was told and waited. When a couple seconds passed and he didn't hear her doing anything, he looked up. She was sitting in the armchair across from him, arms folded.

"You're still wearing it!"

"Of course I am. I told you to close your eyes so that you didn't have to look at me, not because I was going to strip it off in front of you."

Now that sounded fun.

"Come on, are you that hideous to behold?" he asked, trying to egg her on.

"No. At least I don't think so. But, I'm sure I look significantly different than when you last saw me. I was much younger then. And stronger. Oh and tanner, so much tanner," she added wistfully. "I probably look more like death with the cloak off than with it on."

"So that's it. You're worried that I'll be unimpressed," he said with as sly a smile as he could muster with his stomach still in knots. That would get her.

"Why would I have to impress *you*?" she huffed, though he wondered if maybe she was blushing beneath the guise. "Fine. If it scrambles your brain that much to see me then I'll take it off. Please keep any comments to yourself about how weak and ghastly I look."

"On my honor," he responded as he placed his hand over his heart and attempted to appear serious.

He could tell that she was rolling her eyes behind the veil, but she stood up from her chair.

"Well…" he started, when she didn't appear to be doing anything.

"Close your eyes!"

He did what he was told with a disappointed sigh. No strip show today then.

He acted honorably as he kept his eyes closed and didn't peek. Mostly because he wanted to show her respect but also because he was still a little afraid of her. He could hear her struggling with the large pieces of fabric and as she did so, he was hit with the soft smell of roses. Every time he was near her it was a different flower or herb. She smelled like the garden in the morning when he first walked in, before his nose adjusted to all of the scents dancing around him. She smelled like home. It was killing him.

He peeked one eye open to see that she was still struggling with the large cloak and then quickly adjusted himself before she could notice how much she was affecting him without even trying. He cleared his throat before speaking again, trying to remove the husk from it.

"What's with the smell?"

"Really Stefan? Maybe it's the fact that I wear this giant woolen cloak all day, every day. It's hot, I sweat."

"Okay first of all," he scolded, "quit it with the Stefan stuff. Someone could hear you. Second, why does your sweat smell like roses?"

"I didn't take you for being quite that brainless. There's a reason I've sequestered myself down here. It's soundproof," she responded, a bit muffled as she seemed to be fighting with the heavy cloak. He heard her take a deep breath as if she had freed herself finally from the fabric, but he didn't open his eyes. "We couldn't risk Barrett hearing my voice or anything that I talked about with..." she paused as if not knowing how much to share.

"Your sister."

She didn't respond for a minute, and he figured she wasn't happy about him solving that piece of the puzzle.

"Yes," she said finally, apparently accepting that she had lost that fight already. "That's why I chose this room. No windows for secrets to fly out of."

"Well, regardless, just call me Scorpio like everyone else does. I don't want you to get in the habit and then it unwittingly flies out of your mouth one day."

"I really don't see myself getting 'into the habit' of saying your name, but I'm also not calling you Scorpio."

Maybe that wouldn't be such a bad habit for her to have. Especially if she uttered it in that giant bed. Over and over and over. He could feel heat spreading over his face at the thought and he adjusted his tunic better over his lap again in case she looked over.

"What's wrong with Scorpio?"

She didn't answer, but he could tell that she was rolling her eyes again and it made him smile. He could hear her footsteps moving away from him and then the rustle of drawers opening and clothes being thrown about.

"What about Steve?" She said it with the hint of a smile in her voice, but he couldn't tell if it meant she was joking or if she had decided that she would call him that just to annoy him.

"Steve?" he responded, aghast. "Doesn't quite fit a notorious herbalist *or* the rightful heir to the throne of Serenfawr."

"I thought we were worried about people listening?" She was standing close to him now and the way she said it almost sounded seductive, like she was talking about something else, but that was probably just wishful thinking. He felt her foot nudge his boot and he opened his eyes.

He felt fucking sixteen again. Speechless and awkward.

She looked exactly the same as he remembered. Her hair was the same color. A honeyed hue that shone gold in the dark candle lit room. It was plaited into two braids that hung down either side of her chest. Speaking of her chest, *that* did not look that same and was considerably larger than it was back then, but he didn't want to stare too hard at that particular area. She was slightly paler in her complexion, and she had lost some of the softness of youth in her face. Still, it physically hurt to look at her.

He wanted to grab her hand and pull her into his lap. Stick his nose into the crook of her neck and never come up for air. Feast on her lips and see if she tasted as sweet as she smelled.

She looked down at him on the chaise as if waiting for a response and seemed confused when no sounds came out of his mouth. The sweet floral smell of her had completely engulfed him and that was what his brain latched on to.

"You never explained the roses," he finally said, unable to keep the hoarseness from his voice.

She looked disappointed, like she had hoped that he would say something about her appearance. She had let him in on her little secret. Shown him her true face when so few people these days got the chance. He wanted to give her what she wanted, but he wouldn't even know where to start. He would start describing every beautiful piece of her and would scare her away like a frightened rabbit.

She turned away then and walked to the back of the room and into what looked to be some kind of separate washing area. She returned with something in her hands, looking a bit unsure of herself.

"I don't want you to think that anything is happening here other than us strategizing and discussing the need to know information of this situation. But since you asked..."

She tossed the object at him, and somehow, he was able to catch it without looking away from her face. It wasn't until she gestured impatiently to his hand that he looked down at what was a small white square. It had small pieces of dried roses embedded in it and it was obvious that this was where her smell had come from. This small perfumed bar had likely made its way over every generous peak and valley of her body. He couldn't help but look up at her again and imagine its possible trajectory. Probably starting at that long slender neck of hers. Then maybe under and around her full breasts. Down her soft stomach and between her strong thighs. Likely the same path his tongue would take if she let him.

"Soap, Stefan. It's soap." She dragged both hands down her perfect face. "The fact that I took off the cloak doesn't seem to have helped with your scrambled brain."

Definitely made it worse, he thought.

"Where did you get it from?" It probably wouldn't be difficult to make soap. If he requested some lye from the market and got one of the Reds to help him out with the heating process, she could have her pick of floral and herbal scents.

"Odessa brings it back for me whenever her and Eryx go out on a supply run or one of their retrievals. I obviously don't get out much so it's a little taste of the outside world." She looked so incredibly sad when she said it and he didn't like that one bit.

"Could we do something about that?" he asked, thinking of all of the places on the island that he wanted to show her.

"Obviously not. I don't want anyone seeing me," she replied, crossing her arms and bringing his gaze back to her ample chest.

"What if it's night?" he implored, unable to keep the eagerness from his voice. "It won't help with the tan, but I can help you in the sparring ring if you like. Get you feeling stronger again."

"Even if it's dark, someone could hear us."

"Not if we don't speak. Working on stealth at the same time wouldn't be a bad thing. I could come here beforehand. We could plan on what techniques we want to work on and then just use our bodies out there."

She blushed a bit at his last statement, and he had to admit it had sounded a little suggestive.

"Don't you already have enough going on with the garden and the oils and the training and the guard duty?" she asked, looking for an excuse but Stefan detected hopefulness in her eyes.

He stood up, the dizziness issue solved, with a dominant urge to be closer to her. He closed the short distance between them before responding. "The workload in the back garden has lessened. The upkeep isn't as difficult in the colder months, though I would like to show you what I've done before all of the pretty things start dying, even if it is by moonlight."

Her eyes were directly on his and she nodded, "I'd like that."

"I could cut out a couple of those mornings and use that time to sleep in." If it was in her bed, all the better.

Maybe that last thought showed on his face because she took a step back. "If it does become too much you'll let me know. And you really don't have to worry about me in the throne room. I appreciate the thought, but I'm sure nothing like that will happen again. Odessa…"

"Didn't see it last time, and might not see it again," he interrupted. "It's ridiculous that you were alone like that to begin with. Everyone else typically works in pairs or in a larger group. Why should you be any different?"

She opened her mouth to argue, but he could tell that nothing she wanted to say would be an appropriate response. She obviously felt that her own happiness was less important than everyone else's since she was content with living alone in a freezing cold basement just to ensure the well being and safety of others; however, stating that out loud would make her seem like a martyr.

"If Heren or I aren't acceptable, I'm sure I could get Hopscotch to volunteer."

"Please don't." She shivered but then looked up at him curiously. "You can't communicate with him also, can you?"

"Unfortunately I can," he replied. "And he apparently is not a fan of me." He began moving towards the door to leave before she could change her mind about training with him.

"Oh, how sad for you," she laughed. "To have someone who isn't enamored with you." She gestured to the books, raising an eyebrow. "I'm guessing those aren't for your own enjoyment."

You're obviously not. "They're for Echo, I thought I could read them with her while she's stuck inside healing."

Her smile was tinged with sadness, "I'm sure she'll love them."

"If there are any particular ones you think she would like, I could take them to her." He shrugged, wishing he could offer something better.

"Thank you," she said, and he felt suddenly shy at the warmth in her voice. "I'll think about that, and I suppose I'll see you tomorrow night." She said it hesitantly, but he sensed an excited sparkle in her eyes.

He nodded and walked quietly out the door before he overstayed his welcome. Now he had an excuse to see her, possibly every night if he played his cards right. He would make sure that this time, he didn't give her a reason to walk away.

CHAPTER 58
AURA

As Aura left her room the next morning she kept finding reasons to wince at her behavior with Stefan. She had definitely teased him, and flirted with him and showed him her soap. She had basically thrown herself at him. The man who literally tried to bury her alive.

Though he seemed so intent on ensuring their match all those years ago, something must have changed since then. He hadn't looked all that impressed when she took off her cloak. Maybe a smile or some kind of compliment would have been nice, but he couldn't think of one thing to say. Rare for him. She tried not to dwell on it, but it had stung.

Maybe she was just tired of being the third wheel in Odessa and Eryx's non-relationship. She was *definitely* tired of that, and at the moment, Stefan was the only other person who she could actually be herself with, which obviously was making her feel more playful and hungry for attention. That's all this was. She was sure she was looking forward to seeing him tonight only because her usual companions had left immediately after a quick breakfast to pick up a new young one. They wouldn't be back until after nightfall, possibly tomorrow morning.

She just wished that he didn't have to be so good looking. Couldn't he be the scrawny, awkward boy he'd been when she first met him?

She shook her head as she held her skirts, making sure she didn't trip as she made her way up the narrow staircase. Who was she trying to fool? Even at that first meeting all those years ago, she had felt *something*. The need to see more of him. Like he was someone important, not in the royal sense, but someone important to *her*. His smell had been different as well. Not the usual overbearing scent that boys her age used. Something musky and earthy but also sweet.

When she saw him for the second time outside the amphitheater, she had felt a flutter in her heart that he was actually the prince and that there was a possibility they would be matched. She'd needed to remind herself of her plan to play down her abilities so she'd match with Vitus and stay in her village. It was a long and confusing day, in which her head and her heart had been pulled in a variety of different directions. Taking that final step past the barrier line after she'd noticed the mark and saw him watching her from the trees felt like the most difficult thing she'd ever done.

She hadn't regretted her decision. She loved Vitus and the home they had made together and obviously, their children. She was glad that she had been so close to home when their parents died so she could take in Odessa and then Eryx.

That sense of loss had always been there though, and that exciting time every spring when the village was readying for trials always put her in a funk. Though it seemed impossible to mourn for someone who had been a stranger to her, she did so every year without fail. The first spring in the fortress had probably been the worst few months of her life since she had lost practically everyone she'd ever cared for other than her sister and their steadfast friend. She had wanted that frigid icy winter to last forever rather than be met with the season that brought hope for everyone else but only loss for her.

This past spring had been the first one where some hope returned. The realization that Stefan had survived made it seem like maybe things could get better for her as well. That was how she viewed him at first. As a symbol of hope. The more time she spent with him, however, the more frequently she found him infiltrating her thoughts. How he was so eager to please and connect with others. How he looked directly into the hearts of people and somehow knew immediately how to break down their defenses. Something that she had never been very good at. Now that he knew who she was, he was already doing the same with her. She was afraid that while he saw her as just another person to take care of, she was already becoming too attached. She was lonely and craving something that would break her out of the dark, cold monotony she had gotten so used to. She would train with him, get that little dose of exercise and excitement but would close her heart off from anything else.

As she approached the split in the eastern stairway and her heart jumped into her throat, she knew that was easier said than done. She made her way up the steps, expecting to see Stefan on the landing with his cup of coffee, but when she looked up, rather than a verdant colored tunic, she saw one of bright crimson.

Lavender raced down the stairs and took her arm, the girl's silky black hair whipping around her as she turned.

"Good morning Widow," she said, her voice husky with a bit of a southern accent. While the girl was significantly shorter than Aura, her grip on her arm was strong and steady, "I heard Scorpio and Heren talking about taking turns watching out for you and since we were meeting later today anyway, I volunteered."

Aura was mostly meeting with her own children today as well as some of the other younger ones but Lavender looked eager to help and Aura didn't want to turn her down and make her think that she didn't trust her. She liked the fire elemental, though outside of the fortress she likely would have been too intimidated by her startling beauty.

"That's very kind of you," she said, trying to be better about accepting help. "I hope you have something to keep you occupied while you wait."

Lavender nodded while gesturing to the chair she had been sitting in. Aura took notice of a cup of tea that smelled unsurprisingly of lavender, accompanied by two biscuits on the side table and a book on...soap making?

"Scorpio approached me and Yakov about a new project this morning. We'll need to wait on the materials, but I figured I would start reading up on the process."

Aura couldn't decide if she wanted to smile or groan, but the smile won out.

CHAPTER 59
AURA

The days that Aura saw her children were both a blessing and a curse. She loved studying the subtle ways that they changed from week to week. An inch grown here. A voice deepening there. A tighter fitting tunic. A new hairstyle.

She made herself focus on the fact that she was still with them. She had not taken her own life, leaving them behind. She had not gone along with Donovan to the city and abandoned them. Had not married some other stranger who might have hurt or neglected them. She'd taken on this new persona which ensured their safety. Her choices had proven to be even more wise since Jonal stabbed her and ran. If he did speak about where he came from, she didn't think people would be too concerned about a Widow run orphanage. There were others in existence after all.

She often thought about how old the children would need to be for her to trust them with her secret. Though the boys were becoming more mature, she was afraid of how they would take the news and if they would out her for hiding from them out of spite, rather than be happy about their reunion. She felt like they would need a few more years before they would truly understand the plight of a woman in the kingdom and how everything she had ever done had been to keep them warm, fed and safe.

Barrett and Callen were both in self-deprecating moods following Echo's brave rescue. Barrett felt that he should have heard her, even though he had been sleeping and Aura was positive that neither Cassandra nor Echo verbally expressed their plans to anyone else. The only thing he could have heard was the quiet opening and closing of doors, light footsteps on the stones or the gentle splash of the boats being pushed into the water. She was curious as to why Hopscotch hadn't sounded the alarm, yet he *was* just a bird. He might have some level of intelligence, but maybe that didn't include foresight.

Callen was also perturbed by the fact that he hadn't picked up on Echo's intentions. Aura assumed that Echo had heard Cassandra wake up in the early morning hours and followed her, and therefore, Callen wouldn't have been able to pick up that kind of split second decision. Both boys were still figuring out the extent of their powers and were frustrated by the split between what they wanted to do and what they were currently able to accomplish. Barrett mentioned he had been doing some research recently and had read something about "aural manipulators" who were able to whisper into the ears of others and provide suggestions that the person assumed to be their own. Since he was currently able to pick up on others' conversations, he felt like this might be a power that he would eventually be able to work up to. During their session, Aura suggested to him that he start small by attempting to send messages to his brother from varying distances within the fortress.

Echo didn't come up for her meeting, which hadn't surprised Aura but still upset her. She would have liked to see her healing and been reassured that the encounter with the raspberry bush and the men hadn't caused long-lasting emotional pain. Even if she made it up to the throne room with Odessa, she wouldn't have described her harrowing experience herself or expressed her feelings verbally. Echo still didn't speak in "the Widow's" presence, even when accompanied by one of the few individuals who had been given the rare privilege of hearing her sweet whispered voice, namely her aunt, Eryx and her brothers. She wondered whether or not Echo would speak to her once she eventually knew the truth, or if she wouldn't even remember her own mother.

She met with a couple of the other children and then saw Lavender who caught her up on some of the work she had been doing in the garden and greenhouse as well as the forge. Though

Aura had felt a bit down after seeing the boys, she had to admit that she was feeling significantly lighter following that last meeting. She couldn't take all of the credit for the fire elemental's progress but it was another confirmation that they were doing something good here.

Though physically unharmed, Lavender was emotionally distraught when she had arrived at the fortress over a year ago. Though *not* using her power was what got her in trouble in the first place, she was still very hesitant to test her limits and expand on her abilities, worried she would hurt someone else. Aura had assured her that literally "playing with fire" was the best way to learn to control it, especially in a new environment where she wouldn't be as emotionally triggered. Working with Yakov had been the first step since the forge was made of stone and he was a fire elemental as well, who wouldn't be harmed if she did have any accidents. Apart from his fireproof skin, Yakov was also extremely patient as well as warm-hearted and very free with compliments which was another thing Lavender had been in dire need of.

How the girl's husband could have found any fault with her appearance was unfathomable to Aura, and somehow she became even more beautiful as time passed. Whether it was from depression or starving herself in order to better meet her husband's expectations, Lavender's skin looked sallow and her hair was thinning when she'd first walked through the doors of the fortress. Because of her difficult relationship with food, as well as the fact that she likely unwillingly spent much of her time in the kitchen to fulfill her "wifely duties", Aura felt like having her work with Matilda would be the wrong choice. Sure enough, having her do something so different from her old life had seemed to empower the girl and soon enough, her olive skin was glowing and her soft curves had returned.

Lavender seemed very excited about the new project that Stefan had suggested to them at breakfast and she described to her what she'd found while reading up on it this morning. The process would require her to keep the soap mixture heated at a simmer for a full hour. The other projects that she typically worked on did not require as much stamina so this would be an interesting challenge. She was also excited to help out with selecting the different herbs and flowers that went into the bars, though this particular subject made Aura feel a twinge of jealousy for some reason.

In truth, the project would be the perfect stepping stone for what she wanted Lavender to achieve next. For a while she had been thinking about having her try her hand on people; however, she was sure that the girl wouldn't react well. If Stefan and her started working together on the soap making process, maybe he could also talk to her about how her abilities might be used in a healing capacity: lowering a fever or gently increasing a body temperature if there was a threat of hypothermia. If he discussed the possibility with her hypothetically, maybe she would be more willing to make an attempt if a situation did arise.

She thought of the two of them working together in the forge or the kitchen or the laboratory, Lavender slowly testing her power on him by increasing his body temperature by a degree at a time. Maybe the focus and energy required would have Lavender's temperature rising as well until they were both warm and flushed. He would watch enthralled as a bead of sweat made its way down her gently sloped neck until it disappeared into the line of her tunic, between her ample breasts. Their breaths would quicken and the magnetic pull between them would increase until…

A gentle knock on the door pulled her out of her not so pleasant day dream.

She stepped behind the elaborately carved, wooden privacy screen before gently opening the door with a flick of her finger. When she saw Stefan move into the room and close the door, she took a moment to collect herself before stepping out from behind the screen. He would have been concerned if he didn't see her in the room, but for some reason, she couldn't get her heart rate to go down or her breathing to slow. Apparently it was rather obvious because immediately upon seeing her, Stefan furrowed his brows, closing the distance between them.

"Are you alright?"

"Fine," she replied, attempting to feign nonchalance. He didn't look convinced, frowning as he continued to scan her face. He held the backs of his fingers to her cheek which did not help her condition.

"You're warm, but not considerably so." He removed his hand and she felt the coldness in its absence. "Do you just want to stay in tonight?"

She knew that by "stay in" he meant stay in her bed alone to recover from whatever imaginary illness was plaguing her, while he stayed far away in his own room. In her current state, she couldn't help but imagine what would happen if she said something clever like "only if you stay with me" or "only if you promise to help me feel better."

Instead she went with, "I think it's just stuffy down here. I could probably use some fresh air."

"I think that's probably an understatement," he replied smiling. He looked down at her ensemble as if he had just noticed it now that he was no longer concerned about her welfare. She blushed when his eyes took in the too apparent curves of her body in the tightly fitting black leggings and long sleeved dark colored undershirt that she used to wear under her tunics in the cooler months.

"I thought it would allow for better movement and help me blend in with the shadows," she said, almost apologetically. "My usual robes are a bit difficult to get around in and my old tunics would attract attention from anyone who spotted us."

He swallowed and turned his gaze away from her, taking a step back. He sat down on the divan behind him and whatever expression had been on his face was replaced by something more serious.

"Before we go I wanted to discuss something. If we're going to be friends, I want to clear the air first."

She moved and leaned against the arm of the chair across from him. The word "friend" should have made her feel good, but for some reason, it sat uneasily in her gut.

"Alright," she replied, unable to keep the hesitancy from her voice.

He looked up at her and took a deep breath, "I know the first day we met, I wasn't exactly," he paused as if thinking up an appropriate word, "considerate."

"You mean when you pushed me into an earthen grave and then threw dirt on top of me?"

"Yes, that," he replied, sheepishly.

She crossed her arms over her chest, unable to keep the smug look from her face at the fact that he was actually apologizing, "I suppose all's fair in love and war right?" She meant to say it offhandedly. Obviously trials were a combination of exactly those two things and yet after she said it, she could feel the warmth returning to her face. Luckily, he was still uncomfortably looking away from her.

"Even so, it was a little much."

He looked so apologetic that she didn't want to tease him on the subject further. Yes, the stunt had resulted in half a lifetime of nightmares for her; however, she didn't think they would have plagued her so frequently if she had known that like her, he had also escaped his fate. She didn't think she'd had that particular dream since he'd resurfaced.

"I'm not trying to sound cruel, but it seemed that you got what was coming to you." That did indeed sound cruel so she added, "I'm glad that we both made it out alive."

He nodded as he clasped his hands together and she couldn't help but notice that they were nice hands. Long and slender fingers atop heavily calloused palms, the fingernails clean even though he spent so much time working in the soil. She couldn't hold in the tiny shudder that coursed through her when she thought about how they might feel on her skin.

He continued, oblivious to her gawking, "I'm not attempting to make excuses for my behavior, but I just wanted you to know that the reason I was so set on our match was that my father told me his death had been foreseen. He wanted to ensure that I was matched before his death so that the title of king could be passed to me. Obviously my mother could never act as regent on her own, and I suppose that being so young, it would have helped my case if I already had a queen by my side at his passing. I'm sure he wanted to remove Talon as the middleman since he knew that getting him to vacate the throne once he sat his cruel, egotistical ass upon it would be difficult. Unfortunately, my father underestimated him."

She opened her mouth to speak but was unsure of what to say as different emotions passed through her. She could very easily understand why someone she now knew as kind and generous would appear so demanding and unforgiving if he had just been given knowledge that his father was going to die and that he would have to take over the throne at such a young age. He was just trying to gain some sort of control over a situation that seemed incredibly dire.

She felt sorry for him. Then suddenly sorry for herself that her younger self thought he wanted them to match because of something he saw in *her*. He had indeed been that quiet, sweet looking boy she met that day, but the connection she felt with him had apparently been all in her mind. She was just a means to achieve his sense of royal duty. The feelings that were creeping up on her needed to be extinguished immediately.

Stefan was looking up at her pensively as if trying to read the expression on her face. She turned away before she could get lost in the green of his eyes. She searched her brain for something appropriate to say and then his last comment finally registered. "You think Talon was the one who was responsible for your father's death?" She had whispered it, terrified suddenly of being accused of treason herself even though she was the one who had assured Stefan only yesterday that the room was soundproof.

He looked at her disbelievingly for a moment as if he were shocked she hadn't figured it out but then shook his head. "I'm sorry, I just forget that people who didn't grow up in 'His Majesty's' presence aren't aware of how much of a piece of shit he really is."

It felt strange to her that she was learning about the family dynamics of the Serenfawrs and that they apparently had just as many issues as the rest of the kingdom. Likely more.

"You're sure of this? Do you have proof?"

He shook his head, "No. It's just little bits and bobs of information. Pieces that fit together too nicely when I had a week in a cell to think through all of the possibilities. If he hadn't had me to use as a scapegoat, it would have been glaringly obvious that he was the culprit but luckily for him, he did. Someone he hated his entire life who was already distracted by," he looked up at her but then quickly looked away, "other things."

"Well yes, your father's death being foretold the day of your trials, I could easily see you having a lot on your mind."

He nodded and they were quiet for a moment. She tried to form her next question carefully. "Do you think you'll ever go back? Take what's rightfully yours?"

He shrugged and she could see that he felt embarrassed about the situation. Like he thought that he should have done something by now but hadn't. She knew by the way he behaved in the fortress that he would be a wonderful ruler and that maybe he would even want to make some changes to the rules of the kingdom that forced all of the people here to run from it. She stepped off the arm of the chair and sat next to him, gently pulling his hand into hers. She saw him swallow and then threaded his fingers through her own. She tried to tamper down the warmth that was spreading through her. She was supposed to be listening to him and easing his pain. Not getting all atingle about someone who just saw her as a friend.

He spoke quietly and carefully. "Before I came here I didn't think it would ever happen. That I'd ever feel strong or confident enough to do so. I don't particularly care about the power or the title, but I could definitely see ways in which I could improve the kingdom. Give some of the power back to the people," he squeezed her hand and added, "just like you've done here." She scrunched up her face and was about to argue but he continued on before she could. "I also promised my mother that I would come back for her one day, even though she tried to tell me not to." He laughed. "You remind me of her. A little too much actually."

Any flames that had sprung up in her with the touch of his hand were quickly doused. Comparing a woman to one's mother was the least romantic thing a man could ever do. Even if this particular mother was the queen herself.

"It must be difficult being separated from her knowing that she's with him." She rubbed her thumb gently over his skin. "Maybe training together will be good for both of us if it helps you feel more confident. I know you've been spending lots of time with Eryx and the others, but it's probably time you faced a real opponent."

He laughed, turning towards her and she was glad to see a bright smile grace his face again after such a serious conversation. "And that's what you are? 'A real opponent?'"

"Well, we are supposedly equals, aren't we? And last time we faced each other I left you shaking in your boots." She stood up, reluctantly releasing his hand, though for a second it seemed like he wasn't going to let her go. If he held on, there was a very high chance they wouldn't leave the room at all. She could see herself crawling into his lap and lightly playing with the strands of his hair as he told her stories about his past. Just breathing in the masculine, clean, woodsy scent of him, hearing his heartbeat in his chest.

But he did let her go and stood, breaking the spell. "That was fourteen years ago, and your mind tricks don't work on me anymore."

She scoffed, "Or so you think."

CHAPTER 60
STEFAN

Stefan was in trouble.

He had come to Aura's room thinking he was going to have the upper hand and instead, he found himself becoming more and more jelly-headed with each passing moment.

He had stalked into the room with a plan and a swagger and was thrown off immediately just by the look of her. She was flushed and glassy eyed and though initially he thought she was unwell, another thought had come to him: perhaps she was a fellow romance novel reader and had been entertaining herself with something especially salacious. He had almost been afraid for a moment that *someone else* had been entertaining her, but there was no sign of an amorous visitor.

The next deadly strike had been her outfit. Knowing her, she really *had* put the ensemble together based purely on function, but was she really that oblivious about the tantalizing shape of her body and how much it would affect him? If it was anyone else, he would have assumed he was being purposefully seduced.

Telling her the truth about that day helped douse some of the heat he was feeling. He had wanted them to start fresh without any old secrets hanging between them. Strangely, rather than being relieved or understanding, she had looked almost disappointed. When it came to Aura, he obviously had no idea what he was doing.

Just when he thought he had mistakenly upset her somehow, she had stalked over to him and took his hand. She hadn't judged him for his inaction but instead, listened and made him feel warm and accepted. It sparked the hope in him that one day he might be able to face his uncle and rescue his mother. That he had people who believed in him and who might stand with him. People he wanted to change the world for.

If he hadn't already been completely smitten over her, the nail in the coffin was when she'd given him another glimpse of the old Aura by telling him, in no uncertain terms, that she was going to kick his ass. As he followed her silently up the fortress steps, her own ass barely contained within the tight pants and mere inches from his face, he knew he didn't stand a chance.

The large stone patio where sparring practice took place was far enough away from the main fortress that it was likely no one would be strolling around the area so late. As a precaution, Aura fashioned a dark colored scarf around her head and mouth which made her look like some kind of alluring assassin. That only excited him more.

They agreed that before anything else, they would work on getting her body moving again, since the only exercise she had been getting lately was walking up and down the stairs from the throne room to the cellar. If he was being honest, he wasn't likely that far behind her in regards to cardio and strength. Working out with her at night would give him a nice advantage over Eryx during the day.

As they reached the archway that led out of the fortress, she stopped and motioned for him to go ahead of her, either to cover her from anyone coming in the opposite direction or to show her the way. Her footfalls were silent behind him, and he kept wanting to turn around to make sure that she was still following. He led her down the stone stairs that went down to the forge and then back up to the highest point of the island. Though he felt a bit of a chill in the air when they'd first started, he had warmed by the time they reached the top. The moon was bright, only a few days away from being full, and he was afraid for a moment that Aura would be scared off by it; however, as he stopped and slowly turned around, she continued walking as if he weren't even there. She stalked across the stone patio, the edge of which overlooked a steep verdant decline and the river below, and gazed up at the glowing silver orb above. The two had likely not seen each other in quite a while so he gave them a moment to catch up.

When he first laid eyes upon her all those years ago, she seemed to be a daughter of the sun. Golden and bright. Maybe it was because he now only saw her true face in the darkness surrounded by candlelight, but the woman before him seemed so much more a creature of the night. Darkness and starlight. The duality intrigued him.

After a minute he quietly walked up beside her and nudged her with his elbow. Though the lower half of her face remained covered, he could see the excitement and happiness in her eyes as she gazed up at him. A thrill raced through him; he had been the one to encourage her to take this step and she was taking it with him. Too soon, she gave one last look up at the round gibbous and then nodded at him, her features now determined with a single eyebrow raised in challenge as if saying *let's get on with it then.*

This morning, while she was busy, he spent some time in the library looking up books on calisthenics. He took advantage of the flat empty space and led her in lunges and squats, bear crawls and sprints, back and forth across the large expanse. Though apparently his heart and lungs were in better shape than hers, his muscles burned and he was thankful for the light breeze that swept around them. He was sure it was more pronounced due to her reemergence above ground. He didn't know how she did it, constantly being stuck indoors, so far away from the element that fed her power. He figured that the wind still found its way to her through the cracks in the throne room windows. In contrast, it seemed almost joyous now as it swept up some of the leaves around them. The first ones to give in to autumn's call.

Though her dark clothing made it difficult to tell whether she was as sweaty as he, Stefan could hear the sound of her panting through each exercise. Even so, she refused to slow down or give up. He tried not to show too much pride at the fact that he was in better shape than her, but it felt good when she took twice the time to make it from one side to the other. As he waited for her to finish her last set of forward jump squats, he sat down on the large stone wall that surrounded the patio and tried to think of some other ways he could utilize the space to target the various muscle groups. Maybe lunging or stepping up and down from the wall where he sat, which went up to his thigh. Maybe even jogging here from the fortress, though that might make it more difficult for them to notice if someone else was wandering around nearby.

He watched her finish the last few jumps. He was impressed that she still kept perfect form, her backside much lower to the ground than his had been, though he wished she was facing the other direction so that he could get a better view. Finally she stood up and plopped immediately down beside him on the wall. He passed her the canteen he was drinking from, curious if she would take it, and she did, taking a deep swallow without even wiping the spigot. When she passed it back, he fought the urge to take another sip in order to get a taste of her lips.

They sat for a moment and the only sounds were the faint lapping of the river water against the cliffs, the crickets in the woods surrounding them and her gentle breathing. The silence between them was necessary, but for him, it was difficult to just be with someone without filling in the gaps with words. He had spent so many years alone and now he had become so reliant on using words to make connections with the others, proving to them that he was worthy of their company. In the silence he felt naked and vulnerable. Like it was completely up to the other person to decide how they wanted to think of him in the moment, and he couldn't lighten the mood with a joke or impress them with some kind of factoid.

As if she could sense that he was uncomfortable, Aura bumped his shoulder and looked up at him in silent question. He shrugged and attempted to smile, but he knew he probably looked awkward and insecure. She stood and reached for his hand. He couldn't help himself from crowding into her space for a moment as she pulled him up from his seat. They were so close that she had to tilt her head back to look into his eyes. She assessed him just like they had in their very first meeting. Her breathing had slowed after resting, but it quickened again, their proximity making his heart race as much as the jumps and sprints. Though the bottom half of her face remained covered, he could sense a subtle shift as if she were gently opening her mouth or biting down on her lip. He felt his fingers twitch as if they were going to reach up and pull the covering down from her face but as if sensing his next move, she took a not so subtle step back, widening the space between them.

He cleared his throat awkwardly and winced when it was so much louder than any of the sounds around them. She smiled at him though something in the expression didn't reach her eyes. They stood for a moment, wishing for some way to move on from the awkwardness but finding it difficult in the silence. Suddenly she smiled knowingly and held up a triumphant finger. She closed her eyes and when she opened them again, they were the color of starlight. He recognized them as being the same eyes he had seen at their trial and also the ones that he had thought to be cataracts in the throne room. Outside, with the almost full moon behind her, they held less terror and more wonder. He didn't understand at first how she was using her powers since he couldn't seem to take his eyes off of her, but when she gestured in frustration, he shook his head and looked around, noticing that they were now standing in a garden. It was a nice garden. Nothing especially beautiful or unique. He couldn't mask his confusion for a moment, but then he understood. He felt a grin stretch across his face as he leaned into her ear and whispered so quietly that it couldn't be heard by even a bat overhead or other nocturnal predator.

"Mine is much more impressive than that."

CHAPTER 61
STEFANIA

Stefania Gaspard sat on her velvet cushioned purple throne, watching the pale morning sunlight slowly creep across the marble floor of the elaborately decorated imperial sanctuary of the Serenfawrs. She was glad for the heavy, emerald colored gown that covered her body as the chilly morning air whistled in from one side of the immense throne room to the other, the first sign that autumn was on its way to the kingdom.

Her husband kept a highly unusual sleep schedule. He always retired before the sun set and awoke long before it reappeared. When she first found herself in her nightmarish situation fourteen years prior, she was initially relieved that he went to bed so early. She assumed she would be able to spend some of those nighttime hours alone: reading, baking, grieving or scheming. Unfortunately, she learned quickly that Talon still expected her to awaken him with loving kisses and caresses, join him for breakfast in their private dining room and then accompany him to his morning meetings as the sun gradually made its way over the ocean from the east.

Sometimes when he shook her awake in those dark hours, her mind regressed and for a beautiful moment she thought it was Claude telling her that the baby was crying and she needed to feed him. Then she would notice the smell of him, the different feel of his finger pads on her skin, a glimpse of the face in the moonlight that was somehow hideous and handsome at the same time and the illusion was shattered.

She must have unconsciously been staring at that duplicitous face because he reached across the arms of their thrones and took her hand in his. His bright blue eyes shone as if thrilled to have caught her attention. Sometimes she wished that someone would knock her over the head and let her forget everything that happened in the past so maybe she could at least be happy for a few moments. She was sure it wouldn't take long for him to splinter the image of perfection but a minute or two of thinking that she had a handsome, doting, powerful husband would be nice. She gave him what she hoped was a loving smile. Her thoughts and feelings towards him were so putrid she couldn't believe she didn't reek of them, but somehow, Talon never questioned her love or loyalty to him.

Stefania turned her gaze toward her step-son who looked to be counting the tiles on the throne room floor. She wasn't sure what she would do if she somehow did free herself from Talon but was left with Oliver in his place. He didn't seem to have his father's deep seeded cruelty; however, she wasn't sure if she would be able to convince him to follow through with the legacy that her true husband wanted for this kingdom. She felt like she was biding her time until Stefan came back like he'd promised but was unsure when that might happen if at all. It was like holding her breath underwater without knowing how far she was from the surface.

She had considered having another child. She was only in her early thirties when Claude was murdered, but she couldn't bring herself to carry the child of his killer. There were also no guarantees the child wouldn't take after its father, and if it was male it would still be second in line to Oliver. Talon had been confused for a while about why she had never become pregnant, since they apparently had such a vigorous sex life; or so he thought. She had used her powers in a magnitude of ways since saving her son, including the bedroom. Though he never actually touched her body, she still had to live through the scenes she projected into his mind. Sometimes she felt like it might be easier to lay under him like a dead fish rather than put so much effort into her visions, though keeping him satisfied was what had kept her alive and free to do what she wished in the castle.

Her apparent infertility wasn't that suspicious since she and Claude hadn't conceived another child after Stefan; however, that was due to Claude's plans for the kingdom rather than a lack of a healthy womb. It was still to be determined whether they made the right choice when it came to narrowing the line of inheritance, though she knew saving multiple children would have been a much more complicated task. She would have had to kill Talon outright if he actually caused the death of one of her children and that would have surely ended with her own death as well.

At eight and forty, she was seven years Talon's senior. She always wondered if he would eventually tire of her in favor of some lady in waiting or girl from the brothel, but night after night he came to her alone. Part of her felt like he would never leave her in peace. That having his way with her was some never-ending dig at Claude. She often thought that Talon saw her as a strange combination of wife and mother. She had mistakenly taken on that role with him when she and Claude first matched, and Talon was just a sad lonely little boy. If she had ignored him like everyone else, would he have had the same resentment for the men that she'd truly loved? She knew there were other reasons behind his treachery but in the years she spent keeping her secrets to herself, it was hard not to mentally replay her decisions, wondering if different choices might have resulted in better outcomes. It was either that or attempt to make plans for a future that was impossible to predict.

Her thoughts were interrupted by the guards opening the door and the newest of Talon's advisors stiffly walked in. She couldn't fault the man for his nerves since a significant number of his predecessors had "mysteriously disappeared." It seemed as though she and Oliver were the only ones incapable of getting on the king's bad side.

Talon's treatment of his own son had always been a puzzle to her as he had always been so harsh with hers. He rarely gave Oliver a second thought, no matter how much trouble he got into outside of the castle walls. Either everyone was too afraid to complain to him, or he really didn't care what his son did as long as he survived and didn't attempt to overthrow him.

Sometimes Stefania thought that Talon saw Oliver as nothing more than a fail-safe. Like he was some kind of indestructible immortal whose son would only be needed to take over the kingdom in the most unlikely of circumstances. They had apparently made some kind of arrangement to ensure that Oliver was always at these meetings. As was typical the prince's clothes were rumpled, a heavy stubble graced his chin, and his light brown hair was untamed beneath his crown; she was sure he was just arriving home from whatever debauchery he had engaged in the night before. Maybe that was the reason Oliver hadn't yet spent any time in the dungeons. Their schedules were so opposing, this was the only hour of the day he and the king laid eyes upon each other.

It also likely helped his cause that he had made himself scarce following Stefan's death. His older cousin had been the shining star in his world and he hadn't taken his supposed treachery well. If he had attempted to find comfort in his aunt-turned-step-mother, Talon might have seen him as a threat, but he had mostly hidden himself away as a child and then ran wild as he grew into a man. He had yet to find an appropriate match in the five years since his trial, and therefore, there hadn't been any reason for him to tone down his behavior. She couldn't blame the girls who threw themselves at him at every opportunity. He had his father's countenance, strength, and fair eyes and hair with his late mother's slightly darker coloring in his skin. He was Stefan's opposite in every way, which was both a blessing and a curse. A blessing because she didn't have to deal with reminders of her son when she wasn't looking for them. A curse because she missed him endlessly and would kill for the smallest hint as to what he might look like now as a grown man. She knew in her bones he was still alive.

Every morning she held her breath, waiting to hear what the advisor would report; terrified, but also hoping he would say something suggesting Stefan was still somewhere within the confines of the kingdom. She would fret over any tale of a criminal who had jet black hair or a skill in foraging or potion making. When she got the chance, she would quietly visit the dungeons to make sure her son wasn't among the hundreds of prisoners awaiting their death sentences.

The advisor reached the bottom of the dais, and Talon withdrew his hand from hers so the advisor could kiss his ring as he bowed. She kept an unaffected smile on her face though her heart raced for news, and she wanted to gag at the phony display of reverence. The man's hands were clenched before him and his eyes looked everywhere but at Talon, as if there was news he was reluctant to share. His only saving grace was that he was a Red, like the king, so he wouldn't be incinerated alive if the news was ill-received.

"Speak," Talon commanded, the tone firm but not unkind. She could see a fire already burning in his knowing eyes.

The advisor tried to stand straight as he nervously fidgeted with the edge of his tunic sleeve.

"We located a boy attempting to sell a ring at the market. He was bragging about stabbing a Widow in order to retrieve it. A guard overheard him and he was brought in for questioning. Some of the information he provided was…interesting to say the least."

"I don't particularly care for your thoughts on the intelligence," Talon replied, icily, though she could already feel the heat radiating off of him. "I can form my own opinions on the boy's story."

The advisor winced. He needed to improve at speaking to the king's vanities. None of them lasted long enough to tame the beast. She would have been able to do the job flawlessly after so many years of study.

"Yes, Your Majesty. Would you like me to bring him in?"

Talon flitted the man away like a pesky fly and then looked at her with a knowing smile as if it were the two of them against the world. She rolled her eyes at the man's foolishness and smiled back demurely like she knew he wanted her to.

The advisor retreated, though he walked backwards until the very last second, as if making sure the king was not going to do anything to him before he could even finish this simple task. While all were aware that Talon was a talented Red and well-trained fighter, there were rumors about what else he was capable of. Even she was unaware of the full extent of his powers. She sometimes caught him in the dead of night acting peculiar; however, she couldn't be sure if he was hiding something from her or if it was strictly madness.

When the doors reopened, the advisor strode back in followed by two guards with a fair haired, teenage boy between them. He looked as though being brought before the king was quite an inconvenience to him. She wasn't sure if Talon would be amused by his gall or enraged by his lack of respect.

The two guards genuflected and when the boy didn't immediately join them, one of them rose, grabbed him by the neck like a naughty kitten and forced him to kneel. When the guard finally released him, he stood, straightening his tunic and turned to give the guard a dirty look. Talon cleared his throat and the boy finally acknowledged his presence.

"We hear you've gotten into some trouble, young man," Talon started with a smile. Apparently the boy's haughtiness was entertaining to him, though the grin could also be because he had more sinister plans for him that no one else in the room was going to enjoy.

"It was simply a misunderstanding, Your Majesty," the boy said, appearing not at all concerned. A mouse thinking he'd found a friendly cat.

"I'm sure it was," Talon replied, lifting himself from the throne. "Why don't you inform us where the ring in question came from and we'll get everything sorted out."

The boy's eyes shifted between the king, who likely looked more intimidating now that he was pacing around the dais, Oliver, whose disinterest had turned to trepidation, and then herself. She tried not to make eye contact. She didn't want him to see her unease or set Talon off before the boy had even presented his information. She didn't think a stolen ring or a Widow would have anything to do with her son, but there was always a chance.

The boy seemed to understand that he should choose his words carefully, so he gathered himself before speaking; his eyes flickered back and forth as if searching for the best possible response, whether it be the truth or a lie.

"I was at an orphanage, Your Majesty. The Widow gave me her ring so I could give it to my betrothed when I was matched at trials."

A Widow run orphanage wasn't anything out of the ordinary although she wasn't sure if Talon was aware of them.

"And where was this orphanage?"

The boy swallowed, the movement obvious in his skinny neck. He likely knew if he provided the correct name and location they would be able to check on the Widow and make sure that she hadn't met her untimely demise.

"If you were truly living there it shouldn't take you so long to come up with the location," Talon prompted, his arms crossed over his imposing chest.

"It's hard to describe," the boy replied.

"You don't think I'm well acquainted with every corner of my kingdom?" he asked, a hard glint in his eyes.

"Maybe it's not part of *your* kingdom."

Stefania couldn't help the slightest gasp from coming from between her lips. She could see Oliver sinking deeper into his chair in discomfort. She slowly moved her gaze back towards Talon who had a wide grin on his face. He apparently had a good handle on his temper today though that didn't mean the boy would be getting away unscathed after that remark.

"Please enlighten me as to the location so I can make it part of *my kingdom* then," Talon started and then seemed to think for a moment. She knew it was all an act. "If you have come from some uncharted territory then maybe you can earn a place in my militia, lead the next scouting mission. I'm sure you'd like to have a sizable nest egg in order to help earn your match's favor following trials."

She could see the excitement in the boy's eyes. He was sadly oblivious to the fact that Talon had offered him exactly what he wanted based on the crime he had very likely committed. "You would truly recruit me? Even though I haven't yet been to trials?"

Talon grinned graciously, "Everyone needs to start somewhere. The younger the volunteer, the more experienced they become. I'll have Darius bring you to enlist once we've finished here. Now please, where is it that you've joined us from."

Stefania had to give the man credit. If nothing else, he was a smooth talker. He made it sound as if the boy was an invited guest coming to visit with the king for tea rather than a common criminal.

The boy took a step closer. "There's a fortress, right in the middle of the Harridan." He lowered his voice, as if he and the king were sharing a secret. "They say it's an orphanage but there are older people there taking care of the children." He whispered dramatically: "*Unmatched.*"

Stefania felt her heart stop. She saw the flash of anger cross her husband's face, but it was gone in an instant, likely before anyone else had seen it.

"It must be quite far from here to have escaped notice." He raised an eyebrow, asking the question without appearing too eager.

"Not at all," the boy replied, very stupidly, putting all of his cards on the table. "It was right past Steilkopf Mountain."

Talon narrowed his eyes. "And you didn't encounter any ghastly dark creatures in the forest on your way? When every legion I sent that way has returned in pieces or not returned at all?"

"I supposed they didn't have my valor or cunning," the boy replied, sticking out his chest. "I must have stealthily slipped through unbeknownst to them."

"Well the cunning is evidently absent," Talon replied dryly, his smile hard and gaze hungry as if the beast inside him was ready to be fed. "Let's see about the valor, shall we?" He pulled back the collar of his perfectly tailored deep violet tunic. "It's getting a bit warm in here don't you think…what was your name?"

"Jonal," he replied, uneasily, wiping his brow, as if he was indeed starting to feel warmth though Stefania felt nothing but the blast of wind through the windows and a chill creeping up her spine.

"Jonal," He confirmed, "and you were at an orphanage, so I'm guessing there won't be anyone to contact before we send your body to the sea."

"No," the boy replied calmly, as if too confused or distracted by what was going on within his body. "I thought I was leading the troop to the river."

"That's quite a long way," he replied dumbly, as if speaking to a small child. "If the legion isn't as 'stealthy' as you were, it might take them long enough that you start to smell."

Stefania kept her eyes open, so her husband would think that she approved of his "defense of the kingdom" but let her mind wander elsewhere so she didn't have to watch the boy boil to death from the inside. She had watched this particular scene more times than she could count. The reddening of the skin, the rising steam from the orifices. The boy's parents were already in the afterlife or had abandoned him. This was not her son. This is not what would happen to Stefan if the king found him on that island.

She stayed stoic, refused to let the screams infiltrate her mind or the tears to flow.

It was over within a minute and the room remained frozen for a moment.

"Let me go," Oliver said suddenly, breaking the awful silence.

Stefania initially thought he meant as the heir, as his son, as his captive in this throne room.

"Let me look for this island." He stood, moving to face his father while keeping his eyes away from the boy's still steaming body. "Let me be of use to the kingdom." Though he was now even more disheveled, his crown askew atop his head, she had never seen him look so determined; as if he had caught some of his father's flame, even though it hadn't been the power he'd inherited.

She feared for a split second that the prince was about to meet the same end as his fellow Blue, but surprisingly Talon shrugged, the smile returning to his face. "Good thinking, son. Better you than any traitors that might be among us trying to join them." He clapped Oliver on the shoulder before sitting back down and stretching his feet in front of him as if tired from the exertion of murder. "Clear him out, Darius. Wouldn't want to scare the next one."

He reached his hand across the armrests again, placing it on her thigh beneath the velvet emerald of her gown. Oliver took his leave, likely in order to prepare for his sanctioned escape. As poor Darius dragged the boy away by his feet, Stefania hoped that Oliver had heard the threat hidden beneath his father's words. Part of her hoped that maybe he wouldn't heed it.

CHAPTER 62
AURA

"Mine is much more impressive than that."

Aura groaned as she finally forced her eyes open. She wasn't sure if it was due to her aching body or the frustration that stemmed from the sentence Stefan had whispered to her last night.

They definitely had a moment in the moonlit night, and if that small piece of fabric hadn't been covering her face, something might have happened between them.

When they were talking, one of them would always say something to bring everything back into focus, but in the silence they were just two people with a mysterious connection. Though it wasn't tangible like the string that had connected her to Vitus, there was something about him that sucked her in like the current.

Was that what made her take that step back? A stray thought of her husband? The only person that she *had* kissed. Well, other than Donovan and that wouldn't be counted for many, many reasons. Though the kingdom expected her to move on five years ago, she found that not knowing Vitus' fate made it much more difficult. Her sense of loyalty ran deep.

Before this evening, there were always reasons Stefan was someone she would never consider. Initially it was his past treatment of her. Though she hadn't seen any sign of that superior attitude during his time at the fortress, she assumed it still lurked somewhere beneath the surface. Now that she knew the reason behind his actions that day, she could only assume everything about his behavior here was genuine.

The fact that he spent years causing harm to others through his concoctions was also something she initially held against him but that wasn't really fair. Her own conscience wasn't exactly clean. She had seen the regret and disappointment in his eyes last night when discussing the choices he had made. Barrett was only a few years younger than Stefan had been when he was almost killed and sent off on his own, terrified with no one to turn to. She couldn't blame him for trying to survive in the darkness when he had so much to fear in the light of day.

His admission last night suggested he hadn't been interested in her the day they met and only desired to match due to a sense of duty; however, last night, when he leaned in close and whispered those lust-tinged words, she had almost swooned right there. The tickle of his beard on her lower lobe and the feel of his breath against her skin gave her goosebumps. If he had made any kind of advance, she wouldn't have put up a fight. He could have stripped her down right there if she was being honest with herself; instead, he took her hand and led her down to the garden which only made her fall harder.

She had only been down to the garden once or twice. In its initial state, there was no reason for her to visit it other than the intriguing statues of the four demi-gods. Though growing up she heard the stories that were passed down concerning the origins of the elemental powers and the change of seasons, she had never seen any sculptural depictions. The artist's portrayal of Frigus made her smile, since he fit so perfectly into the image she had of him and the wind itself: a bit rough and barbaric but also playful and sweet at times. It saddened her that he and his consort and friends were forced to live in a garden that was so rundown and overgrown and she hadn't had an opportunity to visit again anyway.

When Stefan had led her back there, she hardly recognized the place. She knew he had been working all summer, and yet, she had never imagined something like this. The fountain containing the statues stood in the middle and each of the gods faced a large square section.

Prim, the demi-goddess of the earth and spring, faced a garden that resembled a small portion of the forest floor. In the center stood an elegant crab apple tree, which at the moment was covered in bright green leaves. Surrounding the tree were every variety of the most delicate flowers: sweet blue forget me nots, pink and white cosmos and tiny violets. A small white stone path led to a space beneath the tree perfect for a picnic or some quiet time with a book. Heren must have been in charge of the sparkling crystals scattered throughout: tucked between the cracks in the large pieces of limestone that lined the ground, hanging together in the tree forming delicate windchimes that sang in the midnight breeze, and placed beside mushrooms and ferns as if gifts for the fairies or for Prim herself.

She had blushed a bit when she walked around to Ignitia's garden. The whole thing was a giant field of red, orange and yellow blossoms of various heights that formed the illusion of a sea of flames. Another stone path containing rocks and crystals that formed hearts and flames led to a perfectly circular spot of soft grass, completely hidden from the outside by a tall row of sunflowers. They were barely even visible from the outside due to the sheer volume of brightly colored blooms. The obscured view and the fact that it was Ignitia's garden suggested that rather than a reading spot like in Prim's, this was a place for lovers, though as far as she knew, at the moment no one at the fortress would be taking advantage of it. When her mind had returned to unhappy thoughts of Stefan and Lavender, she'd pushed them away knowing Stefan would see them on her face.

Quiro's garden, though it took the same shape as the others, was more of a pond, though she had not initially realized it, since the water itself was surrounded by a border of calla lilies, cattails and bright blue cardinal flowers. When she peeked through, she could see water lilies and sumptuous pink Lotus Flowers sitting atop enormous green pads. Frogs of all sizes and hues happily chased each other from one to the next, singing nocturnal greetings. Fireflies lit up the scene and she had gasped in surprise when a bright orange koi leapt up from the water to make one his midnight snack.

She had purposefully kept her head down so she could experience only one garden at a time, and saved Frigus' garden for last. As she stepped back from the water garden that spoke of life and fun she had steeled herself so whatever she saw next wouldn't disappoint her. Though she loved everything about being an air elemental, it also felt like the least showy of the four. Air was invisible and while it could be fun making a demonstration with colored leaves or flower petals or even water, it required help from the other elements. While yellow and golds suited her coloring, they also lacked the boldness of persimmon and cerulean and jade, and so while she was sure Stefan had likely done something lovely, it couldn't be as stunning as the other three.

When she hesitated, Stefan came up behind her to cover her eyes with his hands. She pushed back into him, and he moved one hand to her hip while using the other to cover both eyes and steer her towards the final square. When he finally removed his hand from her eyes, he let the one on her hip linger a moment longer before removing that one as well much to her chagrin. She had kept her eyes closed for another second, savoring the anticipation, and then upon opening them, let out an involuntary gasp.

Though the other gardens would have been even more glorious in the light of day, this one was meant to be seen beneath the light of the full moon. There was not a speck of green within the border of the garden and every leaf was the color of night. Almost every flower had a white and black face: petunias, pansies and poppies all completely devoid of color. There were stalks of foxglove whose blooms looked like dark faces with hoods of white. It was eerie and elegant and reminded her of snowfall at midnight.

She had felt tears come to her eyes and turned back towards Stefan who was holding his breath waiting for her reaction. She was sure she gave him an extremely wobbly smile before throwing her arms around his neck. They stood there for a moment, suspended in time, and she realized that she couldn't remember the last time she had held someone like that. When Eryx and Odessa left on their journeys she typically gave them a quick hug and kiss on the cheek goodbye but this was different. They were both desperate for closeness.

She had stepped away and couldn't help but turn back towards the garden, noticing a single speck of yellow in the center.

It had three long dark black petals on top and a large yellow fourth petal that took the shape of an open bulb. It reminded her of a strange toothless old man. She found it odd that this flower was the one yellow one he had chosen, but when she'd opened her mouth and turned around to ask him, she remembered that they weren't speaking.

Rather than part ways at his room, he accompanied her back down to the cellar but hadn't lingered long enough for her to question him about the flower. She had felt anxious and jittery as they silently walked down the stone steps, fully aware that if he looked into her eyes again or put his large warm hands on her body, she would let him stay; however, when she took the step into her room and turned around, he had disappeared, leaving her to wonder if the night had really happened.

All night, she tossed and turned thinking of his words and how her image of him had changed so much in one night. He hadn't constructed that garden because someone told him that was what he was supposed to do. He did so with love and care. He was creative and gentle and apparently very glad to be living here with her and her people. Maybe that was the reason he vanished. He felt the attraction between them but didn't want to start something that might risk his place here. It made sense. She wasn't even sure if she was ready to be in a romantic relationship, but she still felt disappointed. It had been so long since she'd been someone's first choice.

When she heard the quiet knock on her door and the sound of the key twisting in the lock, she stretched, appreciating the soreness in her limbs but also wishing that it had been due to another type of exercise. She supposed there was always another chance. The thought entered her mind that tonight, that chance might come, and she couldn't help but notice the twinge of excitement in her chest.

CHAPTER 63
STEFAN

Stefan sat across the immense wooden table from Heren with Lavender and Yakov beside them. Though he was used to the flavorful array of foods that Matilda orchestrated for their daily consumption, today's rich black coffee and spiced pumpkin bread tasted extra warm and inviting on his tongue. As he inhaled the scent of ginger and cloves, he remembered the feel of Aura's hip under his palm and the unrestrained joy on her face when she saw the black and white garden. It was not an easy thing to create and he felt like some of the others didn't quite understand what he was going for, but Aura was obviously impressed. He was the most proud he'd ever been when he saw the raw emotion on her face, knowing he'd been the one to cause it.

It tore him apart leaving her last night, but he didn't want to rush things. If his assumptions were correct, at least now she no longer loathed him. He even thought it possible that she felt an attraction to him, but there was no way she reciprocated his feelings for her. Not yet anyway. He knew she was lonely and starved for attention, and he didn't want to fall into bed with her only for her to realize that she didn't want anything more from him. It would crush him to have waited all this time and then be rejected. He would take things slow and make himself indispensable to her.

A sudden sharp pain on his shin caused him to spill the hot coffee over the back of his hand pulling him out of his pleasant reverie. "Prim's tits, what was that for?" he asked, shaking off the coffee and glaring at Heren across the table. Lavender reached across the wide wooden surface and grabbed his burning paw.

"May I?" she asked, a curiously excited look in her dark eyes.

Though apprehensive, he *had* seen significant improvement in her ability to control the amount of heat that she sent into, or withdrew from, the plants in the garden. Knowing how anxious he was to use his own powers to heal, he didn't want to show the slightest hesitation that would hamper her confidence. What was there to lose except a finger or two to frostbite?

"Please," he said, letting her examine the wound, "Am I your first patient?"

A guilty smile crossed her full lips as she gently probed the reddening skin, "Yes, but I figure if I make a mistake maybe you'll be able to fix it yourself?"

Her small hands were gentle and soft and he could see that she would be a good healer once she honed her skills curing heat specific wounds. Maybe a job in one of the regions of the kingdom where people were burned by intense sun or frozen to the bone in regions to the north. She closed her eyes, and he exhaled in relief as the irritating spots of heat began to dissipate.

"Impressive," he admitted honestly, admiring her handiwork. "You've been holding out on me. Is Red healing something you've been researching unbeknownst to us?"

She shook her head letting her perfectly glossy black hair dance around her crimson clad shoulders, "No. Actually it was reading about the soap process that made me think about it. That and something the Widow said offhandedly yesterday. I think she wanted to suggest it but didn't want to do it outright in case it upset me."

Stefan was about to take another bite of the fragrant bread but changed his mind upon hearing that Lavender just healed him without even picking up a book on the subject. Though he had suddenly lost his appetite at the fact that he could have just lost a hand, he couldn't help the swell of pride in his chest that formed at the mention of Aura and her wiliness.

"Speaking of soap," Heren cut in, "that's what we were discussing while you were off having intimate daydreams about mushrooms or whatever else you think about in that hairy melon of yours."

"Odessa and Eryx were aiming to leave today to go to the Harvest Moon market but neither one is currently in the state to do so," Yakov explained. "They believe it's due to something they ate on their journey yesterday rather than an infection of some kind. Luckily, the child they retrieved isn't suffering the same fate, but if they don't leave today, they won't make it on time to acquire the lye or sell the goods we've been working on." He didn't sound like his usual easy going self, though Stefan was unsure if it had to do with the severity of the situation or the fact that Lavender's attention and hands had been on someone other than himself.

"Is it feasible for them to skip this one and wait until the next?" he asked, though he knew with the cold season right around the corner the answer was probably 'no'.

"This is the biggest one of the year in Yawning Springs. It has the greatest variety of produce and goods and the largest crowd apart from the Awrymor market in the spring. If we don't acquire the lye now, we won't be able to sell any of the soap that we make at the smaller Hunter's Moon market next month." Stefan could see the disappointment in Lavender's eyes, and was glad that his idea appealed to her so much.

His original motivation behind looking into this particular venture was much more selfish than he would admit, but he was glad they were making it into something that could benefit the whole community. "And I'm guessing our adventurous duo are the only ones who have journeyed so far from the fortress?"

"Their backgrounds appear to be cleaner than most," Yakov answered, looking down into what smelled like strongly spiced cinnamon tea rather than the two sitting across from him in case either of them were offended. "I personally would go, but it would take at least twice the amount of time."

Stefan nodded, thinking about what he and Aura discussed the night before about him trusting his abilities and putting himself out there more to benefit the people he cared about. He swallowed deeply while absently stirring his bowl of cheddar grits topped with sliced portobellos and greens.

"I suppose I could go," he said hesitantly, almost convincing himself, "I don't know anyone in Yawning Springs, and it would be nice to speak with the customers first-hand about their thoughts on the oils we've been working on and what kind of scents they would like for the soaps."

"You can't go alone-" Lavender started and he could see Yakov's hand clench on his fork at the thought that she was about to volunteer to join him.

"I'll go," Heren blurted out, saving everyone from an argument.

He raised an eyebrow at his friend. Though Heren had barely breathed a word about his past, Stefan knew there was likely a good reason for it. "Are you sure that's a good idea?"

Heren shook his head, a sharp glint in his blue-green eyes, "No, but I've been stuck on this rock for much too long. I could use a little trouble."

CHAPTER 64
AURA

Aura tried to control her breathing as she walked down the hallway to the throne room. She knew that Eryx and her sister did a lot for her. They were her eyes and ears and basically every other body part that she had to keep hidden from the world. She wouldn't have survived the past five years without their camaraderie and unwavering support.

At this particular moment, however, she wanted to wring both of their necks.

She was slightly concerned when Odessa told her they needed to pick up a young girl in one of the towns on the other side of the mountain. Luckily it was the shortest of journeys; however, Aura was nervous that they wouldn't be ready to immediately head out again on their longer trip to Yawning Springs. There were crucial goods they needed, and a lot they had to sell in order to have money to stock up on all of the necessary wares at the final market of the year ensuring they would be set for the winter.

Odessa had assured her that everything would be fine, and then she had to go eat a steak and ale pie.

Years of delicious, wholesome, home grown foods and suddenly they thought it would be a good idea to stop in a pub and feast on rancid meat. Eryx as well. The usual voice of reason unable to say no to One-Eyed John's culinary masterpiece at the local tavern.

She hadn't actually scolded them when they showed up green gilled to her room this morning. The fact that they weren't able to look at food long enough to bring her breakfast wasn't helping her anger subside. She would have to sneak down to the kitchen at some point for leftovers.

She was disappointed when she didn't see anyone waiting outside the great hall. Maybe Stefan assumed that after their training session yesterday, she felt strong enough to no longer require a chaperone during her meetings. She couldn't blame him if he was helping out with some of Eryx's responsibilities while he was on the mend.

As she moved further up the steps she noticed that the door was slightly ajar, soft voices floating out. She made sure that she was donning her old Widow persona before slowly hobbling up the last few steps and creaking the door open.

Stefan and Heren were quietly arguing in the center of the room as she stepped in. Stefan was dressed in a forest green tunic and his black hair looked wet and was tied up in a bun on the top of his head. She took advantage of the moment to admire his slight but strong frame and his tanned forearms folded across his chest. She saw his eyes move to her, and she was glad to be covered in her concealing adornments. Though his heavy but neatly trimmed beard hid the lower half of his face in a similar manner as her hood, she could still see the myriad of expressions that he experienced in a matter of seconds: happiness, then hesitancy and anxiety before returning to slight agitation directed at Heren as he whispered something she couldn't hear. He turned back to her with a look of polite neutrality, though it was still tinged with a barely concealed excitement as if he too had enjoyed himself last night and was eager for more.

He quickly closed the distance between them and took her arm in his, leading her up the aisle to her simple wooden throne. His grip on her through her robes was firm but gentle and he smelled clean with hints of mint like he had just bathed. His scent fought with that of something warm and savory coming from the dining room below and her stomach growled in response, though she wasn't sure what she was hungrier for: the man or the meal.

She couldn't see his face through the sides of her veil, but she could hear the knowing smile in his voice, "It sounds like I was correct in assuming that no one delivered your breakfast this morning." He gestured to a covered platter on the window sill directly behind her seat. "It's some kind of white bean and cremini stew with fresh bread. Oh and an apple dumpling for afterwards."

"That was extremely thoughtful of you, but what if I wanted to eat the dumpling first?" she asked, teasingly.

"If you were a child I would think it quite naughty; however, at your ripe old age I suppose you should be allowed to do whatever your heart desires." Heren, who was listening in, probably thought nothing of his response; however, something about his hand on her arm and the way he spoke the words *naughty* and *desires* made her shiver.

"Is the draft in here too much?" he asked, misinterpreting her quivering, "I could bring up a blanket?"

"That's not necessary," she replied honestly, "I'm actually quite comfortable." He helped her step up onto the dais and brought her to the heavy chair, "To what do I owe the pleasure of seeing you two this morning?" She wondered if her emphasis on the word *pleasure* affected him in the same way.

Heren was following behind them and he now crossed his arms over his chest and moved back and forth on his toes nervously. He directed his eyes towards her and spoke with confidence, "We heard that Odessa and Eryx are unable to make the journey to Yawning Springs and we would like to volunteer in their stead."

She opened her mouth, unsure how to respond for a moment. She shifted her eyes in Stefan's direction, but he was looking down at his boots. Had she misinterpreted his joyful expression at seeing her and his teasing, suggestive wording? Had he left in such a hurry last night because she insulted him in some way?

She considered what the Widow would say for a moment, pushing her personal turmoil to the back of her mind. They were in a bit of a predicament and it was reasonable that another set of trusted adults would be expected to make the trip across the mountains; however, where Odessa and Eryx could pass as an inconspicuous, married pair, the same could not be said for these two. Also, though she worried about her sister when she was out on the road, she wasn't concerned about her or Eryx being noticed.

"You're sure this is wise?" she asked, finally. "The risk that you two will be recognized is considerably greater than it typically is with our unfortunately ill duo."

"Lavender told us that the crowds are considerable. I'm sure it would be easy enough to disappear. If there is any hint of a threat, we'll make a hasty retreat," Stefan replied, finally moving his gaze to hers. His look was one of determination and promise. That he was doing this for all of them and that he would come back.

Struggling, she turned her gaze towards Heren, "And what would you travel as? Father and son? Husband and wife?" It was a difficult question but one that needed to be answered.

"Come on, I don't look quite that old," Stefan cut in, jokingly, attempting to diffuse the tension.

"What would you advise?" Heren asked quietly. Aura was surprised that he hadn't taken offense but had seen the query solely as what it was rather than some kind of slight.

She thought for a moment, considering all of the possibilities. "I would be concerned that if you dressed as a female, you may be recognized by someone from your past life. Your mannerisms have become more male in nature and if you keep yourself hooded and keep to the back of the booth without drawing too much attention, you might go unnoticed." She looked towards Stefan, trying not to think about how it felt to have her arms around his neck and his warm hand on her lower back. "I suppose two brothers representing their family's business would suffice."

Heren nodded and opened his mouth to comment, but Aura held up a finger. She looked towards Stefan, unsure of how much he knew about his friend's background but then turned back towards Heren. If the two of them were traveling together, Stefan needed to at least have some of the information in order to know what to look out for. "When you arrived on the island you said you felt like the thread had been severed. When you ventured onto the mainland this summer, did you feel anything? A tug?"

She moved her eyes back towards Stefan. He did indeed look surprised but quickly schooled his features into something more serious.

Heren nodded, also shifting his eyes in Stefan's direction. "No, not since I initially stepped foot offshore for the first time."

Everyone was taught that the thread formed between two individuals during a marriage ceremony was everlasting and impossible to sever unless one party died. When Heren showed up on the island and immediately said he felt as if the thread had been cut, she found it odd. The only explanations were that either *she*, now *he,* had been lying, that the husband had fortuitously met their demise immediately after the parting, *or* that it had something to do with the magic surrounding the river or the island itself. When Lavender arrived saying the same thing, she was sure it was the latter. Heren going back to the mainland had been somewhat of a test, and Aura wondered if the abandoned husband had remarried, therefore replacing the original bond.

"If you feel anything at all, I implore you to turn back. It isn't worth the risk." Heren nodded and she turned towards Stefan. "I'm assuming there isn't a marriage bond you haven't informed us of? If there is, please tell us now." She tried to keep her tone even, but she couldn't help holding her breath as she waited for his response. It was extremely unlikely, but she really didn't know much about where he spent all those years and what romantic escapades he might have been involved in.

"No," he said, the slightest hint of a smile on his face. "Nothing to worry about in that respect, I assure you."

She shifted her eyes back to Heren who also had the hint of a knowing grin on his face in response to that particular comment. She was happy he had recovered from the reminder of his past life but didn't like the idea that he knew something about Stefan's love life that she didn't. And that there was apparently something to know.

"In that case, I'll accept your proposal, but please be careful. Matilda already has provisions set aside for the trip. I suggest you stick with that rather than make the same mistakes as your peers and visit the taverns."

Heren couldn't seem to keep the grin from his face as he grabbed Stefan's arm and started dragging him out of the room, "Thank you, Widow. We won't let you down."

They would be gone for a week at the very least, if they weren't apprehended for some reason or another. She suddenly felt like she was suffocating under the heavy folds of fabric. She tried to keep the panic from her voice as she rose from her seat and called out, "Scorpio, I just need one more minute of your time."

Stefan stopped and clapped Heren on the shoulder as he rushed out the door to start preparing.

"Yes, Widow?" he asked with a sly smile as he walked back up to the dais.

Once they were alone together, she suddenly couldn't think of anything to say. It's not like she could speak anything of meaning up here where anyone could overhear and she had already told them both to be careful. She just had felt the need to say goodbye properly as Aura to Stefan rather than "the Widow" to "Scorpio."

"I've heard talk of the black and white garden you created," she started, knowing she truly wouldn't be able to express what it meant to her but wanting to acknowledge it at the very least.

"Yes," he encouraged, taking another step closer, his green eyes staring into her own beneath the gauzy veil.

How could she feel so exposed when she was covered in so much material? "The golden flower that you chose to include. What is it?"

He looked pleased that she had asked the question. "Cypripedioideae. A lady slipper orchid. Extremely difficult to cultivate. I took it as a blessing from Prim herself that it took."

"I heard that it was rather odd looking," she replied, "Does it have any special significance that inspired you to choose it?"

The grin slipped a bit from his face. For a moment he looked like he was struggling with what to say, but then his face took on a more determined look.

"I acquired one from a market many years ago before my trial. I was planning on giving it as a gift to my betrothed." He shrugged, though he continued looking at her as if it was an inside joke that they shared, "It didn't work out in my favor."

She wasn't sure what to say to that. They had talked everything through and yet this was new. She supposed when he purchased the flower they hadn't even laid eyes on each other, yet she still found it sweet that he had been such a romantic at sixteen. He saved her from forming a reply by continuing as he took a step closer.

"When I first arrived here, Heren and I found a pink one in the forest and took it with us. That was what gave me the idea of adding one to the garden. I thought maybe it was a sign of something positive coming. A future dream that I should pay homage to," and then more quietly, "that she might come back to me." He smiled shyly but that hard look of determination in his eyes didn't fade.

"She..." she started, suddenly feeling a bit lightheaded. "And you chose to plant it in Frigus' garden."

"Well obviously," he scoffed, and then further closed the gap between them, raising a hand to her covered face. "It seems to be working."

He only had a moment to drop his hand before Heren swung the door open with a smack against the wall. He held up a large sack proudly. "I have the provisions. Matilda and Lavender were down there and said they would help us load everything into the boats."

He took a step back and she cursed the crystal seeker for a moment. What would have happened if he hadn't barged in? It was better that he had done so sooner rather than later. If anything was going to happen between them, they needed to be more careful.

Stefan walked backwards, almost losing his footing on the dais, and she smiled as he righted himself and bowed to her deeply before finally turning away. She didn't miss the final glance he directed at her as he left the room, closing the door behind him and leaving her with the steaming bowl of stew and a heart that was warring between anxiety and a comfortable simmering warmth.

.

CHAPTER 65
STEFAN

"Can widows remarry?" Heren asked, as they trudged through the forest. Farther away from the fortress than he had been since the spring.

It should have felt like a breath of fresh air, journeying somewhere new, especially with the gentle sunlight filtering through the leaves that were just beginning to change colors. Instead, Stefan felt like he was being dragged away from the one place he had been trying to get to his entire life. No matter what interesting things he saw or exotic people he met on the road, his greatest adventure would be waiting within those ancient stone walls. If anyone attempted to stop him from getting back there, they would severely regret it.

"Unless something's changed since we removed ourselves from society, I'm fairly certain they have to."

Lavender and Matilda had helped them load their wares onto the boats. The tonics and oils he and Heren had created were fairly light, though they did need to be well packaged so the small glass beakers and jars wouldn't break. The steel and ceramics that Lavender and Yakov crafted were the real issue, though Yakov let them have their pick of the small daggers to carry on their persons for protection against any shady characters. Once they crossed over the mountain range, they would be able to hire horses. For now it would be quite the test of strength and endurance. The way back wouldn't be any better since they would be taking back the lye, cold weather necessities and any delicacies Matilda had requested.

Now he knew how Eryx maintained his incredibly muscled upper body. Once they got back to the castle, he would suggest that he and Aura work on strength training. Maybe he could just stick her on his back and carry her around the island to better prepare for the next time. He pictured her arms around his neck, her breath in his ear and the light floral scent of her all around him. He would have been much more willing to attend training as a teenager if it included carrying around a pretty girl, especially that one in particular.

"I meant the old ones. The ones that aren't forced to. *Could* they still marry if they wanted to?"

Though he wasn't sure where his friend was going with this particular line of questioning, he had to admit it was nice having him as a travel companion. After all their time combing the woods together for mushrooms and crystals, he was used to his constant presence and he had felt his absence last week when he was searching through the forest for Echo.

"I don't see why not. They don't necessarily need to be paired with anyone especially powerful, so I suppose if they met an elder Widower who became enamored with them, a marriage could happen."

"Alright then, so why don't you give it a shot?"

Stefan stopped walking. "Excuse me?"

"I mean you two seemed pretty chummy back there. You're pretty old. She's pretty old. You don't have anything else going on." Heren said it with a teasing smile on his lips and yet he still felt his face reddening beneath his beard. Apparently he was going to have to stay away from Aura unless they were in the safety of her room where no one could hear them. It seemed like it was impossible for him to be around her without wearing his heart on his sleeve where anyone could see it.

He couldn't respond to that comment without his face betraying him. Heren already had all of the pieces of the puzzle, he just needed to put them together. A change of subject was desperately needed, though the one he had in mind wouldn't be well received.

"Speaking of marriage-"

"Don't," Heren interrupted, the joviality in his tone gone in an instant.

"I don't need your full life story but it would be helpful to know if there is anyone or anything I should be on the lookout for," he replied, gently.

Heren thought for a moment, "My family never traveled to the markets outside of Awrymor. They didn't need to. My father used to take us with him on finding expeditions throughout the kingdom though. My skills are pretty pathetic compared to his. He could smell out a diamond quarry half a world away." He said it with a smile and Stefan knew that Heren's father wasn't one of the people he had run away from. He didn't want that smile to disappear just yet.

"You once said you had brothers also. They went with you on these expeditions?"

The smile remained, thankfully. "Yep, all three of them. Even after they went to trial and married. My mother was the only one who refused to come. And who forbade me from coming once I hit 'womanhood'."

"And you listened to her like an obedient young lady?" Stefan asked, unable to keep the smile from his lips at the thought of anyone telling Heren what he could or couldn't do.

"Of course not." He laughed. "The last time she tried to stop me I told her I was just going to get ready for the ladies' tea she had planned, threw on a pair of riding breeches and jumped on my horse to catch up with them. Sleeping under the stars was always my favorite part."

"I've had my fair share of nights in the wilderness, though I think it will be much more enjoyable with a friend," Stefan replied.

Heren nodded, "I'm already thinking about all of the scary stories my brothers used to tell me, so I hope you aren't too squeamish."

"I've generally found that the real world is scarier than any fiction, so don't hold back," he replied, honestly.

Heren nodded, thoughtfully. He took a deep breath and then swallowed.

"My…the man I was with, he worked in Awrymor as well. I don't think it's likely I'll see him in Yawning Springs either."

He waited for Heren to say something along the lines of "If I do, I'll kick his ass" but it didn't come. Apparently whatever feelings he had for the man were complicated. Where he assumed there would be anger, instead there was fear and hurt and sadness in his voice. He stopped him with a hand on his arm. "We can still go back. If this is too much for you."

Heren shook his head. "They've done a lot for me, Eryx, Odessa, your bride to be," he added with a little laugh, though his eyes had the sheen of unshed tears. "I'll just keep to the shadows, let you do the talking. I'm sure you'll be in your element, telling everyone about your concoctions and I wouldn't be able to get a word in edgewise, even if I wanted to."

Stefan smiled. It was probably true. He just hoped that no one from his own past happened upon their booth either. He was sure they were both ready to move on from the heavy conversation but before they did, he pulled Heren into him. He hadn't realized how much he needed a hug until he received one from first Echo and then Aura, and he was sure it was the same for his friend.

"If you see anyone, just tell me and I'll get us out of there, okay?" he asked, feeling Heren's initial stiffness relax as he decided to accept the embrace. For all his usual bravado that made him seem so large, he felt very small and breakable in his arms, and Stefan was no colossus himself.

"Yes, papa," Heren replied, jokingly, before gently pushing him away and wiping at one of his eyes. "Don't forget to add a set of white robes to our list. Your woman will have to change up her wardrobe after the wedding."

CHAPTER 66
STEFAN

Three days passed in the blink of an eye. They had mostly stuck to the forest roads in accordance with the directions that Odessa had given them as she'd nibbled on flavorless biscuits and bland tea. They passed through some small villages. Stefan took notice of all of the goings on he had never been privy to since he had either been within the fortress, behind the castle walls, or sleeping and hiding the days away.

Each village was unique in its own way. There was a slight variation in the way the people chose to construct their homes. Different floral preferences lining window sills and in hanging baskets. Distinct varieties of livestock: black and white spotted chicken, pot bellied pigs, soft brown cows, and wooly sheep just starting to grow in their thick coats.

Though he was sure things would look differently as the months went on and the days grew shorter, everyone seemed well fed and excited about the full harvest and its festivities. Everyone they passed greeted them with a wave and a smile, some stopping to ask where they were journeying from or if they were interested in making any trades. He was sure they weren't the only travelers making the trek to Yawning Springs.

He wondered if these people still thought of the demi-gods portrayed within his garden fountain. The autumn was Quiro's season, and he imagined in the past, his devotees would have given thanks to him for providing the rains that resulted in the final harvests of the year. Maybe they would have left out some of the bounty that grew in abundance with his aide. The only statues he ever saw now were the ones of his grandfather, great-grandfather, great-uncles and so on. He thanked his lucky stars he had yet to see one of Talon, despite being sure one existed somewhere.

He couldn't remember his father ever leaving Awrymor, and it seemed sad that he hadn't. How could a king truly understand his people if he never saw them? How could he govern their lives and take from their coffers without ever giving anything back?

Though he was still looking forward to getting back to the fortress, he couldn't say he hadn't enjoyed the trip. Their conversations hadn't been anywhere as serious as the first day, but Heren opened up about his past, including more about his three older brothers. The oldest was five years younger than Stefan. He hadn't often bothered himself with the other court families, but there were small details that triggered something in his memories, making him think that they had crossed paths before, not that he had told Heren as much.

In order to keep his friend talking, he shared a harmless tidbit or two about his mother and cousin. Treats that she'd made him. The numerous times he tried to involve Oliver in his various hobbies but ended up sopping wet instead. When he used to do his rounds in the shadier places within the kingdom, he always kept an ear out for news about the family members he'd left behind. He never thought twice about the comments concerning his mother's undying loyalty to her husband since he knew the reasoning behind it, and he was sure it was all a farce. The more he heard about Oliver's roguish behavior, the worse he felt about leaving him behind. Not that there was any way he could have acted differently. Since arriving at the fortress, the gossip about the royal family he'd heard was minimal, so he was hoping to pick up on the latest at the festival.

On the morning of the third day, they rose from camp when the sun was only a flat line of gentle tangerine upon the horizon. They walked the final couple of miles with the pair of white and gray horses they borrowed from one of the stables Eryx and Odessa had developed a good working relationship with. They had camped deep into the woods to decrease the chance of being robbed by highwaymen, but as soon as they stepped back onto the road, they became part of a caravan of merchants carrying their wares into town.

Just as the darkness faded, the mist evaporating into the fair morning sunshine, they followed the line of wagons and carriages through the mountain pass and into the still slumbering city. Behind the small buildings, Stefan could see the steam rising from the hot springs beyond, and smelled sharp sulfur hidden beneath a variety of more pleasant aromas.

Though it was significantly larger and obviously richer than any of the towns they passed through on the way here, Yawning Springs still had a sleepy feel to it that spoke of peace and relaxation. Stefan saw cozy inns and upscale cafes that were opening for the day, releasing the scents of freshly baked bread and rich coffee. Small shops lined the streets, showcasing bathing wear and trinkets that would appeal to the ladies who had time on their hands and money to spend. He had heard of the wealthy elite coming to the pools to remedy various ailments and the thought concerned him before he realized that any of the snooty boot lickers wouldn't give him a second glance. Likely, the wealthiest would stay away this weekend and return when they had the place to themselves.

They followed the crowds down the cobblestone streets, eventually leading to an open meadow where the vendors were setting up for the three days of festivities. While many tents and tables already lined the field with a variety of merchants and organizers, the open space made it less daunting than the markets he was used to within the palace walls. Every booth he walked by held something that made him think of Aura. A pair of yellow citrine earrings. A long sleeved Amber colored tunic with sunflowers stitched up the side. A dagger with bumble bee jasper stones embedded in the hilt. Maybe he could get Yakov to replicate that particular item if Heren was able to locate the stones. He held onto the coins in his pocket for now, but he knew he wouldn't be leaving without something that would bring a smile to her face.

Once they set up their own space and Heren assured him he could hold down the fort until the market opened to customers, Stefan took a walk to get a view of the city's natural draw.

The springs were immense. Pools of all shapes and sizes were clustered together, all with different temperatures, compositions and medicinal purposes. He was stopped by one of the caretakers, an elder water elemental named Lewt who, once he found out Stefan wasn't attempting to get a free soak, was eager to describe to him how the springs were maintained and continuously updated by a variety of different elementals. Greens who knew which particular plants, herbs and minerals would benefit each specific pond. Blues who made sure the different springs stayed full and clean. Reds who heated each one appropriately. Golds who helped maintain the air in small saunas. It reminded him of their haven a bit, though this place was sanctioned by the kingdom. All of the proceeds were taxed and went directly into the Serenfawr's treasury. He desperately wanted to stay and take note of all the flora that grew in the uniquely nutrient-dense soil; however, he knew he needed to get back before the market opened and Heren was forced to interact with the public.

By the time he arrived back, the field had filled up with booths zigzagging throughout the space. Enormous multi-colored balloons were being filled, the air directed by the magic of fire and air elementals to provide rides to anyone willing to pay to see the springs and the festival from above. The breeze was filled with the scents of cinnamon, apple and cloves. Though they had stayed away from the taverns on their journey, they couldn't help but indulge in some of the irresistible treats that could only be found in a market: spiced hand pies filled with peas and potatoes, fried apple dumplings topped with fresh cream, sweet maple coated nuts and mulled wine that calmed their nerves and loosened their tongues while conversing with the variety of strangers that stopped to peruse their goods.

Though the customers often asked where they traveled from, Stefan knew that the majority of the time people started conversations so they would be given the opportunity to talk about themselves. He quickly deflected any personal questions back to the askers and in doing so, learned much about all of the different areas of the kingdom. Many were impressed with the craftsmanship of the blades and asked about the process, which Stefan could comment on since he spent a fair amount of time watching Yakov and Lavender's delicate dance of heating and cooling steel. They also received helpful feedback on their collection of oils which they provided samples of and promised to bring a wider variety at the final Hunter's moon market.

By the end of the day, Stefan was exhausted and Heren willingly took over talking with the last few stragglers as well as the bright eyed teenage daughter of the merchants in the next tent over. She had light brown skin and long black hair that was braided into two plaits and hung over her turquoise colored tunic. Stefan tried not to worry as he watched the pair, who were obviously intrigued by one another. Heren kept the hood of his cloak up which hid his face in shadow as the autumn sun moved out of the valley; however, anyone who spent more than a minute or two talking to him would pick up on the fullness of his lips and the fineness of his features.

Stefan was happy to see his friend at ease and feeling confident with someone who had no idea about his background, especially since whatever feelings he harbored for Lavender didn't seem to be reciprocated, at least in a romantic sense. As the girl walked away, a sweet smile on her face, he let his friend bask in that happiness for a moment before bringing him back to reality.

"Watch yourself," he said, gently. "She's either extremely young or already promised to someone."

"Hasn't stopped me before," Heren replied with a grin, "Though it has been a while."

Stefan let out a long breath, shaking his head, "Would have been better off on my own." He said it with a smile on his face and they both knew that he didn't mean it.

"Yes, because you're a bull who could have carried both of the packs." Heren laughed. "You could barely carry your own."

"I'm working on that," he replied, too tired to even feign anger.

"Yeah okay," Heren replied, the smile the girl's visit had brought to his face still present. "I'll behave," he said, and then, "at least until the very last night. It would probably be good for her to get a little experience before she's wed."

"You do like the dark haired beauties huh?" Stefan asked, one eyebrow raised.

"I don't discriminate," he replied, gently packing up the remaining inventory for tomorrow's crowds. "I just throw out the line and see who bites." He winked, and chomped down with his jaws for emphasis.

Stefan swiped a hand down his face but knew that discouraging Heren's behavior wouldn't have any effect on his actions. He would just make sure to be ready when they were chased out of the market by an angry mob of protective fathers and broken-hearted fiancés.

"What did she look like?" Heren asked, curiously. Stefan was unsure who he was referring to until he added, "Like Dessa?"

Though his mind had been occupied all day, the minute Aura was mentioned he felt a tingling warmth rise up his neck. He contemplated his answer for a moment making sure it would be in the past tense. "There were some physical similarities, obviously, but personality wise a load of difference. She wasn't quite as fair skinned. Slightly darker hair. Shorter. A bit more solid."

"So she would have been the one to do the heavy lifting in the relationship." Heren grinned. "Why were you so enamored by her? You obviously still are. You got a lot of interested looks today and didn't even seem to notice."

He reexamined the day and all of his interactions. He thought that the female customers were interested in his tonics and the methodology behind their compositions but maybe Heren was right. Not that it mattered.

He pictured all of the versions of Aura that he knew and loved. *Loved? Shit, he was in trouble.* "Her strength of character. Her determination. I guess you could also call it pigheadedness, but it was balanced with sweetness and kindness. I supposed that was the first thing that caught me. The concern she showed me when I was no one but a stranger to her."

"Will I ever get that story?" Heren asked, hopefully. "Maybe it will trigger those kinds of pathetic monogamous feelings in me. Not that they seem to be benefiting you." A concerned look suddenly overtook his face, and he lowered his voice. "That isn't the reason you ran, is it? You couldn't stand to marry anyone else?"

Stefan guffawed. "If it were only that simple."

"How did you do today?" Stefan turned abruptly to see Lewt running his wrinkled fingers over the remaining daggers that were laid out on the table. He gave Heren a nasty look, hoping that the Blue hadn't overheard the final question.

"Fairly well," he answered, "If you're in the market for a blade or a tonic I'll give you a discount for your hospitality this morning."

"I might take you up on that tomorrow when I get a better look in the light of day, but I was just rounding up some of our regulars for a gathering by the pools and wanted to see if you and your young friend would be interested in joining." Stefan was about to kindly refuse when Lewt continued as if knowing what he was going to say, "The guards will be patrolling the field, I can assure you nothing will be tampered with."

Stefan looked back at Heren who shrugged. "We'd be delighted."

CHAPTER 67
STEFAN

The trail back towards the springs had been transformed since he'd first taken it that morning. Colored lanterns lined the trees, and bright orange pumpkins filled with candles illuminated the paths. Though the moon wouldn't be completely full until tomorrow night, the light of the round silver gibbous lit up the steam coming off the various pools. Whether it was the thinning of the veil or the abundance of magic flowing through the springs, Stefan could feel anticipation in the air. His eyes caught sight of movements between the trees and among the rocks like wayward spirits or fairy folk playing tricks on him. Quiet beside him, Stefan was unsure if Heren was also picking up on the natural sorcery going on around them or if it had to do with thoughts of the young enchantress.

They carefully followed Lewt through the trails that wound around the small natural baths. Eventually they ended up in a clearing in the center that contained a small patio where a number of people were seated with mugs of toddies, the steam mixing with that of the baths around them. The fire and the bubbling water warmed the air nicely, and the scent of burning logs combined with the aroma of the spiced drinks made Stefan want to wrap himself up in a blanket and fall asleep.

Lewt made introductions. Stefan provided a new alias for himself in case his reputation as Scorpio had preceded him. The individuals around them were mostly male, with only a small number of women sitting with their partners. A few men even sat in the nearest pool as they chatted with the others. One of the women offered them bowls of thick chicken stew topped with fluffy biscuits which they both downed quickly. Though he loved everything he was given at the fortress, the taste of the chicken fat that flavored the broth was like an old friend. Afterwards, they were given mugs of steaming liquid which tasted of spiced black tea with a splash of something harder. A star anise floated at the top, and he stirred it with a cinnamon stick as he listened to the conversation around him.

"I'm hoping that we'll even make it back next year. With the tax increase, we're barely making enough to make a profit," a middle aged Red said. His dark brown hands carefully carved something from a small piece of wood, the shavings littering the ground at his feet.

"Forty percent, you would think Talon was performing the labor himself," replied one of the men in the pool.

"Forty percent!" Stefan interjected, choking on the hot, spicy drink. Heren patted him on the back to help him clear the burning liquid from his lungs.

"Do you have some deal with the king the rest of us need to get in on?" the whittler asked, curiously.

"No, it's just that our friends are usually the ones who attend the markets. We typically are more on the production side of things," he replied, though he wondered if Eryx and Odessa had also somehow avoided the tax by living outside of the kingdom proper. He personally had never paid income tax on his poisons. Being legally dead did have its benefits.

"A joint venture? That's rare these days," Lewt commented, eyeing him curiously.

He was glad for the darkness that hid his discomfort at the unwanted attention. "Old family friends."

The old man nodded, but Stefan caught a hint of knowing in his eyes.

"I hope you aren't devoted royalists. Very few of us merchants are these days." An older Green cut in. He said it lightly though there was a bit of anxiety in his gaze.

"Not at all," Stefan replied. "Why such an increase? I would think the king's vanity would make him want the people to love and adore him." It was odd to talk of his uncle with strangers. And to know that he wasn't alone in his hatred.

A fair haired younger man in a gold tunic spoke up, "It's because of the disappearances." He sat before the fire and it caused an eerie glow across his handsome face. "The king keeps sending men into the forest and they don't come back. They're either attacked or go missing, likely either eaten by beasts or taken by the Witch Queen herself to fill her own unquenchable thirst for blood."

Stefan wasn't sure about all of that. Especially since they'd never encountered a single threat. But he remembered the darkness he felt around the king's men when he'd rescued Echo and how spent they'd looked.

"What does that have to do with the taxes?" Heren asked, leaning forwards, his eyes a little too focused on the air elemental. Talk about unquenchable thirst.

"With the soldiers disappearing, there haven't been enough men to match with the young widows who have been left behind. I've heard they can't keep enough of the widow's potion in stock, and there have even been rumors that some of the girls have run off to either find their men or join up with the Witch rather than having to marry a golden-ager or face death. The population is dwindling and there aren't enough young people working to pay the tax. We're making up the difference." He spit into the pit in disgust causing a hiss as it hit the flames.

Stefan held in the rage simmering underneath his skin. Aura could have been taken from him before they'd had their chance, all thanks to his insidious forefathers.

This couldn't go on.

He couldn't *let* it go on. And if there was this much discontent among this small group of unknown merchants who so freely and openly complained about the state of the kingdom, maybe there would be more people behind him if he attempted to come out in opposition to his uncle.

The thought of even laying eyes on the man filled him with dread, but that small red ember in his heart stayed lit as they walked back to their tent and continued to glow as he went in and out of consciousness throughout the night, his dreams filled with rebellion.

CHAPTER 68
STEFAN

The second day of the market passed in much the same way. They returned to the springs again that night and listened to more of the merchant's stories. The elder ones talked about how they had noticed the decrease in magic from generation to generation and how they feared that there would be nothing left for the children of their grandchildren. The summers were sweltering, the winters were frigid. The rains were unpredictable: often either drying out or flooding the crops. No one mentioned the marks or Aura's theories about powers of the mind. He wondered if there was a connection there: how powers seemed to grow only when matches occurred between people of equal abilities, which was in direct opposition to the rules dictated by the palace.

He wondered too if the overabundance of magic in the springs had something to do with the fact that the different elementals were working together, just like on their island. The way of the trials made it so families were often split up. Sons or daughters often had to leave the comfort of home to create their own families, therefore discouraging larger communities of multiple generations living and working together for the greater good. Maybe that was why his friends' magic continued to grow as they collaborated and bounced ideas back upon one another. Maybe they were feeding and nurturing each other's powers.

Though he hadn't had much time to think through everything that had been discussed while he made small talk and bartered with customers, in the few quiet moments, he thought about what the merchant said about people crossing the river, *their* river, to escape the kingdom's harsh rules. Would they have seen anyone? He supposed that there were many places one could cross that would be out of sight of their home. If the Witch was really the one controlling the spirits and beasts of the Stygian, it would make sense that others would have the same ease crossing if they were seeking asylum with that destination in mind. Was the mysterious queen aware that they inhabited the fortress? Would it be worthwhile to join forces with her or were they better off remaining unattached to any kingdom or ruler?

The second night, he literally took the plunge and sat in one of the bubbling pools that smelled of patchouli and citrus, the warm water easing all of the aches in his muscles following three days of traveling and two standing on his feet. Heren strategically placed himself on a chair next to Baron, the young Gold he'd had his eyes on the night before, even though he'd spent the day exchanging sly smiles with Violetta at her booth next door. Though he knew his friend wasn't going to do anything untoward in a crowd full of people, Heren's apparent interest and attraction to individuals of all shapes, sizes and colors made him think about what would happen if the trials were discontinued and relationships were forged of mutual attraction and love rather than dictated by the king. Maybe he would have had less business as a poison supplier.

On the final morning of the market he woke up refreshed from his relaxing soak. Heren slept in with only minutes to spare before the customers started trickling in, and Stefan helped ease his friend's grogginess with cups of hot coffee and light airy pastries flavored with almond. He was almost sure that at some point in the night, he turned over to find Heren's sleeping cot bare. Stefan didn't ask questions; if Heren wanted to share about his exploits, he would have plenty of time on the trek back.

The market was not as full as it had been the first two days as people started heading back to where they'd come. Stefan took a number of trips away from their table to trade with some of the merchants he had become familiar with over the past couple of nights.

He found another soap maker willing to sell him some lye. He also gave him some instructions for making their own. Knowing that she would accept something small without argument, Stefan procured a delicate bar of soap smelling of jasmine and frankincense for Aura. Floral and pretty with a hint of something more unusual. Exactly the way he pictured her, eyes glowing within her beautiful face beneath the waxing moon. Just that thought made him wish for time to speed up. To skip over the next three days of lugging back everything they'd purchased.

Though he felt slightly guilty about it, he did procure a single bottle of wine that he planned to share with Eryx one night in the hopes of getting him to open up a bit. He still had to somehow persuade him that he wasn't interested in the *younger* sister without admitting to being enamored with the *older* sister he wasn't even supposed to know about. He could try to enlist Heren's help without admitting to *him* that his long lost love was no longer lost. He was the only one with all of the information and even he was confused.

As he reached their table, arms full of everything he had acquired, he found Heren sorting through the remaining oils.

"Good, you're back. I was just going to take a couple of these smaller bottles and give them to some of the people we spoke with. Building bridges and all of that."

"The Gold or the Blue?" Stefan asked, slyly. "Or is there a third I'm not even aware of?"

Heren smiled widely, opening his mouth and then looked up at him. Whatever he saw stopped him cold. He appeared like he wasn't breathing for a moment before he adjusted his hood and began fiddling with more of the bottles on the table. He nodded with his head the slightest bit as if to ask Stefan to deal with whoever was pursuing their remaining wares.

Stefan took a breath, readying himself for whoever was standing there. Hoping that whoever it was hadn't noticed Heren before Heren had noticed them. He pasted a pleasant smile on his face and turned around. A tall man in a dark colored cloak stood behind him, his fingers gently running over the blades on the table. Like Heren, the hood of his cloak hid his features even though the autumn day was pleasant and warm. Better to get rid of him as quickly as possible.

"Can I help you?" Stefan asked, brightly. "That's all we've got left so I'd be willing to give you a good price if you've got your eye on something in particular."

The man looked up and Stefan was greeted with the face that haunted his nightmares.

CHAPTER 69
STEFAN

Not his uncle.

While the cloak he wore was dark, it was the dark of navy, not the deep scarlet of blood.

Stefan took an involuntary step back as his mind tried to comprehend what he was seeing. Though the man had his uncle's strong jawline and fine nose, he was much too young. His skin also held a healthy glow that was darker than the usual Serenfawr pallor. His head was bowed as he'd studied the daggers and throwing knives on the table, and when he stood up straight Stefan could see that they were similar in height.

His younger cousin, the man who took over his role as heir to the throne, must have misinterpreted the terror and shock on his face as simple recognition and surprise. He smiled slightly and spoke quietly, his voice significantly deeper but somehow still inherently familiar: "I would appreciate it if you kept my identity to yourself. You're the first one who's noticed and I'm not sure if I should be glad or insulted that my reputation hasn't preceded me."

The initial fear he felt was replaced by a deep sadness as he thought about that last day he spent with the boy who had changed so significantly. How Stefan hadn't been there for him in those formative years leading up to trials when he, himself, felt so lost. How he had no idea who this stranger was before him. He swallowed the giant lump in his throat and attempted to break the awkward silence, unable to think of a single thing to say.

"Are you alright?" Oliver asked, concern sketched on his face.

"Yes, Your High-" he stopped, remembering the prince's words, "Just not used to being in the company of someone so…important."

He steadied himself, taking on the role that he had played so easily the past couple of days. A simple herbalist and merchant. "If we have anything worthy of someone such as yourself, please just say the word. Take whatever you want as a token of our loyalty to the Crown."

"That's very kind of you, but I don't mind paying," he said, as he continued to scan the items, picking up a small dagger with a lapis stone welded into the hilt. "From what I've overheard, you're all paying my father more than you can afford." He shook his head, and there was a gleam of sympathy in his eyes.

Stephan winced, hoping that he wouldn't be taking the list of complaints back to the Awrymor with him. He was sure it wouldn't go over well.

As if hearing his intake of breath, Oliver looked up and gave him a reassuring smile. "I don't go around making trouble." He stopped to think for a moment and his smile turned roguish. "Well, unless there's ale involved."

He recalled one of the last conversations they had about his father's drinking habits. What would it be like to take out that bottle of wine he had bought for Eryx, confess his truth and catch up on the past fourteen years? His heart ached to do just that but he knew it would be foolish to trust Oliver just because he gave smiles and reassurances to a stranger. Who knew what was hiding behind those sharp eyes? How much loathing did he have in his heart for his older cousin who had supposedly committed treason under his nose and as far as he knew, had been buried long ago?

"What takes you so far from Awrymor?" he asked instead, hoping for maybe a little insight about his cousin's life without being too obvious. He was glad to see that he appeared healthy and confident, though maybe that was because at the moment he was miles away from his father. He didn't seem to have inherited

Talon's superiority complex or cruelty, though he supposed it could be lurking there below the surface.

"Oh, you know, leading the troops on the hunt for rebels, defending the sanctity of the kingdom." He ran a finger along the edge of the blade, testing its sharpness. "Trying to actually get a glimpse of the land that I'm supposed to reign over one day."

Stefan heard Heren drop something behind him but stepped in the prince's way so he couldn't get a better look and pointed behind him to the springs.

"Have you gotten a chance to soak in the pools? If you're here you should take advantage."

"Have *you*?" Oliver asked curiously, "I heard it costs a pretty penny for a bath."

"No," he responded, hoping he wouldn't get any of his new friends in trouble for their generosity. "I just couldn't help myself from taking a walk around. I heard there were some unusual species of bedstraw as well as numerous algaes that can actually survive within the hottest of the springs. I had to see for myself."

Oliver laughed. "You Greens are all the same, so obsessed with all of your plants." The brightness of his smile fell as if he were remembering something upsetting.

"Not all of us," he said, quickly, hoping to raise the prince's spirits, and then get him on his way. He didn't think memories of *him* were what had triggered Oliver's change of mood, but if it was, he didn't want him looking at him too closely. He pointed to the stone on the blade he had picked up. "Some of us are more into those things that don't require water or sunlight to grow into their beauty."

"Do you have to purchase the stones through the Magpies? You must not make much of a profit off of the blades if you do." He picked up another blade, this one containing two bright red rubies.

"The Magpies?" Stefan asked, confused, though the name did ring a bell somewhere in the dark recesses of his mind.

"You haven't heard of them? They're the biggest crystal finding family in the kingdom. From what I hear, their talents are fairly rare to come by." Oliver's smile hadn't returned, and there was now a bit of suspicion in his dark gray eyes.

Heren had gone completely still behind him.

"No, we don't go into the city much." This conversation was like a maze with each dead end filled with booby traps. "My wife has a sensitivity to them."

Oliver looked down at Stefan's hands that were splayed out on the table.

"You're not wearing a ring," he stated simply, though there was something dangerous in his tone now. His gaze shifted up behind him to observe Heren who Stefan hoped was safely hidden within the shadow of his cloak.

"Highness!" A red cloaked man came rushing up to the table. Though Oliver hadn't wanted to be noticed, this man was obviously under the crown's employ. The Serenfawr insignia was displayed proudly on his sleeve.

"I'd prefer you not disappear on me like that," he squealed, breathlessly. "Your father would be quite upset with me if we lost you."

"I'm not a child, Darius," he said, annoyance in his tone. He looked back at Stefan as a flush creeped up his neck, though he wasn't sure if it was due to anger or embarrassment.

Stefan took the interruption as the blessing it was and grabbed the dagger that had caught Oliver's eye. He wrapped it within a velvet pouch and added one of their Blue oils that smelled of Bergamot, sea salt and driftwood.

"Please take this as a gift that you can use on your travels." Though it was slightly terrifying, he looked directly into his younger cousin's eyes, pleading with him to move along. As Oliver reached out for the bag he added, "The lapis stone brings truth and wisdom, make sure you recognize it when you see it."

The prince nodded, gazing once more into the back of the tent before stalking away. The advisor stayed behind a moment to drop a handful of coins on the table before chasing after him.

Heren said nothing but released the long unsteady breath he'd been holding.

"Gather what's left, if he comes back I don't want there to be a hint that we were ever here."

CHAPTER 70
HEREN

They hadn't said another word as they packed up their remaining wares as well as everything they'd bought and headed out. Heren would have liked to say goodbye to the friends he made; the ones he'd snuck off to meet with after Stefan passed out. However, the sooner they were on their way and out of the prince's line of sight, the better. If nothing else, at least he'd had a boost to his confidence. The girl's shy smiles and soft sighs when he touched her made him feel strong and like the changes going on inside him were visible to people on the outside. It had been pleasantly validating.

His rendezvous with the Gold was much more risky and dangerous, and yet the man's hard thrusts were everything he was missing from the first interaction. The perfect balance. Apparently whatever he thought about Heren's appearance didn't bother him too much since he'd searched him out this morning, bringing him coffee and asking about his plans for their last night in Yawning Springs. He would be disappointed to find Heren gone, and Heren found that to be extremely satisfying.

Though it was only late afternoon as they walked back down the cobblestone road, the quaint, coziness that he originally felt now seemed suffocating and claustrophobic, the skies an ominous dark gray. The wind howled between the small shops blowing the multi-colored leaves back and forth in a cloud of oranges and reds like the whole place was bathed in flames.

Though he refused to turn his head around to see if they were being followed, he could feel someone's eyes on his back and his hands shook on the reins of his gray horse as they trotted down the street.

Once they reached the road, they picked up the pace and as soon as it was feasible, they ventured deeper into the woods to watch the road from a distance without being seen. The light of the still round waning moon allowed them to continue traveling well into the night until their bottoms were stiff and their stomachs growled in protest.

Rather than build a fire, they shared half a loaf of bread left over from the morning as well as a hunk of hard cheese and some apples. In order to provide some warmth, Scorpio uncorked a jug of wine he'd bought and they each took a couple of swings, though not enough to scramble their wits in case anyone stumbled upon them.

"Well?" Scorpio asked finally, the first word he had spoken the entire journey.

"Well what?" Heren asked, fractiously, his voice harsh from disuse.

"Please tell me that was not your betrothed."

Heren laughed abruptly, the sound scattering a flock of bats that were perched in the trees above them. "You're joking, right? You know who that was? If he was my *betrothed*, I wouldn't have escaped from him so easily, and I sure as hell wouldn't have set foot back in the kingdom."

"But you knew him. And he apparently knew you," Scorpio replied, pointedly. Hearing his family name spoken aloud had been jarring, and he was a bit peeved at his secrets being dropped for his friend like breadcrumbs while Heren barely knew anything about him other than his unhealthy devotion to a missing woman who likely never wanted anything to do with him in the first place.

"They were friends," he said quietly, then seemed to rethink his statement, "Well, drinking buddies. Partners in debauchery. I don't know if it was anything deeper than that."

"Your brothers?" Scorpio asked, clarifying.

Heren shook his head, "My brothers were smart enough not to involve themselves in all of that. It was my..." he stopped, the words that should have come easily feeling awkward on his tongue, "the man who…"

Stefan held up a hand, "It's alright. I got it."

They were silent for a moment as Heren took a bite of the simple yet nourishing feast. The cheese was sharp and nutty paired with the sweet floral taste of the perfectly ripe apple.

"What was he like," Scorpio asked softly.

"How many times do I have to say I don't want to talk about it?" he replied, unable to hold in his agitation. Though Scorpio was annoyingly good natured literally all of the time, he could be so daft.

"Not him," he corrected, waving a hand, "The prince."

Heren thought about it for a moment. What could he say? Well endowed but emotionally distant? He really didn't want to get into his lurid history with the royal.

Heren would have been paired with Oliver if he, then she, hadn't been bested by Luke. For the four years following their trials, there had been no top seeded female for Oliver to match with and throughout Heren and Luke's courtship, the three of them had spent more nights together than Heren could count.

In their younger days, those nights had been mostly innocent. Playing cards while sipping on wine and heavier drinks they pretended to have the taste for. Sneaking into secret clubs using Oliver's position. The fact that they had all been such thrill seekers made the pairing beneficial for all three of them, and Heren had thought that maybe the future wouldn't be as horrible as "she" had expected. Even when their appetites grew and things became more complicated, it still seemed to work. Luke enjoyed Heren's sexuality when it benefited him. Watching his betrothed engage with other women in the brothels. Sharing with his friend who was unsuccessful in finding an appropriate match of his own, even as together they all scoured the widow's balls looking for someone to complete their foursome. For a while Heren thought maybe he could do it. Be someone's wife if this was what it consisted of. That was until their wedding day, and it all stopped. Oliver and Luke still went out and did what they pleased but suddenly Heren was supposed to stay home and act like a proper lady. It had not ended well.

Was there anything he could really say about Oliver though? Did he really know him at all?

"He was someone who would throw money around if you wanted to have fun, but not a person I would go to for help in an emergency. He was…" he paused, thinking it through, "difficult to read. We would do things that obviously were not socially acceptable, and he would encourage it, but then he would see someone else doing the same thing and have them arrested. Like he would remember that he was supposed to be king one day and should be upholding the rules even though he didn't believe in them."

Scorpio let out a long breath.

"Are you surprised?" Heren asked, ripping off another hunk of bread. "Did you assume that the prince would be the perfect upstanding citizen?"

"No, I just…" he shook his head as if the whole thing were his fault somehow, "nevermind."

"You recognized him," Heren stated, an eyebrow raised.

"I'm sure a lot of people would," Scorpio countered.

"Oh, fuck you," he spat out before he could stop himself.

Scorpio's eyes shot up in surprise but Heren went on before he could open his mouth. He knew the whole thing had put him on edge and he shouldn't be taking it out on his friend, but he couldn't help it.

"Everyone we know has their secrets and somehow you keep squeezing out mine. Yet you're too high and mighty to let any of your own slip."

"I told you about," he paused gesturing with one hand as if he couldn't even say her name.

Heren shook his head. "Barely," he cut in. "I figured it out myself and so what? You had feelings for someone a million years ago who's very likely dead."

That had been a bit harsh but Scorpio didn't so much as flinch.

"It's complicated," he said instead, wringing his hands.

"What? I'm the one who's had intimate relations with a Serenfawr and you seem to think whatever you're running from is more dangerous and sordid than that."

Scorpio groaned, shoving his palms into his eye sockets. "Can we not talk about this now? Or ever? Please?"

"What is it? You were locked in a tower and only escaped by growing out your hair and climbing out the window? Someone sold you magic mushrooms that grew high enough to release a giant from the heavens who's been searching for you ever since? You're displaced royalty running from the chopping block?"

Scorpio shrugged his shoulders, his face an uncomfortable grimace.

Heren wanted to scream. "You're not. Things like that don't happen. Only in those dirty fairy tales you read while no one's looking."

Scorpio made the same gesture looking even more pained.

Heren actually screamed, not caring who heard. "I'm taking a walk."

***

He traipsed through the dark forest, far enough from Scorpio to get some space but close enough to still feel the pulsing of the stones that were ensconced in the blades they hadn't sold. The bright green peridot, warming tiger's eye and crystal clear quartz gently vibrated in harmony, stronger than any of the other stones that lay buried within the black dirt of the woods, though maybe it was because they were calling Heren back to his friend. Desiring to bring the two Greens back together.

What made someone a friend anyway? How could you truly be friends with someone you knew nothing about? Had *not* knowing made it easier for them to find that effortless companionship? Would it have been more complicated to form that connection if everything had been out on the table from the start?

Heren was already feeling pretty sorry about his outburst and knew an apology would be forthcoming, but he needed some time to think things through first.

What did he really know about Scorpio? Could he be some pirate king running from the law after murdering a royal admiral and his crew? He definitely had the look of a pirate. Maybe he had infiltrated the group on the island just to find some buried treasure whose location was revealed to him by...

Ridiculous. This was ridiculous.

Scorpio was probably just a sad, last-placed male Odessa picked up because of his medicinal talents.

That statement was hypocritical in itself. Though he could be a bit of a doofus at times, Heren couldn't pretend that Scorpio wasn't a knowledgeable and gifted earth elemental. There was no way he hadn't matched with someone.

He thought about the small crumbs he had been given. The only tiny pieces of his past that he'd shared had been about his menace of a Blue younger cousin and his gentle Green mother who he obviously missed greatly.

The image of Oliver standing in his dark blue cloak came back to him. Scorpio looked nothing like Oliver. Not a single similarity to remark upon. Also, while Scorpio obviously recognized the prince, Oliver treated Scorpio like a complete stranger, which wouldn't have been the case if they were related in some way. Still, something there nagged at him.

What else did he know about Oliver's background? He'd met his mother, the queen. Wait. Not mother, step-mother. Oliver's mother died in childbirth.

Heren's own mother had been prudish and difficult and their relationship was strained for as long as he could remember. He recalled asking Oliver about his feelings towards his step-mother once and he said something along the lines of him "not being her son". Heren assumed at the time that he just meant she treated him distantly because they weren't of the same blood, but had he meant that Oliver wasn't "her son" because there was someone out there who was?

Heren racked his mind for political history. Talon was king for as long as he could remember; however, he could recall something about the last king being felled by fratricide? Patricide? If only he'd paid attention during his lessons instead of drooling over the upperclassmen.

If Queen Stefania had wed the previous king, it made sense that the only appropriate match for her would be his successor, and if he remembered correctly, Talon was the dead king's younger brother.

Another memory came back to him of a late night card game where the subject of traitors came up and someone made a joke to Oliver about it "running in his family". Oliver gave the boy a bright smile then punched him so hard he fell to the floor unconscious. He'd spit on his prone form and stalked out the door.

The autumn air around him was becoming bitingly cold. Heren wanted nothing more than to go back to their camp and cover himself in some of the warm blankets they'd procured but he needed to figure this out first.

Scorpio didn't look like Oliver and therefore didn't look like Talon, whose cloth his son had obviously been cut from. If Scorpio had Serenfawr blood, it didn't show in his appearance.

He thought about the couple of times he observed the queen, always dressed in stunning flowing dresses. Stunning *green* dresses that matched her bright *green* eyes, her dark hair always intricately braided beneath her silver crown. He thought about how there was something about her that always seemed sad: like she always wanted to be somewhere other than the place every other woman in the kingdom wanted to be.

If Scorpio really was the queen's long lost son, could he have really killed his father? Though he supposed his potion-making might have resulted in the demise of a number of people second-hand, the man he lived with never demonstrated any violent tendencies or even anything resembling anger. Saying he wouldn't hurt a fly was putting it mildly. He was sure he had seen him tear up over a stepped upon daisy.

When he finally stepped back into the clearing, Scorpio was still sitting on the log where he left him, staring aimlessly at the spot of dirt before him and sipping from the cup of wine.

Heren walked over slowly and then kneeled before him. He used his right hand to cover his nose and his heavy dark beard and the left to gently push back the long hair covering his forehead. He looked into his green eyes that were lit gently by the full moon and saw an echo of the sadness that he had seen in the eyes of the queen.

"Please don't kiss me," he said, his voice muffled under Heren's palm.

Heren rolled his eyes. "You couldn't pay me all of the coin in your family treasury, Your Highness."

CHAPTER 71
STEFAN

The hasty retreat from Yawning Springs set the tone for the remainder of the journey back home. The strong persistent feeling that they needed to be back within the safety of the fortress walls provided Stefan with a jittery energy and although he was exhausted by the final morning, the trip back had been considerably shorter than the one out.

He was relieved to find that Heren discovering his true identity felt right rather than anxiety producing. It felt as though the air between them had cleared and he knew deep down that he hadn't given his friend enough credit. The information Heren was now privy to wasn't something that would be a fun tidbit to share with others, but rather something precious between the two of them. Whenever they did stop to have a quick bite or let their horses drink at a stream, Heren quietly scanned his face as if looking for more clues but never asked him anything outright as if understanding how terrifying the whole subject was for him.

As they finished up the final leg of the journey, the sky gradually darkened, promising an ugly autumn storm. At first he desperately hoped that the clouds would continue on their way so his time with Aura after nightfall wouldn't be cut short. When they slowly inched over the island and seemed to be staying put, he rethought his plan and decided that maybe the extra time spent in her room wouldn't be so bad if he played his cards right.

Once they arrived back at the fortress, Heren immediately abandoned him, saying that he wanted to check up on things in the library. He was very sure that the books contained within the shelves were too old to carry any mention of his name or tragic history, but he would let his friend figure that out on his own.

Stefan spent the afternoon distributing all of the items they had picked up. He returned the few pieces of hardware they had to Yakov and asked him if he could create a blade similar to the one with the yellow stone he'd seen at the market. The Red looked at him curiously when he made the request but didn't question it.

Lavender was excited about the lye he brought back and Stefan promised that they could start experimenting the next day. Matilda greeted him with a motherly hug and her eyes brightened at the spices, oils and hardy cheeses they had retrieved for her.

He found Eryx and Odessa in the sitting room and filled them in on the market and springs. He passed along the well wishes of the few vendors who noticed their absence and asked after them. He did not include their run-in with the prince as he knew it would bring about questions neither he nor Heren would want to answer.

Finally, he checked in on Echo who was stuck inside because of the promise of rain but who otherwise, was in much better shape and spirits than the last time he'd seen her. When he presented her with the small knit bat that he'd spent way too much coin on, she gave him a big smile and ran off, likely to show it to her brothers or Hopscotch. Though the bird hadn't spoken to him, Stefan definitely heard the sound of large beating wings above them as they had walked through the most familiar part of the forest.

Being back home, having a home at all, made him feel warm and cozy and his body would have been content to just collapse on his bed and sleep for days; however, the nervous energy that filled his chest hadn't evaporated, and he was sure that it wouldn't until he laid eyes on Aura. He washed a week's worth of grime off his body before putting on the tunic that he felt looked best with his eyes and then grabbed the new jasmine soap that he'd purchased. It would smell delicious on her. Maybe she would let him wash her body with it as the rain fell down around them. Probably not, but a man could dream.

He carefully snuck down the stairs making sure to stick to the shadows when passing the library door. When he turned, he was surprised to see that Aura's door, which was typically shut tight, was slightly ajar. The tiniest bit of panic flared in his heart and he hurried more quickly down the hallway. When he reached the door he slowly pushed it open and closed it behind him. The room was darker than usual, the only light a single candle.

"Aura?" he whispered. The room was quiet and he didn't see any sign of her. Maybe she had run out for some reason and forgotten to shut the door behind her?

He heard a muffled groan and then finally saw her body sprawled on the chaise. One arm and one leg hung off of the side and a pool of blood was visible on the floor beside her.

CHAPTER 72
STEFAN

Stefan's feet couldn't move fast enough as he ran over to Aura's prone body.

"Where are you hurt?" he asked, unable to hide the panic in his voice. This woman was going to give him a heart attack before his thirty-first birthday. He ran his hands over her body looking for split seams in her dark clothing or wet patches that might be blood.

"My head," she moaned.

He ran his hands over her hair which he now realized was strewn around her rather than in her usual braid.

She almost purred and he was momentarily distracted. "That feels nice."

"Aura, what happened to you?" he asked, trying to keep his voice calm, but finding it difficult. "I don't see or feel any lacerations. Who did this to you?"

"I supposed Frigus could partly be to blame, but it's not all his fault. It is a bit ironic that he would choose to punish me like this." She laughed softly.

"The demi god of winter? What are you talking about?" Was she delirious?

"Winter *and* wind. The storm. I usually get them at certain times during my cycle but with a thunderstorm it's a given."

He sighed in relief for a moment and then felt the annoyance creep in. She went through this at least once a month.

During the spring and summer rains maybe once a week and she hadn't told him. Even before he knew the truth about her identity, she could have brought it up to him as the Widow but she hadn't.

"A migraine. What you're trying to tell me in your roundabout way is that you get migraines." He looked down at the liquid on the floor that had looked like blood in the darkness but now realized that it was water, likely from the compress she had pressed against her forehead.

"If you're being fancy about it. I just tend to think of them as another plight of womanhood," she replied, moving one of her arms over her face. Apparently the light from the one candle was too much.

"Why didn't you tell me?"

"Why would I tell you? I had my tea, turned off all of the lights. Now I just have to wait until I either throw up, pass out, or the weather breaks."

"So let me get this straight. You knew from the moment I arrived here that I know my way around a tonic."

"Yes…"

"You encouraged me to work with Heren to familiarize myself with crystals as well."

"Uh huh."

"You directed me to look into psychic healing."

"Where are we going with this? I have limited capacity for speech and your yapping is not improving things," she complained, attempting to swat him away with the hand that was covering her face but too disoriented to make contact. He grabbed it so she couldn't re-cover her eyes and looked directly into them.

"I sewed up a knife wound in *your* body *with my mind* and you didn't think I could help you with chronic headaches?"

"I don't know, I've had them for years. I know how to deal with them," she protested, refusing to look at him even though their faces were only inches apart.

"Fighting through it until you throw up or pass out does not sound like dealing with it." He was furious but at the same time hated seeing her like this. By the way she was acting, he didn't think that she hadn't told him because she didn't trust him. She left the door ajar for him after all. It was more likely because she was just used to dealing with everything herself and was too proud to ask for help. A thought suddenly came to him.

"The day you were stabbed it was raining." He pictured her in the vision she had sent him, "the Widow's" head resting on her palm. She nodded again, her eyes meeting his own for almost a moment before moving away again.

"Will you please let me help you?" he asked more gently.

"Fine," she sighed, closing her eyes again.

Impossible, aggravating woman. "Stay right there."

"I'll try, but I might get the urge to go dancing." He could feel a tension headache of his own starting and balled his hands into fists as he started towards the door. "Oh and Stefan?"

"Yes." He replied between gritted teeth.

"If that's soap in your pocket please leave it in your room, the smell is like a needle jamming into my eyeball."

***

A while later Aura had downed a willow bark tonic and was laying on her stomach in bed. Stefan sat on the edge and slowly alternated between rubbing her scalp and massaging the knots out of her upper back. He tried not to think too much about the pleased moans and sighs coming out of her but was finding it difficult.

"You just returned from a week of traveling and sleeping outside. Don't you want to rest?"

"Nope."

"You're lying."

He removed his hands abruptly and she whimpered.

"That's what I thought," he said, unable to keep the satisfaction from his voice. He had found another way to make himself invaluable as well as a perfectly understandable and rational reason for putting his hands on her. Even though there was an annoying thin layer of fabric in the way, he could still feel the warmth of her skin and couldn't help but wish he could wrap himself around her. Her muscles were so tense, her back so full of tightly wound knots it was no surprise that she was plagued by such horrible headaches.

"How was it? You both made it back in one piece?"

He loved the way her voice sounded husky and sleepy and how they were just having a regular conversation like two people

389

who had been apart for a while and were now catching up. Like they were finally part of each other's lives. It didn't even cross his mind to keep what had happened from her.

"We saw my cousin."

She turned over abruptly to look at him and inched her back up until she was resting on the pillow. Her eyes scanned over his face and body as if assessing him for wounds and he felt his heart leap in his chest with her concern.

"Did he recognize you?"

"Do you think I'd be sitting here right now if he had?"

She shook her head and reached for the cup of black cinnamon tea he had brewed for her. He didn't miss the slight tremor as her hands clasped the porcelain.

"What are the chances? What was he doing so far from the palace?"

"He didn't explain his plans to me in elaborate detail. I would assume he had just taken any opportunity available to get away from his father."

She nodded thoughtfully, looking into her cup as she gently swirled the liquid around and around. Finally she raised her eyes back to him, "How did it make you feel? Seeing him?"

"Guilty." She opened her mouth to say something, but he held up a hand. "I know, it's not my fault. I couldn't exactly have broken into the castle and kidnapped a seven year old without letting everyone know that I had escaped, and yet it still *feels* like I failed him."

She took one more sip and then placed the tea back on the nightstand. She scooted over on the bed and laid back down, grabbing his hand to pull him down next to her. He raised his eyebrows as if questioning what she wanted from him, but she patted the space next to her.

"It's cold as death in here and I should let you rest but I want to hear more. It was a dreadfully boring week after you gave me that tease of excitement."

Yes, *he* was the tease. He rolled his eyes but removed his boots and eased himself down on his back covering them both with the warm flannel blanket.

He thought again about that second he had seen Oliver's face and thought that it had been Talon instead.

"The poor bastard looks exactly like his father. I know Heren makes fun of me for all of this hair on my face, but it definitely serves a dual purpose."

"What do you mean?" Aura asked. He wanted to turn on his side and face her in the dimly lit space but was too afraid of the temptation. She wasn't feeling well. It wasn't the time to explore her feelings towards him.

"Obviously it's been a good way to disguise myself. It definitely eased my anxiety about reentering society, but also I was always afraid that I would look like him. My...the king." He had never talked about any of this with anyone and saying it aloud to Aura was like admitting it to himself. "Right now I can look in the mirror and just see me, but if it was gone I think I would be looking for who else was hiding beneath. Wondering if I took after that side of the family in other ways as well."

"I know we often contain echoes of those who came before us, but the strongest, loudest voice is always our own. What you look like on the outside doesn't correlate at all with what's inside." She smiled, and gave a short laugh. "If anyone tried to attack the castle, I bet the first one they would go for as a hostage would be our Lavender based solely on her appearance, and that would be the *worst* choice to make."

He shivered. "One of those first icy looks she gave me," he shook his head, "I almost jumped back in the spring river because I thought it would be warmer."

"And now..." Aura prompted and he could see a small smile on her lips.

"And now we have plans to make pretty soap together."

A frown crossed Aura's face for only a moment before disappearing. "Yes. She trusts you and enjoys working with you because she sees the goodness inside. Even though you still look at times like a hairy creature of the woods."

"Yes well, it's a good thing, because if I had cut it, my cousin might have actually recognized me."

"Thank Frigus for that." He looked over and saw that her eyelids were starting to flutter. Her voice quieter than before.

"So you're glad I wasn't apprehended? That you're stuck with me a while longer?" he asked, gently, knowing she would probably say yes but wanting to hear it anyway.

"I would have said yes before, but even more so now that I've been acquainted with your miraculous hands."

With that last comment he sat up, knowing that he wouldn't be able to keep those "miraculous hands" off of her if she continued talking like that.

"I should let you get some rest but if you're feeling up to it, can we get back to our training tomorrow? If the rain lets up?" He swung his legs off of the side of the bed and picked up his boots, not having the energy to lace them back up.

"Mmhmm," she nodded, and he could tell it wouldn't be long before she closed her eyes for good and that he should leave or he'd end up just watching her sleep.

"Stefan," she questioned, as he draped a second blanket over her almost sleeping form. "Will you bring my soap back tomorrow when my hyperactive nose isn't trying to kill me?"

"Of course," he replied smiling. He quietly tiptoed towards the door of the cold, candlelit room and was about to leave before she spoke once more.

"I don't know if I ever mentioned it, but I'm happy you're not dead."

"So am I," he said honestly, "So am I."

CHAPTER 73
STEFAN

The Harvest Moon waned into darkness and in the blink of an eye was replaced by the Hunter's Moon. The days shortened. The island glowed like its own campfire in the middle of the river and then everything began to fall, filling the slowly moving waters themselves with vibrant dead leaves.

Every evening Stefan came to Aura's room. She consulted with him about the other "orphans" and where else she could attempt to challenge them and their powers. Odessa's dreams continued, becoming more frequent, and Aura believed that it had to do with the coming of winter and that more people would need shelter before the cold weather settled in. Though each new person who walked through the doors triggered his anxiety, he knew that it wouldn't be fair to try and discourage the sisters from their cause. Other than Jonal, they hadn't had any issues and he continued to keep someone stationed at the door to the hall just in case. He didn't like the existence of that one outlier. It suggested something like that could happen again. On the other hand it *was* the way he had found out about Aura's true identity and though he hated the thought that she had been injured, it had brought them together.

He and Lavender perfected the process of soap making. He had thought Aura would be thrilled, but the first couple of times he mentioned their progress to her, she frowned and plastered an interested smile on her face that didn't quite meet her eyes. He recalled Heren's words about Odessa's initial jealousy of the beautiful Red and wondered if her sister suffered from the same affliction. Though she obviously couldn't participate with the hands-on work, he attempted to include her by bringing various dried herbs and flowers to her room with him so she could be part of the process and wouldn't feel as left out. Luckily his prognosis appeared to be right on and the treatment benefited all. Whenever he appeared with a basket of lavender buds or mint leaves or citrus peel, she would rub her hands together, her eyes alight, and begin thinking up combinations that had never crossed his mind.

"You haven't brought up my favorite yet," she said nonchalantly one night, as she sniffed some teas that Matilda suggested might make for some pleasant scents.

"I know," he said, trying to hide his smile.

She looked at him disbelievingly, "You don't even know what it is."

"Of course I do," he replied, rubbing a soft sage leaf between his middle finger and thumb. Her eyes caught on the gesture and a slight blush colored her cheeks before she looked away.

"Well?" she asked, still not looking at him as she took a scoop of Chai and mixed in some faded pink rose petals. The floral, spicy aroma hit his nose and he thought maybe he would suggest to the kitchen mother that the petals be added to the tea as well.

"I don't need you to confirm whether I'm right or not. I'll present it to you when the occasion arises."

She rolled her eyes but a small smile kept at her lips.

For the most part the nights were clear. The temperature continued to drop, making their breaths glow in the moonlight; however, the stronger and faster they became, the less they noticed the cold. They began running from the fortress to the sparring field which would warm their bodies and loosen up their limbs. They would do whatever strength or cardiovascular exercises he had planned for the evening and then moved onto sparring. Initially, they focused only on the physical aspect of fighting. While it took a couple of sessions for Aura to get comfortable again and find her flow, after a few weeks, she was getting some hits in on him.

Typically, in her candle lit bedroom the mood between them was easy and comfortable, like two strictly platonic friends who had known each other forever. In the dark and quiet of the outdoors, though, that deeper, unexplainable connection between them was stronger and more difficult to ignore.

The absence of light and noise allowed space for all of his other senses. He would be completely enveloped in the smell of her: whatever soap she chose to use that day along with the sweet smell of her sweat. Without speech he would hear all of her other sounds: her labored breaths and sighs and grunts which seemed too intimate, making him think of other situations in which she might make those same sounds. Whenever he made contact with her skin, a palm circling her wrist, a swipe of his nose on the back of her ear, a finger on the strip of skin between her leggings and shirt, he would try to prolong the moment for a split second more than was necessary. He would catalog the softness of her and relive those touches after they went their separate ways to sleep wondering if she was doing the same.

As the Hunter's Moon waned and began waxing again towards the Beaver Moon, they experimented more with their powers on and off of the field. If she received a cut or a scrape during their training, he would patch it up with his mind. With her complete faith in him and his abilities, the process of healing became much less daunting. She even encouraged him to use his power in the opposite way: to harm rather than heal, but he refused. Especially on her. If the need arose, he thought maybe he could work it out in the moment but he wasn't going to do so just for the sake of practice. He was done with the business of being the villain, and he wasn't looking into coming out of retirement.

It took very little time for her mastery of her elemental powers to return and she sometimes had to reign them in so he wouldn't be swept off the face of the cliff. On one especially terrifying occasion he was only saved by a strong vine of ivy that grabbed his ankle just in the nick of time; however, it was worth it after the amount of fussing he received afterwards, as she checked him for injuries and applied a balm to his scratches. Using his power on his own person still felt strange and he preferred to heal himself the old fashioned way.

When he complained the next evening that his ankle was still a bit sore she said that they were due for a rest, and so they spent the evening tucked into the quiet library with her mostly robed in a hooded blanket in case anyone walked in. He was happy to discover her reading preference, though a bit disappointed that it was far from his own. The book she delightedly collected from a wooden shelf pictured a frightened looking girl with a dark figure lurking behind her in the shadows of a cobweb filled crypt. He found it a bit odd that she chose to read macabre, dark tales when she was perpetually confined to a frigid, windowless cellar, though it made sense that she enjoyed solving mysteries that helped her to exercise her problem solving skills.

He didn't even consider selecting a book he didn't really want to read just to look more brawny and masculine in front of her. Though he enjoyed doing his research on various topics in the light of day, he knew with her curled up next to him he wouldn't be able to focus on anything too heavy. She raised her eyebrow at him when he returned with *A Courtship of Waves* but obviously kept quiet. He wondered if she would tease him about it when they returned to her room.

While initially she started out sitting up on the opposite side of the couch, somehow, as the hours passed, she eventually ended up with her head on a pillow and her feet in his lap. It happened so slowly and he was so absorbed in his romantic tale that he hadn't noticed. The pirate lord had ordered the young maiden he'd kidnapped to swab the deck and she had just dumped the sudsy bucket of water on his head when Stefan heard Aura make a small happy sound and realized that he had been absently massaging her stockinged foot. He cut his eyes to her to find her blushing, but he only smiled and put his book down to work on both of her feet at once. It wasn't completely selfless of him. He was sure that once the pirate and the maiden had reconciled their differences he wouldn't want her anywhere near his lap. Well he would actually, very much so, but he wasn't sure she would feel the same way.

A while later when Aura had also given up on her book and looked like she was about to fall asleep, he pulled her up from her seat and they padded back to her room. He would have carried her if he wasn't afraid that they would run into someone and she wouldn't be awake enough to disguise herself.

He followed her in and then quietly closed the door behind him.

"Would you like to borrow *A Courtship of Waves* when I'm done with it?" he asked, unable to hide his smile.

"I'll stick with my murder and spirits, thank you very much," she replied, but there was a touch of playfulness in her voice.

"Not one for romance?" he asked, as he tied the boots he left in her room, letting her know that he wouldn't outstay his welcome.

"I never saw the point of it," she replied, watching him from her perch at the end of the settee. "People in our kingdom aren't given much of a choice when it comes to marriage. What's the point of pretending that's not the case?"

He couldn't help but close the distance between them. He stood inches away and she had to crane her neck to look up at him. He tucked a small strand of dark blonde hair behind her ear and looked into her rich golden eyes.

"I don't know if you've noticed, but we aren't in the kingdom anymore."

He had whispered it, and he was so close he could see the goosebumps rise along her neck. She parted her lips and took a staggered breath and he was sure that he had her.

He took a step back and saw a flicker of disappointment cross her face.

"Enjoy your ghastly nightmares. I'm sure my dreams will be a great deal more," he stopped for a moment to think, "pleasurable."

He couldn't stop smiling as he closed the door behind him, knowing exactly who the maiden scrubbing the pirate ship in his dreams would resemble. He hoped that maybe a long haired captain would figure into her dreams as well.

CHAPTER 74
STEFAN

A week later, Stefan sat at the large oak table trying to force his eyes open with his second cup of bitter coffee which was as dark as the cold autumn morning outside.

He had been sneaking back to the fortress in the afternoons to nap, but the mornings were still extremely difficult, especially as he was waking up long before dawn. He was still getting up early in order to have breakfast with the others and then either working on clearing out the outdoor gardens and replanting more hardy varieties for winter, helping Lavender with the soap, taking his turn for guard duty, foraging and working on tonics and oils with Heren, or doing his kitchen duty whenever he was on schedule.

The evenings spent with Aura had been growing longer. It was more and more difficult to leave the cozy comfort of her room and go outside to train but it was also something they were both reluctant to give up. She still seemed to crave that icy breath of fresh air and moonlight each night. He longed for any excuse to touch her. Every time he walked her back to her room, he waited for her to ask him to stay, not even for any especially salacious reason, but just so he could keep her warm throughout the night. He wouldn't ask. It needed to be at her bequest. He could feel it coming. He could see it in the way her eyes lingered on his lips and how her smile grew each night he came to see her. How she played with his hair sometimes when he sat on the floor in front of her and how every day she seemed to put more effort into her appearance. Though perhaps she just looked better and better to him the harder he fell.

He thought about the way she looked last night wearing the dark form fitting outfit that drove him crazy, her hair intricately braided into a crown. She'd used the soap he had brought back for her from the market, and there might have been some rouge on her cheeks but it could have just been the blood rushing to her face from his compliments. Her body had changed over the past couple of months, and even though he loved every line and curve of it either way, he could tell that her confidence was growing and she felt comfortable in her own skin again.

"You can't hide the truth from us any longer," Lavender said perkily from her usual seat, a sly smile on her full lips as she popped a buttery piece of honeyed cornbread into her mouth.

Heren looked up at him from across the table, terror in his gaze, but either he was too out of it or he was comfortable enough with his fiery little friend that he knew she wouldn't out him to the entire dining hall.

"And what truth is that?" he asked, his voice barely more than a rasp.

"You're some kind of bear shifter who usually spends the winter months in a dark cave." She smiled. "I've been waiting for you to give us some kind of excuse as to why you have to disappear until spring."

He couldn't help but smile back. "If I admit that you're right, can I stuff my face with everything on the table and retire to my room until I feel the need to come out again?"

"For someone who's supposed to be fattening up for the winter, you've been looking extra fit lately," Eryx said, forcefully pushing himself into the seat beside him, "Especially considering you haven't been showing up to sparring practice."

"I've been running around this place like a chicken with its head cut off with barely even a chance to eat," he replied evenly, keeping his head down and shoveling in a spoonful of rich yellow eggs speckled with parsley and chives.

"What's your excuse?" Eryx asked from beside him, though he couldn't tell who he was addressing.

Odessa laughed loudly from the seat across from him, "Must be all of the walking around I've been doing in my dreams." Stefan looked up to see her remove a thin, bony arm from her oversized sweater. "Talk about a bear," she laughed again, while flexing her barely existent bicep that resembled the tiniest of gnome holes.

Stefan chortled around his mouthful of eggs, but something about Eryx's comments made him nervous, especially the hint of knowing malice in his tone.

He downed another cup of coffee while they talked about ideas for Cold Moon celebrations for next month. He hadn't had reason to acknowledge the holiday in years, and he tried not to get too excited about what this year's festivities would bring.

Eryx devoured his food even faster than usual and rose from his chair, knocking Stefan's arm with his coffee. Luckily, there was very little left and he avoided any liquid on his hand, so he wouldn't have to worry about another possessive male being upset with him today.

"I want to see both of you up on the field," he said, not even bothering to apologize.

"Yeah, okay," Odessa laughed again, as Eryx stormed off. Though his history with Aura was long and complicated, he supposed things could be worse.

***

As Stefan made his way down the stone steps to the sparring field, he felt a knot of apprehension in the pit of his stomach. He had done this same walk every night. Running the path in the dark with the sound of Aura's labored breaths and quiet footsteps behind him, and yet in the light of day he couldn't help but notice a sense of foreboding.

He tried to brush the feelings away and focus on the beauty around him. The leaves that remained on the trees were golden and the paths and steps in front of him were covered. It would be a good idea to do some sweeping so he wouldn't trip and fall on his face in front of Aura, though she would probably find it endearing. With the sparse tree cover, the afternoon sunlight filtered through the breaks in the trees and he could see

Hopscotch circling ahead. For some reason the sight of the giant bird felt comforting rather than unsettling.

"Good afternoon, your featheriness," he thought, trying to project his message towards the creature above.

He could hear Hopscotch sigh in his mind. *"Why do you humans choose the most ridiculous, derogatory designations? "*

"Do you have an actual name?"

"Your human anatomy wouldn't be capable of reproducing it, and I really would rather not hear you try."

"I never would have thought that someone who feasts on maggots could be so pretentious."

"Good luck at your 'sparring practice'. I placed a bet with a murder of crows that the more well-built Green would get the better of you."

"You wouldn't be the first to bet against me. Unfortunately for you, it's just a practice, not some kind of cage fight. And what are you betting for? Beatles and buttons?"

"An elderly raccoon passed away last night. His eyeballs are ripe for the picking."

Stefan covered his mouth and gagged just as he stepped up onto the flat expanse of grass. Eryx looked at him with a questioning glance from where he stood near the stone wall ahead, but there was no sympathy in his gaze.

"This is why I don't talk to you."

"And that's how I like it." He squawked loudly from above to punctuate his point and then landed on a large branch at the edge of the field.

Heren had offered to come up with him but was already scheduled for lunch preparation with Matilda. Since finding out about his true identity, his friend had become a bit...*over* protective. Like he had taken on the role of personal bodyguard. Stefan wouldn't say it was getting on his nerves but it was definitely unsettling. He was afraid that if Heren saw Eryx getting too rough with him he would step in and say something revealing.

Odessa was unsurprisingly absent, probably reading her cards somewhere warm and cozy with a large mug of tea. Stefan wondered why Eryx had called her out when she never showed up in the first place. He did feel a bit guilty that he hadn't been helping out, and yet, he thought that with all of the extra work he'd taken on Eryx would understand. In truth, he barely saw the other Green with the amount of trips he'd been embarking on with Odessa to retrieve more lost souls. Though the two apparently had an excess of time together lately, it seemed like they hadn't progressed anywhere in their relationship. Maybe that was why Eryx was so grumpy this morning.

The younger ones were clad in warm hats, coats and gloves, their noses and cheeks pink from the biting wind and blazing sun. He walked over to where Eryx stood next to an older teenage boy Stefan had only seen around the dining hall once or twice. He was tall with a mop of curly brown hair and he smiled warmly at Stefan as he approached. Eryx did not do the same.

"Scorpio, this is Bruce. Bruce, Scorpio," Eryx began, "Bruce placed highly at his trial this spring so we thought this would be an appropriate place for him to help out."

"So you don't need my help then?" Stefan asked, unable to hide the confusion from his voice.

"I'm sorry if this is below you, but I thought we could demonstrate some of the techniques we were working on before you suddenly decided you were too good to be here."

He heard a hideous cackling in his mind and looked up to see Hopscotch bobbing up and down. It was a deeply disturbing sight, and he shot him a look that only made the horrible sound and motion escalate.

"I…" Stefan hated conflict, but he also wasn't going to apologize. He had been working his ass off in every way for this community as well as taking care of the one person behind the scenes who made the entire thing possible. Sure it gave him joy as well, but he had seen the light returning to her eyes the more time they spent together and he would never apologize for that.

He turned to look at Barrett and Callen in their matching yellow cloaks and wool hats.

"You boys are looking sharp," he called over, "and warm." He looked pointedly at Eryx as he said it, knowing that much of the money they recently brought in had been from the oils, soap and potions he had been tirelessly working on. Odessa even talked him into making herbal medicinal honeys which had sold extremely well at the last market with the coming of cold season.

Eryx rolled his eyes though he did look a bit humbled. Bruce's smile remained on his face, but his eyes nervously bounced back and forth between the two of them. Stefan wondered what made the boy end up here if he had apparently performed so well.

Eryx walked back towards the small crowd of young ones while Bruce stood with him, asking under his breath, "What did you do?"

"Nothing," Stefan replied, scanning his brain for a possibility. There was that small incident when Heren mentioned that Eryx thought he was staring at Odessa across the table, but that was months ago. "At least nothing I can think of. He's usually not so…"

"Hostile?" Bruce suggested.

Stefan nodded. "That's a good way to put it."

Eryx stalked back towards them and made a shooing motion towards Bruce. "Good luck," the younger boy replied, patting him quickly on the back.

Eryx turned, not looking at Stefan and instead addressed the group. "I know over the past couple of weeks we've been working on techniques that could be used at trial. Ways to artfully, yet harmlessly, spar with an opponent. Today's lesson will be about doing damage. Learning to protect yourself and incapacitate someone who aims to do you harm."

Stefan swallowed uneasily, and Eryx turned his head towards the fortress' path. Somehow, his frown deepened further when he saw that it was empty. Stefan wouldn't have thought it possible.

"As we've unfortunately learned in the past, it could be someone that you trust. Someone close to you."

What was going on? Had Heren spilled the beans? Was Eryx convinced that he was guilty of murder? Maybe he was angry at him for putting them all at risk? If that was the case, maybe his peevishness was founded after all.

He wished the younger man would talk to him alone instead of challenging him to some kind of duel to the death in front of a pack of children, but he supposed communication never had been Eryx's strong point.

"I'm guessing I'm going to be the victim in this fight?" he asked, stepping a couple feet away and turning to face the man he thought was a friend.

"In this scenario? Yes. We're turning the tables a bit."

"What the fuck does that mean?" he asked, fed up with beating around the bush.

"You know what it means," Eryx spat out, and then before Stefan could argue, he launched at him like Hopscotch would a dead goat.

If Eryx thought Stefan would be an easy man to beat after his weeks away from practice, he was wrong. He would not use his mind powers on him, regardless of how angry he was, but he would use the speed and strength he had honed with Aura in the past two months.

Though Eryx was obviously bigger, Aura wasn't a twig by any means and she was definitely faster. Stefan had beat Eryx in their first match together using speed and now he had stamina as well. The only upper hand Eryx had was motivation, and it seemed pretty significant.

"So where is she?" Eryx asked, as they danced around the field of dying grass. "She didn't want to see this? I guess I can understand why. Might be embarrassing for her."

"Who?" Stefan asked, thoroughly confused. He dodged a kick and got a slight hit on Eryx's jaw.

"Odessa," he replied, basically spitting out the name along with a mouthful of blood.

"How should I know?" Stefan replied, unable to keep the irritation from his voice as he continued to block Eryx's punches that seemed to never stop coming. He had to admit that he was proud Eryx had learned from his technique, though it wasn't helping him at the moment. "Can you just explain to me what the fuck you're so pissed about instead of trying to beat the shit out of me? It's not gonna happen. "

"I saw you."

Stefan paused, suddenly realizing why Eryx was acting like some kind of proud stag defending his territory, but before he could explain or correct the mistake, Eryx swung, making direct contact with his left eye socket.

He let out a curse that should not have been uttered in front of the young ones and held his hand to his face, terrified that Hopscotch would collect his winnings on *him* instead of the raccoon.

"You can't say you didn't deserve that," Eryx said, a wide grin now stretched across his face.

"I one hundred percent can say that I did not," he groaned.

"You come here acting like a benevolent healer and then spend your nights seducing girls ten years your junior."

He somehow stood up with surprising speed and grabbed Eryx by the collar.

"It. Wasn't. Her." He spoke through gritted teeth, his eye throbbing.

"I know what I saw," Eryx returned, unflinching.

"You know what you *thought* you saw," he spoke again, grabbing him by the back of the neck and attempting to look him in the eye to express the truth of it but finding it difficult.

"So who was it then?" he asked, disbelievingly. The teasing smile still on his face.

"I can't tell you right now."

"Why not?"

"You know why." He turned towards Barrett and Callen hoping he would finally get the message.

Eryx followed his gaze. Initially, the aggravating smile remained, but realization dawned on him and the look of anger returned. He pushed Stefan off and stormed back towards the fortress. Stefan followed as the crows in the trees around him twittered angrily at the fact that they would be missing out on their feast.

CHAPTER 75
AURA

Aura removed her large black robes and changed into her favorite pair of leggings and her oldest and softest yellow tunic. It was her mother's and even though it was threadbare and she had patched it up more times than she could count, it provided her with more physical and emotional comfort than anything else in her wardrobe.

She had to drag herself out of bed this morning when her sister delivered her morning meal. Eryx wasn't with her, which was highly unusual, but Odessa said he had been in a foul mood during breakfast so she wasn't all that surprised at his absence.

It was the first time in ages she had been alone with her sister and she was tempted to share with her everything that had been going on the past couple of months, but she didn't know where to start. Though she knew Dessa wouldn't tell a soul, she felt uncomfortable sharing Stefan's secrets. Without being able to explain the initial connection they had to one another, it made their story incomplete. *Their story...* like they were already a combined entity.

Like always, Odessa had places to be and Aura had orphans to meet with, so they shared a quiet breakfast together and went their separate ways. The morning was a long one and her meetings lasted until early afternoon. With all of the newcomers, she required more time to make sure they were making positive connections with others and finding their niches. Though it obviously helped the community at large, she found that when these people who'd lost their friends and families and homes were given a new role they could fill, it made the adjustment much easier.

Yakov spent the morning sharpening daggers outside of the hall and she wasn't sure if that was his idea or if Stefan suggested it with the hope that all of the new arrivals would know not to make trouble. She had a feeling it was the latter and it made her smile. Once she stealthily retrieved the lunch that Matilda somehow always knew to leave out for her, she retired to her room for what had become a very routine late afternoon nap.

She sprinkled some drops of lavender and vanilla scented oil on her pillow, covered herself up with her blanket and let her eyes fall closed, a contented smile on her lips, when she heard an abrupt knock on her door. She was grateful for the soundproof walls because the person on the other side would have been offended by her loud groan of displeasure.

She pushed herself back out of bed and looked at the large pile of robes on her chair with lazy despair. Knowing the visitor at the door was likely someone who knew her secret, she decided she wouldn't make the effort. They made it easier to project, but in the darkened room she was sure her powers alone would suffice if needed. There was another loud knock and then she heard the key turning in the lock. Eryx stepped in, closing the door quickly behind him. He looked out of breath and his lower lip was fat and split.

"Is everything okay?" she asked, concerned. Were they under some kind of attack?

He opened his mouth to speak and then closed it, assessing her. "Were you…napping?"

She looked down at her outfit then back at her obviously unmade bed. When she took a breath to respond, the sweet floral smell of the calming oil hit her nostrils.

"I had a headache coming on," she replied. "You stormed in here like the place was on fire and that's what you open with?"

"You don't use scents when you have headaches," he replied, slowly, his eyes scanning hers as if searching for answers. He shook his head as if in shock. "He was telling the truth."

"Who?" she asked, though she didn't think her puzzlement was very believable. She knew exactly who he was talking about but couldn't believe that Stefan would tell Eryx about their nights together when she hadn't even told her sister.

A softer knock echoed through the chamber and the man in question snuck in, apparently much to Eryx's dismay. He crossed his arms over his chest, ignoring the intrusion.

"So you've been sneaking out, putting everything at risk to perform flirtatious acrobatics with *him*?"

She couldn't help herself from blushing even though that was ridiculous. It wasn't like they had been openly fondling each other in a field. They were training. The same thing Eryx regularly did in the bright beautiful light of day.

"Stand down soldier," she replied angrily. "I'm quickly approaching my third decade and…" she let her gaze move towards Stefan for the smallest of seconds and noticed that what she had originally thought was a shadow around his eye in the darkened room was actually an ugly bruise. She looked between them in shock. "Did you do that to him?"

"There was a misunderstanding," Eryx said, very unapologetically.

"He thought you were your sister," Stefan aided.

"Even if it was Odessa, you can't just go around punching anyone that shows interest in her!" she reprimanded, unable to keep the shrillness from her tone.

"I never touched Yakov," he spat back.

"That suggests that he was one of the few. Is there a trail of unconscious men you leave behind everywhere you two go?"

He grimaced a moment, and she had a feeling that wasn't far from the truth. Rather than comment either way, he chose deflection. "Don't tell me that if you thought he was sneaking off with Odessa in the middle of the night you wouldn't have done the same."

She opened her mouth to protest but then side-eyed Stefan with his vagabond appearance and realized he was probably right.

"Oh come on," Stefan interjected, pleadingly.

"I wouldn't because *he* wouldn't."

"Thank you," Stefan replied, "I think."

"How could you be so careless?" Eryx cut in. "What if someone else had seen you?"

"You've known me your entire life, and you mistook me for the person everyone knows you're obsessed with so I'm sure anyone else would have made the same mistake."

His eyes widened as if he was shocked she'd actually mentioned the elephant in the room. "I'm not…"

"Shit or get off the pot," she cut him off, her teeth clenched so hard she was sure they would break.

His body shivered with rage. He turned around, and pushed Stefan out of the way before opening the door and slamming it behind him.

CHAPTER 76
STEFAN

The moment Eryx left the room, and all of that hostile, anxious energy left with him, Stefan suddenly became overwhelmed with exhaustion. He took the few short steps over to the settee and then collapsed onto it.

"Do you want to go and find Heren for your eye?" Aura asked, clearly dismissing him. He took a moment to study her and noticed that she had been about to retire to bed. The tunic she wore was so thin, he could almost see the undergarments through the worn fabric and he was certain it would be soft to the touch.

The thought of leaving so quickly didn't really appeal to him especially since he had found a way into her chambers in the light of day. All he had to do was get a black eye, completely unprovoked for once. "No," was all he replied, shaking his head.

"No?" she asked, incredulously.

"I'm feeling a bit woozy actually. It probably would be best if I didn't get up for a while."

She rolled her eyes but then winced, realizing she was partly to blame for the situation and then *he* felt slightly guilty for playing it up. He was about to cut his losses and get moving when she took a step closer.

"I could maybe help a bit?" she suggested, hesitantly.

He raised an eyebrow. "Does this mean you've actually been listening when I rattle on about healing techniques?"

She blushed. "No, I just have some tricks of my own. Things I used to do with the kids, when…" she took a deep breath, and he could see the pain that the subject brought to her.

He beckoned her forward, and she put a smile back on her face that didn't quite reach her eyes. She went to sit next to him but then apparently thought better of it. Instead, she stood directly in front of him and lowered herself onto his lap, nearly straddling him, but bending her knees and putting one leg on either side of his thighs. He swallowed hard and moved his attention downward so that she couldn't see the blush hiding beneath his beard.

"I can't get to your eye if you're not looking at me." She put her hand on one side of his face and slowly brought his gaze back up to her own. She assessed his eye socket, which was likely red and puffy at this point and then puckered her lips and blew out an icy breath. It was reminiscent of the morning after the Hunter's Moon, when everything was harvested and the wind was allowed to break free. When he closed his eyes, he could smell pine and the promise of snow. Hear the hooting of the snowy owl that lived within the forest around the castle.

"Does that feel any better?" she asked, hopeful.

It did, amazingly so, but he didn't want her attention to leave him just yet. "A little bit," he said instead. "Was there anything else you used to do for your kids to heal their bumps and bruises?"

She gave him a look like she knew that he was full of shit but asked anyway, "What, like a kiss?"

"I mean I'm in a lot of pain so it's probably worth a try."

She let out a sigh which still contained a touch of that cooling air but touched his face gently, pushing back the strands of hair along his forehead and planted a featherlight kiss on his brow. Though it was as innocent as could be, it still sent a shiver down his spine.

"That helped with the top of my eye but the bottom still hurts," he complained, unable to keep the smile from his lips no matter how hard he tried.

She narrowed her eyes at him but pressed her lips gently to his cheek, above the line of his heavy beard. When she brought her eyes up this time they were less focused. She seemed less annoyed and a bit shakier as if the closeness was starting to have the same effect on her that it was on him. He moved his hands gently onto her thighs.

"One more for good luck?" he asked hoarsely. "The best things do come in threes after all."

She flicked her gaze to his lips and then back up to his eyes in silent question. He managed the slightest nod and then she brought her lips down to gently brush his upper one. He moved his hands up to her waist and was immensely pleased when the three kisses turned into four and then five. Her lips were as soft as he'd dreamt they would be and he couldn't help but softly bite the lower one the next time it was within reach. Though this was the closest they had ever been, it wasn't enough, and he grabbed her generous hips roughly, closing the gap between them. She gasped and then moaned as she pressed herself further into him, likely feeling how hard he already was beneath her.

Suddenly the door flew open again to the right of them. "And one more thing-" Eryx started, but then apparently saw them in their compromised position. "Oh for fuck's sake."

Aura shot up but got tripped up on her knees and flew back landing on her behind as the door slammed shut again. Stefan stood to help her but with the blood that was not currently in his head due to its gathering in other places he felt woozy for real this time and immediately sat back down.

When Aura's unabashed laughter filled the room, he knew she wasn't too bad off.

CHAPTER 77
ERYX

Eryx spent the morning walking loops around the island. After seeing Aura and Scorpio wrapped up in each other he had immediately grabbed his pack and then went into the kitchen to pick up one of the bags of non-perishables they usually took with them on their longer journeys. He couldn't hide from Matilda and something must have shown on his face because she immediately packed up a small basket for him with sandwiches, granola and apples. He slept under the stars in an open clearing as far from the fortress as he could get. As it was the penultimate full moon of the year, the air was cold and crisp and it held a sense of anticipation. The usual background sounds of the island: the birds, the frogs, the insects, had been quieted by the cold. The soft sounds of the river remained for now, but, even that would be silenced soon enough with the freezing of the water and the coming of the snow.

Was he happy that Aura had found something for herself after years of being alone? Of course. He didn't hate the fact that it was Scorpio either. If someone had told him when they picked him up in that seedy pub that he would wind up in some kind of relationship with the woman he considered a sister, he never would have believed them. More than that, he would have been horrified at the thought, but the man had turned into an unlikely asset as well as a friend. A friend he had hit unfairly without talking to him first.

He *was* concerned that they were being so careless about it. She had given up more than anyone to make this life work, and it made a monumental difference to so many people's lives. As of late, he couldn't help but feel that things were falling apart. First her injury, which he deduced was when she and Scorpio connected, then Cassandra running away with Echo going out after her, and now this. If he had seen them, who else did too? He didn't need Odessa's powers to know that things were coming to a head.

Odessa. Aura was right; he had to either take his chance or give up, but he didn't even know how to approach the subject. Why had it been so easy for Aura and Scorpio to fall into one another? Was the whole thing some sign that Odessa wasn't meant for him? That if it was supposed to happen, it would have already? She was either completely blind, or really didn't care that his entire life revolved around her.

He was sure the gossip about what happened yesterday must have reached her ears which was why he avoided both dinner and breakfast. He had to show his face again at some point, but the first thing he needed to do was apologize to Scorpio. While it would be difficult and awkward, it would still be considerably easier than explaining his actions to Odessa. His oldest friend whose presence he had missed all night as he'd stared up at the Beaver moon and the shooting stars around it.

The two of them often camped out together when out on their journeys rather than spending their precious coin on one of the dirty, stinking inns around the kingdom; as long as the weather allowed for it. It was the only time there weren't other people or responsibilities distracting them.

Their conversations when it was just the two of them went deeper than they usually did around their small group of friends. She talked about her powers, and what she discovered about their origins. They looked at giant orbs and the constellations and hypothesized how everything was connected. They deliberated about Aura and Echo and Barrett and how they worried about them for different reasons. Callen apparently hit the sweet spot in the whole situation and wasn't one that often came up in conversation since he seemed fairly well adjusted.

Those nights together were important to him, and he would rather keep things the way they were than risk losing that connection with her. Did he fantasize and dream about other possible ways those nights could go? Way too often. There was also the chance that if he waited too long, someone else would take her from him and he would lose it all. For right now he was comfortable with things the way they were and didn't want to rock the boat, though, after yesterday, he might not have a choice.

The giant greenhouse loomed before him and though it usually served as his safe haven, today it made the knot in his stomach tighten. He assumed Scorpio would be in the back garden so he was surprised to find him gathering snippets of herbs from the spiral garden in the corner of the greenhouse itself. The older man didn't turn around when he approached, though he must have heard the sound of the greenhouse door closing behind him.

"I'm just collecting some chamomile to make a satchel for the bruising," he explained without turning around.

"I'm sorry," Eryx replied, hoping there was enough honesty in his voice that Scorpio would know he meant it.

"As you should be," Scorpio replied as he carefully plucked each white and yellow flower from its stem. "Do you have any idea how long I'd waited for that kiss that you so rudely interrupted?"

Eryx rolled his eyes. He had no sympathy for the couple's kiss being cut short. Scorpio had still gotten a kiss, when *he* was still waiting for one and had been for *much* longer. "I was referring to punching you in the face but what, a week? A month? How trying for you," he added in his usually sarcastic, dry tone.

Scorpio smiled a bit, but then it faded and though he still hadn't looked his way, Eryx could see his face was serious. "Fourteen years."

Eryx lifted the corner of his lips, as if waiting for the joke to follow but none came. Scorpio only turned and raised an eyebrow at him as if waiting for him to figure it out. He did the math quickly in his head.

"Trials."

Scorpio nodded as he continued to collect the delicate flower heads.

"But you didn't go up against one another," Eryx stated, fully versed in Aura's matches, and their outcomes, after Odessa had described the day to him excitedly over and over again upon their return. At seven with no older siblings of his own, he hadn't been given the opportunity to take that trip. It wasn't until he was twelve, and his father thought it would be important for him to see some matches in person to begin strategizing for his own trial, that he saw Awrymor for himself.

"We didn't?" Scorpio asked questioningly, almost teasing him.

He shook his head confused. It was risky to be discussing this at all, but if he kept the names out of it, hopefully Barrett wouldn't tune in. "She fought in three matches that day and all of those men are either presumed to be, or definitely dead."

"I think presumed is the key word here," Scorpio replied, finally turning to look at him, his arms crossed over his chest.

He started with the most obvious: "Well you're definitely not her husband."

"Unfortunately not."

Eryx opened his mouth but didn't even know what to say about the next man on the list. The one who had died in front of him. The one Scorpio didn't resemble in appearance or spirit.

Scorpio spoke up as if sensing his hesitancy, "She told me. About that man that followed you, and what happened afterwards."

That was surprising, and implied that maybe whatever was between the two of them was more than just pent up lust. Eryx nodded, not wanting to spend another minute discussing that uncomfortable topic.

"Well that's two down and the third…" he stopped, finally thinking about that final, faceless person Aura had fought. The one that Odessa was the most excited to talk about until the news of what happened to him shortly afterwards reached their village and she never spoke about it again. "The third…"

He unabashedly let his eyes roam his friend's face and Scorpio allowed it without looking away. Not that Eryx would know what he was actually looking for. It made sense now why he chose to keep his hair and beard long and untamed. If anything, the shiner that was now an ugly mix of yellow and purple made him even less princely than before.

"How?" Eryx asked him. How did he escape? How had he been living undetected this long? How had he ended up here with them?

"I don't think that's a story that could be discussed so easily in allusions and nuances," the prince replied. "Maybe another day."

"Why are you telling me this after I gave you a black eye?" He winced, realizing the now more serious implications of his actions, but Scorpio just laughed.

"What, do you think I'm going to have you thrown in the dungeons? If anyone is going to end up there, I can assure you it will be me." He shrugged. "I'm not that upset about the hit. We should have been more careful, and it ended up getting me some sympathy points." He smiled and Eryx could see how the thought of Aura lit up his whole face. Well, the small bit that wasn't covered in hair. "If anything, it shows that you're extremely loyal to your friends, and of everyone here, you probably are the best at keeping a secret."

"So I'm guessing you haven't shared this with your partner in crime yet?" he asked, eyebrows raised, referring to Heren.

"Oh, he's known for about a month now. Figured it out all on his own." Eryx thought he could hear a hint of pride in his voice.

"And he actually kept it to himself?" he asked, disbelievingly, "Or am I the only one who's been in the dark?"

"He hasn't told a soul," Scorpio replied, and there was definitely pride there now. "Our little bird is growing up."

An uncomfortable thought came to him. That someone else had known and kept it from him. That the distance between them had been even greater than he thought. He looked away and asked uncomfortably, "Did Odessa know?"

Scorpio patted him knowingly on the shoulder, "If she does, it's because she read it in her cards or dreamt about it. Other than Heren, we've kept it to ourselves, though now that you know, it's likely we'll let her in on the secret as well."

It was a relief to him that Odessa hadn't kept something so monumental from him and that he wouldn't have to keep it from her; however, he couldn't help but think about the fact that all this time they had been harboring the most wanted of fugitives and that Aura and he were apparently already a "we".

CHAPTER 78
AURA

Aura nervously flitted around her room as she waited for Stefan to arrive. Last night was the first in a long time that they hadn't kept each other company until the early hours of the morning. They agreed it would be wise to take the night off and catch up on sleep. Plus, they didn't want to risk being seen by Eryx when he obviously needed time to blow off steam. He hadn't shown up for dinner last night or breakfast this morning, and Aura thought he probably spent the night outside clearing his head.

This morning, when Aura went to the throne room, Stefan had snuck in to tell her that he would be working in the greenhouse and gardens with the hope that Eryx would eventually show up and that they would talk things through. The night off had also been somewhat of a necessity after their kiss yesterday afternoon. Kisses, she supposed. It felt like something that had been building for weeks. Though he had almost played it off as a joke, it seemed more like something they both wished for but needed an excuse to initiate, too nervous to put their true feelings out there and risk rejection.

Seeing him again in the light of day, after a night alone with her thoughts, she could barely concentrate on his words. Her eyes kept straying to his soft lips and his big strong hands that had so firmly held onto her hips like he never wanted to let them go. Thankfully, his tunic was long and her eyes couldn't drift lower to what had been so hard beneath her. He, on the other hand, seemed so unbothered that she almost started to believe the whole thing had been a dream. Then he'd leaned in close to her ear and whispered so quietly she could barely hear it: "Can I kiss you again tonight?"

When he stepped back to await her answer, his eyes weren't joking and there was no smirk upon his lips. It was a desperate plea. A need in his eyes that showed they were indeed on the same page.

All she could do was nod, incapable of speech. He had smiled shyly and left, and she had been counting down the hours ever since.

For so long, she'd been a ghost haunting the halls. It was only under his hands that she felt solid again. Real.

She had dinner with her sister who looked more frazzled than ever. She wanted to talk to Stefan and find out what he and Eryx discussed before telling Odessa anything, but she was hoping that the air would be cleared by tomorrow morning.

There was nothing she could do about Eryx's possessiveness or her sister's hesitance to settle down. She'd been given much longer than most females, and Aura knew that once one of them took that step, they would be happy together. She also knew that Odessa couldn't be forced into anything and Aura bringing it up would only make things worse. Though she had called Eryx out on it, she knew that putting your heart out there was difficult. Even with Stefan's constant undivided attention towards her, she had still made excuses for his behavior not thinking he could possibly be interested in her. Apparently she'd been wrong on that count.

Finally, when she was about to don her cloak and go out looking for him, she heard the three small raps on the door. She knew that if she stayed standing, she would immediately launch herself at him so she perched on the arm of a chair and sat on her hands.

He opened the door and made his way inside, closing it gently behind them. They looked at each other for a moment unsure how to move forward now that so much had changed.

"So… how did it go with Eryx," she asked finally, hoping it would break the tension.

He smiled gratefully as if happy she had done so. "He's okay. We're okay. I told him everything."

"Everything?" she asked, raising an eyebrow. "You felt comfortable enough to do that?"

"I trust him," he admitted. He stepped closer, and she was wrapped in the pleasant masculine scent of him: a mixture of sandalwood and sage. Her mouth watered, and she felt the sudden urge to pull the dark green tunic over his head and tuck herself into his bare chest. She shifted her gaze up from his body and looked into his eyes which were assessing her curiously. Apparently he had said something she missed.

"What was that?" she asked.

He grinned, knowingly. "I told him we could all meet here tomorrow for breakfast and fill your sister in. He seemed very conflicted with the fact that she wasn't aware."

"I suppose it's time, though she'll probably be pissy at me as well as her spirit guide for keeping her in the dark for so long."

He nodded, taking another tentative step closer. "She can't fault you for wanting to protect me."

"It's more than that," she replied, getting up from her seat and nervously fixing the mussed blanket she had been sitting on. "I never told her any of it. About the mark. About using my powers. She didn't even know what my powers were until I started using them here."

He looked surprised by this. "Why didn't you tell her?"

She shrugged. "She was so young when it all happened. I hated using my powers initially. I didn't understand them and they scared me. I also just didn't like talking about it." She looked up at him and was surprised by the tears coating her lashes and the rasp in her voice. "I didn't like talking about you."

Hesitantly, he took a couple steps closer as she stood awkwardly, her hand on her elbow. "Because I thought it was my fault that you were dead. That I could have saved you."

He raised a hand to cup her cheek and softly caught her tear with his thumb. "You did save me."

She narrowed her eyes at him but also couldn't help but lean into his touch. "How?"

He looked a bit embarrassed but continued stroking her cheek as if unwilling to not be touching her. "It probably sounds a bit pathetic seeing as you kicked my ass and basically told me you wanted nothing to do with me." She winced and he grabbed her hand with his free one in reassurance. "But the thought of you was what kept me going. The few smiles you gave me. The way you tried to calm my nerves even though I was a stranger to you and a bit of an asshole to boot."

"It wasn't-" she started.

"I know," he interrupted, "but you didn't know my reasoning then. All I'm saying is that even though you literally didn't know I was alive, the thought of you kept me going. Imagining your face and wondering how I could make my way back to you kept me warm on my darkest and loneliest days. I didn't fall as far as I might have if we hadn't met."

"And now?" Her throat felt dry but she needed to ask: "Am I living up to the image of that girl you had in your head for so long?"

He dropped his hand to her neck and gently pulled her closer. He brought his nose to her hair and breathed in.

"She didn't smell nearly as good."

She took her free hand and snuck it up the bottom of his tunic until she found the slightly raised bump where Odessa had seen it. She heard him inhale sharply at her touch and knew her hands must be freezing.

"Even though my head kept telling me you were gone, I think my heart still knew."

He nodded then released her hand in order to lift up her fitted black undershirt to find her matching mark. Somehow, in the freezing cold room, his hands were warm and felt like fire beneath her skin. Her lower body moved towards him almost of its own accord.

"I want this. I want you, but I also want to take things slow," she whispered and she could feel tears forming in her eyes again. "I'm sure it's not what you want to hear, but I did love him and even after five years, moving on feels like I'm pushing his body off of that cliff."

He placed his forehead against hers. "He's the father of your children, I'm not trying to replace him or pretend he didn't exist." He opened his mouth but then paused as if deciding whether or not to continue. "I've waited thirty years, what's a little more time?"

She pulled back to look at him in shock. "You mean you've never…" It made sense that someone so afraid of being discovered would be reluctant to be intimate with anyone, but it still seemed hard to believe.

He shook his head and suddenly looked down and away from her though she could feel his hand tightening on her hip, "I don't want to sound like a total sop and say that I was waiting for you but…"

Her eyes widened, waiting for him to continue the sentence. When he didn't, she prompted him and her voice sounded much more shrill than she would have liked, "But what Stefan? You don't want to say you were waiting for me but what?"

He shrugged, reluctantly bringing his eyes back to hers, "I don't know. I guess maybe I was."

She grabbed his neck and pulled his head down crashing her lips against his. They would be staying in tonight. Together.

CHAPTER 79
STEFAN

Stefan woke to a warm palm on his stomach and a messy head of blonde hair on his chest. Though they remained clothed the entire night, it was still the most exciting night of his life thus far. Everything had been laid out on the table during their conversation and therefore there was no longer any reason for hesitancy or holding back.

Though he enjoyed his romantic tales, he never felt the urge to enter a brothel or accept sexual services in exchange for his products despite many propositions in the dark corners of the pubs he called home. While he could appreciate female beauty, he wanted to wait until he could be with someone he truly cared about and trusted. If he needed a release, he was capable of taking care of it himself. When he had told Aura he was fine with waiting, it wasn't a lie, he *had* been completely fine with taking things slow; however, that was before he spent the night in her arms.

Now he had kissed her enough to know the best angle to turn his head for their mouths to perfectly align. He knew how she pushed herself against him when he rubbed his thumbs in circles on the side of her hips above her leggings. He knew the little sounds she made when he did something that felt especially good and what those things were. He knew the cadence of her breath when she slept. Though he would wait as long as she needed to feel comfortable, his lower regions were not getting the message and he needed to calm himself down before she woke up and especially before anyone else came in and found them.

He tried to ease his body off the bed but she grabbed a hunk of his tunic, halting his motion.

"Why are you leaving?" she asked, groggily, and he warmed at the sound.

"Self-preservation," he replied, honestly. "I know I said Eryx and I were on good terms but I have a feeling if he caught me in your bed he would give me another black eye to match this one."

She sat up, leaning on her elbow and turning to assess the eye in question, gently probing at the fluid beneath.

"I would say it did the trick," she said with a knowing smile.

"What trick?" he asked, grabbing her finger and bringing it gently between his lips.

"It got you enough sympathy for a kiss."

"You think I asked for it on purpose?" he asked incredulously. "That it was some highly thought out and orchestrated scheme?"

She shrugged, "I wouldn't put it past you."

"So, just out of curiosity, of course," he started, scanning her perfect face in the still darkened room and committing it to memory for the next time he needed it, "if one black eye got me a kiss, what exactly would two black eyes get me?"

She smiled and brought her head back down until her lips were so close that her breath tickled the dark hairs of his beard, "Why don't you stay and find out."

CHAPTER 80
ERYX

Eryx made his way across the main hallway of the fortress, carrying a tray with a large carafe of coffee and a basket of pastries. Rather than finally face his peers and Odessa in the dining room, he chose to eat with Aura and Scorpio who he hoped would be fully clothed and nowhere near each other when he arrived. Perhaps this evening, after Dessa was caught up on everything and he had somehow explained his actions on the sparring field, he would be more comfortable facing the others. For now, he would rather avoid their curious looks as well as the death stares he would surely get from Heren.

"Eryx, wait up."

He paused, taking a deep breath, but didn't turn around as he heard Odessa's boots swiftly move across the stone floor.

She stopped in front of him looking him up and down and noticing the tray in his hands. "Are you actually bringing that downstairs or are you taking it back to your room so you can keep avoiding everyone?" She said it teasingly, but he thought he could see a sliver of hurt in her eyes.

"Downstairs, are you coming?"

He hoped his voice didn't give away just how glad he was to see her. She wore tawny leggings above her dark brown leather boots and her amber tunic was cut in such a way that the top of her belly button peeked out of the top. Rather than a cloak, she wore a fashionable short brown jacket that matched the color of her boots. He had never seen it before and he wondered if she secretly purchased it at the last market. He wasn't going to call her out on it, but it looked expensive.

She nodded. "I'll walk with you."

He knew it was only a matter of minutes before they would openly speak about everything, but the silence that stretched between them was taught and uncomfortable. For two days he'd avoided her, the longest stretch of time they hadn't laid eyes on each other or spoken in years, and he wondered if she felt it as deeply as he did. The answer was probably "no".

When they had finally reached Aura's cellar door, she reached into her tunic pocket to retrieve the key but stopped before fitting it into the lock.

"Do you want to talk first?" she asked, hopefully, gesturing to the library beyond. "Before we go in?"

He shook his head, just wanting the conversation over with. Hurt flashed in her eyes, but it was quickly disguised by an eyeroll and a shrug of her shoulders as she knocked and then unlocked the door.

She walked in ahead of him but stopped short, almost ending up with a back full of coffee. A gentle movement of air pulled the door shut behind them.

Aura and Scorpio sat at the large table, four mugs already put out in anticipation. He walked over, placing the tray down, and Scorpio stood pouring the steaming coffee into each of the cups.

"What's going on?" Odessa said, nervously. She turned towards him, likely trying to see if he was as in the dark about the situation as she was.

"Have a seat," Aura replied.

"You all look like you're finally going to tell me that Scorpio is the lost prince of Serenfawr," Odessa laughed, flopping down into one of the chairs and grabbing a cranberry scone from the basket.

Eryx swallowed hard. He could already tell this *wasn't* going to be good.

"You knew?" Aura asked, disbelievingly. "How?"

"It wasn't the first time I had seen him," she replied, the smug smile still on her face.

"You came with Aura to trials," Stefan said surely, and there was a distant look in his eyes as if he were recalling that day.

Odessa nodded and opened her mouth, but Aura interrupted her.

"You wouldn't have just recognized him from that day. You were five years old, and he's obviously changed since then."

Odessa was still smiling and yet there was now a bit of worry in her gaze at Aura's building agitation.

"I dreamt of him."

Aura took a deep breath. Anyone unfamiliar with her would assume she was unbothered, but he knew that if they were outside, the winds would be building around them.

"When?" she asked, eerily calm.

"A week or so after your trial." Odessa was playing with her rings now, the smile gone from her lips, her eyes downcast. "And every year after."

Odessa hadn't mentioned the prince again after the news spread to the village about his supposed demise. He always thought she had been upset, but apparently she had instead been trying to keep the secret that he was still alive.

"And you didn't think to tell me?" Aura stood up and paced the floor.

"She told me not to," Odessa said, rising from her own chair. "It kept him safe didn't it?"

"Who is *she*?" Aura spat out, palms slamming on the table. "What are her motives in all of this? How can you have such blind faith in a shadow?"

"She's on our side," Odessa argued through clenched teeth, her fair blue eyes cold as ice. Eryx couldn't think of the last time he'd seen her angry, though he supposed for the most part, she did whatever she wanted without question.

"Is she? She hasn't been all that concerned with our well being. Jonal, Donovan, Vitus. Her directives haven't always been to our benefit. It seems like she picks and chooses for some larger plan."

"You don't seem to have a problem when you're using your own powers," Odessa replied snidely. "You really don't think they come from the same source?"

"I have no idea," Aura replied angrily. "You know I've always had a problem with them. I just did what I had to do to keep the children safe."

Odessa laughed and it was a cruel sound. "You're angry with me for not telling you but if I had, would those same children even exist?"

"What does that mean?" Aura asked. She sounded as confused as Eryx felt.

"I didn't tell you because I was scared!" She looked towards Scorpio with a wince. "I saw the way you looked at him that day and it scared me. It was like you were in some kind of a trance. The ride there felt so long, and I didn't want you to stay there to be with him. I wanted you to be home with us, and I wanted you to be with Vitus. Vitus who gave me piggyback rides and brought me sweets. I didn't want anything to change."

"So what," Aura interrupted, not pacified at all by Odessa's confession, "You thought if I knew he was alive I would try to go out and find him?"

"Yes!" They were standing face to face now across the table and though Eryx had never seen them physically fight before, he was poised to leap in if necessary. He looked towards Scorpio for backup, but the older man looked like he was attempting to use his hair to blend into the shadows. For someone with such honed fighting skills, he seemed to have no stomach for conflict.

"I," Aura started like she was going to deny it, but then looked back towards Scorpio and Eryx could tell just how hard she had already fallen. "I don't know what I would have done, but I should have been given the choice. Maybe as a child you were afraid, but as a teenager? As an adult? Once we knew that Vitus was gone, you still couldn't tell me? Unless there are other secrets you've been keeping?"

"I would tell you if I saw Vitus," Odessa replied, the final sound a hiss through her clenched teeth.

"Not if it somehow went against your agenda." Aura shook her head. "For fourteen years you let me think my," Aura stopped herself, turning away as if she had almost let something slip.

"Your what?" Odessa asked, "What was he to you? After that day you didn't even seem upset about it."

"When was the last time you saw me cry, Odessa? When Vitus disappeared? When I basically gave up my children to you so that they wouldn't be taken from us? Just because I don't 'seem sad' doesn't mean I haven't been." She turned around as if unable to face her sister a moment longer, and then spoke so quietly her words were barely more than a whisper. "You saw his mark that day at the pub. What did you think it was?"

Odessa looked over to him in confusion as if he could provide the answer. He had seen her lift the corner of Scorpio's tunic up quickly but thought it was some kind of old stab wound. Not anything worth examining.

Aura turned slowly, lifting her own tunic. The scar where she was stabbed peeked out, now nothing more than a tiny white line. When she lowered her leggings, she uncovered a small circle with a design he couldn't make out. Eryx thought about the statues in the garden and the matching marks on the two pairs of demi-gods. True mates were just a legend. They didn't actually exist…did they?

He moved his eyes back to Odessa and if looks could kill, Aura wouldn't be long for this world.

"How long have you had that?"

"For about as long as you've been lying to me about my mate."

CHAPTER 81
STEFAN

The next month passed by in a blur, leading up to the Cold Moon, the final moon of the year which was celebrated as a time of letting go to get the most abundance out of the coming year.

Aura hadn't spoken to Odessa since the day of their fight. While Stefan savored each night they spent together, he also could tell how much the separation was bothering her. Personally, he didn't hold any ill will towards Odessa. They all had their secrets, and she had done more to protect her family than he ever had, which actually bothered him a great deal. However, in the early hours of the morning he couldn't help his mind from drifting to the what ifs. What if she had known and went out to find him? What if he hadn't been completely alone all those years?

Whenever his mind did go on those paths, he thought about Echo's small arms around his neck and Callen's easy smiles and Barrett's intensity, and he knew that his loneliness was worth the happy years she'd gotten. He would clear his mind and focus on her warm body against him and her light floral scent and would quickly fall back into a comfortable sleep.

The fact that the sisters weren't speaking meant that he and Eryx had to act as the bridge when it came to passing information back and forth. Maybe it was the fact that Eryx was now sure that Stefan had no interest whatsoever in the younger sister, or maybe he even considered him to now be part of their strange pieced together family, but all of the tension between them had disappeared.

Heren needed some convincing when it came to forgiving Eryx for the hit, especially since he was still in the dark about Aura, so Stefan was unable to truly explain what the fight was about. Eventually, his temper cooled and the three of them spent time together growing and gathering everything that Matilda wanted for the upcoming feast, and figuring out how to decorate the halls with potted plants and floral arrangements.

Heren created ornaments of crystal quartz that looked like icicles hung throughout the corridors. They stuck cloves into oranges and used a needle to thread cranberries on a string for garlands. Matilda kept a pot of herbs and spices boiling in the hearth in the week leading up to the festivities. The entire place smelled of anise and cinnamon, vanilla and pine, whatever bits and bobs she had on hand as she worked overtime with whoever was on duty continuing to cook the daily meals while also preparing for the celebration.

They spent an evening painting round slices of thinly cut fallen pine with images of what they hoped the new year would bring and hung them on the branches of the large tree in the courtyard, along with pinecones and stars made of sticks and twine. Stefan initially couldn't think of anything he wanted to manifest other than Aura's face, but when he looked deeper he couldn't help the feeling of wanting to do more for his community as well as the kingdom that would have been his. Just because he lost his title didn't mean he wasn't a Serenfawr and that he wasn't responsible for the health and wealth of the kingdom's people.

Suddenly, the idea came to him to draw a Jack-o-Lantern mushroom. One that was bold and bright and could be confused with the harmless Chanterelle but actually had poison within. All his life everyone thought him feeble and cowardly, but maybe they were mistaken. Maybe that was why Talon put him down all the time. Not because he really thought him weak, but because of his potential to be strong. Because one day, he could be a threat to him and his position. He would bask in the comfort of his new home until the final moon was fully waxed but as the days began getting longer again, he would start making plans to make things right. He had hidden from his destiny long enough.

On the day of the feast, everyone slept in and in the late morning, met for an extravagant brunch: frittatas and quiches and sweet breads and tarts. Iced buns, shortbread, pancakes and pies. When he complimented the chef, he couldn't help but tell her about his mother, and how he always felt such love and comfort whenever she made something special for him. They were very similar to how he felt now with his stomach full of Matilda's creations.

"Everyone loved her," he said wistfully. "I always felt that somehow she must have imbued whatever she cooked with her magic, to incite that deep fondness and tenderness in people's hearts."

Matilda assessed him knowingly, a slight smile on her lips. "So that's where you get it from then."

He looked at her curiously. "You've seen me in the kitchen, on multiple occasions. How many times have I sliced my finger open just peeling potatoes?"

"I don't think it was the food," she shook her head, chuckling lightly. "Well maybe that was just her particular way of bridging the gap. We have a tough crowd here. A lot of damaged people." He noticed her glances towards Eryx, then Heren and finally Echo, who looked up at that exact moment to smile shyly in his direction. "You disarmed them all rather quickly if you ask me."

He didn't know what to say to that, a lump forming in his throat making any speech difficult anyway. He gave her a hug instead, imagining that maybe for just a moment he was with his own mother, and then presented her with the oil he made for her of sweet plum and smoke.

It was a day of rest and catching up without everyone running off to their jobs. Stefan felt so happily at home that his face began to hurt from smiling. He handed out all of the small personalized oils he crafted for each person based upon their likes and dislikes, which Heren also paired with an appropriate crystal that would bring them confidence, wisdom or healing, whatever it seemed they might need in the coming year.

Rather than another large meal later on in the day, they just nibbled on hard cheeses, dried fruits, nuts and sweets while sipping on mulled wine and fiery spiked cider. Odessa was in her element as she took center stage pulling a card for each person that would represent the coming year from their usual table in the center of the hall. He watched her for a while and then snuck in when there was a break in the crowds surrounding her.

"How is she?" she asked quietly, without looking up at him as she shuffled the cards.

"She misses you." He kept his voice down, even though the raucous hall likely hid their words from any eavesdroppers. "But she's as stubborn as the day we met so don't wait for her to come to you."

"It runs in the family," Odessa replied with a reluctant smile. "I suppose the Cold Moon is a better time than any to make amends, right?"

"Maybe you can bring her breakfast tomorrow morning? Break the metaphorical ice?"

"I can do that." She held the cards out to him. "Now let's see what's in store for your future."

He ran his fingers along the tips and selected one towards the beginning of the fan, in honor of a new start. She turned it over and presented it to him with a grin.

"Is this me literally taming the golden beast?" he asked, laughing at the image which showed a man attempting to wrestle a lion.

She let out a loud cackle and he saw Eryx give a questioning glance from where he was standing. He gave a thumbs up and his friend smiled, shaking his head.

"I suppose it could," Odessa replied after she caught her breath. "Good luck with that. It could also suggest action, bravery, responsibility, not a bad card to pull in anticipation of the coming year."

He nodded his head thinking about how closely the message resembled the ideas that had already been swirling around in his brain.

"I'll keep that in mind." He returned the card back to her and enveloped her in a hug, hoping that she and Aura could indeed reconcile, and maybe he could gain a little sister in the process.

With the warmth of the food and drink in his belly, he took his leave to spend some time with his lioness before the remainder of the night's festivities commenced.

***

When he made it down to the cellar, he knocked quietly on Aura's door and then used the key she had given him to gently open it.

He was surprised to see her still in her oldest pair of clothes, knitting in one of the large armchairs.

"Are you coming up for any of the festivities or to watch the bonfire?" The holiday typically closed with a large outdoor fire that was meant to chase out the last year's worries and regrets and encourage a fresh start.

She shook her head. "Eryx brought me enough food to last a week, and I'm still finishing up the scarves for the children. I'm hoping I can sneak them into their rooms tonight while everyone's out."

He walked further into the room and touched the soft buttercup colored wool.

"Your sister said she'd bring you breakfast tomorrow morning. If you let her in."

She looked up at him, considered it for a moment, then shrugged. "I guess that would be alright."

"Do I get a scarf too?" he asked, admiring her handiwork.

She shook her head, "Maybe next year. I do have a present for you though." He thought he could see a warmth creeping up her neck as she got up to retrieve something from the back of the room. A similar warmth spread through his chest at the thought that someone finally cared enough about him to get him a gift.

She handed him a small rectangular object wrapped in a piece of cloth. It felt suspiciously like a book and he couldn't hide the thrill that he felt that she might have had someone pick up a new romance he wasn't familiar with. He smiled at her excitedly and slowly removed the cloth. He tried not to show his disappointment when he saw the familiar Rapunzel retelling that he adored but was also very familiar with.

"I know you've already read it," she said quickly. "I just thought maybe for your gift, later tonight we could…" she paused, a blush forming on her cheeks, "act out one of the scenes."

He looked down at the book and then back at her, raising a brow, "You're telling me you read this?"

She shrugged. "I've seen you pick it up more than once, I thought if I was going to dive into the genre it would be a good place to start."

"Did you like it?" he asked, honestly curious.

She opened then closed her mouth, as if trying to find something nice to say. "I will probably stick to my thrillers, but I could see why you might have enjoyed it."

He laughed. "Fair enough."

He took a step closer, grabbing her by the hip and pulling her into him. "So which chapter were you talking about exactly? Chapter 17?"

She shook her head shyly, refusing to meet his eye.

"Chapter 29?" His eyes widened.

She shook her head again.

"Surely not chapter 47?"

She nodded gently, finally looking up at him. "Only if you're ready?"

He swallowed hard and could feel his face reddening. It was the moment he'd been waiting for since he'd laid eyes on her, but now that it was within reach he felt incredibly nervous.

When he didn't immediately reply, she nudged him with her foot. "I promise I'll be gentle with you."

"Are you *sure* you read Chapter 47? I'm not sure you could call that gentle."

Now she was blushing. "That was just my way of letting you know that I was ready to take that step. We don't actually have to act it out verbatim with all of the dialogue and..." she swallowed and looked away, "*punishments.*"

"I mean, maybe a little would be okay," he suggested, raising an eyebrow.

She nodded, then let her lips touch his for only a moment before pushing him back towards the door. "Give everyone 'the Widow's' love. I have work to do."

CHAPTER 82
OLIVER

Oliver Serenfawr sat on the shore of the Harridan river under the Cold Moon looking at the land across the water and cursing the Witch Queen. He should be in Awrymor feasting and drinking and corrupting maidens. Instead he was sitting here, hungry, freezing and unbearably sober. If it was up to him, he would have crossed the river and dragged the woman back with them to the castle so his father's thirst for blood might be satiated. Instead he would be spending the remainder of his days parading up and down the eastern shore of the river searching for some kind of orphanage that likely didn't exist in the first place.

He knew he wouldn't be able to convince any of the men to cross the river. He started out months ago with a calvary and was left now with less than a dozen men. For the first few months, anytime they were under attack by a pack of giant wolves or mountain lions or bears, the men would make a formation around the prince, much to his embarrassment, and would be killed, maimed or dragged away as a snack for later. Some were bitten by the enormous spiders or stung by giant killer wasps. Others simply were there one night and gone by morning's light never to be seen again. It was only last month when Oliver had finally had enough and attempted to fight off the beasts himself, that he came to the startling conclusion that they wouldn't harm him. Anyone else was fair game but for some reason his Serenfawr blood meant something to them. Rather than come at him they would growl and slowly back away. It happened again and again and again.

He wasn't exactly sure what it meant. Maybe as subjects of the Witch Queen they were under direction not to harm anyone within the King's family so that peace could eventually be achieved. Maybe she was keeping him alive so they could take him captive and make some kind of ransom agreement with his father. In truth, he wasn't sure if Talon would willingly pay a cent to get him back. Their relationship wasn't difficult, it was basically non-existent.

He wondered if the same special treatment would be given to his father. If he got off his royal ass and actually led his own men through the woods, maybe he also wouldn't be touched, and he could speak to the Queen face-to-face or slay her himself. He debated whether he would tell him what he had learned but was leaning towards not. The harbingers of bad news didn't typically last very long in Talon's presence, and if he found out that the solution to everything had been so simple all along, Oliver would be the one who would feel the brunt of his wrath. Better to make it seem as though he was just so strong and brave that none of the creatures dared touch him.

As he sat on the wet log, his boots encrusted with sand, he played with the small dagger in his hand. It was the one he had been given by the merchant in Yawning Springs and for some reason, rubbing the blue stone with his thumb provided him a great deal of comfort. He supposed it made sense that someone with few actual meaningful connections in life would find solace in a stone, though it seemed like something more befitting of a Green than a Blue.

The oil included in the bag had also become something he depended on. He started off rubbing a bit on his wrists and would bring it up to his nose whenever he felt especially anxious. When the liquid within the small bottle began to dwindle, he kept it in his pocket, uncapping it to take a whiff when no one was looking. Though as a Blue he should have found reassurance in the gentle flow of the river before him, it only made him miss home more. On the other hand, the driftwood and salt in the bottle helped paint a mental picture in his mind of the sun coming up over the docks and the boats gently swaying in the breeze, which brought him an incomparable sense of calm.

It was strange that someone he had never met chose not one item, but two, that he immediately connected with so deeply. He pictured the man in his mind. His slight and sinewy figure and his long dark beard. He had taken his advice and explored the pools of Yawning Springs. Afterwards, Oliver felt the strange urge to find him again to tell him about the unusual flora he had seen there, but when he returned, the merchant was gone. He had a feeling that his prying had scared him away, and he was angry with himself for not even finding out the name of the man or his business or where they were located. He wondered if he would be able to find him at the Awrymor market surrounding the trials next spring. If he survived that long.

The man said the stone would show him the truth, so he continued to rub it while asking for guidance as to where he might find this fortress. He listened to the sounds of the frogs near the shore and the owls and crickets in the woods behind him. He saw a large looming shape flying in the sky above him, the moon reflecting off its large black wings. He watched it dive down onto a piece of land that seemed to jut out of the shore on the other side. As he scanned the area to see if the creature would resurface, he noticed the smallest flicker of flames deep within the forest of trees. He stood, shaking his head to see if his eyes were really seeing what was there or if it was just a trick of the light, but when he started walking further south he could indeed see the fire through the trees and the rising smoke above. Were the Queen's people celebrating the holiday so close to the edges of her kingdom?

As he walked further down the river, he noticed a tower reflecting in the light of the moon. From his prior position it had been hidden by the towering pines, but from this angle it was more apparent. Was what he originally thought to be a part of the other side of the river actually an island that wasn't connected to either side? Was this what he was searching for?

He looked back behind him into the woods. His remaining men were in there along with Darius who had somehow survived, likely by spending the entire journey basically up his ass. He thought about what would happen if he dove into the water and swam to the island. Joined up with whoever was there and left everything else behind. He could tell them to put out the fire and stay hidden and maybe no one would ever find them again.

He remembered his father's thinly veiled threats. The men who risked life and limb to accompany him on this journey and keep him protected. His future as king of this land he had finally started to understand as he journeyed over its hills and meadows and met its people. He sighed as he turned from the river and walked back into the woods to ready his small party for tomorrow's siege.

CHAPTER 83
AURA

It hadn't taken Aura long to finish the scarves she had been knitting for the children. Every year she made them something and Odessa would deliver the gifts saying she had left a store of them before she "disappeared". Maybe Echo believed it, but she assumed the boys just figured their aunt picked the items out for them at the markets. Either way, it made Aura glad to craft something for each of them so they could feel her love in some way despite her forced distance.

Shortly after extricating Stefan from her room, she completed the fringe and crept through the hallways to lovingly place a scarf on each child's pillow. Though she only took the risk because she and Odessa weren't speaking, she had to admit it was nice to get a whiff of each of their scents and a picture of how they kept their spaces. The boys shared a room and while Barrett's side was sparse and orderly with only a single journal on his nightstand, Callen's was a mess of clothing and drawings and crumbs. Echo's room was neat and tidy, the only unique feature a small stuffed bat on her bed which Aura gently wrapped in the scarf so only his tiny head poked out.

Though usually spending the holidays away from her children put her in a melancholy mood, tonight would be different. She wasn't sure how long Stefan would linger at the bonfire with the others so she worked quickly, weaving a soft messy braid down her back and gently filling it with holly berries, poinsettias and sprigs of rosemary. She removed the simple yet elegant red gown she had found in a trunk when they'd first arrived. Other than a couple of holes from moths or mice, it was in fairly good shape, and so she had fixed the worn spots and strengthened the thread on the fine red buttons that went down the front. The bodice was form fitting and showed off the tops of her breasts while the bottom flowed out gently. The sleeves were wisps of gauze that danced as she paced around the room waiting for Stefan to arrive.

She had never worn red and putting it on filled her with a fiery energy. She tried to hold on to that confidence but the second she heard Stefan's key turn in the lock, the nerves came crashing back.

He closed the door and took a few steps in but then stood motionless with a strange look on his face. Not the reaction she was hoping for. She could feel her posture slipping as her confidence continued to drop. "I found this dress ages ago and thought it would help me get into character," she said nervously, "Thought I could try being a Red for the evening."

Though he obviously wasn't dressed quite as fancily as she was, he was still painfully handsome, his green tunic crisply ironed, hair in a tight knot at the base of his neck and his beard neatly trimmed.

"Is everything alright?" she asked when he still didn't move or say anything, a bit concerned about his sudden lack of speech since he usually couldn't keep his mouth shut.

"Don't," was all he said and then began to slowly walk across the room towards where she was standing.

"Don't what?" she asked, annoyed that her effort had not had the desired effect. Her cheeks reddened at her ridiculous attempt at seducing him. It had been too long since she'd bedded anyone and she was obviously out of practice.

"Don't pretend to be someone else. Please. Not tonight."

He was close now, and looking down at her with that same unblinking gaze. Close enough that he took her shoulders and turned her to face the other direction. He reached up and she shuddered as his hand grazed the back of her neck, unplaiting the braid she had so painstakingly put up.

"What are you-" she began, but then he continued.

"When I kiss you tonight I don't want you to imagine that I'm thinking about some fantasy girl who doesn't exist."

She could feel him remove every flower and branch and then he gently brushed through the strands with his fingers until they fell down her back. Just the simple touch of someone playing with her hair felt like such an intimate gesture. He then started on the other side.

"When I fuck you, Aura, I want you to know that the only woman in my head is you. The heroine in every book I've ever read has your face. So even though I deeply appreciate it, I don't need all of this. I just need you."

She couldn't help the small gasp that escaped her lips at his language. Though he made it very clear how he felt about her, something about the desperation in his words in the quiet room as he undressed her made it truly undeniable. He wanted her and even more than that, maybe he loved her.

He slowly slipped the sleeves off her shoulders and let the dress puddle to the ground around her feet leaving her completely bare while he remained fully clothed.

He placed his hands on her waist and bent down to whisper in her ear.

"This has been my fantasy since I can remember. Some form of it anyway." She could feel the softness of his beard on her neck as he took a soft bite on her earlobe and she let out a quiet moan.

"That first day we met all those years ago I thought for a moment that I was afraid of you, and then I realized that I was only afraid that you would never be mine."

He moved his hands down to her hips and stepped back, pulling her back with him until he was sitting down on the settee. He pulled her down with him and then his left hand slowly moved up to cup her breast and toy with her nipple. She could feel the soft fabric on her bare ass and his legs on either side of her boxing her in. She arched her back, pushing into him to cup her more fully.

"Help me," he pleaded softly. "Show me what you want."

She grabbed hold of his right hand and guided it down her body, over her thigh to the place she needed it. The place she hadn't been touched in so long. He kissed her neck while she showed him how to touch her and opened her legs wider to give him more room to work. His hand, already slick with her, moved in perfect circles, and she couldn't help but arch into him and feel his need pushing into her from behind. She wanted to turn and look into his eyes, to feel his lips on hers, to touch him like he was touching her, but she couldn't move as her pleasure continued to mount. All she could do was reach her hand up to touch his face before the wave swept over her. He continued to touch her more and more softly as her body spasmed and she collapsed into him.

He held her for a few minutes as her breathing returned to normal and she turned in his lap similar to the way she had sat upon him the first time she kissed him.

She would give him whatever he wanted, but first she just wanted to look at him. She reached up and softly took his face with both hands. He bent his head down and rested his forehead against hers, staring deep and breathing in the same air.

"I was nothing but a ghost haunting these halls until you found me," she stated, honestly, looking into his deep green eyes that had always been so completely focused on her.

"If you were a ghost, then I was some kind of hairy mythical beast hunting truffles instead of innocent children," he replied in his easy, disarming way that brought smiles to people's faces so easily.

"For a mythical beast you were quite easy to tame."

She smiled and brought her lips up to kiss him softly and slowly. She felt privileged to be known so well and wanted equally. She would let him know what that meant to her. She was fairly sure he felt the same. Even though she would be satisfied with melding her lips with his for all time, she could tell that his body was losing patience. She stood, this time careful not to fall, and held onto his hands to steady her. She pulled him up and along towards the bed, the anxiety fading to excited anticipation.

"Do you have anything?" she asked, as he stepped back and began removing his tunic.

"Done and done," he responded smiling. "I believe I was successful in creating a tonic that inhibits conception through the male."

"It's a good thing I didn't change my mind," she laughed.

"If you refused, I always could have taken the boat out. Rowed to the nearest brothel and tried my luck," he responded, laughing, as he removed his pants and went to lay next to her on the bed.

"And this?" she questioned, gripping his ready and waiting appendage, making him gasp and lightly bite her shoulder. "I fear it would not look half as impressive if you accidently fell in the freezing river."

"True," he responded breathily, "Well it's a good thing you didn't turn me down."

He positioned himself over her and cupped her face as she brought him to her entrance which was waiting to be filled.

"It was all worth it," he said, and she knew he meant all of it. The pain and uncertainty and loneliness.

They were both quiet after that. His movements started slow and she gasped as he pulled almost all the way out and filled her again. As he moved faster, she could feel her own pleasure quickly building, and she reached down to touch herself to meet him at the peak. Once he shuddered and she felt the pleasant heat of his release inside her, she broke for the second time, letting all of the tension of the past few years leave her body.

As she lay there breathing in his warm, now familiar and comforting scent, she felt something deep in her core. It was different from the marriage thread that bound her to Vitus. Thicker like a sailor's rope or the vines of the trees in the library. It felt loose now as it seemed to entwine around her heart. If they were separated, she had the feeling that it would be more strained and taught but still ever strong. For now though, it was relaxed in their closeness. She didn't have to be alone anymore.

CHAPTER 84
STEFAN

Stefan woke to a wretched squawking in the depths of his mind. He sat up abruptly to frigid cold on his bare chest and total darkness. He took in three deep breaths trying to get his bearings. He could hear soft breathing beside him, and feel a warm blanket on his lower body. He was safe with Aura in her bedroom; it was only a dream.

He went to move back into the blankets, careful not to disturb Aura's sleeping form when he heard it again.

"Get up you worthless, lazy fool."

"I don't remember asking for a wake up service," he replied in his mind agitatedly.

"Well then don't lead your kin here and put everyone in danger."

Any remaining grogginess disappeared in an instant. *"Who is it?"*

"Your more pulchritudinous princely counterpart and perhaps a decennial of his guards."

He got up quickly and began searching in the dark for his clothes. *"I get it. You're old and wizened. In the midst of an emergency can you please just speak the common tongue. "*

"Pretty boy plus ten," the condor replied with an exasperated sigh. *"What do you plan on doing about it?"*

What was he going to do? He lit a single candle and turned back towards Aura. He couldn't figure this out while she was in sight. He would just cuddle back up next to her, close his eyes and suck up every last moment until it was too late. She would be angry but he needed to think things through on his own. He snuck quietly out the door, closing it behind him.

CHAPTER 85
AURA

Aura woke to a loud banging on the door. She barely had enough time to cover herself before Eryx burst into the room. She reached out to wake Stefan, but his side of the bed was cold and empty.

"Barrett woke up and heard voices on the eastern banks. He doesn't think it's a full army. Maybe a small collection of men and," he winced, "possibly the prince."

A cold dread spread through her. "Do they know we're here? If we keep everyone within the walls is it possible they'll just continue on?"

She could see Eryx shake his head in the dimly lit room. "They're making plans to come over and soon. Odessa has been making sure everyone is accounted for and gathered."

He looked to her as if waiting for his command, and she couldn't help but feel a tug of love for her ever loyal friend who always put his trust in her so completely. "Give me a few moments to dress."

"And then what?" he asked, not snidely, just with the hope that she had some kind of plan. "Is there anything you can do?"

She gestured for him to turn around, and he did so she could pull on her underclothes and her heaps of robes. She blushed when she saw him notice the red dress discarded in the center of the room but as was expected, he was too respectful to comment.

"I always wondered if the fortress itself was under some kind of enchantment but if they're here and have already spotted it, maybe they were made aware and whatever magic was hiding it was broken. I don't think there's anything I can do to fix that."

"Jonal," he stated and his hands clenched into fists. "If only I-"

"You weren't going to kill a teenager just to silence him, Eryx. You wouldn't have been able to stomach it and I wouldn't have allowed it anyway. That's not what we're about."

"He also stabbed you, in case you've forgotten."

She was surprised to realize that she actually hadn't thought about it, even though the incident was so traumatizing. "There's no point in stressing over the past when we need to come up with a plan for the present."

She placed the hood over her head adjusting it so only her eyes shone through. "I can't hide the fortress but maybe I could hide everyone in it," she suggested. "If we put them all in one place."

He shook his head. "And then what? You really think if they don't find anyone here they'll just leave? That they won't come back? We have a lot of power here. We've been training. We can fight."

She moved to stand in front of him. "So you think killing the next in line is going to make things better for us?"

The mention of the prince suddenly made Aura think of the other one who was currently missing from her room.

"Have you seen Stefan?" she asked, suddenly cold.

He shook his head, a glint of worry in his eyes. "Maybe he just went to grab something to eat?"

She hoped that was the case, but something deep inside her screamed that he already knew what was going on and was about to make a martyr of himself.

"Find him and tell Odessa to bring everyone to the throne room. I'll meet you there."

He ran out, slamming the door behind him and Aura stood frozen for a moment, her worried thoughts paralyzing her. She wasn't sure how she was going to use her power to disguise over three dozen people while also continuing to keep the glamor on herself. The robes would help but she might have to forfeit her false identity for the sake of everyone's immediate safety.

She felt like she had been transported back to five years ago, the weight of the world on her shoulders. She took a deep breath and tried to center herself. When Vitus disappeared, it had been her alone with three children and two young teenagers. Now Eryx and Odessa were grown and she had others: Stefan, Heren, Lavender, Yakov, Matilda…. While they might look to her for guidance, they were a team and they could get through this together. She put her glamor in place and moved as quickly as she could through the deserted halls to meet her people.

CHAPTER 86
STEFAN

Stefan stood in his room in front of the mirror. He had seen Odessa running through the halls pulling everyone from their rooms and bringing them quietly down the hall to the throne room. They couldn't be sure what kind of powers the men accompanying his cousin had so it was good everyone was being as quiet as possible.

Everything that had happened in the past few months, weeks and days had been leading him up to this moment. He knew Aura would attempt to tax her powers to save everyone, but even if she did, this was about more than just their small community. While he loved what Aura, Odessa and Eryx had done here, it wasn't fair that such a small group of people were allowed to live in relative peace and harmony while others were forced to enter into, and stay in, destructive relationships because the kingdom decreed it. Men were dying on the king's ridiculous errands. Women were being killed just for the sake of being women. Children were being orphaned. Families were only barely scraping by.

Maybe he could get Oliver on his side. Or maybe he could put some doubts into the minds of his men. Suggest that things could be better with his uncle off the throne. That if he were in charge he would be willing to get rid of the suffocating control and the taxes and give a fresh start to a dying land. If he was going to do that, he needed to make them one hundred percent certain that he was who he said he was.

He picked up his razor and took a deep breath in. No matter what hid beneath the dark hair on his face, he was still his own person. He might have Talon's jaw or dimples but it meant nothing. It didn't make him who he was, and it didn't have to be how people saw him. The people who loved him would continue to do so no matter what he looked like. He moved the razor slowly down one side of his face, watching the coarse dark hairs fall to the basin below.

As the hair continued to fall, with it went his fears and self-doubts. He was strong. He was powerful. He was a good man who could make things right. His thoughts went back to the last day he had seen his father, and for the first time, he remembered that he had wanted Stefan to be his successor. He had seen something in his son that made him think he could do it and so today, even if Stefan failed, even if he died, he would take this step to try and make his father proud.

He wouldn't think about what he was leaving behind. He couldn't, because then he would never be able to take that first step out the door. He would focus only on the path ahead and return to the haven that he'd found in his mind when the darker moments came because he was fairly certain that they would.

He watched the final stray hairs fall and looked up. He saw his mother's eyes and his father's nose and maybe Oliver's mouth which he recalled from the last time he'd seen him; however, the pieces were just that, pieces, and the whole was uniquely him.

CHAPTER 87
AURA

When Aura pushed her way into the throne room, the remainder of their community was already gathered. The room was dark, only the gentlest hints of light making their way through the narrow windows. As soon as she entered, Lavender ran up to take her arm and assisted her to the throne at the end of the walk. Her tunic was rumpled like she'd just grabbed the nearest one off of the floor and her dark wavy hair was frizzy as if she hadn't had the time to tame it. It was unsettling to see her so unkempt when she was typically the picture of perfection no matter the time of day.

The older teenagers and adults spoke quietly in groups, their hands and arms flailing about in agitation and worry as they attempted to keep their voices down. Bruce and Cassandra had taken charge of the children and were engaging them in some kind of quiet game as far from the thin narrow windows as possible.

"Do you have a suggestion, Widow?" Lavender asked her quietly after helping her to her seat. "Do you think if we hide the unwed and make them believe it's just you alone caring for the children they'll leave us in peace? Maybe separate some of us into pairs and have them believe we were legitimately matched?" She could see the dread in the girl's eyes and knew she had more to fear in being dragged back into the kingdom's clutches than most.

"If they're here, there must be a reason," she said tightly. "I somehow doubt that they're going to just accept our explanation and be off on their merry way."

She scanned the room looking at what defenses and weapons they had at their disposal. Though she was sure that some of them would be able to do some damage, it wouldn't be worth it if even one person was lost. It would make more sense to hide. If she kept everyone in one place, it shouldn't be too difficult for her to make their intruder see an empty room. Her biggest worry was that while she was focused on the interlopers, one of her own people would take notice of the subtle changes in her appearance and react in a way that would disrupt the facade, like a dog barking or a bell ringing in the middle of a dream forcing someone to awaken.

Another concern was that if the men already knew they were here, her powers wouldn't work. A traveling troupe of performers had visited their village once and she had watched an illusionist perform a series of tricks. She remembered being completely enthralled until she had seen a spare ball fall out of the magician's pocket. He held a finger to his lips, and she kept his secret, but her brain couldn't unsee that extra ball that moved between his sleeve and the table and beneath the cups he moved around in circles. She felt like her magic was like that. Once the truth was uncovered there was no more hiding it.

She had attempted to use her powers on Stefan the first day they'd seen each other after her altercation with Jonal but it hadn't worked. She thought maybe he would look at her with confusion and think that whatever he'd seen the week before was a trick of the light, but she knew immediately when his eyes found hers that he was seeing through the illusion. She tested him a couple of times afterwards as an experiment, and he'd complained of a headache like his eyes and his brain were in conflict and taking it out on him. Odessa and Eryx never expressed any issues, though she thought that likely had to do with the fact that the illusion was never properly established in their case. That's what she worried about with the king's men. That since they knew there were people here, she wouldn't be able to disguise them. That they still might see the shapes through the fog. The way the fortress was so obviously lived in wouldn't help and there was nothing she could do to hide each and every piece of evidence.

The thought of Stefan made her scan the room again, hoping she'd missed him but seeing no sign. She couldn't help but feel a twinge of annoyance that he had disappeared from the bed this morning and now wasn't here to help her work through this, especially after what had transpired between them last night. It was possible that he'd truly gone off to get breakfast and got held up chatting with Matilda, but the Fire elemental was here handing out muffins and scones and Stefan was most definitely not.

She looked over and saw her sister arguing with Eryx quietly in the corner. She remembered that they were supposed to be talking through their problems over breakfast this morning. Maybe if they had been talking in the first place, Odessa would have been warned somehow. She wouldn't believe that she *had* been and just hadn't relayed the message. She knew her sister, and even if they hadn't yet worked through their differences, she wouldn't put anyone in danger for spite alone.

She took a long breath in an attempt to steady herself. She was responsible for all of these people, but she couldn't ensure their safety all on her own. If she put the responsibility solely on her own shoulders and the illusion failed it would be a catastrophe. Maybe it was time that she shared the burden. Her children wouldn't be happy with her, but hopefully they could keep any feelings inside until the situation was dealt with. She could come clean and hope that maybe someone else would come up with a solution. She gripped the arm rests of her chair and was about to pull herself up when the door to the room quietly opened. Everyone stood stock still staring in fear at the unfamiliar man who strode through the door.

CHAPTER 88
STEFAN

Stefan softly closed the door behind him before turning to the others in the hall. He grimaced at their repulsion and thought that he must look considerably worse than he had originally believed. The realization then came to him that they just didn't recognize him as one of their own.

"It's just me," he said, raising his hands up in surrender, and the short sentence seemed to carry more weight than it should.

Heren stalked over to him, scanning his freshly shaved face, his eyes a mix of anger and alarm, "What are you doing?"

"Awfully unusual time for a shave," Yakov cut in.

He could see a black shape in the periphery of his vision but refused to look. She would hate him for it, but if he turned his body in that direction, he might not be able to walk out the door. It would be better for her to be angry at him than harmed or separated from her real family.

He kept his voice down, not wanting the trespassers who were making their way over the water to know exactly how many people were hiding within the fortress walls.

"I have strong reason to believe that the prince and his company would be willing to leave everyone here in peace, at least for the time being," he stopped knowing that this wouldn't go over well, "if I give myself up."

"You think rather highly of yourself," Barrett said, suspiciously.

"I can assure you that I don't," Stefan replied, sighing deeply, "And neither do they. That's why this might actually work."

Eryx looked like he was in pain, but Stefan felt like he already understood the rightness of the plan. "There aren't many of them. They would probably be much happier to take one highly valuable willing prisoner rather than engage in combat with a group of people they know nothing about."

"I'm coming with you then," Heren said, and Stefan was both touched and heartbroken to see the tears forming in his eyes.

"If we're both locked up, who's going to come break me out?" he asked, using his knuckle to wipe away a single drop making its way down his cheek. He'd meant it as a joke but knew immediately that Heren wouldn't take it that way. Better if he was able to keep him safe for now and someone else would just have to take over the job later.

"Stay alive until I can," he said, harshly wiping the other side of his face with his sleeve.

"We're not going to be able to convince you otherwise?' Odessa asked, not so subtly looking towards the back of the room.

He shook his head and shrugged. "I guess that stubbornness we were talking about has been rubbing off on me."

Somehow he could sense Aura's fury through whatever bond they cemented last night. It was radiating off of her in such strong waves he was surprised that no one else could feel it.

"I should go," he said, taking a sweep of the still confused glances around him and trying very hard not to cry since he no longer had his long hair or beard to hide his face. "It was a pleasure cohabiting with you all. Keep safe."

He turned to go but was stopped by a tug on the bottom of his tunic. He turned to see Echo standing there before him. He bent down to envelop her in his arms and breathed in the scent of cold winter air and juniper berries, the tears now flowing freely down his bare cheeks.

"Be good, little one," he whispered, before letting her go and stalking out the door without a second look.

He didn't turn even when he heard the sweet tiny sound of her voice behind him, "Good-bye prince."

CHAPTER 89
AURA

Aura stood still with the rest of the onlookers as Stefan turned and walked out the door to his doom. While she obviously wasn't shocked like the others by what Echo revealed in her send off, she was taken aback by his impulsivity in turning himself over to the king's men and that he hadn't consulted with her about what he was going to do. They had no defined relationship, but at least he must think of her as a friend if nothing else. Their lives had been so thoroughly entwined, how could he not even think to tell her what he was planning?

The shock quickly turned to panic and then to despair. What would happen to him? Would she never see him again? Would they have him rot in a dark cell for the rest of his days or dispose of him quickly like they attempted over a decade ago?

Her life was again being turned upside down, and this time, she didn't think she had the strength to survive it. She had lost her parents. Lost her husband. Lost her home. Lost the attachment that she had with her children. She managed all of that by dissociating and focusing on each task that came next, but for some reason, this last loss felt like the one she couldn't handle.

Her connection with Stefan had been like a tiny fire lit in the dead of winter. Small at first but slowly growing and warming her heart bit by bit. And now she felt that fire start to blaze; a burning anger that she had never let herself feel before. Her body went into motion and she lifted her robes to stop herself from tripping as she flew through the hall and down the flight of stone steps, the hall door crashing behind her. As she reached the main hallway, she ripped the hood from her head and threw her mouth covering to the ground.

"STEFAN, "she screamed, the sound coming from her throat almost feral.

He stopped and slowly turned to face her. His freshly shaven face was a strange combination of the boy she had fought so long ago and the man she had grown to care for over the past half year. There was also something she had never seen in him. An inner confidence finally making its way out. An acceptance and pride in the person he had become.

He was the most lovely thing she had ever laid eyes upon and her words caught in her throat as she rasped, "Why?"

He slowly closed the gap between them and scanned her face.

"Why? Because of you, Aura."

"Me?" She choked out a hard laugh as the tears streamed down her cheeks. "Am I truly that insufferable?"

"No," he stated simply. "You're extraordinary."

He stepped closer and looked directly into her eyes.

"After I ran away, I spent a full year terrified. Hiding from invisible enemies who didn't even know I was alive. The years after that, once I felt like I could rejoin humanity again, I survived by fueling the demise of others. Through feeding their addictions and assisting the evil they wanted to inflict upon others. The kingdom, this society, taught me that was the worthwhile part of me. The dark part. The part capable of inflicting the most damage.

"But if I was the dark, you were the light. You sacrificed everything, your own happiness for others. For the ones that you loved and for people you hadn't even met yet. Even if everything falls apart and this place, this haven that you've made for so many, is abandoned, everyone here will be changed because of you. They will know that their lives are worth something and they will know that their power is their own.

"I know all this because of how you changed me. Even all of those years ago, I felt it. That you were someone important. You are my greatest gift, and I know I was given this second chance so I can give you yours. Take them away from here. Find the Witch Queen. Start anew."

"But I can't lose you," she pleaded, barely able to get the words out through the tears.

"There is discontent within the kingdom. I don't think they will allow Talon to get rid of me so quickly this time without a proper trial. Maybe I can convince the people that I *am* the rightful heir and explain to them what you've done here. How we are stronger as equals and how our power should be shared and not hoarded.

"And if that doesn't work and they lock me up, at least I will know that you are safe and I will remember your face and it will make me glad."

He took her face in his hands then and slowly wiped her tears with his thumbs. She grabbed the front of his shirt and rose to bring her lips to his. The boy who had made her so angry and the man who somehow made her even angrier.

"I'm not giving up on you, Stefan," she whispered. "I'm not just going to hide this time and hope for the best. We will see each other again."

He dropped his hands and gave her a final sad smile. Before walking away, he placed something into her hands, closing her fingers around it. He then walked into the cold early morning light falling across the open door. She was still once again. Holding onto the moment before it would be broken by someone who was not him.

"Mama?"

She turned to see Barrett standing at the foot of the staircase. The look on his face was one of confusion and hurt.

"Barrett, love, I can explain."

He shook his head and ran back up the stairs almost crashing into Odessa who was on her way down. Aura turned to look down at the object in her hand. It was white and spotted with small flakes of purple. A bar of lilac soap. When she saw her sister, Aura sank to her knees and buried her face in her hands. Odessa flew down the remaining steps and cradled her fallen sister's head in her lap as she sobbed out five years worth of heartache and pain. The solid anchor who had never left her.

CHAPTER 90
OLIVER

Oliver pulled himself out of the freezing cold water of the Harridan and up onto the small rocky beach. While the temperature of the water didn't affect him much, the frigid cold air that swirled around the island almost in a protective embrace nipped at the skin on his bare back and arms. He stood and looked around the small alcove. A pair of rowboats sat farther back towards the forested incline leading up to the fortress. As he further assessed the land around him, the two remaining Blues left in their company swam onto the shore behind him.

"Take the boats," he instructed them, leaving no room for argument. "Bring back some of the others and some dry clothes and steel as well."

The taller one looked nervous, though he wasn't sure if it was because they feared for his safety or for their own when they returned to the shore without him there to protect them. "You'll be alright by yourself while we're gone?"

"Stop questioning my authority and you'll be back sooner."

They dragged the boats to the shore and he added, "Leave Darius behind."

It would be nice to get away from the man's suffocating presence. The only reason he hadn't followed him was because he wouldn't be able to keep up in the river's rushing waters. If he was taken by a beast in his absence that would be all the better.

Then they were gone and he was left alone listening to the wind scream through the trees. It had taken three laps around the island to find the small bay set into the shore. The fact that it lay on the side of the island that was still untouched by the winter sun hadn't helped. If he had been any other type of elemental, he would have been thoroughly spent; however, the clear cold waters had felt invigorating, and refueled the energy that had been slowly seeping out of him the past couple of months.

As the minutes dragged on, he tried to decide exactly what he was going to do once they reached the fortress. The obvious plan was to take stock of who was present, and deduce whether or not they were living in accordance with the rules of the kingdom. It was possible they would just find the dead and decaying body of the Widow that boy had stabbed, and a number of starving children, but it was also possible that they might find a group of unwed tax evaders and rebels.

The king would surely be impressed if Oliver led the troops in a blood bath; however, the thought made him queasy. He knew he could hold his own in a fight, but the pain and torment he had watched his father inflict on others always left him feeling uncomfortable and hollowed out. Though he didn't mind the occasional bar brawl, especially when he got in a hit on someone deserving, torture and unapologetic murder didn't do the same thing for him that it did for Talon. There was always a light in the king's eyes when seeing a body before him that never appeared when it came to anything Oliver did.

He turned and looked out towards the lands to the west, wondering if the Witch Queen had as much contempt for her subjects as Talon did. If she truly did command the creatures of the woods she obviously had a ruthlessness to her as well. Was it also because she wanted to grow her wealth and her land, or was she just trying to protect her people? The thought came to him that he could just jump back into the waves and swim in that direction. Leave the men to deal with this mess and disappear. Pretend to be a lost soul needing assistance. Start fresh. There sure wasn't anything back home worth staying for. He took the smallest of steps and then heard the sound of feet crunching on gravel behind him. He turned back around slowly, knowing that his men were still far behind and he was completely alone.

He could see a pair of boots coming down the zigzag incline behind him. Whoever it was didn't stop or startle as they approached, suggesting they were already aware of his arrival. Oliver cursed under his breath. The element of surprise was out the window. The person stopped on the last rocky incline before the beach and Oliver brought his gaze up, annoyed to be standing below this stranger like he was the lawless peasant, and they were the one in charge, especially considering the fact that he was half naked, weaponless and alone.

He took in the man's clean green tunic and the worn-looking cloak that still looked warm and comfortable enough to envy in his current condition. He was sure that his narrow, bare face, which was still partly obscured by the hood and the morning darkness, was unfamiliar to him, but there was something about his build and the woodsy smell the wind blew in Oliver's direction that tugged at a memory.

"It's you," Oliver said, surprised. The man smiled like he was glad to be remembered. "I should have realized that you ran away from the market so fast because you had something to hide."

The stranger's face fell like Oliver had disappointed him somehow.

He opened his mouth and closed it again, then used his arm to gesture around the empty beach. "I see you're alone. Does that mean you've decided to join me here rather than drag me back to your father?"

It would have been easier to answer if he hadn't been having those same traitorous thoughts. He decided not to acknowledge the question, "Don't think I'm daft enough to believe that you're here by yourself just because you tried to trick me with your use of pronouns."

"I would never presume to think you stupid Oliver," he said, jumping down from the ledge and sitting himself on the large round stone below.

Oliver could feel his anger growing at the man's lack of respect. "Just because we're on some island in the middle of the river doesn't mean that I don't have reign over you. You will address me as 'Highness' or 'Prince' at the very least."

"How can you be so sure?" he returned, and there was a knowing teasing in his tone that set Oliver's teeth on edge. "You know nothing about me. How can you be so sure you shouldn't be bowing to *me*?"

He was relieved by the sound of splashes behind him and when he turned, he could see the two boats filled with a total of six men. It wasn't much, but it was better than being one-on-one with a madman.

He laughed suddenly, remembering how he had even found the island in the first place.

"The dagger you gave me. You told me it would show me the truth. I was holding it when I saw the fires from your celebrations last night."

"It's too bad you don't have it with you now," the man replied, shaking his head.

Oliver's brow furrowed in confusion. It seemed like a threat, but there was no malice in his tone. Instead he had said it with a hint of sadness. They watched the two boats of men come up onto the beach and then pour out around him. They drew their swords, even though the man hadn't stepped any closer and didn't appear to have any steel on his person. He should direct them, but he wasn't sure exactly how much power the man possessed, or where the others in his company were hiding. As if sensing his internal debate, the Green spoke.

"If you all agree to leave this place now I'll come with you willingly. You can take me all the way back to the castle without a fight."

"Sounds like a pretty piss poor deal," Oliver replied, turning to laugh at the men behind him.

"Highness," one of them suddenly gasped, as if seeing a ghost. He was the oldest of the lot, clad in a yellow tunic so ragged it was falling apart. Oliver was surprised that he'd made it this far when so many younger and stronger men hadn't.

"What?" he asked, annoyed, but when he looked at him, the Gold wasn't even returning his gaze. Instead his eyes were focused on who was behind him

Oliver felt it then. A sudden sense of foreboding. Maybe it was the truth the man had spoken about finally finding its way to him. He didn't want to turn back around for the fear that everything he knew was about to be proven wrong. For one last second, he could be in blissful ignorance but once he turned, there would no longer be any hiding from that "truth".

He took a breath and slowly turned around. The man had removed his hood and the light from the dawning sun was chasing away the darkness. Oliver's eyes went to the man's face again. A traitorous ghost looked back at him. One who, indeed, outranked him.

CHAPTER 91
AURA

Aura sat cloaked in the front of the great hall where she had consulted with her "orphans" so many times before. The previous day had been trying. The king's men all left with Stefan. Their company was small and it was likely that the forest had not treated them kindly. Even so, she knew they would be back eventually and the cold, damp fortress that had turned into a home would have to be abandoned.

The rest of the day was spent planning with Odessa and Eryx and speaking with her children. Barrett stayed in his room, processing things on his own, and she didn't seek him out. The fact that his mother had been living in the same keep as him for the past five years, and that the grumpy, unkempt man he had been training with was the true prince of Serenfawr must have been hard to swallow, and he was not ready to hear anyone's explanations or apologies. With his sensitive nature, and the fact that they had been so close before her departure, she knew he would take her deceit personally. She needed to wait until he came to her.

Callen and Echo took the news surprisingly well. With his intuitive abilities, maybe Callen sensed his mother's motivations for hiding were truly to protect them. Echo seemed unsurprised, like a little bird had whispered the truth in her ear. While fixing her relationship with Barrett would be difficult, and forming attachments with Callen and Echo would be like starting from scratch, Aura hoped that in time they could be a family again.

The silver lining was that her three children had grown up with an aunt and uncle who loved them and she knew she could count on Odessa and Eryx to help her along.

While the children now knew Aura's true identity, she had yet to share it with the rest of the group. Eryx had held them back during her confrontation of sorts with Stefan, and Barrett was the only one to hear it. Whether they would treat her with acceptance or contempt she couldn't say.

She nervously held her hands in her lap as the people she had started to see as family walked in one by one. They already knew that change was imminent and difficult decisions would have to be made. Once she could see that everyone was present, she took a breath and stood to address them.

"As you all know following the events of yesterday morning, this fortress, our home, is no longer a safe place. Whatever magic was keeping out the king's men is no longer protecting us and now that the kingdom is aware we're here, I'm sure they'll be back.

"Our plan is to cross the river to the east and head south. We do not feel it is safe for us to try to reintegrate into the villages at this time, and it is too cold for us to stay this far north with three more months of winter to deal with. That being said, we do plan on returning north and to the city once the snow clears. Stefan is one of our own, and Odessa has been led to believe that he will be held, without being executed until at least late spring so we do have time to regroup. I am sorry if any of you were taken aback by what Echo revealed. It was something he needed to keep to himself for his own safety and not something that I felt I could share."

"How is she so sure that he won't be harmed sooner? Isn't there anything we can do now?" someone questioned from the back of the room.

Aura looked to Odessa unsure of how to respond.

Odessa nodded her head and stood to face the room. "I dreamt of him last night. I saw him in a small cell looking much like he did when he first came to us." Some chuckles were heard and then she continued. "I could smell the scent of cherry blossoms and see morning birds flitting outside the barred window. I take this as a sign that for now we need to keep ourselves safe. While our powers have grown through living together, we could all use quite a bit of work when it comes to our combat skills. Also the castle and city streets are now bare. There will be much more opportunity to infiltrate the palace once spring comes and travelers gather for trials. Please do not feel as though you have to accompany us south or assist us in our future plans. Return to your families or start fresh in a new village; the choice is yours."

"This is our family now," Yakov spoke out. "There is nowhere to go back to and Stefan is part of this family as well."

Aura stood and held up her hand. "Before you make a decision, there is something else you should know. Odessa, Eryx and I brought you all here because we were unhappy with the state of the kingdom. We felt that some citizens were treated better than others. We didn't believe that the worth of a female was only to care for a male and then be disposed of. We didn't believe that someone should be forced into marriage without love. We didn't believe that someone should be made to hide their power in order to fit into the right role."

Members of the crowd began to clap, but Aura again held her hand up to silence then.

"In order to create this place, we needed a guise. An orphanage run by a Widow and a couple was of no threat to the kingdom. I think you've all by now realized the fact that Odessa and Eryx have exchanged no vows."

A number of snickers could again be heard from the crowd. Odessa rolled her eyes, and a faint flush was barely visible on Eryx's dark skin as he looked down at his boots.

"However," Aura continued, "While I am a widow, I am also not quite *the* Widow you have been led to believe." She took a deep breath and lowered her hood. As she did, she knew she would no longer look the same to the people. Her people. There was a gasp or two but mostly shocked silence.

"Did Stefan know about this?" Heren asked, unable to hide the disbelief in his tone.

"He did," Aura replied, uncomfortably.

"That sneaky son of a-"

Aura continued, cutting him off, "My husband was lost over five years ago and rather than take the widow's tonic or marry another man, I chose to leave my village. I took my children, Echo, Callen and Barrett, my sister Odessa, and my late best friend's son Eryx with me on this journey. We found this fortress and then found you all one by one through Odessa's dreams. While my voice, age and stature may be altered, I am still the woman that you know. I give the choice to you whether you will stay or go."

The silence continued. Then Lavender spoke. "I suffered years of abuse at the hands of the man I was forced to marry due to the kingdom's rules. He was supported in his violence by a kingdom who put men over women in all matters. That man is no longer my husband and that king is no longer my king. The Witch Queen, while her magic has favored us, remains a stranger and not someone who has earned my trust. You, though I don't yet know your name, have.

"You are not decked in fancy jewels, feasting on meat at your giant table. You have not been afraid of sharing power with your people. You have encouraged us to become our best. You, my lady, have earned the right to be my queen and I will follow you south or wherever you choose to go."

Lavender lowered herself to one knee and while Aura thought that she didn't have a single tear left to shed, they again started to flow.

"Aura," she said quietly, "My name is Aura."

The others all stood from their places to bend the knee until only one was left standing in the back. A young blond haired boy who was already becoming a man.

"I know how to help Stefan", he spoke, ignoring the scene before him. The others began to rise and looked back at him waiting for him to speak. "The people should know who he is and that he is coming back for them. So the king can't hide him in the tower for as long as he sees fit."

"And how do you mean to do that?" Eryx asked kindly with a knowing look in his eye.

Barrett walked to an eastern facing window, closed his eyes and whispered something out into the lightening sky. While no one could hear his words, somehow, they all knew his message as a cold winter breeze blew back in.

EPILOGUE

Stefan walked at the back of the line of men, taking in the woods around him that still held magic and wonder despite the bare trees encircling them. He knew he wouldn't be seeing any plants or animals other than roaches and rats where he was going.

When Oliver had seen him, truly seen him for who he was, there was a single second of relief and hope before his expression turned to one of betrayal, hurt and anger. Stefan had received his second punch to the face, though luckily Oliver was a lefty, and so it wasn't the same eye.

He deserved it and he needed to feel his cousin's anger just as much as Oliver needed to express it; however, rather than let it bruise and bother him for days, he stepped out of his comfort zone and healed himself. He was confident in his powers now and would no longer bask in his own pain and sorrow. He couldn't help but feel a bit of pride at the fear on the face of Oliver and his crew when they saw how he woke up without even a mark on him. Maybe they all thought he was immortal or had risen from the dead. Inside, he did indeed feel like he had been reborn into someone stronger so maybe that made it even more believable. Though he had been captured and was walking back towards the one place he had avoided for so long, he finally felt ready to face his destiny.

Oliver hadn't given him a second look since this morning; however, that tiny sliver of hope he had seen in his eyes yesterday, paired with the fact that his cousin was so obviously hurt, suggested that Stefan hadn't completely lost him. He was damaged by the past few years, but the bridge between them was still hanging. Ragged but not completely cut.

His connection to Aura was as strong as ever, and he wasn't sure if it was a blessing or a curse. She was hurting badly. He had caused it but at the moment, there was nothing he could do to fix it. Once he reached his lonely cell, he could experiment with it. See if he could use that tie to communicate with her somehow or ease her pain. He knew that as long as that connection remained, she would get him through another period of loneliness and cold. She would be his reason to keep going and to fight for his people.

A cold gust of wind blew around them, shaking the trees as a few light drops of snow began to fall from the sky. As the frigid air blew into his ears, with it came a message that seemed spoken from within his own mind. The men in front of him stopped in confusion as if they too had heard the voice in their ears.

"The rightful prince lives and is being returned to the castle, accompanied by the king's men. He has declared his innocence and will be awarded the trial he was denied so many years ago. If found innocent, he will accept the crown that is rightfully his and bring new prosperity to the kingdom."

He smiled as he recognized the young voice in his mind thinking maybe Matilda had been right: that he did inherit his mother's talent and that if he had finally won over Barrett to his side, maybe the rest of the kingdom would be next.

473

ACKNOWLEDGMENTS

To my magical beta readers: Ciera Abbate, Denise Abbate, Francesca Bury, Jeanne Deyo, Mimi Folco, Morgan Flowers, Danielle Kean, Nicola Mallon and Carolyn Ruszala. Thank you for hyping me up and making me believe that this book needed to be out in the world.

To Emily Puckett for the tough love I needed. Looking forward to lots more manuscript switching and wine and writes in the future.

To Gretchen Cobaugh for being amazingly talented creating the perfect cover to go along with my story.

To Anne D'Amore, Allyse Pulliam and Angela Mazzocchi for reading my anime fanfiction and always letting me be my weird self.

To dad, who was always proud of me no matter what I did or how badly I did it. I like to think that I write a lot better than I ever played rugby or the bassoon and so I'm sure that he would have been impressed.

To mom for taking care of us always.

To my boys for being my inspiration, even though you didn't make the actual writing processes very easy.

To Peter for being my own tall, dark and handsome hero.

THE SIBYL OF THE WIND